A DCI Gilchrist Novel

THE MURDER LIST

T. F. MUIR

CONSTABLE

CONSTABLE

First published in Great Britain in 2021 by Constable

1 3 5 7 9 10 8 6 4 2

A CIP catalogue record for this book is available from the British Library.

ISBN: 978-1-47213-109-6

Typeset in Dante MT by Hewer Text UK Ltd, Edinburgh
Printed and bound in Great Britain by Clays Ltd, Elcograf S.p.A.

Papers used by Constable are from well-managed forests and other responsible sources.

Constable
An imprint of
Little, Brown Book Group
Carmelite House
50 Victoria Embankment
London EC4Y 0DZ

An Hachette UK Company
www.hachette.co.uk

www.littlebrown.co.uk

THE MURDER LIST

Also by T. F. Muir

(DCI Gilchrist series)
Eye for an Eye
Hand for a Hand
Tooth for a Tooth
Life for a Life
The Meating Room
Blood Torment
The Killing Connection
Dead Catch
Dead Still

(DCI Gilchrist Short Story)
A Christmas Tail

In memory of my sister, Rae, the kindest and most loving person.

AUTHOR'S NOTE

First and foremost, this book is a work of fiction. Those readers familiar with St Andrews and the East Neuk may notice that I have taken creative licence with respect to some local geography and history, and with the names of some police forces, which have now changed. Sadly, too, the North Street Police Station has been demolished, but its past proximity to the town centre with its many pubs and restaurants would have been too sorely missed by Gilchrist for me to abandon it. Any resemblance to real persons, living or dead, is unintentional and purely coincidental.

Any and all mistakes are mine.

www.frankmuir.com

CHAPTER 1

6.38 a.m., Monday 17 March
West Sands, St Andrews, Fife, Scotland

DCI Andy Gilchrist's breath fogged the air in thick clouds that burst from his lungs in painful gasps. A quick glance at his Fitbit monitor showed a pulse rate of 112 – higher than he would've liked. But he gritted his teeth and pressed on. About 800 metres to go, as best he estimated – half a mile in old money. He concentrated his gaze on the Macdonald Rusacks Hotel in the distance or, more correctly, a patio window that overlooked the balcony above the Rocca Restaurant, glowing yellow from a bedroom lamp within—

His mobile vibrated. He pulled it from his pocket – ID Jessie – slowed down as he made the connection, his logic warning him that Jessie wouldn't call at that hour in the morning unless it was serious. He drew to a halt, and gasped, 'Yeah?'

'We've got another one,' she said, without introduction.

Gilchrist sucked in lungfuls of air, unable to speak.

'You all right?'

'Yeah,' he managed. Two more deep breaths settled the pounding in his chest enough for him to say, 'Another . . . as in . . . you think it's . . . the same killer?'

'Yes. No doubts. None at all.'

He'd never known Detective Sergeant Jessie Janes to be indirect, but something in the rush of her voice warned him that this recent murder was one of the worst she'd seen. 'I'm listening,' he said.

'Margaret Rickard. Sixty-three. Employed with Santander for fifteen years as an HRD assistant. Retired two years ago. Lived alone. Never married. One brother. Older. Tom. He called it in.'

'Tom found her?'

'Took his dogs for a walk this morning. Popped into her home in Kincaple to make her a cup of tea. Said he and Margaret have been early risers their whole lives. Said they were close and kept in touch mostly every other day. He's a wreck, the poor sod.' She let out a pained sigh. 'No bloody wonder.'

Gilchrist felt that familiar frisson shiver his spine, a sensation he always felt at the start of an investigation. Of course, as he was presently signed off from work, this wasn't his investigation *per se*. Still, he and Jessie had kept in contact over the last four weeks, she on the pretext of asking how he was keeping; he to keep up with Office matters – you could only take so much of not being part of a working unit—

'It's early days,' she said, 'but as best we can tell there's no connection between Rickard and Soutar.'

Adam Soutar, this killer's first victim. 'Was Soutar a customer of her bank?'

'No. RBS.'

'How about Tom? Maybe he knew Soutar?'

'No. According to Tom, the name Adam Soutar means nothing to him.'

Gilchrist didn't want to give up on the idea that Rickard and Soutar somehow knew each other, but his team would uncover a connection if one existed. His breath had settled, his thoughts seemed clearer. 'Where did he find his sister?'

'In the living room.'

'So how did he get in? Does he have a key?'

'He does. Said he rang the bell, but Margaret didn't answer. She's usually up and about at that time. So he let himself in.'

'When did he last speak to her? Did he say?'

'Saturday afternoon. Last time he visited.'

'He hadn't phoned her since?'

'Haven't checked that yet. But there's no reason for him to lie.'

Probably not, although Gilchrist knew from experience that you never could tell. 'Any sign of forced entry?'

'None.'

'So how did the killer get in?'

'Maybe he knew her?'

He pressed the phone to his ear, preparing for the brutal stuff. 'Okay,' he said. 'Let's have the details.'

'Tom found her on her back, on the living-room floor. Naked. Spread-eagled. Hands and feet nailed through the carpet.'

'Post mortem?' he asked, more in hope than curiosity.

'Too much blood. She was definitely alive when the nails were hammered in.'

'Dear God.' He closed his eyes. How anyone could do that to another human being didn't compute. He didn't think that nailing someone to the floor in a crucifixion-like form was intended to send any kind of anti-religious message. No, not at all. He thought he knew the psychopathic mindset well enough to know that this MO was the work of someone who needed to experience ultimate domination, control of life over death, and to inflict unbearable pain – and humiliation, of course. Let's not forget humiliation.

He opened his eyes. 'She was naked. Where were her clothes?'

'On the settee.'

'Neatly folded?'

'Yes.'

Well, there he had it. If ever he had doubts that it was not the same killer, they were quashed right there. And in his mind's eye, he ran through the scenario preceding this latest killing: Margaret Rickard, a retired woman in her sixties, shaking with mind-numbing fear as she is instructed to strip naked – *Take them off. The lot. That's it. To the buff* – her killer-to-be gloating with psychopathic satisfaction as she peels off her bra with hesitant shame, then with a final shiver of resignation steps out of her underwear to stand before him . . .

Now why him? Why not her?

But he cast off that thought. Too much strength needed to overpower a man as big and as fit as Adam Soutar – six two, eighteen stone, known to be a serious hill climber, someone who would not be overpowered by gentle force. No, this killer was male. Strong. And fit. He had to be. So . . .

He pulled his thoughts back . . . she stands before *him*.

Naked. Trembling. Terrified of what is about to happen.

Then what?

Her soon-to-be killer watches with grim-faced impatience, eager now to get on with his murderous task, as she follows his next instruction. Struggling in vain to hide her nudity, she folds her clothes one by one, piece by piece, taking care to press each garment flat – just as Soutar had done – before placing them on the settee in a neat pile.

Then came the part that Gilchrist struggled to comprehend.

'Any signs of resistance?' he asked.

'None.'

'So she lies down on the floor, stretches her arms and legs wide, and lets herself be nailed to the floor?'

'That's what it looks like.'

Just like Soutar, a powerful man who appeared to have simply spread himself out on his bedroom carpet without objection, and let himself be nailed to the floor. It didn't make sense. Doctor Rebecca Cooper, Fife's foremost forensic pathologist, confirmed no drugs in Soutar's system, other than a mild level of alcohol equivalent to a couple of glasses of wine, which Soutar had been known to favour, more or less on a daily basis.

'I don't get it,' he said.

'That makes two of us.'

'Where's Soutar's body now?'

'Still at Bell Street with her Royal Highness.'

Bell Street Mortuary was where Cooper performed post-mortem examinations. If she had unresolved concerns over cause of death, she wouldn't release the body until she'd ticked all the boxes. On hearing about Soutar's murder on the news, then phoning Jessie for details, Gilchrist had resisted the urge to visit the mortuary – after all, he'd only been signed off that week. But he made a mental note to talk to Cooper later that morning, and felt a bitter wave of resolve sweep through him as he prepared for the question he barely had the nerve to ask.

He faced the sea, focused on a light on the horizon, and steeled himself. 'Any other injuries to the body?'

'Her tongue's been cut out.'

'Oh for God's sake.' He emptied his lungs, then sucked in air for all he was worth. He struggled to block out the horrifying image, shifted his gaze to the Eden Estuary, and forced his mind to recall a recent photograph he'd taken from the West Sands – black sea lightening under a heavy-clouded dawn sky, Tentsmuir Beach a sliver of white on the other side of the estuary. It looked as if he'd printed the photo in black and white, but that February morning had been so dull the world could have been devoid of colour.

But it was no use.

Unsummoned images flickered into his mind in blood-red flashes. You couldn't pull out a tongue with your fingers – too slippery – and the body's natural reaction would retract it into the mouth. No, you needed some tool to grip it and stretch it long enough to remove it with a scalpel. He felt certain it had to be a spiked tool of sorts to pierce the tongue and grip it with no fear of slipping – like a carpet fitter's knee kicker. But knee kickers were hefty pieces of equipment, and too big to squeeze into—

'You still there?'

'Yeah, I'm just . . .' He shook his head and turned from the estuary, found his gaze returning to the Rusacks as his fear of the next question grew. Even so, he had to ask. 'Was she alive when her tongue was cut out?'

'Looks that way. Fair amount of blood on her face, neck, and carpet.'

'And the tape?'

'Yes.' Jessie let out a sigh. 'Mouth taped. Nose, too.'

Just like Soutar.

He closed his eyes, squeezed the bridge of his nose until he felt pain. Nailed to the floor, staked out naked and helpless, unable to breathe, the stump of your tongue bleeding profusely, it would take less than a few minutes to drown in your blood – not to mention the pain that would surely push you to the brink of unconsciousness as your body writhed in agony against the nails in a futile struggle to stay alive . . .

He opened his eyes, and realised he hadn't asked the obvious.

Soutar's body had gone through one final act of humiliation – a single vertical cut through his left nipple, confirmed by Cooper to have been done post mortem. No one could explain why the killer had cut through Soutar's nipple, other than to suggest it was some act of depravity from which he took sickening satisfaction, God only knew why.

'Any post-mortem cuts?' he asked.

'Yes,' Jessie said.

Her hesitancy had him asking, 'Through her nipple?'

She let out a heavy sigh, warning him that worse was yet to come. 'Again, it's early days, Andy, but I don't think Soutar's nipple was cut just for the hell of it. The killer was leaving us a message.'

'A message? What sort of message could a sliced nipple leave?'

'He was cutting a number.'

'Ah,' he said, as his sense of logic gave him the answer. The single slice through Soutar's nipple could mean only one thing. Number one. Soutar was his first victim. 'And you know that now,' he said, 'because the number two was cut into—'

'No, Andy. Try *four*.'

His breath clogged in his throat. Four could mean only one thing. Dear God, surely never. 'So there are two more victims—'

'Correct—'

'Nailed to some floor in some building—'

'Correct—'

'And no one has a bloody clue where.'

'None whatsoever,' she added.

The difficulty facing the investigation team struck him with such overwhelming force that his immediate thoughts were of certain failure. Victims one and four had been found in the Kingdom of Fife; Adam Soutar in his home in Cupar, Margaret Rickard in her home in Kincaple on the outskirts of St Andrews. But it didn't necessarily follow that victims two and three had also been killed in Fife – provided, of course, that one and four referred to the order of the killings, and not to some obscure numerical code known only to the killer. But with nothing to go on, he said, 'I need to see Soutar's files.'

'Already on your desk. As soon as I saw the number four, I knew you couldn't resist. Besides,' she added, 'we could really use some help.' A pause, then, 'Where are you? Want me to pick you up?'

'How soon can you get to the Office?'

'Fifteen minutes, give or take.'

'Make it twenty, and bring the coffees.'

She chuckled. 'Want to share a muffin?'

But Gilchrist had already ended the call, and was jogging back to his car.

CHAPTER 2

When Gilchrist entered the North Street Police Station for the first time in four weeks, it felt surreal, as if he wasn't there at all, but was recalling memories through anxious dreams while he convalesced at home like Dr McAuley – his local GP – insisted he should. *Take it easy, and put your feet up for once in your life.* But being signed off for eight weeks due to ill health – even though he had the toughest time acknowledging that exhaustion could in any way be termed *ill health* – was more than he could be expected to handle.

Upstairs, he entered his office and was overcome by the oddest sense of stepping into the room for the first time, or perhaps more correctly, the uneasy feeling that his position of Detective Chief Inspector of St Andrews CID had long been forgotten. Gone were walls that once held tattered corkboards crammed with highlighted memos, dog-eared reports, scribbled Post-its, spiked to the cork with more pins than a hedgehog has spines. Gone, too, was his whiteboard that traced a history of past investigations, older case notes visible only as wiped-out ghostly images over which more recent timelines, places, names of suspects, had been circled, boxed or linked with arrowed lines that swept with investigative certainty from one to the other. Instead, in their place hung two whiteboards, pristine clean, magnetic markers and a row of coloured pens neatly positioned in the boards' trays.

The wall by the side of his desk, on which he'd Sellotaped handwritten to-do lists or blue-tacked crime scene photographs, had been stripped clean, too, patched up and painted. In fact, as he took his seat at his desk he saw that the entire room had been painted. He tried to remember what shade of cream the walls had been – lighter or darker? – but his thoughts were distracted by a loose-leafed folder that sat squarely on his uncluttered desk.

He opened it and forced himself to study the crime scene photographs.

Adam Soutar's unseeing eyes stared out at him, wide and petrified, as if he'd peered over his taped nose and died from shock. Gilchrist flipped onto the next image – another of Soutar's face, not as close-up – which showed trails of blood over his bare chest. He flipped to the next image – more of the same – then the next, and the next, and again until he was turning over the photos like a card shark searching for a missing ace.

Even so, it was no use. He pushed to his feet, reached for the window, and opened it wide. He sucked in clean, cold air. His head spun, his peripheral vision darkened, and for one moment he wasn't sure if he was having a panic attack, or suffering from the exertion of his early morning jog. He found himself placing both hands on the window sill, closing his eyes, and lowering his head until the dizziness passed—

'Got a blueberry muffin to share,' Jessie said. 'Your favourite.'

He turned from the window, tried to give her a smile, but failed.

Jessie frowned for a moment, then caught sight of the opened folder. 'Bloody horrific, isn't it?' She held out his Starbucks. 'Your usual latte. That'll get rid of the foul taste in your mouth.'

'Thanks,' he said, and took a welcoming sip.

She grimaced, nodded to the crime scene photographs. 'I won't challenge you with details of where I've just come from. But I'm sorry to say it's more of the same.' She tore off a chunk of muffin, threw it into her mouth, and downed it with a slug of coffee. 'I was doing well with my diet until this morning. No chocolate. No muffins. Now I know you're to blame.' Another sip, then, 'You not having any?'

He shook his head. 'I'll stick with this for the time being.'

'Are you sure?' Her hand hovered over the muffin.

'Positive.'

'Your choice.' It didn't take her long to devour the rest of the muffin, three bites as it turned out. She dabbed a tissue at her lips, then grinned. 'I'd forgotten how good these are.' She nodded to the folder again. 'You get a chance to read any of that?'

He shook his head. 'Just the photographs.'

She reached for the folder, flipped through the photos one by one. She stopped at a close-up of Soutar's bare chest, then pulled the image closer. 'You know, I hadn't noticed until now, but that cut's sliced right through the centre of his nipple as if he's measured it precisely.'

Intrigued, Gilchrist leaned forward and, with a sense of purpose that time, managed to study the image with professional dispassion. Sure enough, the skin above and beneath the nipple appeared to have been sliced in equal lengths. The open cut went through the centre of the nipple with almost surgical precision. He thought it odd, but said nothing.

'Now I've noticed that,' Jessie said, 'it makes sense of the mess this morning.'

'What do you mean?' It was all he could think to ask.

Jessie removed a pen from her pocket and opened her notebook. She drew a small circle, and crossed two lines through it – left to right, and top to bottom – forming the shape of a cross. Then she drew a diagonal line to create the number four. She held the notebook out to him. 'That's how Margaret Rickard's nipple was cut,' she said. 'With precision.'

'And equally spaced?'

'As if he's measured it.'

'So we're looking for a psychopathic killer with OCD tendencies?'

Jessie shrugged her shoulders. 'All I'm saying is, that it's odd. Don't you think? But now I think about it . . .' She flicked through more images of Soutar's body until she found what she was looking for. 'Here,' she said. 'Take a look.'

Gilchrist stared at Soutar's face, his mouth taped with duct tape, his nose, too. It took several seconds before he thought he saw what Jessie seemed excited about. 'It's as if he's placed the duct tape across his mouth and nose with care,' he said.

'Try precision,' she said. 'See? The tape's been cut with scissors, not ripped.'

'It's duct tape. You can't tear it off like masking tape. You *have* to cut it.'

'But do you have to line it up?' She pulled the photo closer. 'He puts the tape over the mouth first, then stretches another strip over the nose, so that the ends match up.'

Gilchrist had to agree. Soutar's nose had been flattened to one side by the tape being stretched to line up the ends. But something still wasn't right. 'He couldn't do that.'

'Why not?'

'Think about it. He's cut the tongue out. Soutar's alive and kicking, about to drown in his own blood, and the killer takes time to place the tape over his nose and mouth with precision? I don't see how that's possible.'

Jessie stared at the image, as if seeing it for the first time. 'You have a point.'

He took the photo from her, and pulled it close. He studied the image and came to see what he thought everyone, including himself, appeared to have missed. 'Have another look at Soutar's face,' he said. 'And tell me what you see.'

Jessie eyed the photo for a few seconds. 'He looks terrified?'

'Other than that.'

It took five more seconds before she squinted a look at him. 'Is this you back to your old tricks, or what?'

'Your tongue's just been cut out, and you're drowning in your own blood. You'd be coughing and spluttering and spattering blood all over the place.'

She frowned at the photo. 'You're right. There's some blood, but not a lot.'

'Cooper's PM report concluded that Soutar died by drowning in his own blood. So was the tape placed there post mortem? Or not?'

'Post mortem, I'd say. It's too precise to be done when he's alive.'

'Agreed.'

'So he waits until he's dead, then tapes him up with precision.'

Gilchrist nodded, as other thoughts filtered through his mind. 'I'm assuming we still have the tape,' he said.

'We do.'

'If both strips of tape were placed post mortem, then I'd imagine the other side would show minimal blood, rather than being awash in the stuff.'

'I'll get onto that,' Jessie said, then smiled up at him. 'It's good to have you back, Andy.'

He gave a wry smile, and closed Soutar's folder with a finality he longed for. Then he walked from his desk to the window, all of a sudden overwhelmed by his return to the Office. Until that moment, he'd thought he'd been more than ready to get back to work, that he was taking unfair advantage of being signed off for eight weeks, being paid for taking the time to get into shape again; change of diet – less of the starchy stuff, and more fish and chicken; and a composite fitness regimen – light weights, take it easy with the trunk curls, timed jogs along the West Sands. But now he was back at the Office, looking at images that would be cut from triple X-rated horror movies, was he really ready for it?

He let his gaze drift over the old familiar scene below.

Beyond the boundary walls, to the backs of the buildings on Market Street, in winter window boxes that sat on kitchen sills, he could just make out the faintest hints of colour – hyacinths, crocuses, winter aconites, past their best. In drab back lawns, daffodil stems poked through frosted soil as if to insist that winter really had passed, and spring was here at last. He found his thoughts drifting to his garden in Windmill Road, before his late wife, Gail, had left St Andrews and pissed off to Glasgow, both kids in tow, before he sold up and bought a cottage in Crail. He remembered how Gail used to spend hours tending bulbs in readiness for spring – one of the many things he liked about her – which had his thoughts returning to Margaret Rickard, retired, living in her cottage on her own, lonely, harmless, her life snuffed out for seemingly no reason. What had her thoughts been that morning? Now they were gone. She would never again see the heart-warming colours of spring, or smell the promise of summer on westerly breezes—

'What're you thinking, Andy?'

He kept his back to Jessie, and said, 'Can you give me a few minutes?'

'Everything all right?'

'Just a few minutes, please.'

Without a word, she left the room.

He waited until he heard the lock click before he lifted a hand to his face and wiped it dry.

CHAPTER 3

Despite his better judgement, Gilchrist instructed Jessie to make sure that Margaret Rickard's body was not moved to the mortuary before he had a chance to inspect the crime scene. He wanted to do so with her body *in situ*, so to speak.

Now he was there, an almost overpowering sense of regret swamped his mind. He closed his car door and looked around him. The SOCO transit van was parked by the garden gate, doors open, as if abandoned. Metal plates, on which Scenes of Crime Officers and other members of the investigation team were obliged to walk – to preserve whatever forensic evidence might be available – were evenly spaced along the garden path. Cooper's Range Rover, polished and shining good as new, stood parked at the end of the dirt driveway. He removed a packet of coveralls from the boot and pulled them on with thoughtful silence, taking care to tuck in loose strands of hair, all the while fighting off the urge just to turn around and drive home.

'I'll wait for you here,' Jessie said.

He grimaced beneath his mask, thankful that it hid the hard set of his jaw, and hoped she hadn't seen the uncertainty in his eyes.

At the entrance to the cottage, he hesitated, took one last look around him, like a prisoner taking a final look at life before stepping into the hanging chamber, then entered the kitchen area and walked to the living room . . .

He drew to a halt in the doorway, pressed a hand against it for support.

On the floor by the window lay the puce-skinned body of a naked woman, spread-eagled, supine, callused feet pointing to the ceiling. The heads of two six-inch nails protruded from just below her ankles, at the point where the foot's smaller bones made the hammering less difficult. Twin trails of congealed blood painted her skin and ran to blackened pools on the carpet. The calves of her legs were loose-muscled, her heavy thighs, too, flattened and cratered with cellulite. Her pubic hair, greying and thinning, trailed to a stomach scarred with stretch marks that suggested childbirth or major weight loss. A pair of breasts drooped either side of her chest like empty saddlebags, and her arms, soft-muscled and folded in dimpled fat, reached out to the tell-tale glint of nail-heads in wrists striped with blood.

He swallowed a rising lump in his throat as he forced himself to study her face.

In the flesh, death looked different, the impossible stillness of the body difficult to take in. No ticking of blood pulsing beneath blood-striped skin. No flutter of eyelashes at the slightest movement of wind. No hint of warmth from an already stiffening body. He moved closer in a determined effort to view the victim's face with professional dispassion.

Blood spatter ran over her chin, trailed across her chest. He didn't have to peel back the tape to know that it marked the route her tongue had taken as it was removed from her mouth and deposited in . . . ? He couldn't say, could only surmise that it had been taken as a trophy, put in a glass jar, or a plastic container. A tremor took hold of his legs as he imagined blood swelling from the stump of her tongue – an intensely vascular organ – to settle in her throat as she fought against the choking flow and the terrifying sensation of drowning. What must she have felt when the need to breathe or swallow was overcome by the horrifying realisation that she was about to die? But even so, her eyes seemed to lack that look of terror he'd picked up from Soutar's photographs, as if at some point – perhaps at the exact moment of her dying – she had just given up, and succumbed with resolute calm to the inevitable.

Beads of sweat tickled his brow, and he realised he was breathing hard. He pulled himself upright, forced himself to take long breaths, then focused on the furnishings in the room, the often overlooked details of the crime scene.

The first thing that struck him was the tidiness of the place.

Framed pictures of Highland landscapes, rushing waterfalls, snow-covered mountains, adorned every wall. Sets of photographs stood in perfect array on coffee and side tables that gleamed with polish. A two-seater fabric sofa backed onto a wall that faced the fireplace, the coal fire bricked over and replaced by an electric monstrosity that flickered fake flames from fake logs. Whatever heat it was generating was being sucked out the open doors. Plumped up cushions in pastel shades and bold tartan plaid stood against the back of the sofa, or snuggled into its corners. Arm covers folded over the sofa without so much as a crinkled crease, as if they'd been ironed into place. The victim's clothes, neatly folded and pressed flat, lay on one seat of the sofa in the reverse order of their removal – knickers, bra, underskirt, skirt, blouse, woollen cardigan. Other than the body on the floor, nothing seemed out of place. No signs of struggle. No signs that an elderly woman had been tortured and murdered in this room.

No disturbance of any kind.

Which was when he noticed, as his gaze returned to the clothes on the sofa, that she must not have been wearing tights or stockings, or slippers or shoes of any kind. Just that small pile of clothes. Nothing else.

And what about jewellery?

A glance at the body had him thinking she wore none. But he knelt down beside her, just to be sure, eased a finger through her hair at each ear, one by one, to confirm no earrings. No bracelets on her wrists. No rings on her fingers. He puzzled over that, and made a mental note to check with her brother, Tom, who might confirm some jewellery was missing. He pushed himself upright again, and let his gaze shift around the room.

Strangely, or so he thought, there didn't appear to be any signs of the killer having sat on the sofa or either of the two armchairs. In fact, the whole room seemed unusually clean, as if the killer had vacuumed it after he'd carried out the killing. Again, Gilchrist tried to run the scenario through his mind. Had the killer – before he'd nailed his victim to the floor – stood back and watched her undress herself? Had he kept hold of whatever jewellery she'd been wearing as some sort of memento of that killing, her footwear and stockings, too?

It seemed as if he was finding more questions than answers . . .

His thoughts were interrupted by Cooper appearing in the doorway to the hall. She faced him, arms folded, looking at him as if he'd crawled out from under a stone. With her forensic coveralls and face mask on, all he could see were her eyes – the bluest of blues, wide apart, deep set – which seemed to soften from the hint of a smile as he returned her gaze.

'DS Janes told me not to leave the crime scene until you arrived,' she said.

'Not like you to take instruction from Jessie.'

'I was more surprised to hear you were back.'

He jerked a half-hearted smile. 'Want to share your thoughts?'

'DS Janes should learn some manners, and have more respect for her peers.'

Silent, he stared at her.

'Other than that,' she went on, 'I'd say you're looking for a serial killer.' She walked towards him, eyes fixed on his, and for one disconcerting moment he thought she was going to give him a hug. But she turned away at the last second to kneel on the floor, where she took hold of the victim's left breast, eased it from her side, and placed it with care on her chest. 'Did DS Janes tell you about this?'

He kneeled beside Cooper, annoyed with himself that not only had he forgotten about it, he hadn't even noticed. He said nothing as Cooper traced the tip of a gloved finger along the three cutlines, which together formed the number four.

'She did,' he said. 'So what're your thoughts?'

'These cuts were formed post mortem.'

He nodded. 'And the number four?'

'I'm not the detective. That's your job.'

'Well,' he said, 'it suggests that we've yet to find victims two and three.' He sensed she was about to stand, and he added, 'So what do you think about the duct tape?'

She frowned for a moment. 'In terms of what?'

He didn't want to put words in her mouth, so said, 'How did she die?'

‘I can’t say with absolute certainty until I carry out the post mortem.’

‘I know that, Becky, but for crying out loud give me your best guess.’

‘I see time off hasn’t improved your impatience.’

He said nothing, kept his gaze locked on hers, until she turned away and leaned closer to the woman’s face. ‘If it’s the same MO as Adam Soutar,’ she said, ‘then I’d expect to see her tongue missing, her lungs filled with blood, and cause of death suffocation by drowning.’ She faced him. ‘Does that satisfy you?’

‘I think the duct tape might have been placed post mortem,’ he said.

She frowned, stared at the face again. ‘Why would you say that?’

‘When you perform your post-mortem examination, pay particular attention to the other side of the duct tape. If my theory’s correct, there won’t be as much blood as you’d expect to find if her mouth and nose had been taped before she died.’

She seemed to give his words some thought, before saying, ‘Does it matter?’

What could he say? That he didn’t know? Instead, he said, ‘There’s not much blood, is there? With her tongue being cut out, blood should be spattered everywhere.’

‘I thought that, too, with Soutar,’ she said. ‘Which made me think he’d been drugged. But I found no evidence.’

‘You couldn’t have missed something, could you?’

Her eyes cut his way. ‘What do you think?’

He didn’t want to get into it with her, so he pushed to his feet, and offered his hand to help her up.

She ignored it. ‘So what are you telling me?’

'The killer must have been covered in blood. But somehow he's managed to keep all traces of it to a minimum.' He shrugged, ran his gaze along the dead woman's body. 'He'll need to get rid of whatever he was wearing. Bury it. Burn it. I don't know. But until he does, he's in possession of evidence that could link him to this killing.'

'And how are you going to find that?'

'As you said, I'm the detective.' Then he turned and walked from the room, troubled by Cooper's simple question.

CHAPTER 4

Back outside, he removed his face mask and sucked in refreshing wintry air. He'd just slipped out of his coveralls when Cooper walked up to him, pulling hers back from her hair – still a surprise to see it cut short.

'Nice shoes,' she said.

He'd had no time to change out of his jogging gear, and had simply jumped into his car and followed Jessie's directions. 'It takes all sorts,' he said, irritated that he could find nothing more biting to say.

'You look well, Andy.'

'I feel well,' he said. 'At least, until I had a look at that lot this morning.'

She flashed him the tiniest of smiles. 'What I mean is, that the time off has done you good. You look relaxed. More like your old self.'

'Old self?' He grimaced. 'Not sure I like the sounds of that.'

'You were signed off for a reason,' she said. 'You blacked out. You had a breakdown. You'd pushed your body beyond its limits. You'd been overworking.' She sighed, and stared at the cottage, at the front window beyond which lay the tortured body of Margaret Rickard. 'I could see it in your eyes,' she said, and turned to face him. 'I could hear it in your voice. The tightness. The tension. The . . .' She shook her head. '. . . The anger.'

'Anger?'

'Maybe not anger, then. Frustration might be a better word.'

'So what're you saying, Becky?'

'That when you're investigating a murder, you're driven. You're . . . I don't know . . . you become *obsessed* with the case.'

'Is that bad?'

'It is, if the obsession is detrimental to your health, which it clearly had been.'

'Which is why I've taken up jogging again. To run all that *obsession* out of my system.'

She gave him a dry smile, ran a hand through her hair. Now she'd had it cut into a fringed bob, it no longer had the same sensual impact on him. 'That's your most unattractive trait,' she said.

'What is?'

'Minimising me.'

'I didn't intend to.' He should have added – sorry – but somehow didn't feel she deserved that.

'Could I say something to you?'

'If you like.'

'Sir?' Jessie had her mobile to her ear, waving at him.

Cooper tutted.

'Let me know what you find,' he said.

He reached Jessie, who held up her hand as a sign not to interrupt, then said, 'He's here,' and passed her mobile to him. 'It's Mhairi.'

He took the mobile. 'Yes, Mhairi.'

'I'm sorry, sir. I didn't know you were back, or I would've phoned you instead, sir.'

'That's all right, Mhairi. What've you got?'

'I was running some data through the PNC this morning, sir, when I found a post by Strathclyde Police about a murder in the outskirts of Glasgow. The details were similar to a murder we had here a few weeks ago, sir.'

'Adam Soutar's?'

'Yes, sir. Did you know about that, sir?'

He found himself reluctant to mention that he and Jessie had been in contact. 'I read about it in the newspapers.'

'We kept most of the details of Soutar's killing from the press, sir.'

'Always a good move, Mhairi.'

'Yes, sir.'

'And we have another victim in Kincaple,' he said. 'The same MO as Soutar's. Did Jessie tell you about it?'

'Briefly, sir.'

'So it looks as though we have a serial killer in Fife, who may have spread his wings to Strathclyde. Let's have the details.' A tickle of excitement coursed through him as Mhairi read the post from the PNC, which left him in no doubt that they'd found one of the other two victims, already identified as a Mr Albert Forest, a retired school teacher. But when Mhairi made no mention of a number having been cut anywhere on the body post mortem, he said, 'Who's the SIO?'

'A DI Barnes, sir. From the Cumbernauld Office.'

Gilchrist had never heard the name, wouldn't have expected to, but he thanked Mhairi, then told her to locate a phone number for DI Barnes – he needed to speak to him.

'It's DI Ella Barnes, sir, and I have her number right here.'

Gilchrist assigned it to memory. 'I'll contact the Cumbernauld Office. But I need you to get hold of Jackie, and the two of you to find the connection between Albert Forest and our victims in Fife. Maybe they're members of the same golf club, or went to school together. I don't know, but there must be some link. There's no indication that this killer is going to stop anytime soon, so you and Jackie need to work on that as a matter of priority.'

'I'm on it, sir.'

'Let me know the instant you find anything,' he said, and ended the call. He returned Jessie's mobile to her, then using his own mobile tapped in the number for DI Barnes before he forgot it. He'd always had an excellent memory for numbers, but was now finding that the older he became, the quicker the numbers slipped free.

His call was answered on the second ring.

'DI Barnes. Who's this?'

The voice was deep and Glasgow-hard, and took him by surprise. But he introduced himself and said, 'I understand you're the SIO on Albert Forest's murder.'

'I am, yeah. Why? You got a hit?'

'In the past four weeks we've had two similar murders in Fife,' he said. 'So it looks like we could be dealing with the same killer.'

'Never heard nothing about the second one. You post it on the PNC?'

'Not had time to post it. We've only just discovered her.'

'Ah. Okay. Right.' A pause, then, 'Send me what you've got.'

'I'd like to drive down this morning and discuss it with you. That work for you?'

'Sure. I'll be in the South Muirhead Office. Ask for me when you get here.'

The line died.

He nodded to Jessie. 'I need you to come with me to Cumbernauld. And get Mhairi and Jackie to email Soutar's files to DI Ella Barnes of the South Muirhead Office.' He rattled off Barnes's phone number then threw his coveralls into the boot.

'Did you say Ella Barnes?'

'I did.'

'I used to know an Ella Barnes.'

'Used to?'

'A while ago. When I worked in Strathclyde.'

'Might be a common name.'

Jessie raised her eyebrows. 'Did she have a voice like a foghorn?'

'Pretty much.'

'Is that who we're going to meet?'

He hesitated as he opened the car door. 'You don't look happy.'

'I'm fine.' She sniffed, tugged at her collar, then took her seat in the car.

Without a word, he clicked on his seatbelt and eased away from the cottage, while Jessie phoned Mhairi. They drove through Strathkinness and were almost at the West Port mini-roundabout when Jessie said, 'This isn't the way to Cumbernauld.'

'I'm heading home for a quick shower and a change of clothes. Wouldn't want to give Barnes the wrong impression.'

'She's not your type.'

'Metaphorically speaking.'

'Whatever.'

They drove along South Street, and turned into Abbey Road when Gilchrist said, 'Want to tell me why you don't like this DI Barnes?'

'It's nothing.'

'It might help if you talk about it.'

'I doubt it.'

'Give it a try,' he said. 'You used to work together, you said. In Strathclyde.'

'We used to work in the same unit in Pitt Street. Under Jabba.'

'Ah,' Gilchrist said. Jabba the Hutt was Jessie's nickname for DI Lachlan McKellar, her overweight ex-boss in Strathclyde Police, with whom she'd once had a fling, or as Jessie had related it – *a quick shag that I'll regret to the day I die*. It had taken some strong words and the threat of a complaint of sexual harassment before Jabba understood that whatever relationship he thought he might have had with Jessie was over and done with for good.

'Is Jabba the reason you don't get on with Ella?' he ventured.

'One of them.'

'And the others?'

'I never took to her, and she never took to me.'

It took another half mile of silence for Gilchrist to say, 'And?'

Jessie let out a heavy sigh, shifted her butt on her seat. 'We had a run-in about six months before I transferred up here. And what is it with the twenty questions?' She turned her face to the window. 'A heathen bitch is what she is.'

'*Was*,' he said. 'She might have changed since you last saw her.'

She grunted. 'That'll be right. Leopard's spots and all that.'

Gilchrist thought silence as good a response as any, and drove on.

In Crail, he parked in Castle Street and, as he ushered Jessie into his house ahead of him, said, 'Kettle's in the kitchen. Mine's a tea. Help yourself. I might have some biscuits somewhere.'

In his bedroom, he entered the en suite bathroom and switched on the shower, before stripping off. He let the shower run while he brushed his teeth, then scrubbed his hands and fingers with a nailbrush, reddening his skin until he felt as if every single molecule of that morning's crime scene had been washed away.

In the shower cubicle, he turned up the thermostat, let the water run piping hot, almost too hot to bear. Then he lathered himself from head to toe, trying to cleanse every sickening sense from his being. He shaved, too, using a waterproof electric shaver he'd purchased on one of his rare trips to the States. And the hot water worked its magic. When he stepped from the cubicle and rubbed himself dry, he felt cleansed, relaxed, his leg muscles still tight from that morning's run, a minor complaint to remind him that he was getting older, and should be careful not to over-exert himself in his bid to get back into shape – whatever shape that was supposed to take.

In his bedroom, he removed a laundered white shirt from the wardrobe, and pulled on his denim jeans he'd worn the day before. He fastened his belt, pleased to note that he had to tighten it up a notch. Not that he'd been overweight before having his episode, which is what his daughter, Maureen, liked to call it – *You've had a minor episode, Dad. It's your body warning you that you're working too hard. So take heed. And for once in your life do as the doctor tells you.*

Up until that moment when he'd passed out in the Central Bar, he'd assumed that the tiredness that seemed to follow him had been nothing more than not enough sleep or exercise, or from spending too much time at the Office; more like he'd let himself become unfit, even though his weight maintained a steady eleven and a half stones in old money. He used to joke that he wasn't putting on weight, just taking up more space. Now, as he slipped on his leather jacket, his clothes hanging looser gave him a sense of being healthier and fitter.

In the kitchen, Jessie had a mug of tea in her hand. 'Ah, you're still alive,' she said. 'Thought you'd flushed yourself down the loo. Poured you a cuppa, but it'll be cold by now.'

'I'll pop it in the microwave.'

She grimaced as he set the timer. 'Doesn't that stew it?'

'Not enough to make a difference.' He nodded to a ceramic jar on the worktop. 'Did you find the biscuits?'

'I've already had my calorific intake for the week, thanks to you.'

'I thought you liked muffins.'

'That's the problem.' The microwave beeped. 'While you were having your shower, Jackie sent a text. And guess what? Albert Forest used to teach at St John's Roman Catholic High School in Dundee, the same school Margaret Rickard went to.'

'How old's Forest?'

'Seventy-two.'

Hearing that sent a wave of disappointment through him. He'd thought for an instant that Forest and Rickard might have been in the same class, which could have given them the connection they were searching for, perhaps even a motive – classmate seeking revenge after all these years. But he said, 'What school did Soutar go to?

'I've got Jackie working on it.'

'Come on,' he said. 'Let's find out what DI Barnes has to tell us.'

'What about your tea?'

'I'll get it tonight.'

'Jesus, Andy, you'll be telling me you like cold pizza next.'

'Didn't I tell you that's one of my favourites?'

'Are you winding me up?'

But he already had his car keys in his hand and was striding down the hall.

CHAPTER 5

DI Ella Barnes looked nothing like Gilchrist imagined. He'd had a mental image of a heavy-set woman who reeked of stale cigarettes, who could down pints with men, and hold her own in an arm-wrestling competition. What he hadn't expected was a petite platinum blonde with white teeth and lively eyes, wearing tight jeans that squeezed her body.

She shook his hand with a firm grip and a curt, 'Good to meet you,' in a voice that sounded more husky than foghorn, now she was in the flesh.

He introduced Jessie, and they tapped hands in silence.

Whatever fallout they'd had seemed still fresh.

And the way Barnes strode through the Office, heads turning as she passed, not from the sexuality she exuded, but from the way she gave off the impression that she was a woman with only one goal in sight – the top job – and you'd better not cross her.

Jessie, on the other hand, seemed inordinately cowed in her presence.

Barnes's desk was one of several set into the open space in cubicle formation. No real chance of privacy, Gilchrist thought, but when Barnes spoke, she could have been the only person in the entire building.

'Right,' she said. 'Here they are. Photos that would make you sick to your back teeth.'

'Did you get sight of our files?' Gilchrist asked, as he leaned forward to have a look.

'I did, yeah. Looks like we've got one sick fuck out there.'

Jessie said, 'What about his left nipple?'

'What about it?'

'Was it cut?'

A pause, then, 'Why?'

'In a minute,' Jessie said, and flipped through the crime scene photographs, one by one, as Gilchrist handed them to her.

More of the same, Gilchrist thought – naked body stretched out on the floor, nailed wrists and ankles, taped mouth and nose, both lengths of tape cut to the perfect match, eyes wide and fearful – just like Soutar's – and not a lot of blood. But the scene was different in one critical way. The body was bloated, the skin discoloured. Putrefaction had already set in by the time Forest's body had been discovered.

'Estimated time of death?' Gilchrist asked.

'Last seen on Friday the twenty-ninth of February,' Barnes said, 'at the Post Office collecting his pension. Then not seen again until a neighbour called in saying there was a bad smell coming from his house. The heating had been turned up high, too, which we suspect was deliberate, to expedite decomposition. Best we can tell, he'd been dead for twelve days.'

'Did the neighbour hear anything? See anything?'

'Just come back from two weeks in Tenerife the other night. Called it in yesterday morning.'

'So, if we assume he'd been alive when his neighbour went on holiday, that gives us a two-week window.' He flipped through more photos. 'Do you think it's significant he was killed in his neighbour's absence?'

'Meaning that the killer knew the place was quiet? That the neighbour's away? Nobody to disturb him?'

'Him?' Gilchrist said.

She nodded. 'That's what we're thinking.'

Jessie said, 'We're pretty sure it's a male perpetrator. His first victim, Adam Soutar, was a heavy man, someone you couldn't shove about without having muscles.'

'You sure Soutar was his first victim?'

'We believe so,' Gilchrist said. 'Which is why DS Janes was asking about the left nipple. Any photos of the clothes?' he went on, before Barnes could question him.

'Not with that lot.' She opened a folder, and removed another batch of photos. 'Here they are. What're you looking for?'

Gilchrist eyed the neat pile on the kitchen table. 'Same MO,' he said. 'No signs of a struggle. No defensive wounds. Nothing. Just stretched out and nailed to the floor.' He shook his head. 'What makes the victims do as they're told? What hold does he have over them?'

'Fear?'

'It's more than that, I'd say.'

'Drugged,' Jessie said. 'They have to be.'

Barnes tutted. 'We've found nothing so far.'

'Neither have we,' Gilchrist said, then added, 'I don't see any photos of his nipples.'

'What's with the nipples?' Barnes complained.

Jessie said, 'He leaves a message in the shape of a post-mortem cut.'

'Message?'

'A number.'

'Ah,' Barnes said, as if some switch had clicked on. 'I wondered what that was. You don't see it too well from the photos, but it was mentioned in the PM report.' She opened another file, and riffled through it. 'Here.' She read it out. 'Subcutaneous post-mortem cuts on the left chest in the shape of a Z.'

Gilchrist took the file from her, and gave it a quick scan, noting cause of death – *suffocation by drowning in his own blood*. He passed the file to Jessie. 'I suspect the letter Z is intended to be the number two. It's easier to cut three straight lines with precision, rather than trying to form an exact two.'

'Is that important?' Barnes asked.

'We think so,' he said. 'Our two victims have the numbers one and four cut through their left nipple. Yours has the number two—'

'Shit in a bucket,' Barnes said. 'So there's a third one still out there?'

'How would you describe the crime scene?' Gilchrist asked, as if she hadn't spoken.

'In what way?'

'Any mess?'

She frowned, puzzlement reaching her eyes. 'No. The room was spotless, well, as spotless as it could be, given the circumstances.'

'Nothing out of place?' he said. 'Every piece of furniture as it should be?'

Barnes shook her head. 'Nothing,' she said, but Gilchrist didn't expand on his theory in case it came back to bite him. Instead, when Barnes excused herself to take a call, he and Jessie spent the next thirty minutes reading door-to-door interview reports, and the written statement of the neighbour who called it in.

By all accounts Albert Forest had been a quiet man who kept himself to himself and bothered no one. He lived alone, his wife having died from Alzheimer's four years earlier. Married for forty-plus years, they'd had no children, and Albert's only living relative – his older brother, William – who'd emigrated to Toronto, Canada, in his early twenties, had kept in contact – if it could be called that – by sending Christmas and birthday cards once a year.

Which had Gilchrist's thoughts powering into overdrive.

All three victims had lived alone – both Forest and Soutar had been married to women who predeceased them. And Margaret Rickard had never married. Was that the connection – no matter how tenuous – that this killer chose only elderly people who lived alone? Or was the most slender of connections the fact that they were all retired? Soutar from a career in law. Rickard from Human Resources with Santander Bank. And Forest from a teaching position in St John's Roman Catholic High School in Dundee. And again, something shifted through his thoughts. Both Forest and Rickard attended St John's RC High School as pupils, but he hadn't heard back from Mhairi regarding Soutar's education. His thoughts were interrupted when Barnes returned, face tight, eyes alive with anger.

'Problems?' Gilchrist asked.

'Nothing that can't be solved with a stiff disciplinary hearing,' she snarled. 'I'm going to have to cut our meeting short.'

Something seemed to shiver through the air between Barnes and Jessie at that, which prompted Jessie to gather her notes and say, 'I'll meet you outside.'

Silent, Gilchrist watched her walk to the door and push through it without a backward glance. 'You and Jessie used to work together,' he said. 'In Pitt Street.'

'*Used to* being the operative words.'

When he realised that Barnes wasn't going to offer more, he thanked her for her time, gave assurance that his team would advise her Office of progress in the investigation, and told her that he expected reciprocal cooperation.

A grimace for a nod, and a soft handshake for agreement, ended the meeting.

Outside, he found Jessie standing by his car, backside resting on the bonnet. He beeped his remote fob, and she jerked with surprise.

'You really don't like DI Barnes, do you?' he said.

'Surprised you noticed.'

'Care to explain?'

'Forget it, Andy. It's nothing.'

Neither of them spoke until he accelerated onto the M80. 'If there's anything between you and Barnes that could rear up to bite us,' he said, 'I need to know about it. I can't have her casting up something that could . . .' He shook his head, as he searched for a polite way to say it. '. . . jeopardise the integrity of this investigation.'

It took two more miles of silence before Jessie said, 'It's nothing that could jeopardise your investigation, Andy. It's just that it's . . . it's so bloody embarrassing, that's all.'

He nodded. 'I'm listening.'

She turned away, and spoke to the countryside. 'You know all about Jabba, aka DI Lachie Fucking McKellar, and my one-off affair with that fat bastard.' She waited until he grunted acknowledgement. 'Well, what you don't know is that Lachie'd once been a rising star in Pitt Street, someone who was climbing the ladder, destined for the top of the shitpile, until we had that knee trembler in his office.'

'Ah,' Gilchrist said, thinking he knew where this was going. 'The Office is never a good place in which to conduct . . . how do I say it . . . passionate relations.'

'And don't I know it.' Jessie lifted her hands and clutched both sides of her head, as if trying to squeeze a headache away. 'Well it was that bitch, Barnes, who caught us.'

'Caught you? As in . . . reported you?'

'No. Nothing like that. My God, I can feel my face flushing at the thought of it.'

Gilchrist was about to tell her to forget it, he didn't need to know the details, but she beat him to it.

'She opened Lachie's office door, and there we were. Me with my bare arse wobbling like a vat-load of jello, and that fat bastard grunting and slathering all over me like he'd never had his nookie in ten years.'

'Was that what the *stiff disciplinary hearing* comment was hinting at?'

'There was no disciplinary hearing, stiff or otherwise.'

Gilchrist frowned. 'I don't understand.'

'She had to rub it in, the *bitch*.' If ever Gilchrist held any doubts of the hatred Jessie had for Barnes, they were dispelled right there. She wiped spittle from her chin, and carried on. 'She held the door open for longer than was decent, and said in a squeaky-clean voice – Sorry, sir, I see you're busy – then she took her time shutting the door.'

'And did she report it?'

'She didn't dare. She'd been known to give out now and again, but not to anyone as fat or as ugly as Jabba.'

'I don't understand,' Gilchrist said. 'So why the ongoing feud?'

Jessie turned from the window, face flushed, eyes brimming. 'She laughed, Andy. That's what was so embarrassing. That's what hurt. After she closed the door all I could hear was her high-pitched laugh as she pissed off down the corridor. And to add insult to injury, that fat bastard never missed a beat. Not one. He just gripped me tighter and shuddered and grunted all the way to the end. I'll never forget it. It was horrible. It was *beyond* bloody horrible.'

In the silence that followed, Gilchrist was lost for words. McKellar's reaction when Barnes had opened his office door didn't just speak volumes – it screamed. Not what you would do if someone interrupted your illicit shag. Not at all. Which did more than give him a hint that the incident had been set up, with Jessie being the scapegoat.

But why would McKellar do that?

He let his thoughts shift to what he thought was the obvious conclusion, that Barnes and McKellar had been having an affair of their own, and being caught *in flagrante delicto* with Jessie had been McKellar's way of ending it. For a moment, he toyed with the idea of throwing his thoughts out to Jessie, then decided not to. Instead, he would tell her to forget it, it didn't matter, they were both adults and DI Barnes should've had the decency to have said nothing and closed the office door. He glanced at Jessie to take his cue, but her head was turned away from him again, her focus on the sodden countryside.

'Don't worry,' Jessie said, as if sensing his eyes on her. 'I'll be professional. But you'd better not leave me alone in a room with her.'

'Got it,' he said, and drove on in silence.

CHAPTER 6

By the time they arrived at St Andrews, Jessie had recovered – not her usual cheeky effervescent self, but a flattened version, like a bottle of sparkling water that had been left with the top off, and lost its fizz. She'd livened on the drive back when Gilchrist instructed her to get hold of Tom Rickard and arrange for an interview, the sooner the better. But despite that, her encounter with DI Barnes seemed to have stifled her.

When Gilchrist entered the North Street Office, he was pleased to find Tom Rickard already seated in Interview Room 1, with his back to North Street. A single frown ran like a ploughed furrow across his forehead, and his hands massaged his fingers as if trying to work up a dry lather. He froze for a surprised moment when Jessie opened the door, then jumped to his feet at the sight of Gilchrist who introduced himself and Jessie, and thanked him for coming in at such short notice, and do please take a seat.

Jessie offered Rickard, 'Coffee? Tea? Anything? Water?'

'Naw, hen, I'm fine. I just . . . I just cannae believe it.'

Gilchrist let several seconds pass until Rickard composed himself. 'We're sorry for your loss, Mr Rickard—'

'Tam. Please. Just Tam. Everybody knows me as Tam.'

'Sure, Tam.' A pause, then, 'We'll do everything we can to find out who did this to your sister, Margaret, and bring him to justice.'

'Aye, I've heard all that shite before.' Tam's eyes burned. 'Justice? That'll be the effing day. What effing justice is there for poor Margaret, eh? Never harmed a soul. Never had a bad word to say about no one. A kinder person you couldnae find in the entire effing world. Justice? What effing justice can replace the life of someone like my Margaret? Can you tell me that? Eh?'

Gilchrist made a point of modulating his tone, keeping his voice soft. 'No, Tam,' he said. 'Regrettably, we can't. We know there's nothing we can do that will ever replace your sister. But what we can do, and what we *must* do, is to stop this man before he has the chance to take the life of some other innocent being, and to prevent some other family going through what you're going through at the moment.' He wasn't sure if his words had worked, for Tam massaged his fingers again, as if intent on breaking a joint or two, maybe all ten.

Jessie helped him out with, 'Did your sister have any enemies?'

'Enemies?' Tam's eyes bulged. 'Have you no listened to a word I've said?'

'Well someone didn't like her, Tam. You can't deny that.'

Gilchrist almost winced at her bluntness, but sometimes the only way forward was to press a point home.

She went on with, 'So what I'm asking you, Tam, is . . . can you think of anyone, anyone at all, who might have held a grudge, no matter how small, against your Margaret?'

Tam's eyes narrowed. His brow folded like a landslide.

'Someone she'd maybe had an argument with in the bank?' Jessie pried. 'Someone she worked with, maybe? She worked in

Human Resources. Was she the person who did the hiring and firing? Maybe she let someone go, Tam, and that someone then held a real grudge against her.'

Tam's eyes shimmied left and right, then stilled. 'Years ago, maybe. But it couldnae be him. It's too long ago, and he's moved out of the area. To Glasgow, somewhere.'

'It couldn't be who, Tam?' she asked.

Tam looked at Jessie, eyes moist and bright. 'She'd nearly got herself engaged.' He shook his head. 'But that was thirty-odd years ago.'

'Who to, Tam?'

'Ron somebody-or-other. I cannae remember his full name, that's how much of an impact he had. I told Margaret he was a useless effing wanker. He'd hang around and just take take take, and never give anything back in return.'

On hearing that Margaret's relationship ended some thirty-odd years ago, Gilchrist didn't think it likely that her ex-fiancé, -lover, -whatever, was this present-day serial killer, but he would have to check him out regardless. 'Ron who?' he asked.

Tam shook his head. 'McKenzie. McKechnie. McKintie. Something like that.'

He scribbled the names down, disappointed that they were so vague.

'So how did Margaret end the relationship with Ron?' Jessie again.

'Just slammed the door on him one night, and that was that.' Tam chuckled. 'By Christ, our Margaret had a temper on her when she put her mind to it. If you fell out with her, hell mend you.'

Well, Gilchrist thought, so much for being the kindest person on the planet. Even after only a few minutes, he had a sense that

Tam couldn't provide anything that would advance his investigation. But he resisted the urge to bring the interview to an end, and said nothing while Jessie continued to pry a little here, nibble a bit there, but all in all getting nowhere. Not until ten minutes had passed did Tam's memory seem to recover.

'There was one other person,' he said. 'Where she worked.'

Gilchrist leaned forward, as Jessie pressed on.

'In the bank?' she asked. 'Santander?'

Tam nodded. 'Aye. But I dinnae know the name. It's just came back to me. It was one of the reasons she retired when she did. She was gonnae go at the end of the year, but then something happened and she took the humph and left six months early.'

'Did she tell you what happened, Tam?'

'She didnae give me the details, like, just said that she wisnae happy with the way they were treating her. Something to do with her final redundancy package.'

'They?' Gilchrist said.

'Well, one person in particular I think it was.'

'Did she say who?'

'Didnae get the name. Just some manager that had transferred frae another branch.'

'Male or female?' Gilchrist tried.

'It was a woman. Some young thing trying to make a name for herself. Margaret said she had a face like a torn sheet.'

Jessie said, 'We'll contact the bank and take it from there, Tam. Okay?' She shook his hand. 'Thanks for all your help, and again, we're sorry for your loss.'

Gilchrist sat back, not quite ready to leave – just one or two more questions that Jessie hadn't brought up. 'Before you go, Tam, did Margaret wear much jewellery?'

Tam's lips downturned as his mind ransacked his memory. 'I was never one to pay notice about any of that stuff, you know? She might have worn the odd necklace, or earrings, or something like that. But no, she wisnae into baubles and stuff.'

'How about rings?'

Tam shook his head.

'Did she inherit any rings when your mother passed away?'

His eyes widened, as some memory came back to him. 'Aye, now you mention it, she did have a wee diamond.' He shook his head. 'Although I wouldnae've said it was valuable, more like a cheap piece of glass, if I knew my mother well enough.'

'So Margaret wore it daily?'

Tam grimaced. 'I couldnae say. As I said, I dinnae pay attention to all they baubles and bangles and stuff.'

But Gilchrist gave it one last shot. 'Would you recognise it if you saw it?'

'Maybe.' Tam twisted his mouth. 'Maybe no.'

Well, if he was looking for an observant witness, he wasn't going to find one in Tam. He pushed to his feet, an indication that the interview was over. 'If anything comes to you, or if you think of anything we might have missed,' he said, 'let us know, Tam, okay?'

They shook hands.

Then Tam cast his gaze to the floor, and shuffled from the room.

Alone with Jessie, Gilchrist said, 'So, what do you think of Margaret's fiancé, Ron whatsisname?'

'I don't think there's anything there,' she said. 'Too long ago.'

'Agreed. So get hold of Mhairi and have her talk to someone in Santander, see what upset Tam's sister to make her leave six months early.'

'From the way Tam described her, Mother Teresa would've had some competition. I mean, *nobody's* that nice.'

'She did have a temper, though, once she got going.'

'Everybody's got a temper,' she said. 'Talking of which, I think I'll give that bitch Barnes a call, and have it out with her once and for all.'

'Not a good suggestion. You're likely to resurrect a call from Jabba. The last thing you'd want.' Which seemed to do the trick, for Jessie tightened her lips. 'Besides, didn't you say you were going to be professional about it?'

She hissed something under her breath, which he failed to catch, then said, 'Bugger her. Let's see if Mhairi and Jackie have come up with anything.'

He followed Jessie upstairs, and found Mhairi peering at Jackie's monitor as she typed away, oblivious to all around her. Something in the way both Mhairi and Jackie were focused with intensity on the screen gave off a strange sense of familiarity – silence, except for Jackie's fingers tapping the keyboard; her crutches in their usual place, standing upright in the corner of her office closest to her desk; her rust-coloured hair like a dyed Afro – longer than he'd ever seen it before – bouncing as if in time with the keyboard. As he approached, she glanced at him, did a double take, then gave a smile that stretched her lips wide as she struggled to push herself back from her desk.

'No need to stand, Jackie,' he said, and she laughed in response, a staccato chuckle that sounded all the more childlike because of her stutter. He leaned down to her and pecked her cheek. 'Happy to see me?'

She nodded. 'Uh huh . . . s . . . s . . . sir.'

'I'm happy to see you, too, Jackie. So,' he said, 'got anything for me?'

She nodded to the screen as the clipped voice of Chief Superintendent Diane Smiley said, 'Good to see you're back, Andy.'

Smiler – as everyone called her behind her back – stood in the doorway, immaculate as usual, more blonde than he remembered. And was that gel glistening her hair? Her uniform could have been picked up from the laundry minutes earlier. 'Thank you, ma'am.'

'Thought you were signed off for another couple of weeks.'

He didn't want to mention his phone calls with Jessie. 'I feel well, ma'am,' he said. 'Much better. So I thought I should stick my head in and see what's what.'

'Well enough to have a chat in my office?'

The fact that Smiler turned and walked away, heels clicking with authority on the corridor tiles, warned Gilchrist that she hadn't thrown out an invitation for him to consider at his leisure, but instead had given instruction. She did leave her office door open behind her, which was a first. Even so, she was settled behind her desk by the time he entered.

'Take a seat, Andy.'

Which he did, feeling oddly uncomfortable, like a truant schoolboy being asked to explain his absence by the headmaster or, in this case, the headmistress. The room, too, had an unfamiliar taint to it, until he realised it had been recently painted, the same colour as his office as best he could tell.

'I take it that DS Janes has brought you up to speed with these God-awful killings,' Smiler said.

'She has, ma'am, yes.'

'And your initial thoughts are . . .?'

'Too many similarities for it not to be the same person.'

'We have a serial killer on the rampage, is what you're saying.'

Again not a question. 'Regrettably, I am saying that. But if I could just pick you up on one point, ma'am?'

She frowned. 'Yes?'

'The *we* you refer to is not only Fife Constabulary, ma'am, but Strathclyde, too.'

'Yes, I heard about Albert Forest.'

'We've also determined that the killer is leaving a message in the form of a number,' he said. 'Cut into their chest, which we suspect is intended to represent the numerical order of each killing.'

Smiler was known for being up to speed, even well ahead of the game. But what he'd just said had her eyebrows searching for shelter in her fringe. 'Good Lord,' she gasped, then recovered with an anguished grimace and a hard-eyed stare that warned him to be careful.

'But we can't be sure,' he added. 'If we're right, ma'am, then we're missing victim three, which makes me suspect that this killer may stray farther afield, and perhaps already has, ma'am.'

She frowned for a long moment, as if struggling to comprehend what he was saying, then said, 'Which is what I want to discuss with you.' She entwined her fingers, pressed them to her mouth, elbows on her desk, and eyed him over imaginary spectacles. 'We need to keep the wraps on this. Keep certain details of the killings from the public domain.'

He nodded. His earlier phone calls with Jessie had given him information he hadn't been able to pick up from local or national papers.

'We can't let the public know what these poor victims have gone through.' She shook her head. 'God help us if the press get hold of the details. It utterly defies imagination.'

'I agree, ma'am.'

'I've already been in contact with the Chief Constable, and expressed the need for a joint investigation team that encompasses a number of our police forces, with one person in command. I've already put your name forward for that role, Andy, which I'm sure you'll be happy to agree to.'

'Yes, ma'am,' although he wondered how she'd managed to put his name forward when, strictly speaking, he hadn't been expected back at the Office for a few more weeks.

'Chief Constable McVicar is expected to get back to me later today with approval for that joint investigation unit. Assuming we're good to go, you'll have an initial briefing with Tayside, Strathclyde, and Lothian and Borders, first thing tomorrow morning, at Glenrothes HQ.' She held his gaze in a look of steel. 'Any questions so far?'

'Yes, ma'am.'

She stared at him in puzzled silence.

'I'm intrigued as to why Tayside and Lothian and Borders have been called in, when we've found two victims in Fife, and one in Strathclyde.'

'Because of Adam Soutar,' she said.

Now it was his turn to be puzzled. 'Ma'am?'

'Soutar began his law career in Dundee, and had a two-year stint in Edinburgh Sheriff Court, before setting up a private practice in Edinburgh. His firm provided a lot of *pro bono* services, as well as legal aid work, and he personally took on a number of difficult cases for the defence. He did a lot of good work over the years, and retired two years ago and returned to St Andrews, where his wife was from.'

'If ever there is such a thing as an honest solicitor,' Gilchrist said, 'it sounds as if he would have to be it.'

'Quite, DCI Gilchrist.'

The shift to formality took him aback for a moment, until he recalled that Smiler's father had been a small-town solicitor – oops. 'What I'm saying, ma'am, is that as a defence solicitor he would not necessarily leave himself open to threats of revenge which sometimes prosecuting solicitors receive. Often defence solicitors are seen as being more helpful than . . .' He searched for the correct word. '. . . aggressive, ma'am.'

'I see you haven't lost any of your wile.'

'Well I do feel refreshed, ma'am.'

'I'll let you know of McVicar's decision by close of play.'

Gilchrist nodded.

She pushed a typed sheet across her desk to him. 'This is a draft statement, with certain elements of the crime scene not mentioned. Have a look at it, but I want this on all the main news channels this evening.'

He picked it up and folded it without looking at it.

'That'll be all, Andy.'

'Yes, ma'am.'

CHAPTER 7

Back upstairs, Gilchrist studied the press release in his office, noting no mention of Soutar's murder – after all, in today's digital world, news more than a day old was considered history. And strangely, nothing of Albert Forest's death, either, only Rickard's, identifying her as Margaret Gillian Rickard, a retired Santander employee who lived alone, and whose body was discovered in the early hours of that morning by her distraught brother, Tam. The gory details of her murder had graciously been omitted, and substituted with – *Margaret Rickard's naked body was found by a family member in the living room of her one-bedroom cottage in Kincaple on the outskirts of St Andrews. There were no signs of any break-in or disturbance to the property. A post mortem will be carried out shortly to determine cause of death* – as bland a description of a brutal and grisly murder as he'd ever come across.

Reading through it once more, he came to understand that Smiler had not mentioned Albert Forest's or Adam Soutar's murders because, firstly Forest had been killed within the jurisdiction of another police region; secondly she hadn't wanted to forewarn the press of the formation of a multi-regional investigative task force; and thirdly no police force wanted to admit – at least in public for the time being – that a serial killer was rampant and on the loose, apparently murdering his victims randomly, and numbering them along the way. Pen in hand, intent on minor editing, he realised that the press release as written by Smiler covered all that needed to be addressed, and was good to go. He folded it, stuffed it into his jacket pocket, and went looking for Jessie.

He found her in Jackie's office – along with Mhairi – staring at the monitor. Jackie's fingers moved in a blur. The room was silent, save for the frantic clicking of the keyboard and the rhythmic shuffle of pages being pushed out of a printer at the edge of Jackie's desk, just as fast as Jessie could remove them from the tray.

'Here,' she said, and held out a handful of pages. 'What do you think?'

A quick scan told Gilchrist they'd been downloaded from some blog. A slower flick-through showed they were not all from the same blog. And not much writing in any of them, either. The right-hand margins of every page listed ads and hyperlinks that appeared to cover everything from penis enlargements to equity release, which were a far cry from the theme of the blog, the significance of which he failed to understand – *A successful day requires us to stop taking our children's sin personally and help them find Jesus in the middle of it. Success is when we watch hearts and souls changed and reshaped.* The reference to Jesus had him flipping through other pages expecting a Jihadist blog to appear, spouting vitriol and death to non-Muslims. But after thirty seconds, he said, 'Okay. What am I missing?'

'All of these are by the same blogger,' Jessie said. 'Different blogs. Different styles. But all originating from the one blogger.' She gave a dry smile. 'Want to try a guess?'

'Go on. Surprise me.'

'Fiona van der Stoor.'

'I'm duly surprised. Never heard of her.'

'That's her married name.' A smirk, then, 'She married Ruud van der Stoor two years ago in a registry office ceremony to which her father wasn't invited.'

'Ah,' he said. 'So you're going to tell me we know her father?'

'Adam Soutar.'

The name seemed to come at him at a tangent. For a moment his mind stalled. Then he recovered and flipped through the printouts. But whatever Jessie was expecting him to find seemed lost in translation. He flapped them at her. 'So this is important because . . .?'

'Ruud van der Stoor married Fiona Soutar one week after he was released from prison after serving twelve months for drug-related offences.'

Gilchrist thought that maybe he'd been away from the Constabulary for too long, that his four weeks' absence had obliterated his sense of logic and rationale, for nothing came to him. 'Keep going,' was all he could think to say.

She handed him a printout of an Amazon book sales list. Three thumbnail covers ran down the left margin in a vertical row. 'Ruud van der Stoor, under the pseudonym of R. S. Vander, wrote and self-published a nasty little booklet with the innocent title – *Where Now?* – but which was really a how-to-manual on Islamophobia before the book was reported and Amazon pulled the plug.'

How-to-manual? He almost scratched his head. 'How to do what?'

'Rid the world of Muslims.'

'For God's sake,' he said.

'Try for Allah's sake.' She held up more pages. 'And here is how Adam Soutar's son-in-law, Ruud the bigot, proposes to do it.' She passed them to him. 'Well, *one* of the ways actually.'

Gilchrist's breath caught in his throat at a crude drawing of a crucifixion, the victim naked, flat on his back, arms and legs spread-eagled with spikes for nails protruding from his wrists and ankles. For a fleeting moment, his mind seemed to stall with the significance of what he was seeing. Was this how Ruud van der Stoor intended to rid the world of Muslims? Did it matter whether the victim was male or female? And the title of the booklet and this sketch proved what, exactly? That Soutar's son-in-law intended to rid the world of Muslims by crucifying them? Even so, the rough sketch didn't portray someone of ethnicity, but a white male. Was the drawing intended to be a caricature of Adam Soutar? What he was looking at didn't make sense. Nothing added up.

In restrained desperation, he said, 'There's no tape over the mouth.'

Jessie seemed deflated. 'I thought you'd notice that. Here.' She passed him six pages of more amateurish sketches – a male body hanging by the neck from the branch of a tree; another standing upright and blindfolded facing an invisible firing squad; one of a decapitated body with a hand in the foreground holding a dead-eyed head dripping blood.

Gilchrist had seen enough. 'What the hell is this?' he snarled.

'I don't know,' Jessie said. 'All I can tell you is that Ruud van der Stoor is one sick excuse for a human being, on top of which he's married to Soutar's one and only daughter.'

'I assume you have an address.'

'Thought you were never going to ask.'

As it turned out, Ruud and Fiona van der Stoor lived less than sixty miles from St Andrews, in a two-storey stone mansion in the village of Cambusbarron, on the outskirts of Stirling. When Gilchrist parked half-on half-off the pavement, he noticed they were within walking distance of the Bruce Memorial Church. Its proximity had him wondering if they should be taking Ruud van der Stoor's Islamophobia more seriously. Was that what the killings were about? Islamophobia? Or just plain old religious hatred?

He stood at the front door, Jessie by his side. 'Any thoughts?' he said.

She chinned the grounds. 'They don't like gardening.'

He had to agree. The gravel path was matted with weeds, the front lawn spread brown with flattened grass. 'Or painting,' he said, scraping a fingernail over the outside storm doors and flaking off dried wood and paint.

'Reminds me of my mother's place,' Jessie said. 'God rest the heathen bitch's soul.'

'I thought she lived in a flat.'

'She did. But this is what it would've looked like if she hadn't.'

'Right.' He thumbed the doorbell, and a melodic chime echoed back at him. He was about to ring the bell again, when he caught movement from within. 'Sounds like someone's here.'

'What is it with your ears?' Jessie said.

'Always had good hearing.'

The lock clicked, and the door cracked open with a stiff-hinged creak.

The days of psychedelic flower-power were long gone, but the woman who faced him could have been a reincarnation of a sixties San Franciscan hippie. A floral bandana tied in a tight knot circled a head of shoulder-length blonde hair, and matched a loose-fitting dress that covered no more than a few inches of freckled thighs that were way too thin and lacked muscle tone. White suspender-less stockings, or long socks – he couldn't say which – rode high above her knee-line.

'Mrs Van der Stoor?' he said, holding out his warrant card.

Without a word, the woman pulled the door wide open, and bumped her back against the wall. If she hadn't been holding the handle, or the wall hadn't been there, he was certain she would have toppled over. High on drugs, or drink. Maybe both.

'Is Mr Van der Stoor available?' he said.

'Enter,' she said.

Jessie rolled her eyes to the ceiling as she walked ahead of Gilchrist.

Through to the back of the house, in a room that smelled of burnt toast and a hint of something less pleasurable – the musky skunk-like odour of marijuana – a man was seated in a tall-backed Gothic bishop's chair. Eyes that seemed too big for a face as gaunt as a skull studied Gilchrist and Jessie with malevolent suspicion. A black velvet robe, thrown over his shoulders like a toga, covered a body that had to be skeletal thin for all the space it seemed to be taking up.

Gilchrist jolted at a metallic click from behind, and turned in time to see Fiona – if that's who she was – locking the door.

'What do you think you're doing?' Jessie asked.

'What does it look like?' Her eyes smoked. Her voice sounded low and come-on sexy, as if she were trying to imitate some Hollywood starlet of bygone days.

'Unlock it,' Jessie ordered.

The woman's lazy gaze drifted to the man in the bishop's chair, and at the instance of some signal that Gilchrist failed to spot, she reached down and turned the key.

'Are you for real?' Jessie said to her, as she glided across the room to stand next to the man in the bishop's chair.

'Ruud van der Stoor?' Gilchrist asked him.

A bony hand appeared from under the black cloak and tapped the material, whereupon the woman shifted from his side and sat down on his knees. She adjusted her legs as if trying to make herself comfortable, but in doing so revealed that she wore no underwear.

'Oh for God's sake,' Jessie said.

'Ah,' said the man. 'In times of despair, I see you beseech your god, which is who? What god do you believe in?'

'I'll ask you again,' Gilchrist said. 'Are you Ruud van der Stoor?'

'And if I am?'

Jessie said, 'Put it this way, Sonny Jim, you are one question away from being arrested on suspicion of murder.'

Lips parted to show teeth far too long for his mouth. 'Welcome to chez Van der Stoor,' he said. 'I am Ruud, and this is my wife, Fi.'

Fi – short for Fiona – smiled. But she was too far gone to hold it for long.

'Care for a drink?' Ruud asked, and produced an unbranded bottle of clear liquid from a table at his side, which Gilchrist hadn't noticed until then.

'We'll pass,' Jessie said, then held up the Amazon printout. 'This your book?'

'Oh, that?' he said. 'Just a passing phase we go through.'

'We?'

'The general *we*.' He swept an arm wide before him. 'No one specific.'

Gilchrist said, 'Why do you hate Muslims?'

'Do I?'

'According to that book, you do.'

'Oh, that wasn't me who wrote it. I mean . . . *I* wrote it. Of course I did. But I take on different personae when I write, and in that instance, I found myself in the mind of someone who hated all religions. Not just Islam. Quite a discovery, really.'

'And the point of writing this book was what . . .?'

'It's fiction. That's all. If you'd care to read it, you'd understand that.'

'And the sketches that show . . .' He searched for the right word, but in the end settled for '. . . executions? What's their significance?'

'They say a picture is worth a thousand words.' He smiled at his wife balanced on his knees. 'And Fi is such a wonderful sketch artist. Isn't that right, darling?'

Fi tried another smile, but it seemed too difficult.

'Why didn't you invite your father to your wedding?' This directed at Fiona.

'I hate him.' Again, the affected voice.

Even though Gilchrist felt sure he knew the answer, he still had to ask. 'Did you have anything to do with your father's death?'

'No such luck.' She placed her hands either side of her husband's head, and kissed him on the mouth, hard and long.

'When you come up for air,' Jessie said, 'maybe you can tell us why you hated him – past tense.'

Her eyes flared. 'I *hate* him. I will always hate him, whether he's dead or alive.'

'We gathered that. But why?'

'He was cruel to my mother, and he was cruel to me. He was a terrible, terrible father, and a terrible, terrible husband.' Her eyes creased, as if about to cry. But no tears came.

Despite everything about the Van der Stoors ringing alarm bells in Gilchrist's sense of logic, he could see no way for someone as slim as Ruud to have overpowered a man as large as Adam Soutar. He stepped in again, all of a sudden keen to get some answers, and bring this interview to an end.

'Where were you on the night of February eighteenth?'

'I'm assuming that's the night Adam was murdered?' Ruud said.

The first name reference surprised Gilchrist, but he said, 'It is.'

'We were in the Caribbean, Barbados, at a religious gathering, spreading the good Christian word. We didn't hear of Adam's death until we returned home seven days later. Didn't we, sweetheart?'

She nodded.

'Which hotel?'

'The Radisson in Bridgetown.'

He thought the answer too quick, too prepared, but just noted it in his notebook.

'And what did you do when you found out he was dead?' Jessie asked.

'Do?'

'Yeah. Do. Did you pray for his soul? Light a candle? Or shit on his headstone?'

'We prayed for his soul, of course.'

'Why?'

Ruud seemed puzzled by the question. 'The lighting of candles,' he said, 'is to honour the departed soul, in the belief that the light of the soul shines on as bright as ever in the spirit world. Light is a symbol of life.'

'Even though your father-in-law was a terrible, terrible person?'

Gilchrist thought it intriguing how Ruud's face hardened.

'Maybe I should light a candle for your soul,' Ruud said.

'I wouldn't waste the effort,' Jessie said, then addressed Fiona. 'You must have been disappointed, losing out on your inheritance.'

Gilchrist watched confusion flit across Fiona's face. He was confused himself, having no idea who'd been the executor of Soutar's estate, or how it had been distributed.

'Your father's house and all his money just left to the Law Society,' Jessie went on. 'Not a single penny coming your way. I mean, it must have been so disappointing.'

'The only thing that was disappointing,' she said, her words sharp and precise, as if a rush of anger had sobered her up, 'was that Papa hadn't died sooner.'

'For crying out loud. He didn't just die. He was murdered. Brutally, too.' If Jessie had been hoping to hurt her with her words, she was disappointed, for Fiona threw an arm around Ruud's neck, pulled herself closer to him, and whispered in his ear.

Ruud nodded, then said, 'Unless you intend to charge or arrest one or both of us, you're going to have to excuse us. We have much to be getting on with. I'm sure you can find your own way out.'

Jessie reached for the door handle, but Gilchrist didn't move. He turned to Fiona, and said, 'After your mother passed away, did your father continue to wear a wedding ring?' He had no idea if

Soutar ever wore a wedding ring or not, but thought it worth a shot.

'How should I know?' She shrugged, then said, 'But I do know Papa always wore a St Christopher's medallion.'

'How do you know that?'

'Because I bought it for him with Mama. Before she passed. It was terribly expensive for all the size it was. Over four hundred pounds. But Mama always spent more than she could afford on Papa.' She frowned. 'Why are you asking about Papa's wedding ring?'

'Your father might have left everything to the Law Society – money, house, that sort of stuff – but not jewellery, surely. So I wonder what became of his wedding ring.'

'Why don't you ask his old law firm? They were executor of his estate.'

'How do you know that?'

A shadow of sorts seemed to sweep across her face, as if at the memory of some dark thought. Then she turned to Ruud and kissed him hard on the mouth.

'Christ on a boat,' Jessie said, and pulled the door wide.

Gilchrist let himself be ignored for a few seconds more, before following Jessie.

CHAPTER 8

As Gilchrist bumped his car off the pavement, Jessie said, 'Bloody hell, I thought they were going to have it off in front of us. And what's with the wedding ring?'

He powered up to thirty before realising Jessie's question was directed at him. 'I don't recall seeing jewellery on any of the victims. Do you?'

'You think he's taking jewellery as trophies?'

'Could be.'

'If they're trophies, he'd want to keep them, not pawn them or sell them on eBay. So we'd never find them, because he'd never sell them. So that line of investigation would get us where, exactly?'

Jessie had a point. Whatever trophies the killer was removing would in all likelihood remain just that – trophies – for the killer to look at from time to time, to touch, to smell, to put rings on fingers, slip bracelets over wrists, dangle necklaces around his neck, in order to relive the delicious memory of that most unique of moments when life fades with absolute certainty to disappear with the exhalation of a final breath, the subtle flicker of an eyelid, the glazed dulling of dying sight, until all that is left to witness is the morbid stillness and utter silence of death – the end of a human life. No, whoever the killer was, he would hold onto his trophies. But they were forgetting something else.

'What about the tongues?' he asked.

'God knows what he does with them. Stores them in jars of formalin most likely.'

For a moment, he thought that sourcing formaldehyde could give them a lead, maybe some place to start. But there were so many different uses for that liquid now that it was sold over the counter or through the internet in any multitude of forms. He wondered if sourcing the jars could give them a lead. But a sliced-off human tongue would fit into any old jam jar, and he cast that idea off as he slowed down at the junction with Main Street.

'You think it's worth talking to Soutar's old law firm?' he said.

'To find out what happened to his wedding ring?'

'Maybe the killer's got a wife, or a partner, and he gifts it to them. If we knew what the ring looked like, we could put a call out on national TV.'

Jessie shifted in her seat, looked around her. 'Isn't Stirling that way?'

'We're going to Edinburgh.'

'What's there?'

'Soutar's old law firm. See if you can find an address.'

'How do you know his old law firm's in Edinburgh?'

He didn't, but Smiler mentioned Adam Soutar once worked there. He said nothing, just floored the accelerator and powered up to seventy.

* * *

Soutar's old law firm in Atholl Crescent no longer bore his name. A polished brass plate fixed to one of two stone pillars either side of the entrance doorway identified it as *The Law Offices of KTIF & Associates*. The outside storm doors lay opened to a black and white tiled vestibule. Through the glass-panelled inner door, the reception area glowed with welcoming warmth from soft lighting of table and desk lamps.

Gilchrist presented his warrant card to the receptionist. 'Mr Dickson is expecting us,' to which he and Jessie were invited to take a seat while she checked to see if Mr Dickson was available.

He was; a handsome white-haired elderly gentleman, with ruddy jowls and piercing blue eyes that somehow reminded Gilchrist of the Hollywood actor Paul Newman, except that Newman would never be seen dead in a pinstriped double-breasted suit buttoned up all the way to a wide-striped pink and blue shirt with a white buttoned down collar. A waft of after-shave, or perhaps perfume, choked the air around him. He presented himself to Gilchrist with a tight smile and a firm handshake that exposed a gold bracelet that had to be priced in the five-figure range. He gave a short nod to Jessie, who seemed happy to keep her distance.

Conference Room 3 was empty save for a circular glass-topped table around which six stainless steel chairs were positioned. An original oil painting as disjointed as a Picasso and as large as a venetian blind took up most of the facing wall. Dickson held out an arm as an invitation for Jessie to sit there, and for Gilchrist to sit here. Then he took a seat opposite, clasped his hands, and said, 'You wanted to ask me about Adam?' and before Gilchrist could speak, added, 'Utterly tragic what happened to him. Shock to us all.'

Gilchrist let a few seconds pass, then said, 'I understand you and Adam started the law firm together,' which generated a solemn nod of a white-haired head.

'We did, yes. Twenty-five years ago last year. It's appalling how time flies.'

'And I see the name's been changed, even though as one of the original partners in the firm, you're still here.'

'Yes, it has, and I am.'

Jessie said, 'I didn't see your initials on the brass plaque. Why?'

'Because we were taken over by a multi-disciplinary German law firm with ambitious plans to expand into the UK, but which wanted existing clients without the bother of carrying existing partners. They felt the original name, Soutar Dickson, did not sound . . . how do I say it? . . . *international* enough. They preferred to keep their German name, and don't ask me what the initials stand for.' He smiled, as if pleased by his humour.

'So they made you an offer you couldn't refuse?'

'They did, yes.'

'So why are you still here? Why didn't you retire with Adam?'

'They wanted one of us to stay on, keep our clients happy, that sort of thing. Adam decided he'd worked long enough, so he retired, and I stayed on.'

'So you and Adam were long-time friends?' Gilchrist asked.

'You could say. When we started out, we worked as junior solicitors in the same company, and we hit it off. We had a lot in common, but also complemented each other in terms of the law. Adam had aspirations in criminal law, defence solicitor, whereas I was more inclined towards domestic law, house conveyancing, divorce settlements, that sort of thing.'

'And as a defence lawyer, would Adam have made enemies?'

'Enemies?' Dickson made the word sound filthy.

'Yeah. Enemies,' Jessie interrupted. 'You know, people who might wish him harm. After all he was murdered in his own home.'

Gilchrist almost flinched, but Dickson shook his head. 'I'm sorry, but I can't think of anyone who would've wanted Adam dead.'

Gilchrist pressed on. 'And as part of your remit in domestic law, when Adam . . . eh . . . when Adam died,' he said, 'you were executor of his estate?'

'Yes.'

'I mean, not the company, but you personally?'

'That's right. Yes.'

'I understand he left his estate to the Law Society of Scotland. Is that common?'

'No. First time I've come across it, I have to say.'

'How much are we talking about?' Jessie again.

Dickson's pink forehead folded into a frown. 'What's the value of Adam's estate got to do with how he was killed?' he asked. 'I thought that's why you wanted to meet me.'

'We're looking into all aspects of Adam's life,' she said. 'Hoping to find something that might help us understand why someone would want to kill him. Money's a powerful motive.' She gave a quick smile. 'So, with the sale of the business, Adam must've been a wealthy man. What're we looking at? Six figures? More?'

Dickson cleared his throat. 'Two million and change.'

Jessie mouthed a silent whistle. 'Including the sale of his house?'

'Yes.'

'It's already been sold?'

'Yes.'

'Don't mind me asking, but wasn't that a bit quick?'

'It was sold without going on the open market.'

'Who to?'

'One of our German partners.'

'Name?'

'Marina Bühl.'

'What about furnishings?'

'She made a generous offer for the house as is, which was accepted.' He smiled, and added, 'She was looking to buy a second home in the UK. Despite the tragic circumstances, she jumped at the opportunity. Not knowing Adam personally, helped of course.'

'Of course,' Gilchrist said.

Jessie was less deferential. 'She pay market price?'

Dickson cleared his throat again. 'As good as.'

Which told Gilchrist that Ms Marina Bühl had got herself a bargain, maybe a bargain and a half. 'And what about Adam's personal effects,' he asked. 'His books, clothes, golf clubs, that sort of thing?'

Dickson almost flushed. 'Given to charity, I believe.'

'You believe?' Jessie again.

'I didn't deal with the minutiae, but instruction was given for it all to go to charity.'

'Surely not *all* of it. What about personal items of value, watches and rings, or even his late wife's jewellery?' Gilchrist didn't know if Soutar owned any such items, although it did seem a reasonable assumption. But the stiffening in Dickson's posture had him thinking that perhaps some items of value had been sold below market price, maybe even slipped through the cracks altogether, and found their way into some . . . ex-partner's pockets.

'All sold to an Edinburgh jeweller,' Dickson said.

'Name?' Jessie said, pencil poised over her opened notebook.

'I'd need to check my records.'

'We can wait.'

Gilchrist said, 'You have an inventory of these items, I presume.'

'We do, yes.'

'That would be helpful, too.'

Dickson harrumphed, excused himself, and left the room.

Gilchrist raised an eyebrow at Jessie. 'Penny for your thoughts?'

'Solicitors make my skin crawl. I'd like to find out what that Fräulein Bühl paid for the house. Nowhere near market value, I'd bet. And dumping clothes and stuff to charity? Just giving it away? Anything to get the job done. Did you see the way his face flushed when you mentioned jewellery? I wouldn't be surprised if some of it was just pocketed.'

Gilchrist nodded his head in silent agreement. With no next of kin to monitor the sale or disposal of an estate, most solicitors would contact a removal company and instruct them to clear the property. Furniture might be auctioned, even scrapped if it was not considered suitable for resale. But in most cases the settled value of an estate would be well under market value.

Dickson returned with a manila folder, which he placed on the table. 'I've taken the liberty of having Adam's last will and testament copied in its entirety. I wouldn't normally do that, but this is not a normal situation.'

'No, it's not,' said Jessie. 'What about the inventory?'

He removed a single sheet and slid it across the table to

Gilchrist. 'This is a list of items of value, although you'll see that not much is of any great value.'

'I thought Adam was loaded,' Jessie said.

'He wasn't ostentatious in any way.'

'No solid gold bracelets, you mean?'

Dickson's lips pressed to a scar.

Gilchrist spent a minute or so studying the list. The most expensive item was a Seiko watch valued at £300. Five sets of cufflinks ranged from £20 to £80. Four gold tie-clips – when had he last seen one of these? – each priced at £60. And there was his wedding ring, a simple gold band valued at £120. He turned the list around and slid it across the table.

'Whose signature's this?'

Dickson scowled at it. 'That's Fairfax & Radcliffe.'

'Not an individual's signature?'

'On behalf of.'

'Did Fairfax & Radcliffe prepare the inventory?'

'They did, yes.'

'And price these items, too.'

'Yes.'

Jessie said, 'What, you trusted them?'

'We've used them before.'

Gilchrist said, 'I don't see his late wife's jewellery here. What happened to that?'

Dickson frowned as he looked at the list. 'I uh . . . I uh . . .' Then he looked at Gilchrist. 'There couldn't have been any.'

'But you're not sure.'

'I'm sure. Of course I'm sure. All items of value were listed and sold, so if there's no jewellery listed, then there couldn't have been any.'

'Couldn't have been . . . or *weren't* any?' Gilchrist said, and watched the subtlety of his words flit through Dickson's mind.

'There weren't any,' he said at length.

Jessie said, 'But you don't know for sure, do you?'

'All I can say is, that if nothing was listed, then it wasn't in Adam's estate.'

Gilchrist retrieved the folder, pushed his chair back. 'Thanks for your time. If you think of anything else, let me know.' He placed a business card on the table, and left the conference room.

CHAPTER 9

Fairfax & Radcliffe was not the upmarket jewellery shop the name suggested. Instead, a faded poster on the window of a ground-floor flat on Blair Street identified the company in swirling Victorian scroll as *Designer of Jewellery and Timepieces*.

'What're you hoping to achieve?' Jessie asked, as she opened the car door. Rain as fine as a sea haar fogged the air on a chilled wind.

'We're in Edinburgh,' Gilchrist said, 'so we may as well check it out.'

'Whatever.'

He pushed the shop door open to the tinny clatter of a cheap bell, and stepped into a musty room that seemed to double as a reception area cum workshop. The front counter had a weakly lit glass panel that displayed a poor man's selection of jewellery – silver and gold bracelets as thin as thread, silver lockets as small as pinkie nails, gold bands that looked for all the world like brass washers. A hundred quid for the lot, Gilchrist thought.

A young man with a shorn head and red beard was seated at a workbench, examining a ring, a loupe pressed against his right eye. The air was tainted with a hint of cleaning spirit and burning rubber – an overloaded plug socket, Gilchrist would bet. The young man continued to eye the ring for a few more seconds, before he placed it on the workbench, removed his eyepiece, and stood.

At the counter, he said, 'Yeah?'

Gilchrist showed his warrant card, introduced himself and Jessie, who returned her card to her jacket, and said, 'Are you it?'

'Am I what?'

'Fairfax & Radcliffe's designer of jewellery and timepieces.'

'It's just a name.'

Gilchrist placed the inventory on the counter. 'Did you sign for this?'

The man squinted his eyes. 'Looks like my scrawl.'

'No name?' Jessie said.

'Company only.'

'I was asking, what's your name?'

'Rab Tinto.'

'Okay, Rab,' she said, voice rising with more than a hint of impatience. 'Have you still got any of what's on this list?'

'You want to buy any of it?'

'No, just look at it.'

Rab sniffed, and shuffled back to his workbench where he opened a drawer, ruffled about inside, and removed a battered tobacco tin. He opened it, fingered around the inside as he carried it to the counter.

'Let's see,' he said, and removed a pencil from his apron. He ran a finger down the inventory and put a tick beside some items, and scored through others. Then he pushed it back to Gilchrist.

The Seiko watch was struck through, as were the wedding ring and the gold cufflinks. All that was left were ticked tie-clips. 'You sold the watch?' he said.

'Yeah.'

'The wedding ring and cufflinks, too?'

'Melted them down. Just nine carats. Not worth much.'

'And the tie-clips?'

'They're ornamental. Worth more as tie-clips.'

Gilchrist could sense Jessie's unease. She was right. They were getting nowhere. But he thought he would try one more push. 'You remember preparing this inventory?'

'Of course, yeah.'

'There's no jewellery. No other rings, bracelets, necklaces, all the items that a widower might keep as mementoes of his wife?'

Rab shook his head. 'There wasn't any. Only what's on the list.'

'What about the St Christopher's medallion?' Jessie said.

'The what?'

'Gold. Twenty-two carats. Worth four or five hundred quid.'

'And?'

'And it's gone missing, Sonny Jim,' she snapped. 'You nick it, did you? Couldn't resist pocketing it when you were sorting out the inventory?'

'This is a reputable business—'

'Aye, it looks it.' She turned to Gilchrist. 'Want me to apply for a search warrant?'

Gilchrist kept his gaze locked on Rab's eyes, looking for signs of guilt, then decided that Rab was either too good an actor, or innocent of theft. 'Do you have any St Christopher's medallions?'

'Sorry. Not something we keep a lot of.'

Gilchrist removed a business card from his pocket and placed it on the counter. 'If you come across it,' he said, even though he knew it was a waste of breath, 'give me a call.'

Outside, the haar had changed to a steady drizzle, that light rainfall that seemed to exist only in Scotland and soaked through everything. Jessie slid into the passenger seat and rubbed her hair with a paper tissue she'd pulled from her pocket.

'I've got a windscreen cloth,' Gilchrist said. 'If that'll help.'

'No, this'll do. I've caught it in time.'

'In time for what?'

'It goes all frizzy in the rain.'

'Why don't you carry a small umbrella? It's Scotland, after all.'

'Why don't you just start the car and get us out of here? I feel as if we've wasted a whole morning following up on jewellery and rings and stuff.'

He almost agreed with her, but he'd learned over the years that murder investigations can often turn on leads from the least expected sources. Instead, he said, 'Call Mhairi for an update, and put her on speakerphone.'

Jessie got through on the second ring, and without introduction said, 'You found anything yet?'

On the car's system, Mhairi's voice boomed. 'Jackie's managed to find more blogs from the same blogger,' she said. 'But I've had a look through them, and I don't see how they're going to help us.'

'Forget them,' Gilchrist said, lowering the volume a touch. 'We've spoken to the Van der Stoors, Ruud and Fiona, and they say they were out of the country when Adam Soutar was murdered—'

'And out of their heads ever since,' Jessie chipped in.

'Have Jackie check that out,' Gilchrist carried on. 'Radisson Hotel, Bridgetown, Barbados, around the time of Soutar's death.'

'Will do, sir.'

'Anything else?' he asked, eager for something that might recover some of the wasted morning. But he was disappointed.

'We've been searching the records of St John's school in Dundee, sir, but we can't find any meaningful connection.'

Well, no luck there, he thought. 'How about Santander?' he tried.

'I'm just about to head up there, sir.'

Jessie said, 'You need any help?'

'I'm fine. I'll manage.'

Gilchrist pulled the conversation back on track with, 'Ruud van der Stoor got married one week after being released from prison. Can you find out which prison, and what he was in for?'

'Got it right here, sir.' The cabin filled with the sound of paper rustling, then Mhairi came back with, 'Barlinnie in Glasgow, sir. Served one year of a two-year sentence for possession of a Class B drug. Cannabis.'

'That's light,' Jessie said. 'Did he have a good lawyer?'

'He was charged with intent to supply, but claimed his cannabis was necessary for pain relief. Medical reports confirm that he fractured several vertebrae in a car crash ten years ago. His lawyer argued that the pain was so severe that Van der Stoor had reluctantly reverted to smoking cannabis in his home, only for medicinal purposes, sir.'

Gilchrist nodded. That was the smell he'd picked up in the Van der Stoors'. It might also explain why Fiona had been in a drug daze. Clearly Ruud's spell in Barlinnie had taught him nothing. For a moment, Gilchrist thought of sending a uniformed officer to make an arrest on suspicion of possession of a Class B drug, then realised that the man was street-smart enough to hide, or dispose of, whatever stash he had as soon as Gilchrist and Jessie had left their home earlier. Instead, he thanked Mhairi, and told her to let him know if her meeting with the Santander manager uncovered anything worthwhile.

He ended the call, and drove on in silence, already feeling the pressures of returning to work, and worried that his investigation was on the verge of stalling.

CHAPTER 10

By the end of the day, Gilchrist was no further forward when Smiler called him to her office with the blunt news that the Chief Constable had just confirmed that a detective chief inspector from Strathclyde Police had been assigned to take charge of the joint task force.

'Chief Constable McVicar felt that you weren't up to it quite yet, Andy, having only just returned to work.'

'I see, ma'am. Anyone I know?'

'Detective Superintendent Rommie Frazier.'

'Did you say, Ronnie?'

'Rommie. With two m's. He's a rising star by all accounts, and I've assured the Chief that Fife Constabulary will do everything in our power to assist. And by Fife Constabulary, I mean you.'

He returned her hard stare for a long moment, then said, 'I'll do what I can, ma'am.'

'And that means DS Janes, too.'

'Ma'am?'

'Since she's not had you to protect her these last four weeks, I've noticed . . . how do I say it? . . . how *abrasive* she can be—'

'She's an excellent detective—'

'So you've assured me on numerous occasions, DCI Gilchrist. But my concern now is she needs to soften her approach if she's going to work alongside Detective Superintendent Frazier.' She eyed him over the rims of imaginary spectacles. 'Can I make it any clearer?'

'I suppose not, ma'am.'

'Good. Glenrothes HQ. Tomorrow. Seven sharp.'

Back in his office, Gilchrist phoned DCI Peter 'Dainty' Small. Having started their police careers together with Fife Constabulary, Dainty had since upped sticks and moved to Strathclyde Police, Glasgow. They'd kept in touch over the years, helping each other from time to time with inside information on one investigation or the other.

'Better make it quick, Andy. I'm up to my oxters in alligators and horseshit. Par for the course down here in this fucking midden.'

'Maybe it's time to retire,' Gilchrist offered.

'What for? Hate fucking gardening, and the wife would have me mowing that lawn of ours three fucking times a week. So what d'you need?'

'Detective Superintendent Rommie Frazier. You know him?'

'Don't tell me you've crossed paths with that bastard.'

'Bastard?'

'Turn of phrase.'

'I haven't come across him yet. But he's heading up a joint task force that's being set up tomorrow.'

'Aye, I heard about that. He's a flier for sure, Andy. Got eyes on the top job, and he won't let anything stand in his way, and by that I mean nothing or no one. Ambitious as fuck. And I hate the bastard.'

'So you don't get on with him?' he joked.

'Pushy bastard went over my head about six months back. I was SIO on a serious assault investigation. Some punter from the south side who fancied himself as a pimp was giving his girls a hard time, and by hard time, I mean beating them black and fucking blue. These girls have it tough, you know, really tough. But it's a job, and for many of them it's the only way they know to make money.

'Well, one night he goes too far, this punter. Puts one of them in hospital with broken ribs and a fractured arm. She's had enough, so she coughs on him. Problem is, she doesn't do it through me, even though she's one of my snitches, and she knows it. She goes straight to Frazier, and before I can say Bob's your fucking uncle, a warrant goes out for the punter's arrest, and he's pulled in. That's not the worst of it. I find out later that Rommie fucking Frazier's been cosying up to the girls, nothing illegal like, just making sure that in times of trouble he's their go-to guy. And next thing I know, none of the girls will have anything to do with me, even though I'd been nurturing them for years.

'I was fucking livid, let me tell you. Read Rommie the riot act. But it was like water off a duck's back. Next thing I know, the bastard's promoted. I tell you, I could've fucking jacked it in there and then. Teflon-proof doesn't come close. Friends in high places. So my advice to you, Andy, would be to ca' canny.' The phone rattled for a moment, then Dainty's voice came back with, 'Got to go.'

'Thanks,' Gilchrist said, but Dainty had already hung up.

That day's debriefing led him nowhere. The Van der Stoors had been in Barbados at the time of Soutar's murder, and Mhairi's meeting at Santander turned up nothing out of the ordinary. The bank manager confirmed she'd been transferred from the Kirkcaldy branch to St Andrews, and found Ms Rickard too set in her ways and somewhat difficult to work with. She couldn't recall why Ms Rickard retired six months early, but said she did remember a sense of relief throughout the branch once she'd left. As far as she was aware, Ms Rickard might not have been the most popular employee in the branch, but she was certainly not disliked enough for anyone to want to harm her in any way. Well, if he was looking for a couple of dead ends, that was them right there.

He was reviewing Soutar's crime scene photographs for the fourth time when his mobile rang – ID Mo. He took the call.

Before he could speak, his daughter said, 'I bumped into Jessie in Market Street, and she said you were back at work.'

Her accusatory tone put him on the defensive. 'Well, yes, I feel a lot better, and I needed to get out and about.'

'And you're still there, aren't you? At the Office.'

'I was just wrapping up when you called.'

'Have you eaten yet?'

'That's why I was wrapping up,' he lied again. 'Stomach's rumbling.' But if the truth be told, once he focused on a case, food lost what little appeal it had to him, and he found he ate simply for the purpose of staying alive. 'Would you like to join me? My treat?'

'Sure, Dad. The Central in ten minutes?'

'See you there.'

But by the time he finished reading just one last report, and shut down his computer for the night, it was closer to twenty minutes later when he pushed through the College Street entrance into the Monday night din of a St Andrews pub.

It never failed to amaze him, the number of people who could afford to eat or drink or do both any day of the week. Not only was St Andrews a university town, which more or less guaranteed that the bars were frequented by thirsty students for most of the year, but the fact that it was also the home of golf, and the town in which Prince William met his then-to-be-princess, Kate Middleton, resulted in the town being plagued by overseas visitors keen to soak up the quasi-royal atmosphere, and stand side by side with groups of ruddy-faced caddies who carried bags for golfers on package tours from all around the world.

He found Maureen seated at a table by the window with her back to Market Street in conversation with a woman he hadn't seen before, older than Maureen, somewhere in her forties he'd say.

Maureen caught his eye and waved him over.

He gave her a hug and a peck on her cheeks, loving the fresh smell of her hair. He was pleased to see that at long last she was beginning to put on weight – not much, but no longer the stick-like creature of recent years. Her face was filling out, too, less gaunt, more rounded, with that soft-skinned dark-eyed look that reminded him of his late wife, Gail.

'Remember I told you about Joanne?' Maureen said. 'This is her mother, Irene.'

Gilchrist struggled to place the name, failed to pull it up, but smiled and nodded as he took Irene's outstretched hand.

'Irene, this is my dad, Andy.'

Introductions over, Gilchrist said, 'Can I get you anything from the bar?' Maureen's wine glass was half-full – always a treacherous time to ask for a refill – but she surprised him by declining. He turned to Irene. 'How about you, Irene?'

She looked at her drink for a moment, a clunky glass of clear liquid – could be tap water or straight vodka – then smiled. 'Oh, go on, then. I'll have what you're having.'

'I was going to have a beer?'

'Perfect.'

'A pint?'

She nodded. 'Why not?'

'Anything from the menu?'

'I've already eaten, thank you.'

'How about you, Mo?'

'I'll stick to this, Dad.'

As he turned to the bar to place his order, he glimpsed Mo and Irene giggling together like naughty schoolgirls. He ordered fish and chips, without the peas, and a couple of pints of Deuchars, which he carried back to the table.

'There you go,' he said, and took his seat.

They all chinked glasses together with a Cheers, lovely to meet you, and he watched Irene take a sip of her beer with the tentative unfamiliarity of a non-beer drinker.

She replaced her pint on the table. 'Not bad,' she said. 'In fact, it's good.'

'Not better than good?' he joked.

'It's *very* good.'

He nodded to her, ran a finger back and forth over his mouth to let her know her lips were striped with beer froth. She pulled a paper tissue from her handbag, and dabbed at her lips with embarrassed fuss. He had a sense that Irene had chosen to have a beer with him just to be polite. He took a sip of his own pint, revelling in the coldness against a hot throat – was he hatching something?

When his food arrived, he sprinkled salt over his chips, conscious of Maureen's eyes on him, as if ready to work up her common complaint that he took too much salt. Then he squeezed the lemon over the fish, and finished off with a dollop of brown sauce – not HP, which pubs never seemed to have any more – to the side of the chips. The first mouthful of fish tasted divine, making him realise he'd been hungrier than he thought, and that he needed to pay attention to his diet.

'You sure I can't get you anything?' he said to Irene. 'Share a chip or two?'

'I have to say it looks lovely,' she said. 'Would you mind awfully?'

'Not at all.' He sliced the fish, pushed his plate towards her, but she reached out and fingered a chip, dipped it into the brown sauce then lifted it to her mouth, one hand under the other like a drip-tray.

'I can't resist chips,' she said, cleaning her fingers on another tissue.

'Some fish?'

'Would you mind?'

'Help yourself, please,' he said. 'I'm not all that hungry.' He pushed his chair back, and stood. 'In fact, I'll get another plate.'

A few minutes later, Irene and Gilchrist were sharing his meal, and downing beer, mouthful for mouthful, as if in sync. Light chatter intermingled with forkfuls of fish or chips, and he was intrigued by the way she tried to catch his eye with each forking. He glanced at Maureen, and she stared back at him with a wide smile. Whatever was going on between the pair of them, he knew he would not be made privy to, but had the sense that Maureen had set him up with a quote unquote blind date.

Food finished and beer glasses empty – Maureen's wine glass, too – he said, 'Anyone like another drink? Mo, some more wine? Irene, another beer, or something else?'

'I'd love another beer,' Irene said, and dug her hand into her bag.

'I've got these,' he said. 'Mo? Another glass?'

But she surprised him again. 'I'm all right, Dad,' then grabbed her jacket and scarf from the back of her seat. 'I've got to catch up on some studying.' Before he could respond, she pecked him on the cheek. 'Love you.' She twiddled her fingers at Irene, made a *phone me* sign with her hand, then strode to the Market Street entrance with purpose – or perhaps too much haste, he thought.

Looked like he'd guessed right. Mo had set him up with Irene.

He smiled at her as he pushed to his feet. 'Still fancy that beer?'

'Of course,' she said. 'Just one more, then I've got to be off.'

As it turned out, they each had two more, and Gilchrist was surprised to find himself warming to Irene's company. She smiled, she laughed, she tried to crack a joke or two, and burst out laughing when she fluffed the punchline. And again, she matched him mouthful for mouthful.

'It's unusual,' he said, 'for a woman to down beers like that.'

'I don't normally drink beer. Except Maureen told me that was all you drank.'

Not exactly true. By choice he would drink beer, but often, when he was at home and had had perhaps a beer or three too many, he'd change to liqueur – Drambuie, or the odd Glayva – and sometimes the occasional half of whisky, although how he measured a half at home he had no idea.

'I don't go out much these days,' she said, 'and I've really enjoyed your company.'

'Likewise.'

She smiled at him then, and he was taken by the darkness of her eyes, the irises so black they were almost indistinguishable from the pupils. She reached for his hand. 'Thanks, Andy, you've been a real gentleman. I'd like to offer to buy the drinks next time, but that would be a bit presumptuous of me.' She threw a scarf around her neck, gathered her coat, and stood.

Like the gentleman she'd said he was, he helped her on with her coat, one arm at a time, and surprised himself by flicking her hair out from under her upturned collar.

Her eyes squeezed with friendliness. 'I don't mean to be so forward, but would you mind escorting me home? I don't live far. South Street.'

'Of course,' he said, and with that, he followed her to the door.

CHAPTER 11

Outside, the air had chilled. Frost glistened on the cobbled street. Stars sparkled in a black sky. About to step off the kerb, Irene said with a husky whisper, 'It looks slippery,' and surprised him by taking hold of his arm. He held her firmly, and together they crossed Market Street without a word, and without mishap, and stepped onto the pavement at Church Street.

The air seemed less chilled there, the road less frosty.

Even so, Irene held on.

It felt nice being in the company of a woman again, the freshness of her unfamiliar perfume, the shortness of her step, the awkward bumping of hips before he adjusted his own step to match hers. Despite their silence, not having said a word since crossing Market Street, as if each of them were lost in their own private thoughts, he felt comfortable. He realised he hadn't been with a woman for . . . well, he couldn't really say . . . since Cooper had ended their on-again-off-again relationship once and for all, a year or so ago, if memory served.

They reached South Street, and he let himself be guided as Irene pulled him left. The noisy chatter from the Criterion almost had him suggesting a quick one for the road, but he had to drive home to Crail, and had an early rise in the morning. But now he was in South Street, it struck him then, the reason why Mo had befriended Irene.

'Do you live close to Maureen?' he asked.

'I couldn't tell you. I don't know where she lives.'

He almost stumbled. 'She has a flat in South Street.'

'I didn't know that. I first met her when Joanne brought her home, oh, I suppose about two years ago. We took to each other straight away. She's such a lovely girl.'

Inwardly, Gilchrist smiled. If Maureen heard herself being described as a *girl*, he didn't think she would be overjoyed. He felt pressure on his arm, as Irene took a turn to the right, preparing to cross the road.

On the other side, she said, 'I bumped into Maureen recently in Fraser Gallery. She was looking at a collection of photographs. With the lighting – Fraser's great at that – they looked stunning, even if I say so myself. And Maureen and I got talking, and the rest as they say, is history. Ah, here we are. This is where I live.'

The three-storey terraced residence reared into the night sky like a castle battlement. He wasn't sure if the building was flatted, or if she owned the lot as a single home – surely never. He waited until she slotted her key into the lock, before saying, 'Well, thanks again for the evening, Irene. I thoroughly enjoyed it.'

'I'd like to show you something,' she said, as if he hadn't spoken. She opened the door, and stood back. With some reluctance, he had to say, he crossed the threshold. As it turned out, the building was indeed a single family home – owned by Irene as he would later find out – and had been maintained to the most exacting standards. Wide-planked wooden flooring throughout, which looked like the refurbished original, chipped and varnished, was covered with an array of rugs, from the smallest at around four feet in length, to the largest – a Persian, possibly Isfahan – that almost covered the entire lounge.

Upstairs, the living room was redolent of smoke and pine, and warmed by a log fire that slumbered behind a fine-mesh fire guard. Irene clicked a remote, and the lighting softened, which had Gilchrist thinking that perhaps it was time to leave. Not that he didn't find her attractive, rather it all felt too rushed, too set up, too . . . *fait accompli* . . .

'Would you like anything?' Irene said, walking into the kitchen. 'Beer? Something stronger? I'm going to have a glass of red. Can I entice you?'

'A cup of tea would be nice.' He hoped he'd sent the right message, but she seemed not concerned, and switched the kettle on.

'How do you take it?'

'Milk. No sugar,' he said, then added, 'What did you want to show me?'

She glanced at him then, as if disappointed by his question, but recovered with a smile that creased her eyes. 'This way. Follow me.'

He did, along a darkened hallway, up a flight of stairs, and through a door that led off the top landing. She clicked the light on.

'What do you think?' She stood back to let him survey the room. 'Maureen told me that you fancy yourself as a bit of an amateur photographer. She said you've bought a new camera, and that you've been shooting some landscapes. She says you're very good.'

But not as good as this, he thought, as he walked into the room, eyes fixed on a series of matching black and white photographs that lined one wall, all in black frames with cream-coloured black core bevelled mounts. An adjacent wall was crammed with colour landscapes, panoramic seascapes, and streetscapes that seemed expansive, too. He recognised the East Sands, the cathedral ruins, the stone pier, and cliffs and stretches of Fife Coastal Trail. Other photographs, which appeared more focused on specific items within the frame, created that soft out-of-focus Bokeh effect – a cannon with the Culdee church ruins in the background; a wooden bench on The Scores close to Martyrs' Monument, the sea a haze of white horses and spindrift in the misty background. Another, of rusted chains by a capstan in the harbour, ropes lying around it like stiffened snakes, looked out of place with other framed images, more painting than photograph with a hint of colour spilled here and there. He leaned closer to find it was indeed a photograph, but printed on paper with a canvas texture. The result was an image of professional standards.

'Are all of these yours?' he asked.

'They are.' She stood by the open doorway, a hint of a smile at her lips. Confidence seemed to exude from her, as if she knew her work was first class, and could stand scrutiny by any of the world's top photographers – powerful thoughts indeed.

'Well,' he said as he shuffled to the next wall to examine a line of macro-photographs of flying insects stilled by a high-speed shutter. He knew enough about macro-photography to know that the skill was in capturing the perfect image within an extremely shallow depth of field. A bumble bee taken along its length, one of its pollen-covered legs in sharp focus, the hairs on its body softly focused, busied itself over an azalea. Two butterflies, the closer one in focus, the other a shadowed haze in the background, stood atop purple lilac blossom. A wasp, wings outstretched as if about to take off, seemed to stare with alien-like malevolence into the camera lens.

'I don't want to insult you by asking if you use automatic focus and shutter speed, but I have to.' He faced her, and raised his eyebrows.

She laughed, and said, 'Automatic focus only.'

'Ah,' he said. 'What shutter speed did you use?'

'Two-thousandth.'

'The quality's stunning. What camera do you have?'

'I have several, but I shot the close-ups with my twenty mega-pixel Nikon and an f/2.8 macro lens. Once the image is on the computer screen, you can zoom in to an amazing extent without loss of quality.'

'Twenty mega-pixels will let you do that,' he said, adding, 'You print them out yourself?'

'After spending money on a decent printer. Upgraded to Adobe software on a backlit Apple screen. It makes all the difference.'

'These are excellent,' he said, feeling as if he was repeating himself.

'Thank you.'

He thought he was beginning to put two and two together. 'So it was your display in Fraser Gallery that Maureen liked?'

'Yes. Which was when your name came up.'

He turned to her then, and was taken by an impish grin that hinted of . . . what? A self-assurance he hadn't noticed in the pub? Or maybe a sense of pride and achievement at having taken and produced such a fine photographic display?

'What do you plan to do with these?' he asked.

She crossed her ankles in a shy little girl pose, shrugged, then leaned against the doorframe. 'Take some more photographs, I suppose. I haven't really given it much thought.'

'You should,' he said.

'Take more photos?'

'Give it much thought.'

She laughed at that, pulled herself off the doorframe, turned to the staircase. 'That's the kettle boiled. I'll make that cuppa for you.'

Downstairs, in the kitchen, she filled a solitary mug with tea, which she topped up with a splash of milk, just the way he liked it.

'Any biscuits?' she asked.

He declined, and took a sip of tea, watched her eyes watch him from over the rim of her wine glass. Something in the way she studied him, felt disconcerting. He took another sip, placed his mug on the counter, and noticed a set of three framed watercolours mounted on the kitchen wall – the West Sands from different points of view. He was struck by the subdued colours – beiges, peaches, blues – that lent a misted atmosphere to beach scenes of oatmeal sand. The initials JT hugged the bottom right hand corner of each.

'They're impressive,' he said. 'JT?'

'Jamie. My son. Joanne's older brother.'

He glanced at her, but saw only sadness in her eyes. 'My son Jack paints, too,' he said. 'But never with watercolours. Mostly oils. He's more of a sculptor now, I suppose – large pieces, chunks of metal and steel rods shaped into God only knows what. Nothing as subtle as these.' He turned to her and said, 'Maybe they know each other.'

'Jamie committed suicide three years ago,' she said. 'Drug overdose.'

He stilled for a moment, then said, 'I'm sorry, Irene, I had no idea.'

'Neither had I,' she said. 'Had any idea that he took drugs. I thought I knew him, but I'd also no idea how depressed he'd been. Two days before he took his own life, he destroyed all his work.' She looked at the watercolours on the wall, her face tight. 'These are all I have left of him.' Then she gave him a smile, didn't quite pull it off, and removed the top from the bottle of wine. 'I'm having another. Sure I can't persuade you?'

He almost accepted, but sensibly said, 'I'll pass, thank you. Busy day tomorrow.'

'I really shouldn't have had as much to drink in the bar, but it was just nice to go out of an evening, even if it was only for an hour or so.'

Gilchrist saw an opening, and took it. 'Talking of which,' he said, and made a show of looking at his watch. 'I've an early start. So I really should be heading off.'

'Of course.'

He thought he detected disappointment in her tone, but again she seemed to recover with a smile as she lifted her coat off the back of a chair and reached into a pocket.

'It's all right,' he said, 'I can see myself out,' which pulled a chuckle from her throat.

'Here,' she said, handing him a business card. 'Give me a call if you'd like to chat some more about photography.'

He took her card, and nodded.

'Or we can chat about something other than photography,' she said.

He had a sense that she was struggling to find common ground, searching for some reason to keep in contact with him, and he wasn't making it easy for her. But he helped her out with, 'I enjoyed tonight, Irene. It was lovely to meet you. Maybe another beer or two?'

'I'd love that,' she said, and leaned up to peck his cheek.

For just that moment he could have changed his mind, agreed to share a glass of red wine, maybe two, chat some more about photography or . . . something else. But after being escorted downstairs to the door, common sense prevailed. 'I'll be in touch.' He tugged his collar to his neck, and strode across South Street without a backward glance.

CHAPTER 12

5.30 a.m., Tuesday

The morning arrived to the hard rattling of loose slates on his roof. The weather forecast was for heavy rain and high winds, gusts touching seventy – a hurricane in any other part of the world, but a normal spring day in Scotland – which could strip his roof clean in a matter of minutes if more slates worked loose. He made a mental note to call Tony – his local handyman – and have him repair the slates as soon as.

In his car, he phoned Jessie.

'Where's summer when you need it?' she said.

'The forecast for May is supposed to be good.'

'Aye, right. Did they say which year?'

He chuckled, and said, 'I'll be with you in about ten minutes. You ready?'

'No, I always stand fully dressed at five-thirty in the morning. Of course I'm ready. But Starbucks or Costa won't be.'

'We'd better get to Glenrothes sooner than later, then.'

As soon as he drew up to Jessie's home in Canongate, she came running down her driveway with something in her hand. Instead of opening the car door, she turned to the side and bumped the passenger window with her elbow. He leaned across, clicked the handle, and the door blew open to a chilly wind.

She slid in and handed him a carton of coffee. 'That's yours,' she said, and closed the door with her free hand. 'Homemade, which is a lot better than that cheap stuff they dish up at Glenrothes.' She took a sip, then said, 'Drink up then, and let's go.'

Gilchrist had to say that Jessie's homemade coffee was better than good, much the same as a Costa latte, but at least twice as strong.

'You like?' she asked.

'Makes me wonder why we waste money on Starbucks and Costa.'

'Flattery'll get you everywhere,' she grumbled.

But he could see his comment pleased her.

Glenrothes HQ is a modern building, set back from Detroit Road, and offering plenty of parking spaces. It has no detention facilities, which are provided by Glenrothes Police Station about half a mile away. But HQ is where all emergency calls within the Kingdom of Fife are first received, recorded into the computer system, then assigned a duty status. It is also where the CCTV Control Centre is housed, in a subdued, windowless office with one wall an array of screens through which all of Fife can be monitored. At the press of a button, the screens can shift from Kirkcaldy to St Andrews, from Cupar to Dunfermline, in the blink of an eye. Gilchrist recalled one of the CCTV technicians showing off the system by targeting a camera across the Firth of Forth where it picked up, in surprising detail, the Royal Yacht

Britannia harboured in Leith on the northern outskirts of Edinburgh.

Once through security, Gilchrist and Jessie mounted the staircase to the upper level, where the Task Force was scheduled to meet in the largest of the conference rooms, one that overlooked the countryside to the rear of the HQ building.

Despite arriving well ahead of the scheduled time of 7 a.m., they were not first there. He recognised a few faces – DCI Solomon Reef from Strathclyde – a friend of Dainty's – in close conversation with an attractive woman he hadn't seen before. DCI Freddie Danson – whose prominent buck-toothed grin had earned him the nickname 'Mercury' after the lead singer of Queen – stood alone at the back of the room, mobile phone to his ear. Others he didn't recognise, but it seemed that McVicar had assembled a powerful task force.

Jessie found her way to the coffee machine, and poured herself another coffee. She seemed to be enjoying the taste of it until her gaze shifted over Gilchrist's shoulder to settle on another invitee to the Task Force meeting – DI Barnes, who looked as if she owned the place, striding into the room ahead of a more senior-looking detective.

'Bloody hell,' Jessie said, then hid her face in her coffee as she turned her back to Barnes. Gilchrist caught Barnes's eye, and gave her a smile with a nod of recognition, which she reciprocated, then steered her senior detective to the far corner.

Despite being one of a number of persons of colour in the Task Force – parents from Jamaica, Gilchrist remembered hearing – Detective Superintendent Rommie Frazier was instantly recognisable when he entered the conference room fifteen minutes before kick-off, accompanied by two female detectives carrying laptops and thick folders. He strode behind a table set at the front of the room, while the two female officers set their folders down, removed several files, and went about connecting a laptop to the projector.

What struck Gilchrist about Frazier was the energy that seemed to spill off the man's six-three frame. With shoulders out to here, and a suit that had to have been made-to-measure to fit a massive 50-plus inch chest – at least – and bulging thighs that looked as if they'd been created on the velodrome, Frazier possessed the demeanour of an NFL linebacker fired up from having sacked the quarterback with a loaded hit. He spent a few minutes gathering his papers, talking quietly to the women who'd taken their seats either side of him, and glancing up now and again as if to make sure the full team was present.

Two more pairs of detectives entered, with only minutes to spare, which earned them a scathing look. But Frazier waited while they took their seats before clapping his hands, and saying, 'All right, listen up, everyone.' He scanned the room, waiting for absolute silence. It worked, as all eyes turned his way.

'For those of you who don't know me,' he said, in a voice the match of any barrister's bluster, 'I'm Detective Superintendent Rommie Frazier of Strathclyde, and I'm the SIO in this murder investigation, which from now on will be known as Operation Calvary.'

Jessie whispered to Gilchrist, 'What are we, the cavalry to the rescue?'

'Probably more to do with Calvary being the place where Jesus was crucified.'

Jessie mouthed an Ah . . . then scribbled in her notebook.

Frazier nodded to the woman seated to his left. 'Assisting me are DC Agnew.' He nodded to his right. 'And DC Pollard.'

Both DCs flashed cold smiles at the room.

'Every one of you has been selected as part of a Task Force set up to bring Operation Calvary to a successful conclusion. And by successful conclusion, I mean that the perpetrator of these brutal murders will be found before he can commit any others.' He paused, referred to his notes, then continued. 'We'll now go round the Task Force team, with everyone stating their name, rank and office.'

One by one, introductions worked their way around the room, with DCs Agnew and Pollard striking each name off an attendance list. When it came to Gilchrist's turn, he said, 'Detective Chief Inspector Andy Gilchrist of Fife Constabulary,' followed by Jessie. 'DS Jessica Janes – Jessie for short – of Fife Constabulary, ex-Strathclyde,' she emphasised.

Introductions over, the next two hours were spent going through the details of each of the three murders, with crime scene photographs being displayed on a projector screen that rolled down from the ceiling. DC Agnew had control of the laptop connected to the projector and with every nod from Frazier, tapped the touchpad for the next image.

When the display ended, Frazier said, 'These murders were committed by a serial killer.' He scanned the room. 'Anybody disagree with that?'

No one did.

'We're looking for a male perpetrator,' Frazier went on, 'someone strong enough to overpower the likes of Adam Soutar.' He paused when a hand rose, before looking at his notes, then saying, 'Yes, DCI Gilchrist.'

'I don't believe we should rule out a female perpetrator . . . not just yet, anyway.'

Frazier shook his head. 'Female serial killers are the rarest of the rare, and don't have the physical strength to commit these murders.'

'With all due respect—'

'Let's stick to the facts, shall we?' Frazier snapped. 'Right, first task is to establish a connection. What do Soutar, Forest and Rickard have in common that would make them victims in the eyes of this killer?' He nodded to a woman at the back of the room. 'Yes, DCI Mercer?'

'Both Forest and Rickard attended the same school in Dundee,' Mercer said. 'And we've already established a list of possible victims based on class friendships and common studies.'

'How many potential victims?'

'Six so far, sir, and possibly more.'

'Okay, track down these potential victims and interview them. For all we know, this killer has already selected his next victim, so time is of the essence. I want to see interview statements of each of these six potential victims by close of business today.'

From the look on DCI Mercer's face, she regretted having opened her mouth.

'Anyone else?'

DI Barnes stood. 'We suspect that the cuts through the left nipples are numbers in the order of sequence of these killings,' she said. 'That being the case, we have victims one, two and four, and another victim out there – number three.'

'And victim number three is . . .?'

'Sorry, sir, we have no way of knowing who or where—'

'Precisely,' Frazier said. 'Which is why we need to focus on finding that common connection between these victims. Once we establish that, then we've a better chance of finding who victim three is.' Another scan of the room. 'So, what kind of person are we looking for? Anyone?'

As Gilchrist listened to the others offering their thoughts, he had a sense of them all jostling to be noticed, as if trying to stand out, perhaps in the hope of making a name for themselves in the eyes of Frazier. But Frazier said nothing, just jotted down notes. When the collective group appeared to have run out of ideas, and Frazier scanned the room, Gilchrist pushed to his feet.

'One thing that seems to have been overlooked, if I may?'

Frazier nodded. 'Let's have it.'

'I believe we're looking for someone with an OCD complex. Can you pull up Margaret Rickard's crime scene photographs again?' he asked DC Agnew.

She glanced at Frazier, who nodded, and within seconds Rickard's supine naked body appeared on the screen, spread-eagled.

'Someone dim the lights again,' Frazier demanded.

Gilchrist said, 'Can you click through the images until we see one with a good view of the living room. There. That's it.' He eyed the image that had been taken from an angle that showed Rickard's outstretched arm and nailed wrists, with the sofa in the background. 'Now look at the surroundings,' he said. 'Just like Soutar's and Forest's home, nothing's out of place. The cushions on the sofa don't have a crease in them. They look as if they've been fluffed up and set side by side in perfect alignment. And the living-room carpet looks as if it's been hoovered clean—'

'Have we found that hoover?'

'Already on it, sir,' Jessie said. 'We've sent the contents to the lab for analysis, but so far they've come back with nothing incriminating.'

'Stay on it.'

'That goes without question, sir.'

'If anything comes up, let me know pronto, okay?'

'Yes, sir.'

'Okay, DCI Gilchrist. It's slim, but I take note that the perp could have OCD issues. But again, we need to be focusing on that missing common connection.'

'Which is how this serial killer's OCD behaviour might help.'

'Explain.'

'Soutar's body was found in his home in Cupar, Rickard's in her home in Kincaple, which suggests that this killer lives locally, or at least lives somewhere in the Fife area.'

'And what about Forest's body in Cumbernauld? That's nowhere near Fife.'

'But only an hour's drive, sir.'

'I'm not convinced—'

'I'm not asking you to be convinced,' Gilchrist said. 'I'm suggesting that it might be worth interviewing psychiatrists in Fife, and find out if any of their patients have an OCD complex, along with psychopathic tendencies. Sir.'

'That's a long shot.'

'I'm not saying it isn't. But it would be worth establishing if any of the victims attended a psychiatrist within the last, say . . . five years.'

'That's all good and well, but it assumes that the perpetrator lives locally.'

'We've got to start somewhere.'

'DS Janes,' Frazier said. 'Do you agree with your boss?'

'Yes and no,' she said. 'I believe we should be focusing on Adam Soutar. Why was he the first victim? Why was he chosen? We need to chase down Soutar's medical records, even hospital visits, anything that might give us a connection to his killer.'

'Okay,' Frazier acknowledged. 'I want you and DCI Gilchrist to follow up on Adam Soutar's medical records. Again, I need something back by close of business today.'

'We'll see what we can do, sir.'

'I'm not asking you to see what you can do, DS Janes. I'm instructing you. Have a typewritten report on my desk no later than six this evening, after which I'll decide whether or not to continue with that line of enquiry.' He cast his gaze across the room. 'Anyone else?'

DI Barnes raised her hand again. 'CCTV footage, sir. We have a good estimate of time of death for each victim. I've already set up a team to review footage around the time of Albert Forest's murder. But we also need to review CCTV footage on the roads leading to Soutar's and Rickard's homes. If we can establish a vehicle common to all three victims, we could run the number plate through ANPR. For coverage of Soutar's home, any footage is likely to have been stored in the National ANPR Data Centre. I'd need your authorisation, sir, to access these.'

'You've got it.'

'In writing, sir.'

Frazier seemed unconcerned by Barnes's request. He looked down at DC Agnew, who nodded in response, then he said, 'It'll be with you at the end of this meeting.'

'Thank you, sir. And if . . .' Barnes paused as if for theatrical effect. 'If we find that common vehicle, it might lead us to the missing third victim.'

'Excellent, Ella. That's more like it. I want you to take charge of coordinating all CCTV footage for Strathclyde and Fife. And let me be clear about this.' He scanned the room again. 'I want teams in each CCTV Control Centre working 24/7. Overtime's approved. Keep track of your costs, and let me have them. If I need to increase the budget, I'll take care of that.' Back to DI Barnes. 'Let me know the instant you find anything, Ella.'

'Will do, sir.'

Gilchrist sat back, amused by the smile that creased Frazier's face. With the use of DI Barnes's first name, Frazier had made it clear that he not only knew her, but admired her – maybe even more. Who knew? But big plans ahead for both of them, for sure.

Frazier's imperious look around the room resulted with another clapping of hands. 'All right everyone. Let's adjourn for a coffee break. Be back here in thirty minutes. We need to have a joint statement prepared for the press, so we're all on the same page. I want to make sure we have the media covered. And again, let's be clear on this, no one other than myself is to talk to the media. If I need any of you to assist me in a press conference, I'll let you know. Everybody got that?'

The room gave a general mumble of affirmation.

'Thank you.' And with that, Frazier in-gathered his notes, and strode from the room, Agnew and Pollard scrambling after him.

Gilchrist and Jessie remained seated until the room cleared.

Jessie blew out her breath. 'Bloody hell, this is worse than being back at school. Did you see the way he spoke to that bitch? Excellent, Ella. Well done, Ella. Three bags full, Ella. Meanwhile the thieving bitch stole your idea about victim three still being out there. I tell you, I'm going to have her for that.'

'Professionalism,' Gilchrist said. 'Isn't that what you promised?'

'Yeah, but some promises are meant to be broken.'

He stood. 'Let's get out of here. We've got work to do.'

Jessie's mouth dropped. 'What, you're leaving the meeting?'

'We've been given our assignment, so let's get onto it right away.'

'What about the debriefing tonight? We'll need to attend that.'

'We can email the report, assuming we complete it in time.'

'Jeez, Andy, you're flying too close to the wind for my liking.'

'Well, why don't you find out when the debriefing is, and attend it? Give them my apologies when you get there.'

Jessie fumbled with her notebook and files, and managed to catch up with him as he exited the conference room and strode across the entrance hallway to the main doors.

CHAPTER 13

On the drive back to St Andrews, a thought struck Gilchrist.

'I like your idea that we focus on Adam Soutar,' he said to Jessie. 'He was the first victim, so we need to know why. He's the key. But here's what I'm thinking.'

Jessie shifted in her seat to face him.

'Soutar was a defence lawyer who presumably defended all kinds of criminals.' He eyed the road ahead, not sure where he was going with this, but knowing that he had to test his rationale against Jessie's. Something stirred in his memory banks, a murder trial years ago in which Soutar had defended his client. Being the arresting officer, Gilchrist was required to attend court to give evidence. How long ago the trial had been, he couldn't remember.

But what he did remember, was Soutar being a larger-than-life character, a bombastic lawyer seemingly comfortable in High Court surroundings, doing his best to get his client off all charges. But to no avail. The prosecution had reliable witnesses, three of whom had allegedly watched the victim being almost pummelled to death. Every argument proffered by Soutar was vehemently argued against by the prosecution team, and at the end of the trial the jury unanimously found his client guilty.

But . . .

And this is what had triggered Gilchrist's thoughts; the memory of Soutar's client screaming as he was led from the dock – *These bastards are lying through their back teeth. I'll have youse all for this. Every last fucking one of youse.*

Had Soutar's client been released from prison, only to murder his solicitor because he'd failed him? But if that was the case, surely his client would have been set on killing the three witnesses he'd claimed had lied . . .

'Earth to Andy? Are you still there?'

'Sorry, yes, just thinking.'

'Care to share it?'

He grimaced, let his thoughts simmer a tad longer. If he told Jessie, would that taint her own view on the ongoing investigation, send her logic down the wrong path? He thought of telling her it was nothing, just a fleeting idea, then changed his mind.

'What if one of Soutar's clients felt he'd failed him,' he said, 'that he hadn't done a good job of defending him? And was then found guilty, and sent to prison.'

'So he does his time, gets released, takes out his revenge on Soutar by crucifying him to the floor and cutting out his tongue. Is that what you're saying?' Jessie said.

'Well . . .'

'So why kill Forest and Rickard? And this missing number three?'

'That's the million-dollar question. I don't know.'

'And why stop at four? Who's number five, if he's not already onto six?'

'That's another million-dollar question.'

'I could retire on two million dollars if I knew the answers.'

Now he'd aired his thoughts, he had to move them on. 'Get hold of Mhairi and Jackie and have them look into Soutar's old cases. Start off by looking in the region of ten to fifteen years ago. If one of Soutar's clients killed him because he'd failed in his defence, then he's likely to have been put away for murder, or assault to severe injury.' He wasn't sure if he should mention that he'd been the arresting officer in the case which led to that defiant client of Soutar's being sent to jail – partly because he couldn't remember the defendant's name, but also because he wasn't convinced he was on the right track.

'What about Frazier?' Jessie asked. 'This other stuff he wants on his desk tonight?'

Gilchrist smiled. 'Unless I heard to the contrary, overtime's been approved, with 24/7 teams working around the clock. So we can throw bodies at it, spend as much as we'd like as part of the Task Force.'

'Who do you want checking out Soutar's medical records?'

'Get Norris onto it. And Baxter, too.'

'That should keep them out of trouble for a while.'

Gilchrist settled down to the remainder of the drive to the North Street Office, while Jessie phoned in and set the balls rolling.

Back in his office, he accessed his computer and searched for that old case file. What age had he been when he'd made the arrest? Mid to late thirties? So, in the region of fifteen years ago?

After twenty minutes, he found it.

Tap McCrear, nicknamed *Dancer*.

Gilchrist had come up against many an insidious criminal, but he recalled Tap being one of the most vile. Foul-mouthed, offensive, and unpredictably aggressive, Tap seemed to carry a burden of hate for all things human. And now that he'd recovered his name, the case came flooding back to him.

A black winter's night in the suburbs of Dunfermline, and Gilchrist carrying out door-to-door interviews for a crime committed in St Andrews. The suspect had entered two shops in Market Street, one after the other, bold as brass, brandishing a butcher's knife, and made off with over £2000 in cash. The first shop had only £300 in the till, which was presumably why he'd robbed another shop. But CCTV footage picked up the suspect's car, and from its number plate they identified the owner as a small-time criminal with an address in Dunfermline.

Gilchrist had driven to the suspect's address, only to be told that he'd left home and hadn't been seen around for a month or two. So he decided to carry out door-to-doors on neighbouring properties. He was about to knock on his sixth door when he heard a woman screaming, followed by a commotion of voices, deep, angry and swearing.

He'd jogged towards the end of the terraced building and rounded the corner as a man in a denim jacket rushed past him, almost knocking him down. It took only a few seconds to interpret the assault scene in front of him. A young woman on her knees tending to someone – her boyfriend, or husband, he didn't know. What he did know, was that the man who'd bumped into him was responsible for the assault.

He pulled out his mobile and took up the chase, the suspect now no more than a slim shadow that threatened to disappear into the deeper darkness of terraced buildings. When the connection was made, he reported the assault, and gave the address as best he could explain it – just around the corner from the houses he'd been interviewing. Fifteen years ago, he'd been leaner and fitter, and although he would never describe himself as a sprinter, what he did have was stamina, and an ability to settle into a jog and run for miles. Just as well, because the man he was chasing was fleet of foot, and shifted through the dark streets like a flying wraith. For several minutes Gilchrist thought he was being outrun, but then he sensed the man tiring, the distance between them shortening. So he dug in, kept running, closing the gap until, with less than ten feet between them, the man stopped, and turned to face him, breathing hard, but not prepared to give up readily as he widened his stance.

Gilchrist's blood chilled as he caught something in the man's hand – a knife? He took a step back. 'I'm a police officer,' he shouted. 'You'll only make it worse for yourself.'

'Fuck off.'

'You don't want the assault of a police officer on your record.'

But the man stepped forward, arm lifting, and in that instant Gilchrist saw it was not a knife but a hammer. The man cursed, swung the hammer hard, and Gilchrist only just stepped back from it, feeling the draught of its passing, missing his head by no more than an inch. He took another frantic step back as the hammer came at him again in a backhanded slash. But the blow missed, and its momentum caused the man to stumble.

Which was enough for Gilchrist.

He rushed forward, grabbed the arm that held the hammer, tucked his leg behind the man's. Unable to step back, the man toppled to the ground and thudded onto his back with a force that cracked his head on the asphalt, and pulled a grunt from his throat. Still holding the hammer arm, Gilchrist rolled him over. Knee on the back, and a twist of the wrist, and the hammer fell to the ground with a dull clatter. On automatic now – one arm pressed up the back to the sound of gristle crunching, then the other, and with two clicks the man was cuffed, and going nowhere.

As it turned out, Gilchrist had caught a young up-and-coming criminal by the name of Tap McCrear who, at the age of twenty-five, had a record of fifteen charges of assault, none of which had been proven because every single witness had withdrawn their statement for fear of retaliation. McCrear had psychopathic tendencies, a man who would seek revenge on those he believed had wronged him. But on that occasion, the young man whose skull he'd cracked open in Dunfermline never recovered. Despite spending six weeks in hospital, he failed to regain consciousness, and with a DNR in place – Do Not Resuscitate – he contracted pneumonia and died a week later.

Had Soutar's murder been carried out as revenge for his failing McCrear in court? Having been found guilty of murder, had McCrear's mental state been so warped that all he could do was harbour resentment and anger all these years behind bars, only to launch an explosive attack on an unsuspecting Soutar upon his release from prison?

In theory, Gilchrist's rationale worked.

But in practice, it didn't.

It failed to explain why McCrear targeted Forest and Rickard. And until he found the answer to that question, and established an irrefutable connection, he was reluctant to share his thoughts with anyone other than Jessie.

He found her in Jackie's office, reading something fresh off Jackie's printer.

'Is Mhairi around?'

Jessie shook her head. 'Gone with Norris and Baxter to interview Soutar's doctor, as well as a number of local psychiatrists.'

'Right,' he said. 'Jackie? You got a minute?'

Jackie stopped typing, and nodded. 'Uh-huh.'

'Take a note of this name,' he said. 'Tap McCrear, aka Dancer. Sent to prison fifteen years ago for murder. I need to know when he was released, and where he's living now. As soon as you can. Got it?'

'Uh-huh.'

'And I need bank and credit card statements, name of employer if he has one, and place of employment, work records, tax returns, the usual.'

'Uh-huh,' she said, fingers back to rattling the keyboard in a constant clatter.

'So you think it's him?' Jessie said.

What could he say? That he didn't know? That it was a shot in the dark? 'Let's see if he's out first of all,' he said. 'And if he's back inside for some other crime, well that'll be the end of it.'

'You look concerned,' she said.

'Just intrigued.'

'I can tell when you're holding something back.' She returned his gaze with a direct stare of her own. 'Care to share it?'

'I'm kind of hoping it's not McCrear.'

'You seemed so sure a few minutes ago.'

Rather than continue to hide his fears from Jessie, he decided just to tell her. 'Adam Soutar was his defence solicitor. But I was the arresting officer.'

She stilled, as if struggling to understand. Then just as quickly recovered. 'It can't be McCrear,' she said. 'Why would he kill Margaret Rickard? It makes no sense.'

'It might,' he said, 'if she was one of the jury that found him guilty.'

'Oh, for crying out loud,' Jessie said. 'You mean . . .?'

'But only if he's still out.'

'Right. I'm on it.'

Gilchrist left them to it, and walked back to his office.

CHAPTER 14

By 3 p.m. Gilchrist had his answer. Not only had Margaret Rickard been a member of the jury that had found McCrear guilty, she'd been the spokesperson. Just as damning was the fact that Albert Forest had been on that jury panel, too. But more worrying, there were another thirteen jury members on the list of potential targets, not to mention Soutar's legal team – three, as best he could recall.

And of course, there was Gilchrist himself, the arresting officer.

If he had indeed found the connection between all three victims, then it was likely that McCrear had at least sixteen more to kill. As the sickening truth of what he'd uncovered revealed itself to him, he came to see how cruel McCrear was, someone without remorse or compassion, who could, through the most cruel and violent acts, take the lives of innocent people on the basis of his twisted perception that they'd done a bad deed against him.

And the more Gilchrist thought about it, the more certain he became.

Tap McCrear was the man they were after.

But what to do with the information? Speak to Frazier immediately, and tell him of his concerns? Or wait until that day's debriefing? He needed time for his thoughts to mature. He glanced at his computer screen – 15:12 – which gave him less than three hours to pull a detailed report together. But if he waited until that day's debriefing, for all anyone knew, McCrear could be setting off to kill his next victim.

With these thoughts, the answer seemed crystal clear.

He returned to Jackie's office. 'Any luck with Tap McCrear?'

Jackie pointed to her printer tray, from which he removed a sheaf of paperwork, and flipped through it – mostly bank statements that seemed healthy, credit card statements through which several hundred pounds were spent monthly, then paid in full before interest charges kicked in. He studied the photo of an enlarged copy of McCrear's driving licence. Just as he remembered him, but older, leaner, harder. Cheeks so sunken they looked rutted. Blue eyes, so light they were almost white, stared at the camera with malevolent defiance. A square chin sported a three-inch scar that ran in a crooked line through the corner of his mouth towards his left ear – the result of a confrontation with a drunk outside a public house in Edinburgh, who was threatening everyone with a broken bottle, or so McCrear had claimed. He noted the address on the driving licence. 'Is this where he still lives?' he asked Jackie.

'Wha . . . wha . . . ?'

He read the address out to her – a street in Dunfermline – and she opened up another screen and typed it in. Ten seconds later, he had her answer.

It was.

He found Jessie in her office, opening a bar of chocolate. When she saw him, she gritted her teeth. 'Why do I feel as if you've caught me with my knickers down?'

'Because you're blowing your diet?'

She cracked off a square of chocolate. 'I can't help it if I've got a sweet tooth,' she said, and slipped it into her mouth.

'Let's go. You can finish it on the way.'

Without asking, she grabbed her jacket off the back of her chair, and managed to catch up with him as he pushed through the back door into the car park.

'What's the rush?' she said.

'We're going to interview the prime suspect.'

'Anyone I know?'

'Tap McCrear.'

She hesitated, almost stumbled. 'Just the two of us?'

'For the time being.' He clicked his remote fob and his car's lights flickered.

Jessie scrambled into the passenger seat. 'Bloody hell, Andy, if he's who we're after, don't you think we should have back-up? I mean, as soon as we turn up at his door, anything could happen.'

Gilchrist entered the address into his satnav. 'I don't think he'll see it that way.' He slipped into gear, powered through the pend, and swung a hard left onto North Street. 'He's left no forensic evidence at any of the crime scenes. So he thinks he's clever. He thinks he's smarter than us. So he'll just listen to what we say, and deny everything.'

'If it's that easy, why don't we just arrest the bastard?'

Gilchrist grimaced. He was working on a hunch, not much more. Arresting someone under the pretext of being a suspect, without first running it past Frazier, could put him in serious trouble. No, best just to question McCrear, let him know he was being looked at.

So he focused on the road ahead, and drove on.

But unknown to Gilchrist, the murder investigation had just taken a turn for the worse. The Force Control Centre at Glenrothes had received a call from a hysterical woman less than an hour ago, sobbing her heart out. She'd come home early from work, and found her father on the floor, naked, staked out, and unequivocally dead.

The first Gilchrist heard about it was when he received a call from Frazier.

'How fast can you get to Kilconquhar?' Frazier said.

Kilconquhar was almost directly due south of St Andrews, and as best Gilchrist could remember, some ten or so miles away. Luckily – if that was the correct word in light of the circumstances – he hadn't driven too far. 'About twenty minutes,' he said. 'Why?'

'We've got another one. Laura Detling, the victim's daughter, called it in. It's on your patch.' Frazier rattled off an address.

'What's the victim's name?'

'John Matthew Moorhouse.'

Gilchrist ended the call, pulled to the side of the road, and entered the Kilconquhar address into his satnav. The shortest route was back through St Andrews, then onto the B845 south. He swung the car around, and floored the pedal. Then he phoned Jackie through his car's system.

'Got another name for you to check out. Write it down.'

'Uh-huh.'

'John Matthew Moorhouse. Can you find out if he was on the jury panel that found McCrear guilty?' He took a fast right into

Abbey Walk, and accelerated to fifty, too fast for the town's speed limit – but sometimes it didn't matter – and listened to the clatter of Jackie typing on her keyboard.

Then her voice came back with a breathless, 'Nuh-uh.'

He mouthed *What . . .?* 'He wasn't on the jury panel?'

'Nuh-uh.'

'How about plain John Moorhouse? Check that name.'

'Nuh-uh.'

'Anyone by the name of Moorhouse?'

'Nuh-uh.'

On the off-chance that they'd somehow got the names mixed up, he said, 'How about Detling? Anybody on the jury panel with that name?'

'Nuh-uh.'

Shit and damn it. He gripped the steering wheel tight as he powered through the mini-roundabout at Lamond Drive, and raced up the Kinkell Braes. He'd reached seventy by the time he said, 'I need you to find out how Moorhouse is connected to the others, Jackie. He just has to be. And let me know as soon as you find something. It's important. Got it?'

'Uh-uh.'

The call disconnected with a clatter.

'Damn it,' he snarled. 'Just when you think you're onto something, the rug gets pulled.' He shook his head. 'I can't believe it.'

'Maybe he was someone McCrear met in prison,' Jessie said.

He didn't reply, just gritted his teeth. If Moorhouse hadn't been on that jury panel, then his theory, which had sounded so plausible a few minutes ago, was worthless. 'Let's wait until Jackie gets back,' he said, which was all he could think to say.

They found the address in Kilconquhar without difficulty. A white Transit van parked outside, forensically suited SOCOs milling around the front door, and crime scene tape across the road, flapping in the wind like bunting, were a certain giveaway. Two constables stood by the tape, either side of the SOCO van, keeping spectators back from the crime scene. Three Fife Constabulary police cars were parked at awkward angles, as if to make it more difficult for spectators to approach.

'Looks like we're last to the party,' Jessie said.

Gilchrist parked on the opposite side of the road, some distance from the SOCO van. He removed two plastic packages from the boot, handed one to Jessie, and tucked the other under his arm. As they strode towards the address, warrant cards at the ready, he caught Frazier standing next to a top-of-the-range Mercedes Cabriolet with the driver's door open, mobile to his ear. When he saw Gilchrist, he ended the call. Then he slammed the car door shut, beeped a remote fob, and advanced towards him like a lion eyeing prey.

'What kept you?' Frazier said.

'Who found the victim?' Gilchrist asked, ignoring Frazier's snipe.

'Already told you.' He nodded to a parked car. 'His daughter, Laura Detling. She's with the FLO at the moment.'

Gilchrist glanced at two females sitting in the front seats of a Ford Fiesta. The Family Liaison Officer was already here? That was quick. But something didn't feel right, as if he'd arrived at a dinner party at the scheduled time only to find everybody well-oiled and halfway through the second course.

'So she's already given her statement?'

'She has.'

'To whom?'

'That doesn't matter. What does, is that we have another victim.' He glanced at the front door. 'Get booted and suited and let me know what you think.'

'When was it called in?'

'You're here now. It doesn't matter.'

'I should've been informed earlier. As you said, this is my patch.'

Frazier narrowed his eyes and squared up to him. 'Don't play territorial games with me, DCI Gilchrist. You've now been duly informed. So get on with it.'

'Any closer to making the connection between the victims?' Gilchrist said.

Frazier's eyes burned, as if he knew he was being made a fool of, but couldn't figure out how. 'I've had a look, and there's something not right about this one.' Frazier tilted his head to the opened door. 'I want to see if you agree.'

When Frazier walked away, mobile to his ear again, Gilchrist had the sense that he'd been set some kind of test. *Something not right about this one.* Was the MO different? Was it another killer? If Moorhouse had not been a member of the jury that found McCrear guilty, why had he been murdered? Too many questions, not enough answers.

He turned his back to Frazier, and suited up.

CHAPTER 15

He was about to cross the threshold when Colin, the lead SOCO, stepped outside.

Gilchrist gave him a grim smile. 'Any thoughts?'

'Yeah. I'm thinking I've just about had enough of it all.'

Gilchrist could only nod in agreement. No matter how many dead bodies you came up against in your career, you never became inured to it – the metallic smell of blood, the rotting aroma of putrefaction, the unmistakable stillness of the body confirming a life gone from this world. You almost had to be inhuman to take it in your stride, and for many there came a point where they simply reached their limit. It seemed like Colin was fast approaching his.

He squeezed Colin's shoulder. 'Try to remember that it's more than just a job. You're doing it for the victim. We all are. If not us, then who else would see justice done? If you can, hang onto that.'

Colin lowered his eyes.

Gilchrist stood aside to let him pass, a heavy feeling warning him that he might not be able to stomach much more himself. He forced his thoughts into focus – *you're doing it for the victim*. That's what he'd told Colin. *If you can, hang onto that*.

He and Jessie found Moorhouse's body through the back of the house on the carpeted floor, supine, naked, arms and legs stretched wide in a horizontal crucifixion. His face could have been a human effigy, skin plaster-of-Paris white, eyes half-shut in the out-of-focus look of the dead. Not much hair, a widow's peak that swept back to thin white strands too long at the ears. And no tape over the mouth either, lips not pressed tight together, but parted as if to let his final breath pass unhindered.

And no sign of any blood.

Gilchrist said nothing as Jessie kneeled on the carpet, and moved her face close to the victim's, as if she were about to place her lips to his. Then she touched his lips with gloved fingers, and eased them farther apart.

'The tongue's not been cut out,' she said. 'It's still there.'

Well that would explain the lack of blood. He looked along the victim's bare arms to gleaming nail-heads protruding from both hands and a trail of blood that pooled in the carpet. He then shifted his gaze down both legs to the bloodied feet. Everything appeared the same, except that the tongue had not been cut out.

He cocked his head at the sound of music in the background, the volume so low that Jessie seemed not to have heard it. It took a few seconds to catch the tenor vocals of Andrea Bocelli reaching the high notes of 'Nessun Dorma'—

'Rigor's not set in yet,' Jessie said. 'Time of death probably no more than a couple of hours, although I'll let Queen Becky's thermometer determine that.'

Gilchrist rested one knee on the carpet, pressed his fingers to the side of Moorhouse's neck. Not that he was searching for any kind of pulse, rather he was confirming for himself that death had only recently occurred. The skin was not stone cold, but still possessed the latent warmth from a beating heart only recently stilled.

'Jeez,' Jessie hissed. 'He's a right skinny bugger. Look at these washboard ribs. You could run a stick up and down his sides and pull in the crowds.' She pushed to her feet. 'What do you think killed him? Heart attack, maybe?'

Silent, Gilchrist let his gaze shift over the body. Jessie was right. Moorhouse could not have weighed much more than seven stones, if that. On its back on the carpet made it difficult to estimate the body's height with certainty, but the more he looked at the skeletal figure before him, the more he came to suspect that Moorhouse had not been in the best of health. Blue veins streaked his arms and legs like inked lines. Grey chest hair clumped in thick tufts interspersed with black skin lesions that looked like crusted moles.

Gilchrist stood upright, stretched his back, and looked around the room.

A pile of clothes lay on the sofa, neatly folded, not stacked in the reverse order of their removal as the others had been, but laid along the sofa side by side. Did it matter that they hadn't been piled on top of each other? The cushions, too, seemed a tad disorderly, not plumped up to crease-free perfection. An indentation in one cushion and a dishevelled settee cover gave a hint of where Moorhouse might have last been seated. The TV in the corner confirmed that.

Gilchrist twisted his head to the side, and inhaled through his nose. 'What do you smell?' he said.

Jessie sniffed once, twice, then shook her head. 'Not a lot. Why?'

'I don't know. There's something in the air that I can't quite put my finger on.'

'Like what?'

'An aftershave that I've smelled before.' He grimaced. 'I don't know. Something's not right. And the music, too.'

'What music?'

'In the lounge.'

'There's music on?' She stepped beyond him. 'Jeez, Andy, have you got bat ears or what? I never heard a thing.'

'Don't touch it.' He hadn't meant to shout, but his words had Jessie standing still, hand poised by the Bose remote control.

'Okay. I get it,' she said.

'I can't see it clearly yet,' he said, searching for some way to put his thoughts into words. 'But what happened here . . . is a mistake I think. It's as if McCrear's slipped up.'

'Been taken by surprise?' Jessie said. 'I'm thinking that old Johnny died of fright, thereby screwing up McCrear's perfect plans for victim number five.'

'It's more than that.' He looked around, moved to the patio door that opened onto a small slabbed area which in turn led to a trimmed lawn. Despite the wintry month, the grass looked as if it had been recently cut. A square concrete block with a round hole in it defined the location of the whirligig for hanging out washing in warmer months. A covered barbecue stood in one corner of the patio. A metal table with four chairs stacked to one side stood in the other. The lawn itself was surrounded by a wooden fence, about six feet high, beyond which the hills fell off to the distant Firth of Forth. He tried the patio door handle, pressed it down – unlocked – then pushed the door open.

He stepped onto the slabbed patio, struck by how symmetrical the small garden space was – the table stacked in the corner, just so; the barbecue positioned so that it was square to the slabs and the back fence; the fence itself, no more than a year or so old, he figured, wood-stained to keep it looking fresh and new, but which also left the tell-tale scuff mark of leather on wood, where someone – McCrear? – had scrambled over in his rush to escape after being disturbed. A look over the fence confirmed the land spread off to open fields and barely a neighbouring house in sight. No CCTV cameras or domestic webcams, too. Still, with all the rain they'd had, they might be able to lift a footprint or two, if they got lucky. A gust of wind picked up, sending a chill through him, and he returned to the living room.

He walked around the body to stand close to the feet. The left foot lay in a small pool of blood, but the right showed only a trickle, making him think that Moorhouse died before his right leg was nailed to the carpet. Had he died from shock, or suffered a heart attack? Or had he just simply expired? Because by the looks of the man, there couldn't have been much flesh to cling onto life. But Cooper would determine cause of death, maybe even pin down the moment in his crucifixion at which Moorhouse had died.

Even so, Gilchrist was sure he was missing something. They all were. But what, he couldn't say. He studied the body for a full minute, let his gaze drift away and shift around the room until it settled on Jessie with such directness that she said, 'What?'

'Just thinking.'

'Thank God. I thought you were trying to turn me to stone.'

'He's been disturbed,' he said, as if Jessie hadn't spoken. He walked to the sofa, and with his thumb and forefinger lifted one edge of a folded shirt. Despite it having been worn by the victim that morning, it appeared clean and smooth enough to have been removed fresh from the wardrobe. He let it go, pressed it flat again, and faced Jessie.

'I'm thinking that his MO was disrupted.' He still didn't have it clear in his mind, but hoped that talking to Jessie would iron any flaws in his logic. 'Firstly, the victim dies on him before he can complete his ritual.' He looked around him. 'But that's not enough to have him scampering out the patio door.'

'You think he left that way?'

'Yes. It's unlocked.'

'So what? I leave my back door unlocked if I'm at home, or hanging out washing.'

He nodded to the patio. 'There's nothing out there. Not even a whirligig. Everything's been stacked away for the winter months.'

Jessie seemed deflated.

'Think about it,' he said. 'He overpowers Moorhouse, strips him, then nails him to the floor. Like the others, Moorhouse doesn't put up any kind of a fight. The clothes are folded, but McCrear hasn't placed them in a pile. For some reason he wasn't ready to leave when he did.'

'Well, old Johnny died on him. That would spoil his fun.'

'I don't think it was just that. There's more.'

'There's a lot of assumptions in that.'

'Go with me on this. Hear me out.' He closed his eyes, tried to visualise the scene in the darkness of his mind, to urge that sixth sense of his into action. He opened his eyes, and looked beyond Jessie, into the lounge. Andrea Bocelli was still on low, the Bose player likely set on shuffle repeat mode. He walked into the lounge, steering clear of the body. The music was louder there, but not by much. Most people would have to strain to make out who was singing, especially the elderly. Even John Moorhouse?

He glanced at the TV, then eyed the TV remote on a side table at the end of the settee. He reached for it, clicked on the TV, and waited until the screen came alive. *BBC News* came on, much louder than comfortable for such a small room. He clicked it off, and returned the remote control to the table.

'Moorhouse didn't put on the music,' he said. 'McCrear did. It's unlikely we'll be able to lift any fingerprints from the remote. He'll have been wearing gloves; I'm sure of that. But I'm also sure he was interrupted.' He eyed the patio door again. 'And if he had to leave in a hurry, he wouldn't have been able to cover his tracks so well.'

Jessie gave a non-committal nod. 'Okay . . .'

'Let's find Moorhouse's daughter,' he said, 'and have a chat with her.'

CHAPTER 16

Gilchrist found Colin by the rear door of the SOCO Transit van, forensic coveralls pulled back from his head, cigarette tight between his lips, cheeks pulling in with the effort. Despite having not smoked for nigh on twenty years, Gilchrist was struck by how strong the urge to have a quick puff still was. He reached Colin, breathed in the acrid air, held it in for just that second or two longer, savouring the moment, trying to eke out some infinitesimal sense of unpermitted pleasure.

Just then, Colin crushed the dout between thumb and forefinger, and flicked it into the wind. It never failed to amaze Gilchrist how inconsiderate smokers were – a despicable habit altogether. He eyed the sky. Clouds were folding in from the east, low and dark, threatening rain. They didn't have much time. 'I think he made his escape out the patio door and over the fence into the fields. If he did, you might find footprints before the skies open up.'

Colin's gaze drifted to the house, then up at the clouds. 'Right. I'm on it.'

Gilchrist watched him call out to one of the SOCOs, a young woman he hadn't seen before, and together they entered the house. Gilchrist then walked across the road, and tapped the car's window.

Startled, the FLO jerked him an angry look, then wound down the window. 'Yes, sir?'

'If you're finished, we'd like to have a chat with Mrs Detling.'

'Of course, sir.' She spoke to the woman in the front seat, then folded her notes.

Gilchrist walked around the car and opened the passenger door. 'Laura Detling?' He held up his warrant card. 'We'd like a few minutes with you,' he said, 'to help us understand what happened earlier,' then stood aside as she slid out.

She gave a pained smile, and crushed a tissue under her nose. He introduced himself and Jessie, offered their condolences, then led her to his car, where he opened the door and helped her into the passenger seat, while Jessie clambered into the back. Seated behind the steering wheel, he couldn't fail to catch the young woman shiver – from the cold or the stress of what she'd just experienced, he didn't know – but he switched on the car's engine, turned the heater up.

'It'll warm up in a minute,' he said. 'If it gets too hot, let me know.'

She nodded, and pressed the tissue to her eyes.

He opened his notebook and made a show of flattening a clean page, noting the date, time and place of interview. He would put her in her late forties, and physically nothing at all like her father. With her round face and double chin, he had to assume that she took after her mother. And her red hair, too, thick with waves that curled at the ends, reminded him more of Cooper than the loose strands of white hair of the man lying dead in the house behind them.

He adjusted the temperature controls. 'You comfortable?' he asked.

She sniffed. 'Better.'

'You popped in today to see your father?' he began.

She nodded. 'I look in on him most days now. Make sure he's got food in the fridge. That he hasn't spilled anything. Or left something on the stove. I also pick up his laundry. I wash and iron his clothes at home. That sort of thing.'

'Most days, you said. The same days every week?'

'Usually every other day. Mondays and Wednesdays. Then I'll take him for shopping on Fridays. Sometimes have him over to ours for Sunday lunch.'

He was aware of Jessie scribbling in her notebook behind him. 'But today being Tuesday, he wouldn't have been expecting you, would he?' And neither would McCrear, he thought. He'd been caught out by Laura's unexpected arrival.

'No, I suppose not. On Tuesdays, I usually go to my yoga class after I've finished school. But Dad's not been feeling well. And his memory's not as sharp. So I thought I'd pay him a quick visit. Make sure everything was okay.' Her voice broke then, and she choked a sob into her hands.

'Here,' Jessie said, and handed her a couple of fresh tissues.

Silent, Gilchrist waited while she recovered. 'You have a key for his house?'

She sniffed, and nodded.

'When you let yourself in,' he said, 'do you ring the doorbell first? Or do you just slot the key in and enter?'

'Ring the doorbell, of course.'

'And does your father usually answer? Or do you then let yourself in?'

She frowned again, puzzled by his question. But with McCrear's crucifixion having been disturbed, Gilchrist was trying to establish how long McCrear thought he had in which to abandon his gory task. Or, put another way, how narrow an escape Laura must have had, for if she'd stumbled upon McCrear in the middle of his murderous act, he had little doubt she would have been an unintended addition to the murder list.

'I wait for a little while,' she said, 'then I'll let myself in, in case he's in the toilet.'

'So, run through it with me,' he said. 'Just as it happened. From the moment you rang the doorbell, to when you let yourself in. Tap your hand for every second you waited. As best you can.'

She mimicked pressing the doorbell, then tapped her hand on her thigh seven times, before mimicking ringing the doorbell again. Had McCrear panicked when he first heard the doorbell? Or had he tried to brave it out, and simply waited? After all, it could have been a cold caller, a salesman trying to promote landscaping services or solar panels, someone who would wait for only a half a minute if the door was unanswered, before walking to the next address. But when the doorbell rang a second time, McCrear would've realised that it was no salesperson. Would he have abandoned his task then? Or had he already left?

Laura mimicked slotting her key into the lock.

'So about fifteen seconds between the time you first rang the bell, and unlocked the door. Give or take. That about right?'

She nodded. 'Yes.'

'When you pushed the door open, and stepped into the vestibule, what did you do?'

'What do you mean?'

'Did you shout out anything? Did you call out a welcoming Hello?'

'No. Nothing. I just took off my jacket and hung it over the hook.'

Gilchrist nodded. Her silence on entering her father's home that afternoon might have saved her life. If McCrear had heard a woman calling out, he might have chosen to attack her, kill her too. But silence had been his enemy. He couldn't risk being confronted by someone unknown, someone who could possibly overpower him. But even so, he would have been armed with a hammer for the crucifixion, and a knife or scalpel for the tongue.

So why run at all? Why not stay and chance it?

Which was when Gilchrist found his answer.

Because Moorhouse, the intended crucifixion victim, was already dead. He'd died during the hammering in of the nails. And without a living person to identify him, and most likely without a reason to complete his gruesome task, McCrear had made a snap decision – to cut and run.

Gilchrist grimaced at Laura. In her mind's eye she was still in the vestibule. But he had to know what she saw or heard. 'Keep going,' he said to her. 'You've hung up your jacket. Your scarf, too?'

She nodded.

'What about your handbag?'

'I was carrying it.'

He nodded. 'And the house keys?'

'In the handbag.'

'So you'd removed the keys from the lock and returned them to your handbag?'

'Yes.'

Jessie said, 'It's important that you don't miss anything out.'

'I'm sorry. I didn't think that was important.'

'That's all right,' Gilchrist said. 'What happened next?'

'I walked into the hallway—'

'Was the vestibule door unlocked?'

'It's never locked.'

'Did you push it open?'

'Yes.'

'Did it make a noise, like a catch clicking?'

'Yes.'

He scribbled in his notebook. McCrear would have had no doubts that someone had entered the house, that it was only a matter of time before he was discovered. 'Then what did you do?' he said.

She took a few seconds to gather her thoughts. 'I pushed the vestibule door open. It clicked. I shut it. It clicked again. Then I checked the thermostat.'

'Why?'

'I thought it was cold.'

'What, the hallway?'

'It's usually warm. Dad doesn't like the cold. He has it turned up. He gets a heating allowance from the government. But it didn't seem as warm, somehow.'

Had a blast of wind swept through the living room when McCrear opened the patio doors? 'And did you turn up the thermostat?'

'No, it was already set at twenty-two.'

Well, he had his answer. McCrear had escaped in the nick of time. And so had Laura – with her life. 'Okay,' he said, easing into it. 'Take your time, and tell us what you did next, if you noticed anything odd, or out of the ordinary before you entered the living room . . .' He let his words fade.

She shook her head. 'I can't think of anything odd.'

'Except the temperature.' Jessie again.

'Well . . . I suppose so.'

'It's important,' he said. 'The smallest thing, the tiniest sense of something not being right could help us.'

She frowned, as if puzzled, then brightened. 'Oh, yes, I heard music playing. I thought it was coming from the telly. But when I entered the living room, the first thing that caught my eye was the telly. It was switched off. Which was odd. Because it's usually on all day long. And that's when . . .' She pressed her hands to her lips, squeezed her eyes shut.

Gilchrist gave her arm a gentle squeeze. 'It's all right, Laura, you're doing really well.' He waited while she recovered, then said, 'What sort of music did your father like?'

'What?' She looked at him as if he'd asked her to strip.

'What was his favourite group, or band?'

'He didn't really listen to music. He'd spend most of his time in front of the telly.'

'What about the Bose CD player?'

'That was mine. It's an old one. We gave it to him when we upgraded.'

'If he didn't listen to music,' Jessie said, 'why did you give him a CD player?'

'He'd listen to music sometimes. Not a lot. At Christmas. Or maybe when the mood took his fancy. Which wasn't often, mind. Someone told us that listening to old songs could be good for the memory. Not that it would ever improve. More like it made him feel good.'

Gilchrist nodded, while Jessie scribbled. 'What about CDs?'

'We gave him a few to tide him over. The Beatles. Abba. That sort of stuff.'

'Andrea Bocelli?'

'Oh, God, no. That wasn't his style at all.'

He had his answer. He pressed on. 'You said your father hadn't been keeping well.'

She nodded. 'He's never been in the best of health. Been frail most of his life. And recently his heart was giving him trouble.'

Well, he thought, if anything would stop an ailing heart in its tracks, being nailed to the floor had to be top of the list.

'He was scheduled to have heart surgery next month,' she said, and choked back a sob. 'He wasn't looking forward to it. Now it's . . . it's . . .'

Jessie said, 'How long's your father been retired?'

Gilchrist almost cringed at her directness.

But Laura seemed unfazed. 'About six years,' she said. 'He was a clerk of the court, about as boring a job as you could ever imagine. But Dad seemed to like it.'

Gilchrist closed his notebook. 'Thanks, Laura. We know it's been difficult for you, but you've helped us build a picture.' He smiled, but she shook her head as if unable to take in what he'd said. 'DS Janes will take you back to the Family Liaison Officer.' He thought of handing her one of his business cards, but didn't think she could offer anything else.

When Jessie helped her from his car, he recovered his mobile. 'Got another one for you, Jackie.'

'Uh-huh.'

'Find out if John Moorhouse was a clerk of the court during Tap McCrear's trial. I think we've found our connection.'

CHAPTER 17

It took Jackie less than five minutes to get back to Gilchrist with a positive result. John Moorhouse had indeed been the clerk of the court in attendance at Tap McCrear's trial.

So, now Gilchrist had his connection.

He called Jessie over and told her.

'That's it,' she said. 'Let's get an arrest warrant and a team together, and head off to his house and cuff that dancing bastard.'

But Gilchrist had his doubts. Having been disturbed before he could commit his latest murder, would McCrear have run straight home? He thought not. 'There's no guarantee he's going to be there,' he said.

'So what? We raid his house and find all the evidence we need. Jars of tongues, for one. Piles of nicked jewellery, for two.'

But that sixth sense of Gilchrist's was niggling at him, warning him that all was not as it seemed. 'He's slippery,' he said. 'He won't have any evidence at home. He'll have it stored somewhere off-site, in a place that only he knows.' He faced Moorhouse's home, and tried to imagine McCrear pulling himself over the patio fence to flee into open fields. Where would he have gone? Straight home did not seem like the correct answer.

'Uh-oh,' Jessie said. 'Here comes trouble.'

Frazier reached them, and squared up to Gilchrist, shoulders twelve inches wider, it seemed, eyes two inches higher. 'What d'you think?' he asked, ignoring Jessie.

'It's different, all right,' Gilchrist said. 'I believe he's slipped up.'

Silent, Frazier glared at him, as if to intimidate him. But Gilchrist wasn't in the mood for being trodden on. He also wasn't in the mood for sharing his thoughts on the possibility of having found the connection between the victims – still too early, and maybe just a tad unsure of it all – until he'd done some more homework.

So he said, 'He was disturbed before he could go through with the murder.'

'What makes you think he was disturbed?' Frazier asked. 'He didn't go through with it because his victim died on him. Plain and simple.'

'The patio door was unlocked—'

'We got that. Unlocked, and probably the way he came in.'

'Not if the key was on the inside.' He watched Frazier's eyes watch his, as if he was being tested with the simplest of questions. Start off with the easy ones, then move onto the more difficult ones.

'So how'd he get in, then?' Frazier asked.

'The front door.'

'Which has a key on the inside, too, doesn't it?'

'It does, yes. But it's also got a doorbell.'

Frazier gave a lopsided grin. 'So he presses the bell, and is invited in?'

'I'd say so.'

'And why would Moorhouse let him in?'

There was a myriad of reasons to invite someone into your home, but even if you hadn't, once the door was opened, you didn't have to be a heavyweight lifter to overpower a man as frail as Moorhouse. Gilchrist almost shrugged. 'Why wouldn't he let him in?'

'So front door, not patio door?'

'That's right.'

'Still not convinced.'

'If he'd come in by the patio door, there would've been mud on the carpet. The place is clean.'

Frazier narrowed his eyes, slid a glance Jessie's way. 'You agree with your boss?'

'Of course,' she said. 'It's obvious, isn't it?'

Back to Gilchrist. 'I need more convincing.'

'How about the Andrea Bocelli CD, then?'

'The what?'

'The killer brought it with him. But when he was disturbed, he forgot about it in his rush to leave.'

'He brought his own CD?' He almost snorted. 'What, like music while you work?'

'That's one way of describing it.'

'And another?'

'Evidence from which we might lift prints.' Frazier's eyes locked onto his, and for just that split second, Gilchrist wanted to wipe the smirk off his face, share his thoughts on Tap McCrear being the prime suspect. But he needed to be more assured of his reasoning before he planted his head on that executioner's block. Instead, he said, 'I've asked Colin to check it out.'

'Who?'

'The lead SOCO. One of the best we have.'

'He'd better be.' Frazier seemed to catch someone's eye over Gilchrist's shoulder, then said, 'Get back to me with something more conclusive.' And with that he strode off.

Jessie came up to Gilchrist's side. 'I thought he was supposed to be a high flier.'

'Isn't he?'

'He's not smart enough. He's next to useless. Look at him. Giving out orders, making it look like he's in control, the wanker.'

'He *is* the Task Force Commander. You've got to give him that.'

'Doesn't make him any smarter.'

'So you don't rate him?'

'If he'd two brains he'd be twice the arsehole.'

'Right,' said Gilchrist. 'Let's see if McCrear's at home.'

They located McCrear's home in a rundown crescent on the outskirts of Dunfermline, rows of semi-detached council houses that had seen better days. He drove past the property, taking in the overgrown grass, the uncut hedge, abandoned toys in a weed-ridden driveway – evidence of a lower-class family living there, and not someone with OCD – leaving him with a burgeoning sense that something didn't fit. From what he'd seen of the crime scenes, he'd had it in his mind's eye that McCrear – if he was indeed their serial killer – would be a clean freak, someone who kept the house spick and span, lawn mowed and free of weeds, hedges trimmed to within an inch of their lives. But the address noted on McCrear's bank statements, the house number to which all his mail was delivered, couldn't be more dilapidated.

Gilchrist parked some fifty yards beyond the property, and switched off the engine. The skies had darkened. Rain spotted the windscreen. The dashboard put the temperature at close to freezing. It could turn to sleet, even snow, in a matter of hours, maybe minutes.

'What do you think?' Jessie said.

'I think we're dealing with someone who's smarter than we're giving him credit for.'

'Should we knock on the door, and see what's what?'

'And who's who?' he joked.

'That too.' She craned her neck to look at the address. 'Someone's in. The lights are on upstairs. Could be his granny, for all we know.'

Which had Gilchrist wondering just how many steps ahead of them McCrear was. His driving licence was registered under the address they were looking at. But if he'd forged his licence, what else had he faked?

He phoned Mhairi. 'I need you to look into McCrear's NI status, and his tax returns. What address do HMRC and DWP have for him?'

It took Mhairi thirty seconds before she rattled it off – the same address.

Gilchrist killed the call. 'Right. That's it. He's probably using the address as a mailbox. So whoever lives there has to know him.' He ran his gaze along the row of terraced houses again, and wondered if McCrear lived in one of the adjacent homes, making it no more than a short walk to collect his mail from the delivery address.

'Let's go,' he said.

CHAPTER 18

Gilchrist and Jessie walked towards the address, heads down against a whipping wind.

Jessie hissed a curse, and said, 'Why couldn't you have parked so we could walk *with* the wind, instead of *into* it?'

'Then we'd have to walk into it on the way back.'

'You've always got a bloody answer.' She tugged her collar in annoyance. 'So how'd you get on with whatsherface the other night?'

He caught a glimmer of a smile, and wondered if her question was meaningful, or was just being thrown out there to see what came back. He decided on the latter. 'If I knew which whatsherface you were asking about, I might be able to tell you.'

But she hunkered down into the wind, leaving him to ponder what he was missing.

As they neared the house, the more signs of distress the building displayed. Wooden window frames hadn't seen paint this side of the millennium. Weeds grew from roof gutters holed with rust, dripping water. The front door could have been painted once, but that might have been when the house was first built over fifty years ago. Grass and weeds and gravel blended into a hardened, trodden mess pooled with muddied puddles littered with kids' toys, plastic bags, orange peel, cigarette filters. Against the side wall, an overfull wheelie bin spilled pesto-stained pizza boxes, crushed tinfoil containers, crumpled takeaway cartons flattened and sodden by the incessant rain. By comparison, the house next door – not exactly a sales model – could have been advertised as home of the year.

He had his warrant card out as Jessie rattled the letterbox.

From inside the house, the pained wail of a child echoed back at them. The door opened with a sticky slap and a whiff of fried bacon, a tad on the burnt side. A woman with brown hair as dry and broken as threshed straw, and in need of a shampoo and conditioning, or a comb-through at least, eyed them with a grim look. A bedraggled child clung over her shoulder. A crumpled roll-your-own dangled from lips dotted red and black with cold sores. She took a hard drag, acned cheeks drawing in. The roll-up glowed as it burned to nicotine-stained fingers. Then she squeezed the dout between her thumb and finger and flipped it into the garden.

'What're youse wanting?' Her voice sounded as if she'd smoked sixty Capstan Full Strength a day since birth.

Gilchrist held out his warrant card, gave their names as DCI Gilchrist and DS Janes from Fife Constabulary, and said, 'We're looking for Mr McCrear. We understand he lives here.'

She ignored the warrant cards. 'That's news to me.'

'You don't know him?'

'I didnae say that.'

Jessie said, 'So what are you saying?'

'He disnae live here.'

'You collect his mail for him, though, don't you?'

'Says who?'

Jessie eased forward, one foot almost on the threshold. 'D'you mind if we come in?'

'What for?'

'It doesn't look good, two police officers standing on your doorstep.'

'What? You think the neighbours are gonnie be complaining?' She turned her head away from the child on her shoulder and coughed, a gravel sound that produced a throatful of phlegm. Her Adam's apple bobbed up and down, and that was that – better than any spittoon if you thought about it. 'Ah couldnae give a fuck about the neighbours.' She leaned to the side, for a moment out of sight behind the door, and shouted, 'Shut your traps, the effing lot of you, or you'll be feeling the back of my hand in a minute.' Back to Gilchrist and Jessie. 'And ah don't give a fuck about youse lot either.'

Gilchrist said, 'We can apply for a warrant, if that'd make you feel happier. Or we could just have a quick look around and be out of your hair in no time at all. Your choice.'

Something shifted behind the woman's eyes, as if giving weight to her options. She coughed again, dandled the child as if wishing she'd never had it, then said, 'Yeah, why don't youse fucking do that? Get the fuck off my doorstep and go and get yoursels a warrant.'

The door slammed shut with a hard crack.

'Want me to rap it again?' Jessie said.

'No. Let's wait a minute.'

He retraced his steps over the gravelled mess, and crossed the road to stand on the pavement opposite. As he turned to face the house he thought he caught an upstairs curtain flicker. He could be wrong, but he had a strong sense that the woman was not alone. Houses either side showed evidence of having been purchased from the council – gleaming double-glazed windows, modern doors, porch additions, freshly painted roughcasting, new roof tiles – making McCrear's address the odd one out. Was that why he'd selected that address as his mailbox? Did he live in anonymity with a short walk to collect his mail? Or was he related to the woman in some way – sister, girlfriend, lover, or God knew what else?

'What're you thinking?' Jessie asked.

'That it's an odd choice for a mailing address.' He gave the upper windows one final survey – no one there – before deciding that maybe his instincts were wrong.

Seated inside his car, he switched on the engine, and drove off.

'Are you going to apply for a search warrant?' Jessie said.

'If I do that, I'd have to come clean with Frazier about McCrear. And I'm not sure I want to share my thoughts with him. Not just yet anyway.'

'So you fancy doing a bit more digging?'

'If I had something to dig for, yes.'

'How about the Golden Panda?'

He let a few seconds pass, then said, 'I'm listening.'

'It's just a thought, but what if we went back and wound that trollop up, then left her dangling in a rage. What do you think she would do?'

'Doesn't bear thinking about.'

'Wrong answer. I bet she'd get straight on the phone and call somebody.'

'Who?'

'That's what I'd like to know. Wouldn't you?'

He glanced at her, but her attention was focused on her mobile, a tight smirk on her face. Her suggestion was worth considering, but it came with a number of flaws. Firstly, they didn't know the woman's phone number, which was likely to be her mobile, not a landline. And secondly, he couldn't see Frazier agreeing to a phone tap, which in effect was a fishing exercise so they could listen in to a call she might or might not make. Weak as water didn't come close. The stakes were high, of course, but there was a limit to how far Frazier could go, and that was surely beyond it—

'Here's the Golden Panda's address,' Jessie said, and tapped it into his satnav. 'There you go. Less than a mile away.' She sat back, pleased with herself.

'So, what happens at the Golden Panda? We discuss the case over a sweet and sour and a Singha beer?'

'Not quite.' Again that smirk on her face.

'Okay . . . what am I missing?'

'Nothing, really. Just that trollop's mobile number.'

'Right,' he said, and settled down for the short drive.

CHAPTER 19

The Golden Panda looked like any other of a thousand ethnic restaurants. A converted ground floor of a two-storey terraced stone building – owners living on the floor above – that fronted a busy road. Wide windows either side of the door displayed menus and a view of hard-surfaced tables and vases of plastic orchids as good as wilted. The problem Gilchrist could see, was that the restaurant was closed.

'Just park outside,' Jessie ordered.

He didn't think they would have any success with whatever she had in mind, so he pulled up on the double yellow lines, and switched his hazard warning lights on.

'Let's go,' she said, and jumped onto the pavement.

At the door, she rattled the handle, thumped the heel of her hand against the glass.

'Any harder, and they'll think you're trying to break in,' he said.

Undeterred, she returned to his car, opened the door, and leaned across the passenger seat. The sound of the horn blaring resounded off the buildings either side, loud enough to be heard in St Andrews, he thought. Back to the restaurant, and that time she battered the glass with her mobile in one hand, and shook the door handle with her other.

They didn't have long to wait.

From the depths of the interior appeared the shuffling figure of a small man, apron round his middle, face pale. He approached with some trepidation, and frowned at the sight of Jessie's warrant card. He peered at her through the glass.

'What you want? We close.'

Jessie shook the door handle. 'Police. Open up.' Then knuckled the full-length glass panel with a force that should have broken it.

'Okay okay.' He held a finger up to the glass, then scurried through to the back of the shop. Thirty seconds later, he returned with a jailer's set of keys which he used on four separate locks.

When he opened the door, Jessie stepped inside. 'What is this? Fort Knox?'

The man frowned. 'No unnerstand.'

'You don't have to, Ho Chi Minh.' She held out her warrant card, introduced herself and Gilchrist – from Fife Constabulary – and said, 'We're involved in a murder investigation. Now do you understand?'

The man nodded, although Gilchrist wasn't sure he did.

'You delivered takeaways to this address.' She held out her mobile, and let the man read the address from the screen. 'Okay?'

'Okay.'

'I want you to check your records, and give me the phone number of the person that placed the order. Okay?'

'Okay.'

She returned the man's empty stare for several seconds, then said, 'Preferably before the sun sets. Okay?'

'Okay.'

Gilchrist was about to step in when a voice from the back of the restaurant said, 'Can I help you?' A younger man with thick black hair strode towards them, arm outstretched for an introductory handshake. 'I'm the owner. Eddie Wang. What seems to be the problem?' His accent was strong Scottish, with an Edinburgh lilt, and no hint of the Far East. At six one, he levelled with Gilchrist, then faced Jessie. 'Ho Chi Minh was the Prime Minister of Vietnam,' he said. 'My father and I are both Chinese. And this is a Chinese restaurant.'

Jessie bridled. 'And . . .?'

'And how can I help you?'

She held out her mobile. 'You deliver to this address. It's local. I want the phone number of the person that called in recently for a takeaway.'

'Don't you need a warrant for that?'

'We can get one, if that would cheer you up. But that might piss me off, and have me asking questions about illegal immigrants.' She glanced over his shoulder. 'You got any back there?'

'This is a family-run business, and everyone in my family is a UK citizen.'

'What about the delivery boys? They family, too?'

Gilchrist said, 'We're asking for your assistance in a murder investigation, Mr Wang. We can apply for a warrant, of course we can. But that takes time, and time is something we don't have a lot of, if you understand what I'm saying.'

Wang stared poker-faced for a few seconds, then said, 'What's that address again?'

Jessie showed him.

'Jeannie Findlay's,' Wang said.

'You know her?'

'She orders a takeaway every week, at least once, and sometimes three times.'

Jessie said, 'Now we know her name, have you got her number?'

'I should have,' he said, and stepped behind the counter. It took him less than a minute to come back with, 'We have two mobile numbers for that address.'

'We'll take both of them, thank you,' Gilchrist said.

Jessie scribbled them into her notebook as Wang read them off.

Back in his car, Gilchrist switched off his hazard warning lights, then eased his way into a line of traffic.

'Is Vietnam anywhere near China?' Jessie said.

'It borders it.'

'Geography was never my strong point. Okay?' A couple of hundred yards farther, she said, 'Now you've got the numbers, are you going to do that magic trick of yours?'

'What magic trick?'

'You know, the one where you work behind the scenes and come up with stuff that you can't come up with by going through the normal channels. That magic trick.'

Gilchrist drove on in silence. He'd always tried to keep Jessie distant from his calls to Dick, but she was no fool. Far from it. And if he thought about it, he realised it had to have been only a matter of time until she found out.

When the traffic thinned, he turned into a side street, and drew to a halt. 'Let me make a call,' he said, and opened the door.

He tightened his scarf and pulled his collar up around his neck to ward off the chill. Rain as fine as mist was icing up as soon as it landed. But what heat there was in the ground melted it. A deep freeze was forecast for that night. By morning, the streets could be sheets of black ice.

He removed his mobile from his pocket, and dialled the pre-set number.

It was answered on the second ring.

'Long time, long time, old son. What can I do you for?'

Even though Jessie was little more than a shadow through the rain-misted windscreen, he turned away in case she could lipread. He was about to break the law, and even though he now knew Jessie had a good idea of what he was up to, it was something he didn't want her to be involved in, or in any way be guilty by association.

'Got another favour to ask, Dick.'

'Shoot.'

Whenever he had an urgent need of phone records, or a number tapped, or a mobile phone traced, Dick was Gilchrist's go-to guy. You could go through the process of applying for any number of warrants, but sometimes you just couldn't spare the time. 'Take a note of these two numbers,' he said, and rattled them off. 'I need to know all incoming and outgoing calls for the next, let's say, couple of hours.'

'Can do.'

'And I'd be especially interested in who calls who in about fifteen minutes or so.'

'Got it.' A pause, then, 'Anything else?'

'Any chance of the first few calls being recorded?'

'No problem. Want me to send the recordings to you?'

'Not yet.' He didn't think it a good idea to have evidence of illegal phone recording on his own mobile. 'I'll also need details of the numbers being called, names, the usual.'

'I'm on it.'

'Thanks, Dick.'

The line died.

He slipped his mobile into his jacket, and walked back to his car.

CHAPTER 20

Nothing had changed in the time they'd been away. If anything, clouds had gathered above a weakening wind. Other than that, the house that was McCrear's mailing address was as dilapidated as ever.

Jessie rapped the door with the corner of her mobile phone's case. She paused for two seconds, then rapped it again. Another pause, then again, until Gilchrist heard a disgruntled, 'Haud your effing horses. I'm on my way.'

The door cracked open.

'What the fuck? It's youse again.'

'Well spotted,' Jessie said.

'I know youse don't have a warrant. I'm no that fucking stupid. You cannae get one that quick. It takes hours to get them things.'

'You're Jeannie Findlay, right?'

The woman's eyes narrowed. 'And if I am?'

'We forgot to ask you to pass a message onto Dancer for us.'

Jeannie paused for a split second, but long enough for Gilchrist to know the name meant something to her. 'Who? Dancer? Never heard of him.'

'How did you know Dancer was a man?'

'What the fuck is this with the questions? *Who Wants to Be a Millionaire?*'

'How about – who wants to go to jail?'

'How about – who wants to fuck off?' She made to shut the door, but Jessie pressed her foot to the threshold.

'You listen to me, you little trollop. I'm going to get that search warrant, and I'm going to come back here and turn this midden of yours inside out. You're a lying wee bitch, and I'm going to have you, good and proper.' She pulled her foot back. 'You got that?'

'Aye, fuck you.'

The door slammed, and Jessie walked back to the car.

She clipped on her seatbelt.

'That looked like it went well.'

'Just drive, will you? That slut just does my nut in.'

Gilchrist slipped into gear, and drove off. Several seconds later, he pulled off the road, and parked out of sight of McCrear's address.

'What now?' Jessie said.

'We wait.'

It took just over ten minutes for his phone to ring. He recognised Dick's number, took the call off speaker, and opened the door. Outside, he stepped around the back of the car and onto the pavement. 'Okay, Dick, what did you find?'

'Two quick phone calls one after the other.'

'From different numbers?'

'No, the same one.'

'Who did she speak to?'

A pause, then, 'Not she, *he*. And his first call was to a woman.'

The upstairs curtain. A man in the house, keeping an eye out, checking to see who the two policemen were. Had it been McCrear who'd spied on them?

'Want me to send them to you?' Dick said.

'Let's hear them first.'

'Hang on.' The line clicked, then a moment later the sound of a call being connected, and a woman answering.

Yeah?

You were right, Deeps. We got a visit from the polis. Two of them.

Get their names?

Useless bitch cannae remember. But I seen him afore. That fuckin arsehole, Gilchrist, and some fat wee cow.

You sure?

I'd recognise that cunt anywhere. D'you think I need to call Tap?

Aye. Right away. Tap said this would happen. So get yoursel ready. He's gonnie tell us to move it up. Nae messing. To just get it done.

The recording clicked.

Gilchrist held his breath as the next call was connected, followed by an electronic silence that spoke of someone having answered the call, but saying nothing.

It's that cunt Gilchrist. He's onto you.

The line filled with digital silence for five seconds, before the connection died.

'I've got both numbers,' Dick said. 'The first call was made to a mobile registered with Tesco Mobile services, account name Terence Garson, pay as you go. And here's the interesting thing. The first *and* second calls were also made *from* a mobile registered under the name Terence Garson, also pay as you go.'

'So he's got two mobiles?'

'At least.'

'So we've no idea who he was calling?'

'None. Other than the reference to Deeps in the first call.'

He thought for a moment, then said, 'Was the second call made to a Garson number?'

'No. To a mobile that's going to take me a while longer to trace. Might not be able to. Most likely a burner.'

'Can you triangulate a location? See which masts it pinged?'

'Already on it.'

'And that other number I gave you. Who's that registered to?'

'Jean Findlay. Mean anything to you?'

'No. That's legit, I think. Thanks, Dick. Get back to me if you find anything.'

'It could take some time.'

'I'm going nowhere,' he said, and ended the call.

Time. It was always about time. And from the sound of those calls he might not have much time at all. For if his logic was correct – and he gave a silent prayer to a God he didn't believe in that his logic had failed him miserably – what he'd just listened to – *To just get it done* – was another murder being ordered. He tried to still the hammering of his heart, make sense of what he'd just heard, glean something from it, no matter how small.

Something in the way the man had spoken niggled deep within him. He'd heard that voice before. He was sure of it. But he couldn't place it. Without a doubt, the man had known him – *That fuckin arsehole, Gilchrist, and some fat wee cow*. Had they met around the time of McCrear's trial? He couldn't say. He would need to have Jackie work her magic on that name, and see what she came up with.

After the door had slammed on Jessie, he'd expected Jeannie Findlay to make a call or two. Not a man. And with both mobile numbers registered under the name Terence Garson, was it Garson himself who'd made those calls? Jessie's idea of winding Findlay up had been a bit of a longshot, so he hadn't expected a result, and certainly not the result he'd got. And as he thought back to the crime scenes, the unnatural tidiness, and his suspicions that McCrear was OCD, what was worrying was his belief, however slight, that McCrear was devious. And smart. Much smarter than any criminal he'd come up against.

If that second call had indeed been to McCrear, did his silence mean anything? Had the call been unexpected? Had it broken some unwritten protocol?

It's that cunt Gilchrist. He's onto you.

And the first call, to someone called Deeps.

He's gonnie tell us to move it up. Nae messing. To just get it done.

His mind replayed the end of that message, over and over.

Just get it done . . . Just get it done . . .

Just get what done? And as his logic worked it out, ice chilled his spine.

Had he just listened to his own murder being ordered?

Was he next on the murder list?

CHAPTER 21

The question now was – what to do about it?

Turn the car around, and drive back and arrest the man who'd made the calls?

No, how could he explain how he'd come across a burner number without exposing his illegal tap, which could ensure that all evidence provided by Dick would be inadmissible in court, and would jeopardise the integrity of any legal action, not to mention the likelihood of Gilchrist's suspension or sacking, or even court action against him personally.

He slipped his mobile into his pocket, and returned to his car.

Once behind the wheel, and the engine switched on, Jessie said, 'You look pale.'

He mustered up a shiver. 'It's cold out there.'

'Penny for your thoughts?'

'I'm thinking about whether or not to tell Frazier about McCrear, and the possible connection between the cases. I'm still not one hundred per cent sure it's him.'

'I'd say you're ninety-nine point nine per cent sure.'

He grunted his general agreement, then said, 'So what do you think?'

'One hundred per cent that McCrear's the man we're after.'

He glanced at her. 'Why so confident?'

'Because I was called a fat wee cow.'

He jolted in his seat. She'd overheard his call with Dick. How had she? He tried to keep his tone level, his voice even. 'Who called you that?'

'The same guy that called you an arsehole and that other word, the c-word.' She tried a smile. 'You left the key in the ignition, Andy. All I had to do was press that button there, and I could listen in.'

Gilchrist puffed out his cheeks, emptied his lungs. 'So you heard it all?'

'Every word of it.'

Shit. This could be trouble for both of them.

'Don't look so worried,' she said. 'I'll pretend I never heard a word.'

He felt annoyed with himself for being so careless. Was this lack of awareness the result of growing older, or of being out of the Office for the last four weeks? He could trust Jessie, he was sure of that. Which wasn't the point, really, for if it ever came down to it, what she'd overheard could make her an accessory to any disciplinary, or even worse, any criminal action raised against him—

'So we need to come up with some story as to why we think McCrear's behind these killings,' she said. 'We can't say we heard his name in an illegal phone tap. That's a big no-no. So I'm thinking we just slip Jackie a lead, and let her come up with the answer.'

'Such as . . .?'

'I don't know. But we've got the connection to McCrear's trial. Everyone who's been killed was involved in it in some way. Defence solicitor, clerk of the court, member of the jury.' She raised an eyebrow as she shifted in her seat. 'Arresting officer?'

He could feel her eyes on him, studying him, waiting for his response. 'That's the dilemma. At some point we're going to have to let the SIO know, and once we do, then . . .'

'He'll pull you off the case.'

'Precisely.'

'Which isn't necessarily a bad thing. I know, I know, I'm just telling you what I'm thinking, so there's no need to look at me like that. But until we know how these guys are all connected to one another, we need to tread with care. We're dealing with three people now. Up until those calls, we believed McCrear worked alone. Correct?' She waited for his nod. 'Now we've got two possible accomplices – some punter by the name of Garson, and a woman by the name of Deeps.'

Listening to Jessie's straight talking helped him with his dilemma. They'd bent the rules before, and would no doubt bend the rules again. But – and here was the crux of the matter – they had to be careful. Frazier was still an unknown quantity, someone who'd been presented to them as a hot-shot high-flying detective aiming for the top spot, but who came across as more of a bruiser than a detective. Even so, they couldn't keep what they'd found out from him and his Task Force forever. Frazier had to be informed.

But how, and when to do so, were the troubling questions.

One step at a time seemed as good an answer as any.

'Three names,' he said. 'We tell Frazier that the common link to all killings to date is a fifteen-year-old court case in which Adam Soutar defended McCrear. From that, we back out and find the link between McCrear and Garson. We need to ask around, put feelers out. Check with your past work associates in Strathclyde. Get them to rattle their snitches' cages. Someone somewhere knows what they have in common. Get Mhairi and Jackie to find out all they can on Garson. Who is he? Does he have form? Somewhere in his past, he's crossed paths with McCrear. We need to find out how, where, and when. And Mhairi and Jackie need to treat it with urgency.'

'And what about the guy who made the phone calls?'

'I'm betting he's Garson.'

'Bloody hell. How do we explain that, then?'

'If we know the common factor in the killings is McCrear's court case, and we know where he lives, or what address he uses as a mailbox, we say that door-to-doors uncovered him, and his mobile followed on from that.'

'But that still doesn't get *you* off the hook,' she said. 'As arresting officer back then, Frazier's going to pull you off the case, on the basis that your life could be in danger.'

'Let me worry about that.'

She paused for a moment, then gave him a knowing grin. 'Now I get it. You're not going to tell him that you ever arrested McCrear, are you?'

'Not for the moment.' He slipped into gear, tugged the wheel hard right, swung his car round in a circle. He parked out of sight of the front door, and dialled the number Dick had identified as Garson's mobile.

'Let me take care of this,' Jessie said, as he put the call on speaker.

It was answered on the second ring.

'Yeah?' a man's voice said.

'Dancer?' Jessie said. 'Is that you?'

'Who's this?'

'Are you Tap Dancer McCrear?'

Silence.

'I need to speak to Dancer. Today,' she said. 'Nae messing.'

It took two seconds for the call to be disconnected, and another twenty seconds for the front door to open, and a man to emerge in a hurry, struggling to pull his hoodie over his head as he half-walked half-jogged down the path. When he reached the pavement he turned left, then veered off across the road and into the driveway of another house.

Gilchrist pulled himself upright, fully alert now. Was this where McCrear lived? Then he felt a stab of disappointment when the man opened the door of a white van parked on the driveway, and jumped inside.

'Get the number plate,' he said.

'You might have bat ears, but I don't have eagle eyes.' Jessie peered through the windscreen, and shook her head. 'You're going to have to get closer.'

He eased onto the road, kept well back as the van worked its way out of the housing estate. At the junction, he let three cars pass before he pulled onto the main road and followed the van. At a set of lights on red, he drew to a halt close enough for Jessie to note the number, and for him to see the man's face in the wing mirror, but not clear enough to identify him.

Jessie phoned Mhairi on the car's system. 'Check out this number.' She read it off. 'We need to know who it's registered to, and if the owner has any history.'

Gilchrist said, 'And check out ANPR footage and see if the van was anywhere near Kilconquhar earlier today, or last night.'

When he ended the call, Jessie said, 'So, if McCrear has accomplices, you're thinking that one of them might be the driver, while McCrear does the killing.'

He nodded. 'And if so, we might be able to lift DNA from the back of it, maybe even some evidence of the murder weapon.'

And with that thought, he settled down for the drive, keeping well back from the white van ahead.

CHAPTER 22

The white van worked its way through the back streets of Dunfermline, Gilchrist no more than four cars behind. Once, he almost got caught out when it accelerated through a set of lights that turned to amber, leaving the cars behind when the lights changed to red.

'What now?' Jessie said.

'We wait. He's not going far.'

Sure enough, a hundred yards farther on, the van drew to a halt at another set of lights. When the lights turned to green, the traffic eased forward, and the stop-start journey through town continued at a slow rate, Gilchrist safely hidden by a tail of cars in front. But beyond the town's limits, the traffic speeded up, thinning out, and he had to keep well back when they entered the countryside.

Jessie had her mobile in her hand, and was tapping the screen. 'Do you know where this road goes to?' she asked.

'Afraid not.'

They passed through Gowkhall, nothing more than a row of houses on one side of the road. A road sign gave directions to

Alloa and Stirling straight ahead on the A907, and Saline and Dollar to the right on the B913. But Jessie seemed not to notice, her attention focused on her mobile as the van drove straight on.

He said, 'Could be Alloa or Stirling.'

She glanced up for a moment, then back to her mobile.

The van drove through the country towns of Carnock, Oakley, Blairhall, at a steady ten miles an hour over the speed limit. A few miles farther on, they passed another sign, and this time Jessie was alert.

'Coming up to a roundabout,' she said. 'This should help us.'

Ahead, the van's brake lights flickered as the driver prepared to enter the roundabout, and Gilchrist feared he might be noticed if they entered the roundabout too soon. But the van accelerated through, peeling off at the second exit – the A907 to Stirling and Alloa.

Another moment of worry as they neared the town of Clackmannan – construction works and temporary three-way traffic lights had cars backed up in a line at least thirty long. The van idled seven cars ahead, and a row of vehicles trailed past in the opposite direction. From the length of the tail of cars, Gilchrist knew the lights were set for lengthy stages, but when it came to their turn, and the cars eased forward, he cursed when the lights turned to red and the van was the last vehicle to make it through.

'We've lost him this time,' Jessie said.

'He'll stick to the main road,' Gilchrist said with a confidence he didn't feel. 'We'll catch up with him once we're past this lot.'

But it took two full minutes before their light turned to green, and Gilchrist had to admit that he shared Jessie's concerns. Through Clackmannan, he flew along country roads, powering past slower vehicles, working his gears with the paddles on the steering wheel, pushing his car to hit high revs, even touching ninety on one stretch, as he tried to make up for lost ground.

But it was no use. By the time they came to the A91 roundabout, the van was nowhere to be seen. Had it turned off into one of the many side streets in the small towns they'd driven through – Sauchie, Glenochil Village, Tullibody?

He had no way of knowing.

'Shit,' said Jessie.

'My sentiments entirely.'

He entered the roundabout, and on instinct took the exit to Stirling. 'Get hold of Mhairi and see if Jackie's got anything on the van's number plate.'

One minute later, Jessie said, 'We've got a hit. It's registered to Terence Garson. Lives in Stirling. Queen Street.'

'You got the house number?'

She did, then entered it into the satnav.

As they neared Stirling on Alloa Road, the River Forth ran alongside them on their left, nothing at all like the seven-mile-wide mass of water that formed the Firth of Forth some thirty miles to the east. He followed the directions on his satnav, and wound through the outskirts of Stirling, easing ever closer to the congestion of town traffic.

Queen Street rose gently uphill. Old stone terrace buildings bounded either side like walls. Cars were parked nose to kerb along one side, and it didn't take Jessie long before she spotted the white van ahead. 'There it is.'

But Gilchrist wasn't so sure. The van looked like the one they'd been following, but with no signage on its panels, it could be any one of a thousand. 'Check the number plate,' he said, as he eased past.

She did, then said, 'Got you, you bastard.'

Gilchrist drove on, and found a parking spot in Upper Bridge Street, round the corner from Queen Street, out of sight of prying eyes.

'Let's go,' Jessie said, and opened the door.

'Hang on.'

She hesitated, one foot on the pavement. 'What?'

'We've more to gain by waiting and watching.'

'How about we just arrest him—'

'For what?' He hadn't meant to snap, but experience had taught him there were times to make an arrest, and times to sit back and watch. And his gut was telling him they should be careful around Garson, who had a direct line to McCrear and a woman called Deeps. Had all three taken part in the murders? But even if they hadn't, their link to McCrear told him they were dangerous, and without knowing exactly who he and Jessie were up against, he didn't want to risk a face-to-face confrontation. Not just yet anyway.

'Why did Garson drive straight here?' he said.

'Duh . . . Andy. It's where he lives.'

'But why drive here immediately after you phoned him about McCrear? Ask yourself that. Maybe he's not the only one heading this way?'

'You think they could all be meeting up here?'

What could he say? That he was only guessing? So he tried to explain his thoughts as best he could. 'We can detain Garson now, for whatever reason you make up. But he's driven straight here for a reason. Not because this is where he lives. But he's here for something.'

'Maybe to collect something?'

And with these words, Gilchrist knew that the time he'd spent mulling over their next step was enough time for Garson to have picked up whatever he'd returned home to collect.

'Damn it.' He opened the door and stepped onto the pavement.

Sure enough. When they rounded the corner of Queen Street, the van had gone.

He phoned Mhairi. 'Put a marker on the PNC for this number plate.' He read it off to her. 'With a warning not to apprehend. Occupants of vehicle are considered dangerous, and likely to be armed. Just report location and follow.'

'Got it, sir.'

'And I need you to track it on the ANPR, and get back to me the instant you find it.' He walked with Jessie back to his car. 'Last seen at this address in Stirling.' He rattled out the Queen Street address. With some luck, they would locate the van in only a matter of minutes with the help of ANPR, which uses alphanumeric recognition to read plates in real time through CCTV cameras.

By the time Gilchrist had driven the length of Queen Street, Mhairi called back.

'Got several sightings in Stirling,' she said. 'The most recent one being on Goosecroft Road, sir, about thirty seconds ago.'

'Keep me posted on his whereabouts,' he said. 'We're on our way.'

Jessie entered Goosecroft Road into the satnav and, within two minutes, they drove into it. Despite his best efforts to ignore the speed limit, traffic was heavy, and he was soon trapped in a slow-moving pack. The outside lane widened, and a number of vehicles peeled off, freeing up the road ahead. He saw an opening, and floored the pedal.

'Anything from Mhairi?' he asked Jessie.

She shook her head. 'Nada.'

'Put her on speaker,' he said, knowing with a sickening feeling that they'd been given the slip. It had been the parking signs that did it, the exit from the main road into a shopping centre. He hadn't caught the name of the centre, but knew that if Garson had driven in there, he was going to do one of two things – change his vehicle, or his number plates—

'Nothing, sir,' Mhairi said. 'Last sighting was that one I gave you on Goosecroft.'

'There's a shopping centre just off Goosecroft. Do you know what it is?'

'My sister lives in Stirling, and she shops a lot in the Thistle Centre.'

'Is that off Goosecroft Road?'

'I don't know, sir. Hang on.' A pause, then, 'It is, sir, yes.'

'That's where he went,' he said, and indicated left, searching for the first available exit. But he ended up doing a U-turn at a set of traffic lights to the noisy blaring of angered motorists, and raced back the way he'd come.

Inside the Thistle Centre multistorey car park, his tyres squealed as he powered up and down lanes on one level, then accelerated to another level, to repeat the exercise. When he finally emerged onto the roof level, he realised Garson had outfoxed them. The van wasn't there. Which meant only one thing. Garson had parked the van out of sight of CCTV cameras and changed the number plates. With an electric screwdriver, the job would have taken less than thirty seconds a plate.

'That's what he was picking up at his home,' Gilchrist said. 'A set of fake plates.'

'Next time, why don't you just let me cuff the bastard?'

'Noted.'

A sedate drive to ground level, checking each level in case they'd missed something, turned up nothing, and ten minutes later, they were back on the A91 to St Andrews.

Phone calls to the CCTV control centre in Glenrothes HQ initiated a search for white vans leaving the Thistle Centre car park within the last twenty minutes, to try to identify the new plate number. But Gilchrist didn't hold out much hope. He settled down for the drive, thinking over that day's events, and feeling as if it was one step forward, and two steps back.

All in all, not the best of results for all their effort.

But he and Jessie had some work to do before that day's debriefing, which he hoped might help make amends.

Or at least improve the odds.

CHAPTER 23

6.20 p.m., Tuesday
Glenrothes HQ

When Gilchrist and Jessie arrived late for that day's debriefing, Frazier seemed to bristle with irritation. But rather than spit out the usual quip – *Nice of you to turn up* – he stood at the whiteboard in silence, and waited while they took their seats. When he caught Gilchrist's eye, he said, 'I want a word with you two later,' then turned his attention back to the whiteboard, one of three on which photographs, names and birth dates of each of the murder victims were littered.

Other photos of people Gilchrist didn't recognise were pinned to the board, connected by lines that looped from one image to another. Not until he recognised Laura Detling and Tom Rickard did he come to understand that he was looking at a list of each victim's family members, which now appeared to be the focus of Frazier's strategy, based on the well-established fact that most murders are committed by those closest to the victims.

But not in this case, surely. With nothing substantive to go on, Frazier's investigation was floundering, and would stall if time and effort was wasted interviewing family members.

After five minutes, Gilchrist had heard enough. He raised his hand.

Frazier stopped mid-sentence. 'Yes, DCI Gilchrist.'

'With all due respect, sir, we shouldn't be focusing on family members.'

'And why's that?'

'We believe we've found the common factor in these murders, sir.' He pushed to his feet, and approached one of the white-boards – the least cluttered of the three – which listed mobile phone numbers and bank accounts.

He picked up a marker, and printed one line after the other:

Tap McCrear, aka Dancer. Tried and convicted of murder.

Released August last year.

Adam Soutar – Defence solicitor.

John Moorhouse – Clerk of the court.

Margaret Rickard – Member of the jury.

Albert Forest – Ditto.

He was aware of a murmur in the room as he circled McCrear's name, then drew a line to a point where he printed another name – *Terence Garson* – and circled that, too. He drew a second line from McCrear's name to a third circle in which he printed *Deeps?* – emphasised with a question mark.

Marker in hand, he faced the room.

'We now believe that the common link between each of these victims is a nasty piece of work by the name of Tap McCrear. Prior to his conviction for murder, he was a criminal who'd been in trouble with the law since his teens. He was released from prison last year, and we suspect is out for revenge against all those who he sees as having failed him at his trial.

'Adam Soutar, his defence solicitor, failed him by losing his case. Margaret Rickard and Albert Forest were members of the jury panel who found him guilty. John Moorhouse was the clerk of the court during his trial. Why McCrear targeted Moorhouse is anybody's guess, but it's clear that anyone involved in that court case is in grave danger.'

He turned back to the whiteboard and tapped *Deeps?* and *Terence Garson.*

'We believe McCrear has two accomplices. Whether they're someone he trusts to help him hide the evidence, or participate in the killings, we don't know yet. We believe the former, but we can't say for sure.' He tapped the question mark. 'This accomplice we believe to be female, although we don't know her surname. The other we suspect is a petty criminal.' Under Garson's name he wrote – *white Ford van.*

'Garson owns a white Ford van, registered in his own name. His driving licence gives his address in Stirling.' He wrote the Queen Street address. 'We placed a marker on the PNC this afternoon for that white van, but we suspect the number plates have been changed.' He put a question mark beside the van. 'Without knowing what that number plate is, we're as good as shooting in the dark. We've applied for warrants to search Garson's home, as well as the home of a woman we believe could be his girlfriend.' He wrote the Dunfermline address, placed the marker pen in the whiteboard tray, then faced the room.

'We have two lines of enquiry. One, find McCrear and his associates before they kill anyone else. Two, identify everyone who participated in McCrear's trial, locate them and make sure they're safe.' The room buzzed with whispered conversation. By his side Frazier shuffled his feet, but Gilchrist pressed on.

'I believe our primary effort should now be on locating everyone on the jury panel, as well as identifying and locating everyone involved in the court proceedings during McCrear's murder trial. That includes everyone who worked for both the defence and the prosecution solicitors, and includes Sheriff Conniston and his staff.' He nodded to Jessie, who held aloft a sheaf of papers, then proceeded to place them on the desk behind which DS Agnew and DS Pollard sat, bemused smiles on their lips, as if intrigued as to how Frazier was going to respond to Gilchrist's commandeering of his investigation.

'We've printed out a list of names of everyone on that jury panel,' Gilchrist said, 'including what contact information we had at the time of the trial. We're still in the process of identifying employees of the Procurator Fiscal's office, and Adam Soutar's law firm, and court officials who may have been in attendance during McCrear's trial. But we ran out of time.' He faced Frazier. 'Hence the reason for our delay.'

Jessie waved a stapled report in the air. 'This is a start. There should be enough copies to go around, but we'll leave it to Detective Superintendent Frazier to assign who does what.' A quick glance at Frazier, then she returned to her seat.

'Presuming I agree with what you've just presented,' Frazier said, facing Gilchrist.

'Of course, sir.'

Frazier scowled. 'Seems a bit of a *fait accompli.*'

'It's far from a *fait accompli*, sir. There's still a great deal of work to be done – first locating, then interviewing everyone on that list. As well as identifying who was working in the court that day, and tracking down everyone employed in the prosecution and defence teams. We also don't know where McCrear and the two potential accomplices are, or what their involvement in these killings is.'

'When were you first aware of this link to McCrear?' Frazier said.

'This afternoon, sir.'

'And why was I not informed immediately?'

'I needed to be sure of the connection first.'

'And you're sure now?'

'I am, sir, yes.'

'Why?'

'It'd be too much of a coincidence if it wasn't McCrear, sir.'

Frazier held Gilchrist's gaze for a long moment, then narrowed his eyes and looked at Gilchrist's printing on the whiteboard. 'Who did McCrear murder all these years ago?'

This was the area Gilchrist didn't want to get into, his personal involvement in the case, which could lead to his removal from the Task Force on the basis that his life was clearly in danger. 'The original charge was assault to endanger life,' he said. 'The victim was a young man called Michael Beaton, who was attacked and beaten unconscious for no reason other than being in the wrong place at the wrong time. He never recovered from a coma, and subsequently died.'

Frazier gave a vague nod. Then he approached the desk, and DS Agnew handed him a stapled copy of Jessie's jury list. Silent, he looked through it. Then he grimaced, and nodded.

'This is good work, DCI Gilchrist. Good work indeed.'

'DS Janes was instrumental in—'

'And DS Janes, too, of course.' He smiled at her. 'Well done.'

'Sir.'

'Right.' Frazier turned to face the room. 'We need two independent teams, working side by side, but together, through me. We need everyone on this list traced and interviewed as a matter of priority. And we need to find McCrear and his two associates before they can do further harm.' He nodded to the assembly. 'DI Barnes?'

She raised her hand. 'Yes, sir?'

'I want you to take the lead in locating McCrear and his associates.'

'Thank you, sir.'

He turned to Gilchrist. 'And I want you to take the lead in locating everyone involved in McCrear's trial. Both of you will report directly to me. Let me know if you need additional resources. Media contact will be through me only. Got it? We have to keep this tight. DCI Danson?'

'Sir?'

As Gilchrist listened to Frazier take back control of the room, Dainty's words echoing in his mind – *He won't let anything stand in his way . . . nothing or no one. Ambitious as fuck* – he came to understand the strengths of the man. Frazier wasn't a detective. Not at all. He was an organiser, a specialist in logistics, someone who could see the big picture and break it down into smaller tasks. He was also a politician, a manipulator of facts and figures to suit his own needs, to stand on his self-made pedestal like a demagogue, and listen to the sound of his own voice reverberate around the room, arousing passion and emotion.

As Gilchrist returned to his seat, Frazier rattling off instructions like a shopping list, he was surprised to see the magisterial figure of the Chief Constable, Archie McVicar, slip from the room.

CHAPTER 24

7.39 p.m., Saturday
North Street Office, St Andrews

The following four days passed in a blur of phone calls, interviews, meetings and reporting – always reporting, verbal and written, to the Task Force Commander. True to his word, Frazier pulled in extra resources from other police forces around Scotland, and even from the north of England. How he'd managed to do that was anyone's guess.

Gilchrist had a team of thirty staff, dedicated to identifying and contacting everyone involved in McCrear's trial. With that number assigned to the task, he'd felt confident that they could track down and interview everyone in a matter of days. But he was surprised by how many had moved home, changed employment, or simply died. Adam Soutar's law firm had been bought out by the German firm, KTIF, and moved office. Of the six lawyers who'd formed his core team, only two remained with that firm. Of the other four, two now worked in London, one had retired to Hereford, and one had died from cancer. The procurator fiscal's employees, too, proved to be as elusive. The procurator fiscal at the time, Christine Dugard, had died four years earlier, and of her team of seven – five lawyers and two paralegals – all had found alternative employment and were working in the private sector. They'd managed to locate all seven, but interviewed only five. The other two were confirmed to be on a cruise in the Caribbean, and were to be interviewed immediately on their return.

Fife Constabulary, too, came under scrutiny. A young DS Gilchrist, as the arresting officer, and all members of the investigation team – five, as it turned out – had to prepare written reports for Frazier. Gilchrist objected to having to submit his own report; wasn't the purpose of his team to make sure that anyone involved was safe and had not been killed? And would his time not be better spent looking for that missing victim number three?

But Frazier was having none of it, and Gilchrist had no alternative but to complete the task of identifying, locating, and interviewing everyone on what Frazier was now calling the murder list.

And so it went on.

Of the original fifteen jurors, in addition to Rickard and Forest, three had died – two from natural causes, and one in a car crash. Of the remaining ten, two had moved to England, and one had retired to Spain. By Saturday evening, his team had located and interviewed nine of them. Officers from the north of England had travelled to Birmingham and Torquay for the formal interviews. At Frazier's insistence, the juror living in Murcia, Spain, had to be located and interviewed in person, and Gilchrist had assigned Jessie to fly to Spain, not because she'd asked for a day in the sun, but because her constant complaining about not being part of the *real* murder inquiry – locating and arresting McCrear and his associates – had grated on his nerves.

And the *real* murder inquiry seemed to be going nowhere fast.

From what he'd heard at debriefings, the investigation was stumbling along. Terence Garson and his white Ford van had, for all intents and purposes, disappeared. For all anyone knew, he could be sunning himself on the Costa del Sol along with McCrear. A warrant had been granted to search the address in Dunfermline, where it was confirmed that Findlay was an ex-girlfriend of Garson's – her youngest child of fifteen months had been fathered by him. But there was no love lost between her and Garson – *When you find that lazy bastard tell him he owes me three months' maintenance.*

As for the third associate, the woman called Deeps, no trace of her had been found.

Although they had an address in Kirkcaldy for the final juror, attempts to interview him at home had resulted in door-to-doors with neighbours who, despite confirming old Jay Dempsey was a lovely gentleman, seemed to resent the fact that he spent much of the year holidaying in the Far East. Gilchrist had read five of the six typed transcripts of DC Norris's interviews with Dempsey's neighbours, the only reports in which the juror hadn't been talked to in person. Reading them was eye-straining, but he persevered, and with only one more report to go, he was almost finished.

Mrs Alice Black: Old Jay just gets up and flies out every now and then like he's won the Lottery.

DC Tom Norris: How often does he holiday overseas?

AB: At least three times a year. Maybe more. I think he's got one of these Thai girls on the side, giving him what he can't get here. He's far too old for any of that nowadays.

TN: So he flies out every what, three months or so?

AB: About that. Aye. Maybe four times a year.

TN: How long does he stay there?

AB: Usually he disappears for two or three weeks. Then he turns up all tanned and smiling, like he's been having you know what.

TN: When did you last see Mr Dempsey?

AB: Maybe a couple of weeks ago.

TN: Maybe? You're not sure?

AB: I don't really pay attention. Like I said, he's off as often as he likes.

TN: When was the last time you can remember he flew out?

Gilchrist's mobile rang then. He glanced at it, and frowned when he didn't recognise the number. It could be a call from any one of his temporary staff, so he swiped the screen and placed the phone to his ear. 'DCI Gilchrist.'

'You sound so serious, Andy.'

For a moment, he couldn't place the voice.

'It's Irene,' she said.

'Of course, Irene. Yes. I'm sorry. I just . . . you took me by surprise.'

She chuckled at that, a warming sound that had him smiling. 'Where are you?' she said. 'Surely not still at work?'

'Afraid so.'

'Maureen told me you were a bit of a workaholic.' She chuckled again. 'Which is better than being a bit of an alcoholic.'

He sent a chuckle of his own down the phone to let her know he got her joke.

'I don't mean to sound presumptuous,' she said, 'but do you have anything on tonight? After work, I mean.'

'Hang on a second.' He cupped his mobile as Mhairi stuck her head into his office.

'You wanted me to hand deliver these final reports, sir?'

'Yes, Mhairi.' He sat his mobile on his desk, gathered a bundle of reports together, and held them out to her. At the last second, he removed the one he'd been reading. 'I haven't finished this yet. I'll take care of it myself.'

'Yes, sir.'

When Mhairi left, he returned to his mobile. 'Sorry about that.'

'You sound busy, Andy. I didn't mean to interrupt you. I'll leave you to it.'

All of a sudden he realised he didn't want her to hang up. 'No, no, it's okay. I . . .' He glanced at the time on his computer screen – almost eight o'clock. 'I was just about to have a break. It's been a long day.' He pushed to his feet, muscles stiff from sitting too long at his desk. 'I suppose you've already eaten.'

'Yes, I have.'

'Ah.'

'But that's not why I was calling.' She paused, and he was unsure if she was waiting for him to say something. 'I wanted to ask a favour of you actually. But now I've got you on the phone, it sounds so silly, what I'm asking.'

'I'm sure it's not,' he said. 'If I can help in any way, I'd be glad to.'

'Are you sure?'

'Yes, I'm sure.' He wasn't really. He still had that final interview transcript to read, and phone calls to make. But as if to remind him that he hadn't eaten since breakfast – other than a nibble of a cranberry muffin with a cup of coffee – his stomach rumbled. Besides, his eyes felt tired, and his bones ached. He really was becoming too old to work such long hours.

'I feel as though I'm taking you away from your work.'

'I've got to eat.' He remembered that Irene already had. 'And I could do with a light refreshment,' he added. 'A beer or two, to cheer me up. You could join me.'

'I wasn't meaning for you to take me out, Andy. I'm sorry if I gave that impression. I was phoning to ask if you could help me with some photography.' She chuckled once again, and he found himself being pulled closer by the husky whisper of her voice. 'To be my assistant, as it were.'

'Help you lug your camera equipment about, you mean? That sort of thing?'

She hesitated, as if his directness had somehow offended her. 'There's a full moon tonight. And not a cloud in the sky.'

He found himself walking to his window, looking up at the night sky. He remembered being a young boy, going out for late night walks with a school friend of his, Henry Bamford, with Henry's dog – Roy, it was named – and on nights like this being amazed by how many stars sparkled in the sky; galaxies' worth, it seemed back then. Now, modern-day electricity sent too much reflective light skywards, and you could count the number of stars on one hand. But tonight, for whatever reason, the sky could be studded with diamonds.

'What did you have in mind?' he said.

'The town centre,' she said. 'I'd like to take a set of photographs with no flash on a long exposure. Besides,' she added, 'I've just treated myself to a new camera. A Leica. I've had Nikons and

Canons, but never a Leica. I have to say I'm impressed with it so far.'

'So you want to give it the ultimate test,' he said. 'No flash. And at night.'

'You have to live dangerously.' She chuckled again. 'So are you up for it?'

'Of course. What time?'

'Any time that works for you.'

'Well, I'm going to have a bite, and a pint, so we're looking at an hour, maybe less?'

'Which pub?'

'I thought I'd try the Central for a change.'

'A man of habit, I see.'

'More like, becoming too set in my own ways.'

'Well, we'll see about that.' She let out a breathless sigh. 'I'll meet you there.'

And with that, she ended the call.

Gilchrist remained staring at the sky for several seconds longer, a frisson brushing his skin, causing an involuntary shiver. He smiled as he collected his jacket from the back of his chair, and slipped his mobile into his pocket. At the last minute, he stuffed Norris's report into his jacket pocket, to read at home.

He found Jessie in Jackie's office. 'Where's Jackie?' he asked.

'Off home, where we should be,' she said, without taking her eyes from the monitor.

'I'm having a break, heading out for a pint. Want to join me?'

'Can't. Got to complete this report on the prosecution team, and get it over to His Highness, or else my balls are for the chop, if I had any. Then I'm going to go out with my wee boy for dinner.' She glanced at him. 'It's a special occasion. He's completed another manuscript, and he wants to buy me dinner.' She smiled. 'My wee boy buying *me* dinner? What can I say?'

'Congratulations?' he suggested.

'I'll tell him you said that.'

'Please do. I mean it.'

'Go. You're putting me off.'

'Catch you tomorrow.' And with that, he stepped into the hallway.

CHAPTER 25

Gilchrist found a seat at the corner farthest from the Market Street entrance, and hung his jacket on a hook under the bar. He ordered a pint of Belhaven Best, a side of fries, and a bowl of the soup of the day. Whatever hunger he'd felt earlier had left him, but he had to eat – Maureen was always on at him about not eating enough. He thought of giving her a call, as he hadn't heard from her since . . . well, since she'd introduced him to Irene, then thought better of it. She might ask about Irene.

He was toying with the idea of phoning his son, Jack, whom he hadn't spoken to for well over a week, which was par for the course, he supposed, when his soup and side order of fries was placed before him. He thanked the barmaid, a young dark-haired student he hadn't seen before, and asked for brown sauce, and salt and pepper, which were promptly presented on the bar with a white-toothed smile. As he watched the barmaid slide within the tight confines behind the bar, he couldn't help thinking that students were becoming younger. Or maybe he was becoming so much older.

He picked up a chip, dipped it into the sauce, and took a nibble. A dash more salt, and they were perfect. He peppered his soup

– far too heavily, according to Maureen. But he liked the spicy nip. On a TV screen in the corner, he eyed a muted game of football, Newcastle and Spurs, as best he could tell, and thought it must be a recording. Or did the Premier League play at eight o'clock on a Saturday night? He wasn't sure.

He had just finished his soup, when Irene said, 'I see you've left me some chips.'

He jolted with surprise. He hadn't seen her come in, then realised she'd entered by the College Street door to his side. He slid off his stool, and pushed it to her. 'Here,' he said. 'I'm happy to stand.'

'Ever the gentleman.' She slid onto the stool, skirt riding high, and he had to divert his eyes from a meaty length of black-stockinged thigh before she placed her jacket over her legs. 'Do you mind?' she said, and sneaked a chip from his plate. 'I love them salted, too.' She ate it *sans* brown sauce. 'That's another thing we have in common.'

'What's that?'

'We both like chips.'

He struggled to remember what the other thing was they'd had in common, but came up with nothing. Maybe he'd missed what she'd said. 'Can I get you anything? A wine? An order of fries? Bowl of soup?' She leaned towards him as she adjusted her position on the stool, and an arousing aroma of freshness – shampoo, soap, perfume – engulfed him.

'I'll pass,' she said, shuffling her butt on the stool. 'Have to watch my figure,' and let out another whispery chuckle.

He breathed her in, loving her fragrance, and the way her eyes crinkled when she smiled at him. Her lips pulled his gaze, too, moist and fresh with lipstick that stained glossy teeth. This wasn't a date, he chided himself, but instead was a favour of sorts; a photographic assistant, if he could call himself that. Even so, the unspoken intimacy of her closeness stirred something within him.

'But on second thoughts,' she said. 'Maybe I'll have a wine.'

'I've talked you into it, have I?'

'Leading me astray, more like.'

He chuckled to share her joke. 'Same as last time?'

'No, I'll have a dry white. A small one, though.'

He kept his gaze on the barmaid, trying to make eye contact, all the while conscious of Irene looking at him, as if studying him from close range. He ordered a small Chardonnay, and when it arrived, chinked his pint against it.

'Cheers.'

'Up yours,' she said, and took a mouthful.

The sound of a stool grating the floor had him looking behind him. A couple were leaving, and he took hold of the vacated stool, and pulled it under him. Comfortably seated, he sipped his beer. 'So where's this Leica of yours?'

She tapped her handbag. 'In here.' She fumbled with her bag's clip, and handed her camera to him.

An M8, whatever a Leica M8 was, felt heavier than it looked. He removed the lens cap and read the specs – F2, 35 mm – a wide-angle lens, preferred for streetscape shots. He'd seen Irene's work, and knew how proficient she was. He held the camera to his eye, and was surprised by how comfortable it fitted into his hand – solid, compact, typical German precision and perfection.

'Nice,' he said, handing it back to her. 'What photography did you have in mind?'

'I've had a change of heart, and thought I might try the harbour first. Or the pier, looking back to the shorehead.' She shrugged.

'I'm never really sure what I'm looking for until I get there. Then something just catches my eye.'

'The perfect moment?' he said.

She raised her glass. 'With the perfect gentleman.'

He didn't know how to take that, and felt a flush warm his face. He tried hiding behind his pint, but her eyes followed his, and creased as if on the verge of laughing. He felt annoyed with himself for being so . . . so clumsy with her, and it unsettled him that she seemed to have that effect on him.

'I like that you're shy,' she said. 'It's what Maureen likes about you, too.'

Well, there he had it. Coming across as shy? He thought he'd grown out of that, but he supposed old habits died the hardest, particularly where women were involved. 'I'm going to have another beer,' he said.

'Why not have a wine? Here. Try this.' She held the glass to his lips before he could object. 'A cheeky little white?' she said.

After the smallest of sips, he said, 'Very cheeky.'

She chuckled again, that whispery rush of hers sending a frisson down his spine. Then she frowned, as if something had come to her all of a sudden, and reached for her handbag. 'Here. Let me get this.'

'It's all right. I've got it covered.'

'No, I insist. Really. I'll be so cross with you if you don't let me buy you a pint. You bought all the drinks the other night, if you remember.'

'Did I?'

'You most certainly did. Which was so kind of you. What's that? Regular beer?'

Well, what could he do? Her insistent tone hinted of a toughness she hadn't shown before. So rather than make a fuss, he said, 'Belhaven Best, if you don't mind, thank you.'

'Of course, I don't. My pleasure.'

She placed the order, then swung around on her stool to face him. 'Are you involved in this big murder investigation that's going on at the moment?'

'Sort of.'

'A terrible state of affairs. I've been watching it on the news, and I have to say that I don't particularly like that detective, the one who's always at the press conferences, with his huge shoulders and his slick suits and his sticky-out ears and his mightier than thou attitude. He seems far too big for his boots. I really can't stand him.'

'Too big for his boots?'

'By far.'

Gilchrist's chuckle almost evolved into a laugh. 'You know, I never noticed.'

'What? That he's too bossy?'

'No. That he had sticky-out ears.'

She coughed out a laugh that pulled tears to her eyes. She dabbed them with a tissue that appeared as if by magic. 'Maureen told me you had a cheeky sense of humour.'

His pint arrived then, and he said, 'Have you seen her recently? Maureen?'

'Not since she was in here earlier in the week. She keeps herself busy. Just like you.' She took another sip of wine, almost finishing it. She frowned again, reached out and set her hand on his thigh. Not the politically correct thing to do, but her uninhibited intimacy felt nice. 'You know, Andy, I could just forget about the photography, and chat with you all night. I think I might have another wine.'

'Passing up a full moon and a cloudless sky? That's a rare combination in Scotland. Particularly at this time of year.'

She paused, smile frozen on her lips, eyes shifting as if she were trying to calculate some mental arithmetic. Then the moment passed, and she removed a tenner from her purse. 'You're right,' she said. 'It is such a rare event. But you know what?'

He waited, then realised she was expecting him to reply. 'What?' he said.

'Sometimes you just have to grab the moments as they come.' She ordered a wine, paid for the round, then sat in awkward silence until she received her change. She scattered the coins into her purse with a flourish. 'You don't get much for ten pounds nowadays.'

He tipped his pint to her in agreement. 'You're right.'

'Everything's so expensive now.'

'I wasn't meaning that.'

'You weren't?'

'No. You're right about having to grab the moments.' He chinked his pint against her wine glass. 'Drink up,' he said. 'We should go.'

She livened at that, and took a mouthful that almost emptied the glass. Then she fluttered her eyelids at him. 'What did you have in mind?'

He hadn't really thought it through, other than the fact that he needed a break from the constant pressure of the current investigation, the perpetual grind of Frazier being on at him every hour, it seemed, as if he had nothing better to do. Just to get away from it all, if only for an evening, or less. Even for just an hour or two.

'It's a beautiful night,' he said. 'Why don't we go for a walk?'

Her eyebrows raised at his suggestion, and he couldn't tell if she was surprised, or just disappointed. Then she said, 'That sounds like a grand idea,' then downed the remains of her wine, and reached for her jacket. 'That's me. I'm ready when you are.'

He returned his half-finished pint to the bar, removed his jacket from the hook by his knees, and slipped it on.

She surprised him by steering him towards the exit onto College Street.

CHAPTER 26

Outside, the temperature seemed to have dropped ten degrees. He brushed off a shiver and dug his hands deep into his pockets, Irene clinging closer as he did so. Without a word, they walked down College Street like two lovers, crossed North Street and stepped into Butts Wynd in case someone from the Office noticed him and called him over. He glanced behind him. The lights were on in all the windows, and he had an image of everyone at their desks, working away. Despite the urgency associated with the investigation, he felt no guilt.

After all, it was a Saturday night.

'Where are you taking me?' Irene asked.

'You never told me you were impatient.'

'Just curious.'

At The Scores, he turned left, and he pulled up his collar as a westerly wind did what it could to chill him to the bone. Unlike Irene, who'd come well prepared for an evening of photography – quilted jacket, scarf, gloves – he wasn't dressed for the weather. His leather jacket stood up well against most foul weather, but in a wind like this he needed heavier clothing.

'You're shivering,' Irene said.

'I'll heat up in a bit.'

She pulled him closer. 'I'll keep you warm.' She chuckled again. 'I always think it's odd that while we shiver in this bitterly cold weather, there are thousands of people sunning themselves on a beach somewhere. Doesn't it make you want to move?'

He laughed at that, as his mobile vibrated in his pocket. He removed it – ID Frazier – and thought of ignoring it. But personal dislikes aside, he was part of a task force that was trying to stop a serial killer from claiming another victim's life, and he had a professional responsibility, if not a moral obligation, to do everything in his power to prevent that.

'Sir?' he said.

'Where are you?' Frazier said without introduction.

'About to have a bite to eat,' he lied.

The snort at the other end of the line could have been one of derision, or of envy at being able to afford the time for such luxuries as food. 'Thought I'd check in with you and see if anything new has come up.'

Gilchrist released Irene's arm, and stepped onto the road for some privacy, or more correctly to avoid the possibility of a civilian overhearing gruesome details of an ongoing multiple murder investigation. 'No change from this afternoon, sir. How about at your end? Anything on McCrear or Garson yet?' Until that moment, he hadn't questioned Frazier on the handling of the *real* murder investigation, but the lack of response warned him that Frazier did not like being challenged.

It took a few seconds of silence before Frazier said, 'I've been thinking about your past involvement, DCI Gilchrist. About you being the arresting officer.'

'Yes, sir?'

'I've spent some time going through the reports. I hadn't realised that you had a bit of a tussle with McCrear during the arrest. Two cracked ribs, fractured wrist, a laceration on the back of his head that needed six stitches.' Frazier sent a whistle down the line that could have been a warning signal. 'You don't mess about, do you, Gilchrist?'

'He was armed with a claw hammer, sir, with which he'd already assaulted a member of the public.'

'You received training in unarmed combat did you not?'

'I did, sir, yes.'

A grunt that could have been the opening to a question, or the end of one, or someone sticking a knife into Frazier's gut – Gilchrist couldn't say. What he could say was that he was in no mood to be challenged over his efforts to disarm a testosterone-crazed, drug-livened McCrear whose clear intention had been to resist arrest by hammering Gilchrist's brain from his head. He'd been only too relieved to disarm the man without receiving serious injury to himself, and was prepared to further defend his actions, when Frazier surprised him.

'I've been in touch with one of the world's foremost forensic psychologists, Doctor Fern Weinstein from the FBI Training Center in Quantico, Virginia. I've tasked her with reviewing the murder list and analysing these reports your team has been preparing.'

Gilchrist almost gasped. When Frazier said that resources were not an issue, he hadn't expected the man to come up with experts from overseas. But it troubled him that he was calling him at eight-thirty on a Saturday evening to tell him . . . what?

'So what did Doctor Weinstein conclude?' he asked.

'I asked if there was any way she could identify from these reports who might be next on the murder list. And she came up with two likely suspects.' A pause, then, 'One of which was you.'

Gilchrist felt something heavy and thick turn over in his stomach. His worst fears had just been confirmed. This was what every policeman dreaded, that the person they'd helped put away for some serious crime years ago would nurse their hatred during their time in jail, until all that remained in their twisted mind was to seek revenge on release.

'And the other suspect?' he said.

'Sheriff Pryce Conniston.'

Gilchrist remembered Sheriff Conniston, a portly man with a puffed up appearance and lips that always seemed too wet for comfort. In private, he'd been a polite gentleman, but under that white wig, his body adorned with his robes of office, Conniston could have been the epitome of the arrogant upper class. He'd been brutal in his pre-sentencing assessment of McCrear, but the fact that McCrear had since been released was testament to the powers of authority vested in the Parole Board and the suspect manner in which decisions to release dangerous criminals were considered. Some of the most violent offenders could pull the wool over the eyes of the Parole Board, and calls had been made to the government for a formal review of the entire process.

Of course, none of that helped Gilchrist at that moment. Whether he liked it or not, McCrear was out and about. 'So what are you suggesting, sir?'

'I've organised a couple of uniforms to keep a twenty-four-hour watch on Sheriff Conniston's home. But Doctor Weinstein's of the opinion that of the two suspects, you're more likely to be targeted.'

'Meaning?'

'Meaning, that I'm going to pull you off the investigation, and have you moved to a secure location.'

'*No.*' The word came out louder than intended, but he couldn't allow himself to be removed from the team, effectively suspended, no matter the reason. 'That's a bad idea, sir.'

'I'm not asking your opinion, Gilchrist, I'm instructing—'

'Listen to me.' He turned to face the wind, and struggled to keep his voice even, his tone level. 'If you take me off the case and house me somewhere safe, what do you think McCrear will do?'

'This isn't up for discussion, DCI—'

'You're not listening to me, dammit. Think, for God's sake. What will McCrear do if I'm taken out of circulation?'

A heavy sigh warned him that Frazier might be about to hang up.

But Gilchrist persisted. 'If he can't find me, what'll he do? And don't try to tell me he'll move onto his next victim.' He paused for breath. 'He knows I have a daughter who lives in St Andrews, and a son who lives in Edinburgh. Believe me when I say this, I know that he knows that. So I can't put them in any danger. Suspend me, treat me differently from everyone else, and you're putting the lives of my daughter and son at serious risk.' He didn't know if Frazier was buying it, or even if he was listening. But he wasn't finished.

'What we do is, we carry on as before. In fact, you need to put me more upfront, make me a part of the main investigation, speaking at press conferences, where McCrear and his associates can see me. Up the ante. Force him out of hiding, and make him come to me.' He found he was breathing hard, partly from anger, and partly from the rush of adrenaline that coursed through his system. He'd had these thoughts before, but kept them hidden. Now they were out in the open the sound of his voice lent strength and credibility to his logic, and with a clarity that stunned him, he saw how deep in danger he really was.

At last Frazier spoke. 'Sacrificial lamb is what you want to be. Is that what you're saying, Gilchrist?'

'I have no intention of being a sacrificial lamb, sir. But in light of what you've just told me, or rather, what Doctor Weinstein has just told *you*, then I see no alternative.'

'Let me think about it.'

'No, sir. *No*. There's no decision to be made.'

The line died.

Gilchrist let out his breath in a steamy gush, and stared off beyond the cliffs, across the North Sea. Irene had continued to walk along The Scores, but stopped when he hadn't followed. She faced him then, a silhouette against the moonlit backdrop. From the stillness of her posture, he sensed she'd heard him raise his voice, witnessed his anger.

He stuffed his mobile into his pocket, and approached her.

'Trouble at mill?' she said, affecting an English accent.

'You could say.' He was conscious of his breath steaming in white puffs, and tried to still his pounding heart. But dammit, Frazier was a fool if he tried to suspend him from the case. Wasn't it obvious what he'd argued? It bloody well should be.

'We can do this another time, if you'd like,' she said.

He nodded. 'D'you mind?'

She shifted her bag on her shoulder, tugged at her gloves. 'Well, I'll leave you to it.'

'No, please, I'll walk you back.'

'No need.' She took a deep breath, as if relishing the cold. 'As you said, a full moon in a cloudless sky. I can't let that go to waste.' She faced the wind, looked down the length of The Scores. 'Maybe I'll grab the moment and shoot the town from Bruce Embankment.' She made a phone sign with her gloved hand. 'Call me if you want. Once trouble at mill's sorted.'

Then she turned and strode away from him.

CHAPTER 27

On the walk back to the Office, Gilchrist phoned Frazier, but couldn't get through. Either he'd taken his SIM card out or powered his mobile down – the wrong thing for a Task Force Commander to do during an ongoing investigation. He crossed North Street, slipped his mobile into his pocket, and in doing so fumbled with the folded report from DC Norris. He was about to enter the Office to read it, when he had a change of plan. He was still fired up from Frazier's call, and the thought of spending any more time behind his desk just didn't appeal.

He changed tack, and walked through the pend to the car park in the rear. He pressed his key fob, and his car beeped at him. Behind the wheel, he clicked on the reading light, and unfolded the report. He scanned down the page until he came to where he'd last read.

TN: When did you last see Mr Dempsey?

AB: Maybe a couple of weeks ago.

TN: Maybe? You're not sure?

AB: I don't really pay attention. Like I said, he's off as often as he likes.

TN: When was the last time you can remember he flew out?

AB: I can't really remember. Maybe a month ago?

TN: He flew out, or flew back about a month ago?

AB: Flew back. I remember it now. I was getting ready for Tony's birthday party, when the taxi pulled up, and old Jay got out all tanned and smiling like. So, let me see, that would've been about three and a half weeks ago.

TN: And how did Mr Dempsey appear?

AB: What do you mean?

TN: When he got out the taxi was he drunk? Did he look frightened?

AB: Nothing of the sort. He just looked like he was happy to be home. Old Jay goes through life like he couldn't be arsed doing anything. He spends all his money going away on holidays, or getting drunk down the pub then pissing it down the drain, or on you know what, when he's away.

TN: I see. Can you think of anyone who might want to do Mr Dempsey any harm?

AB: Not really. He's not my cup of tea, but he's never done me no harm.

TN: Did he owe anybody any money?

AB: How would I know that?

TN: Do you know if he'd fallen out with anybody?

As he read on, he realised DC Norris had asked Alice Black just about every question he could think of asking, then some. But he would need to wait until Jay Dempsey returned from whatever holiday he was on before he could interview him in person.

He glanced up at the lighted windows. His office light was on. Which was odd, he thought. He'd switched it off when he left to meet Irene. Or had he? He stared at it, straining to catch movement through the glass, when it switched off. Had one of his team dropped a report into his in-tray, something that could make a difference to the case? He thought of nipping upstairs and checking it out, then decided against it. He'd had it for the day.

Whatever it was could wait until the morning.

Decision made, he fired up the ignition, and eased through the pend onto North Street. He took it slow through town, thinking of his lost evening with Irene. He'd raised his voice within earshot of her. What had she thought? Had she seen a side of him she hadn't liked? It troubled him, but he could do nothing about that now.

On St Mary Street, past the New Inn, he drove through the double mini-roundabouts and accelerated onto the Kinkell Braes, with the thought that he would call her tomorrow if he wasn't overloaded with work, and offer to buy her lunch.

As he drove on, his subconscious worked in the background, touching on one event, then the other, toying with this idea, then that, and in its own mysterious way sorted through that day's investigative detritus until . . . until . . . until he was driving past the Castle Course and realised what he'd missed. He hissed a curse as he reworked the logic.

Old Jay Dempsey took four holidays a year, each about two weeks long. Which meant he would fly off every third month on average, and be back home for ten weeks before flying off again. Even if Alice Black had it wrong, and Dempsey took, say, six holidays a year, that worked out at old Jay staying at home for six weeks before flying off again. But hadn't Alice said three and a half weeks since his last return?

Shit. He thudded his foot on the brakes, slid to a halt.

He clicked on the reading lamp, found the report, and unfolded it.

He read it again, and saw he'd made no mistake.

Unless old Jay Dempsey had changed his habits of a pensioned lifetime, Gilchrist's rationale could not be wrong. Dempsey wasn't on holiday. The time at home was too short. And if old Jay wasn't on holiday, was he the missing victim number three?

Only one way to find out.

He checked Dempsey's address on Norris's report – Newliston, on the outskirts of Kirkcaldy – entered it into his satnav, and accelerated into the country night. Kirkcaldy lay on the Fife coast some twenty-five miles due south of St Andrews, a distance Gilchrist was determined to cover in as short a time as possible.

He found the address easily enough, his satnav leading him directly to Dempsey's house, a tidy modern bungalow at the end of a dead-end street. He switched his headlights onto full beam to reveal a gravel driveway bordered both sides by neatly trimmed hedges that ran into the property in a sweeping curve. He eased between a pair of roughcast gate pillars and into the driveway, tyres crunching gravel, and drew to a halt in front of a garage separated from the gable end of the bungalow by a slabbed path that led to the back of the house.

He removed a torch from the glove compartment, and stepped outside. As he walked along the concrete path to the front door, torchlight brightening the garden area to his left, he came to understand that Dempsey might have been a spendthrift abroad, but he certainly took care of his garden. Bushes and hedges were trimmed as smooth as topiary. The lawn looked as if it had been freshly edged. Not a weed or a dead leaf in sight.

At the front door, the entrance stoop was clean, as if it had been brushed in the last day or so. He kneeled down, pulled the letterbox to him, and shone the torch inside. But the angle was too tight, the letterbox too low, for him to see much of anything. He pushed to his feet again, and stepped off the path onto an area of soil beneath the front window. Daffodils, crocuses and the withered remains of winter hyacinths crowded the area. He shone his torch at the window to confirm the curtains were open, pressed his face against the glass, but saw only a clean dining room with a polished table and six chairs around it.

What he did notice was a vase of flowers in the centre of the dining-room table, which had drooped to the point of terminal exhaustion. Now why would someone who took care of their garden leave a vase of flowers unwatered if he was flying off on holiday? And if he was flying off on holiday why would he have purchased the bouquet in the first place? He tried pressing an arm against the windows, but they were all secured.

He stepped off the soiled area, scraped the soles of his shoes on the grass, and walked around the side to the garage. He rattled the door, but it was locked, and having no windows he couldn't tell what was inside. He made a mental note to find out if Dempsey owned a car.

Not that any of that would matter if his worst fears were realised.

The back garden was another tidy area, with a bricked barbecue in one corner, and a small deck area next to it, cleared of garden furniture probably still stored in the garage for the winter months. He tried the back door, but it was locked, too. He backed onto the lawn and shone his torch at the windows. From the curtain material, he was able to work out the rooms – utility room and kitchen to the left of the door, living room to the right.

He pressed his face to the living-room window, but his torch picked up nothing untoward. He did the same with the kitchen. Again nothing. Then the utility room. Nothing there, either.

As he walked to the door the light from his torch picked up movement to the side. He froze, shone his torch at the kitchen window. Had he imagined it? Had it been only a trick of light? He held the torch beam steady for a moment . . .

Which was when he saw it.

He stepped closer, torch to the glass, and watched fly after fly come to the window attracted by the light. He knew it took anywhere from two weeks to a month for maggots to morph into flies – sometimes earlier, depending on the ambient temperature. He placed the flat of his hand to the glass, and realised that the thermostat had been turned up.

The correct protocol was for him to call it in – suspected death – and wait for back-up to arrive. But that phone call from Frazier still irked, and he decided that if he wanted to be a player in the ongoing investigation, he was just going to have to get on with it. He switched off his torch, walked to the back door, and shouldered it. Solid. He stood back, raised his leg, and booted the wood with his heel as hard as he could. Not quite so solid. Another kick, and he saw movement in the door. He tried his shoulder again, put all his weight behind it – one thud, two thuds – and the door-frame splintered as he tumbled inside.

The first thing that hit him was the heat, a wall of warm air that slapped him on the face, then wrapped around him. The second was the smell of putrefaction, a sickening guff that seemed to coat itself on his tongue with his first breath. He covered his mouth with his hand, fumbled the wall with his free hand, found a light switch, and clicked it on.

To his left, the kitchen door was closed. As he watched, flies seemed to seep from the gap beneath the door, attracted to the light. He leaned forward, opened the door, and clicked another switch. The room exploded with brightness to reveal the bloated figure of a naked man lying spread-eagled on the floor. Flies spilled from the body into the air like black dust. His stomach lurched, and he backed out of the room, slammed the door shut, and retreated to the garden.

On the deck, the air smelled clean, fresh, but did little to shift the coating of death that covered his tongue. He coughed up phlegm, spat it into the hedge, wiped his mouth. For some reason an image of Cooper carrying out a post mortem on Dempsey's body entered his mind with such clarity that he had to close his eyes. Maybe her ability to work on the most horrific of cases had something to do with her personality, which could explain her coldness when it came to matters of the heart. He spat out more phlegm, then removed his mobile from his pocket.

As he placed his phone to his ear, the distant sound of police sirens came to him on the night air, no doubt called in by neighbours concerned by someone creeping around old Jay's house late at night, or having been awakened by the noise of a back door being battered in. He glanced at the neighbouring houses beyond the boundary hedge, lights in all the windows, doors open to reveal concerned faces.

This time, his call was answered with an abrupt, 'Frazier.'

'I've just found victim number three, sir.'

CHAPTER 28

The first to arrive at Dempsey's home was a pair of uniforms in a squad car, who'd been called to the scene by Dempsey's next-door neighbour, Mrs Black, the same Mrs Black who'd been interviewed by DC Norris. Despite Gilchrist holding a pack of forensic coveralls under his arm, they challenged him, but he held out his warrant card.

'Sorry, sir,' the smaller of the two said, his hi-viz jacket glistening from Gilchrist's torchlight. 'So, what've we got?' A gust of wind shifted, carrying with it the stench of decay. The constable placed a hand to his mouth, and gasped, 'What the hell is that?'

Gilchrist didn't need a couple of inexperienced uniforms making a scene, so he said, 'I want you to set up crime scene tape at the entrance to the driveway. No need for door-to-doors, but if any of the neighbours show up, see what you can glean from them. Did they see anything suspicious? How well did they know Jay Dempsey? That sort of thing.' Despite DC Norris having already interviewed most of the neighbours, Gilchrist thought it would keep the uniforms interested and busy. Besides, you never could tell what they might turn up.

Next to arrive were the SOCOs, shortly followed by Frazier, who walked up to the back door, and peered inside. The fetid stench seemed not to bother him. One of the SOCOs pushed past, and Frazier turned from the door and walked towards Gilchrist. 'You. Over here,' he said, then strode to the middle of the lawn.

Gilchrist turned his back to him, and retrieved his mobile from his jacket. Strictly speaking, the body couldn't be moved without the police pathologist first confirming that life was extinct. But old Jay Dempsey was dead beyond any doubt, and nothing Cooper could do or say would change things. Even so, he decided to phone her. And Frazier's attitude was grating on his nerves.

'Nice to hear from you,' she said. 'And on a Saturday night? Business or pleasure?'

Even from these few words, Gilchrist could tell she'd had a few wines. 'Regrettably it's business. Looks like the third victim. There's no need for you to be here. The body'll be transported to Dundee tonight, and you can carry out your PM in the morning.'

'That's good of you, Andy, but why are you calling to say I'm not needed?'

'To follow protocol.'

'Ah.' She let the word fill his silence. 'Frazier keeping you on your toes, is he?'

That was one thing he could always say about Cooper. She was sharp. 'He keeps everyone on their toes,' he said.

She remained silent for a moment, then said, 'I've been reviewing my PM notes, and have some additional thoughts on the killer's MO.'

Gilchrist felt a spurt of hope. 'Such as?'

'Patience is a virtue, Andy.' She smiled, then said, 'I'll complete my review, then call you tomorrow.'

The line died.

'Finished?' Frazier said.

Gilchrist walked up to him. 'Sir?'

'My patience is stretching thin, so run it through me in excruciating detail how you just happen to find our missing victim when the rest of my Task Force are scratching about in the dark like headless fucking chickens.'

'DC Norris's report, sir.'

'Who the fuck is DC Norris?'

'The member of Fife Constabulary who interviewed Jay Dempsey's neighbours.'

'Don't fuck around with me Gilchrist, I'm warning you. Why didn't you report to the Task Force before you arrived here and kicked the door down like Super-fucking-man? You think the rest of us are a bunch of arseholes who don't have a clue how to shit.'

Gilchrist had heard much profanity over the years, but never before had he heard it delivered with such levelled and angry coldness. He retrieved Norris's report from his pocket and slapped it against Frazier's chest, harder than intended, he had to confess.

'There it is, *sir*. Norris's report. All the answers are in there. *Read* it.'

Give Frazier his due. He didn't bat an eyelid, just took hold of the report and stuffed it into his pocket without looking at it. As Gilchrist walked away, Frazier said, 'You're off the case, Gilchrist. Effective immediately.'

Gilchrist stopped mid-step. 'Take me off the case, and you'll be putting the lives of my daughter and son in danger. I've told you that, and I won't stand by and let that happen.'

Frazier narrowed his eyes, as if trying to see through Gilchrist's calm demeanour, the matter of fact way he spoke, that what he was being told was an indisputable fact. 'I don't stand for insubordination, Gilchrist.'

'Neither do I. *Sir.*'

Something shifted behind Frazier's eyes at that, as if calculating the loss versus the value of having Gilchrist on his team. He looked as if he was about to reply in kind, when one of the SOCOs, a woman, shouted out, 'Sir? I think you should see this.'

Gilchrist opened the pack of coveralls, and slipped them over his jeans.

Frazier said, 'I said you're off the case.'

'Then let this be my last involvement.' He pulled his mask up and over his mouth and nose, and followed the SOCO indoors.

The kitchen reeked of putrefaction. Ceiling spotlights, too many for the size of the place, flooded the room with light that almost blinded. Any heat that had been generated by the thermostat being turned to high, had dissipated through windows thrown open to let flies out. Some still crawled over work surfaces, or buzzed around the room.

Jay Dempsey was small in stature, which was just as well, Gilchrist thought, or he wouldn't have fitted into the narrow space provided by the kitchen floor. He lay naked, not in the typical arms-wide form of crucifixion, but with his arms outstretched above his head as if trying to reach for the utility door. His bare feet were no more than a metre apart, toes purple and swollen, heels in a blackened pool of blood from being nailed through his ankles. Even from where Gilchrist stood, he could make out the cut nipple, the wound open, skin peeled wide where the gases of putrefaction had bloated the body.

He stood in the open doorway and let his gaze shift around the small room. Something about the scene didn't make sense. Why kill Dempsey in such a cramped space? Why not do the deed in the living room, like Rickard and the others? He couldn't answer these questions, and had a sense of missing something. And where were Dempsey's clothes?

In the living room, a pile of clothes sat on the sofa, neatly stacked in the reverse order of their removal. He swatted a fly from his face as he walked to the sofa for a closer look, and had a feeling that the clothes were not as tidily folded as the others had been. Did that matter? He couldn't say. But it was different.

He walked the length of the room to the front window, and surveyed the scene from a different angle. Two-seater sofa, matching single chair, coffee tables either side. In the centre of the lounge in front of a gas fire, a woven rug large enough for a spread-eagled body to lie upon. So why not crucify him there? With the blinds drawn, and the curtains closed, no one could see inside. The room would have been perfect.

He returned to the kitchen.

The forensic-suited SOCO, a young woman with brown eyes that looked at him with keen interest, was kneeling on the linoleum flooring by Dempsey's head. 'You wanted to show me something?' he said to her.

'This, sir.'

He stepped alongside the body and kneeled beside her, taking care to keep clear of a black trail of hardened blood which ran from Dempsey's nailed wrist along the length of his arm. At first, he couldn't make out what he was being shown, an object being pointed out to him by a latex-covered pinkie.

'What is it?'

'I think it's a broken Stanley knife blade, sir.'

He couldn't say for sure. It was metal, he could tell that much, but blood trailing from the wrist had all but engulfed it. He glanced at Dempsey's taped mouth, his face bloated and swollen around the tightness of the tape. Back to the metal object. Was this part of the knife they'd used to remove Dempsey's tongue? If so, what had happened to snap the blade? And as his thoughts fired a thousand questions at him, he came to understand that he was referring to *they* – not one killer, but two.

Is that what was different about this crime scene? The clothes? The broken blade? The tight confines of the kitchen floor? The different form of crucifixion? His mind screamed at him – Why? Why here? Why not in the living room? It would have taken considerable force to snap a blade like that. So what had happened? He ran his gaze along the body, then looked around, trying to visualise the killers working in the cramped space, stepping over the body, bumping against the kitchen cupboards in doing so. And he realised there could have been only one killer in this room. The space was too cramped for two. Had it been McCrear? Or some other person who'd tripped, and in doing so snapped the blade?

Back to the blade once again. It shouldn't be there. McCrear would have known it had snapped off, so he should have found it and removed it. But the fact that it was here, in the kitchen, by the body, was a mistake. It had to be. So, maybe not McCrear?

'It must've snapped off and got lost in the blood,' he said. 'It's been missed.'

The SOCO nodded. 'I think so, sir. You can hardly see it.'

'Could we lift prints from it?'

'Maybe a partial, sir. But I wouldn't hold my breath.'

'Bag it, and have it analysed. Maybe we can identify which store it was bought from.' A long shot, he knew, but the broken blade was their first and only solid piece of evidence from any of the crime scenes, other than the tape – if that could be called evidence.

He pushed himself to his feet, grunted as he did so. His knees felt stiff from squatting by the body. As he reached for the counter top to steady himself, he saw it, a messy streak of something, a mark that ran across the glass door of the oven.

He stepped over the body for a closer look.

'Looks like something's brushed against the door,' he said.

The SOCO leaned across, tilted her head as she studied it. 'Can't say for sure, sir, but could it have been made by a hand?'

'Dempsey's?'

'I don't know, sir.'

He eyed the oven handle, the surrounding cabinets. If the mark hadn't been made by Dempsey, could it be McCrear's? He'd concluded from other crime scenes that McCrear was meticulous. But this scene was different, less tidy, more cramped, just . . . just . . . just *wrong*, as if someone had been experimenting—

'Here's something else,' the SOCO said, and pointed to a cut in the face of a cabinet door. 'I think this might be where the blade snapped, sir.'

He leaned forward. 'It could be,' he said, then tried to imagine McCrear losing his balance. But if the blade was snapped there, and the mark on the oven door was here, then it couldn't have been a hand reaching for support, but . . .

Which was when it came to him. 'It's not a hand mark,' he said. 'It's from his face. Could be a sweat mark, or saliva. You might be able to recover DNA from it.'

'I'll certainly try, sir.'

'Keep me posted.' And with that, he retreated from the kitchen.

Outside, Frazier advanced on him again, face grim, eyes wild, Norris's report in his hand. 'Explain,' he said, and slapped it against Gilchrist's chest.

Gilchrist peeled off his face mask and breathed in the cold night air. Despite a rising wind, the smell of putrefaction still hung around him. Rommie Frazier might be a rising star with expertise in logistical management, but he was sorely lacking in basic logic. He took the report from Frazier. 'Jay Dempsey flies off on holiday every second month or so. He'd just come back a few weeks ago. So he should've still been at home. Not away on holiday.'

Something shifted across Frazier's face – disappointment in the answer, perhaps, or in his own failure to work it out. Gilchrist pulled the coveralls from his head, and nodded to the house behind him. 'This scene is different,' he said. 'Not by much. Just . . . different.'

'What d'you mean?'

He sucked air through his teeth, not sure how much he should tell Frazier, or even if he could trust him. 'It's as if we're looking at another killer,' he said. 'I don't think McCrear killed Dempsey—'

'A copycat?' Frazier livened at the prospect.

Gilchrist burst his bubble with, 'No. We've kept certain details from the press, so a copycat wouldn't know about them.'

'So you're saying what?'

Gilchrist knew that Frazier's investigation was floundering, that he was searching for something, anything, a new line of enquiry he could pin to the incident board. But he worried that airing his gut feelings might end up with Frazier altering the course of the investigation in the wrong direction. Even so, they really needed to change their line of enquiry.

And he thought he saw what that new approach should be.

'Dempsey was murdered in his kitchen,' he said. 'Not in his living room. Which was the killer's mistake.'

'How come?'

'The kitchen was too cramped. He tripped. He broke a knife blade. And left his DNA on the oven door.' He didn't know that for sure. But he had Frazier's attention. 'Don't think we'll lift any prints from the knife blade. But if it's McCrear, his DNA will be in the system.' He stepped out of his coveralls, and said, 'Moving forward, you need to keep me on the case, sir. And you make me—'

'No chance, Gilchrist. You're out. Finished. You've blown it.'

'And so will you if you don't listen to me.'

That seemed to grab Frazier's attention.

'How many man hours have you spent on this investigation so far, sir?' The question was rhetorical, of course, and Frazier didn't need reminding that money was tight, that police budgets nationwide were being cut, and what was left was being scrutinised to the nth degree. 'And for all that expense, what has the rest of the Task Force uncovered so far?'

'You don't have all the answers, Gilchrist, if that's what you're suggesting. We have a good team assembled, a great team, one of the best—'

'And you want to weaken that team by suspending me?' He shook his head. He could explain his thoughts on how to progress the investigation, but needed to hold them back until he'd strengthened his position. Moorhouse's patio door being unlocked had been the trigger. How had McCrear escaped across the fields without being seen? You couldn't get far from Kilconquhar without transport. So there had to have been a car. Which meant that Garson or Deeps – one of them – must have been the driver. They just had to be.

Which was key to the shift in focus of the main line of enquiry.

'Rather than kick me off the case, why don't you let me head your investigation? I'm not interested in fronting the Task Force through the media. That's your job. Meanwhile, I've got some ideas as to how to move this forward.'

'And these ideas are . . .?'

'Do we have a deal?'

'Don't try to fuck me around, Gilchrist. If you're withholding evidence, I'll have you charged with obstruction of an ongoing murder investigation.'

'I'm withholding nothing that isn't already in plain sight, if you'd just look.'

'That's it, Gilchrist. We're done.' And with that Frazier pushed past him and strode towards the gable end of the bungalow, no doubt heading to his car from where he would place a call that would initiate the paperwork to suspend Gilchrist from the case.

Well, sometimes you need to have friends in high places.

He removed his mobile, and placed a call of his own.

CHAPTER 29

5 a.m., Sunday
Fisherman's Cottage, Crail

Gilchrist groaned as he wakened to the sound of his alarm. He rolled onto his side, reached for his mobile on his bedside table and swiped a finger across the screen to *Snooze*. As he returned his head to the pillow, sleep enveloped him again, pulling him down, deep into its warm embrace . . .

Seconds later, it seemed, his alarm beeped again.

This time he slid his feet to the floor before swiping the screen and shutting the alarm down. He sat on the edge of his bed for thirty seconds while he pulled himself awake, rolled his head, lifted his arms, stretched his muscles, his mind sifting through last night's turbulent events. It had just gone 2 a.m. by the time he'd crawled into bed, exhausted, frustrated, and still nursing his anger at the way Frazier had tried to treat him. The pair of them had argued for a full hour about the correct way forward, but in the end it had taken a midnight call from Chief Constable Archie McVicar before Frazier had relented.

On the drive home, Gilchrist had been surprised to receive another call from McVicar, who thanked him for the effort he was putting in, and told him that Frazier was now in agreement that Gilchrist was the man to take charge of the Task Force.

'You've reassigned Detective Superintendent Frazier, sir?'

'No, Andy. You'll be his second-in-command. Which is the best I can do.'

Gilchrist had thanked him, and pondered over what he'd just been told. *The best I can do?* Which warned him that Frazier was indeed a man to be watched, a star who had powerful friends in high places, too high up the chain of command for even someone as revered and respected as Chief Constable McVicar to argue against.

Hence the early rise on a Sunday morning.

Now he'd been reassigned as Frazier's second-in-command, effectively taking over control of the Task Force in their attempts to locate and arrest McCrear, he had much to do. He'd decided to focus on two separate lines of enquiry, each as important as the other, and both needing many man hours assigned to them to see them through. One line of enquiry was to pull out all the stops in finding Terence Garson. The other was to review CCTV footage around each of the victim's homes, starting with Moorhouse's, in an attempt to locate the associate who must have driven McCrear to each of the murder sites. That line of enquiry was the most dubious, the one based on conjecture, not facts. So, despite his need to have both lines of enquiry equally manned, Gilchrist had the sense to know that he might have to rein in the search for the driver.

Showered and shaved and seated at his kitchen table, he opened a copy of the files he'd insisted Frazier give him last night, and began to read through them. It didn't take him long to understand that Frazier's method of investigation was to cover himself in paperwork, smother the office with report after report, all for the purpose of ensuring that nothing could ever come back to bite him in the rear end.

Reams and reams of the stuff, almost too much to take in.

But Gilchrist persevered and dug through the files until he found what he was looking for – the typed transcripts of Jeannie Findlay's interview at the police station, questions and answers relating to her relationship – or lack thereof – with Garson, highlighting sentences that helped summarise pertinent points.

No, he disnae live with me. He just pops in now and again to see his kid.

Last time I seen him was about three or four days ago.

Aye, he sometimes gives me money, but it's no enough, the lazy bastard.

Naw, I don't know where he gets the money. Probably steals it.

On and on he read, marking bits here, others there. He paused for a moment when the interviewer – DI Ella Barnes – asked where she and Garson had first met.

In a pub. Cannae remember which one.

Aye, I was right pished, so I was, or I wouldnae have let him shag me.

Naw, I wasnae going out with nobody else.

Cannae remember the name of my last boyfriend.

Aye, Terry knew him all right. They used to be friends.

Gilchrist read on, eager to find out if Barnes had asked the one question he needed to have asked. But it never was, which was why he should have been analysing the interviews, making sure nothing was missed. That sixth sense of his was niggling at him, telling him that the key to finding Garson had to be through Jeannie. Yet the police interviews fell short.

In the end, Jeannie had been released and sent home.

He closed the file, and stood up. He felt stiff, tired, and slightly bemused by Frazier's tactics. As Task Force Commander, the man had missed a beat, maybe half-a-dozen beats. He should have focused on Findlay's children – three in total – the oldest a girl of six years old. But Garson had fathered only one, the youngest. The key question as far as Gilchrist was concerned was – Who fathered the other two children? One man, or two? And did Garson know him, or them? He noted bullet points to remind him to have that question answered.

He checked the time – 07:18 – and gathered in his notes. Once McVicar had spoken to Frazier, and an agreement of sorts had been reached, Frazier agreed to hold a briefing that morning at eight, in which he would announce Gilchrist's new role. It had been left to Frazier to set up the Sunday morning briefing, with each of the team leaders advising their own staff. In that matter, Gilchrist had texted Jessie and Mhairi, rather than wake them up by phoning the other side of midnight: he would pick Jessie up from home at 7.30; Mhairi was to review CCTV footage around Kilconquhar as a matter of urgency, and was given a short explanation of what she should be looking for.

He phoned Jessie.

'Got your text, Andy. Did something happen overnight?'

'We found Jay Dempsey, the missing third victim.' He went on to tell her where and how, and when she started firing questions at him, he said, 'We've got a briefing at eight this morning in Glenrothes HQ. You'll hear all you need to hear then. I'll pick you up in ten.'

'That'll give me time to put on some makeup, then.'

'No coffees?'

'Already done.'

He was a tad late picking up Jessie, but at that time on a Sunday morning, the roads were clear, and he made the twenty-mile trip to Glenrothes in just over fifteen minutes.

'You ever get caught for speeding?' she said, when he pulled into the car park.

'Now and again.'

She tutted, finished the remainder of her homemade coffee, and stuffed the empty cup – a reused Starbucks – into the holder in the centre console. Gilchrist hadn't finished his, so took it with him.

In the conference room, Frazier was already there with his two female DCs – Agnew and Pollard – seated at the top desk, busy typing on their laptops. Only two others had arrived – DI Ella Barnes with a chubby man in a scuffed suit who looked as if he'd been on the binge the night before. Well, it was the weekend after all.

By 8 a.m., everyone had arrived, and the room stilled when Frazier walked to the wall chart on which Jay Dempsey's details had been added.

'We had a busy night, last night,' he began. 'One in which DCI Gilchrist, using his own initiative, established that Jay Dempsey, who we believed had not been available for interview because he was on holiday, had in fact been murdered in his home.' He tapped the board with a pointer. 'Mr Dempsey's body had undergone severe decomposition due to the thermostat having been turned up to full for a period of some three weeks, or so.' He nodded to the DCs behind the desk, who started to distribute files to each of the attendees.

Gilchrist almost gagged at the close-up of Dempsey's bloated chest, the nipple sliced through leaving a swollen cut and skin peeled back to expose a layer of white fat and rotting flesh beneath. A quick flip through the remainder of the images brought him to a biography of Dempsey – age, address, next of kin, summary of work experience – followed by a copy of DC Norris's door-to-doors with every neighbour, it looked like. Which had Gilchrist thinking that Frazier must have been up all night preparing for that morning's briefing. If he hadn't been such a pain, he could have been impressed by the man.

'We know that Dempsey was the third victim of this serial killer,' Frazier said. 'The number three was cut through his left nipple in the same straight-lined manner as the others.' As Frazier talked on and referred them to the crime scene photographs, Gilchrist flipped through the images – taped mouth, face bloated and blue; nailed wrists, left and right, blackened with blood; nailed ankles, ditto – each image made more gruesome by the decayed condition of old Jay's body. As he riffled through the pages, a groan came from behind him, and a few whispered curses hissed around the room.

Frazier tapped the incident board.

The room stilled.

'That is where the similarity to the other victims ends,' Frazier said, looking around the room as if trying to catch each and every attendee's attention, until his gaze arrived at, then settled on, Gilchrist. 'DCI Gilchrist has some interesting theories about the nature of Dempsey's murder, theories which I discussed with the Chief Constable in the small hours this morning.' He pulled his shoulders back, appeared to give a triumphant smile, then said, 'And we have agreed that DCI Gilchrist will join me as *Deputy* Task Force Commander.'

A murmur rushed through the room for a long moment, then stilled.

'DCI Gilchrist?' Frazier said, and stepped aside.

CHAPTER 30

At the incident board, Gilchrist introduced himself again as a matter of courtesy, then gave a brief summary of events leading to his discovery of Dempsey's body, referring to DC Norris's transcripts, 'Which you'll find in the reports you've been given this morning.'

Rather than ask if anyone had any questions, he pressed on.

He assigned detectives from Tayside, Northern, and Lothian and Borders, to locate Terence Garson as a priority. 'We must find that white van. Revisit CCTV footage in Stirling. He hasn't vanished off the face of the Earth,' he insisted, although Garson and his van could be halfway across Europe by now. He emphasised the need to locate and arrest McCrear, even though not one shred of evidence put him in the country, let alone at the scene of any of the crimes. And the mystery woman whom Garson had called Deeps, and who Gilchrist now believed could be the key to the case, was being tracked through phone records, the only lead they had.

He was relieved that warrants had been issued to recover records of Jeannie Findlay's landline – which kept Dick's illegal involvement secret. The Task Force had already gone to considerable effort tracking phone numbers, with teams tasked to identify addresses and follow up with interviews of each of the owners. Four numbers could not be identified, calls to untraceable burners which Jeannie Findlay maintained she never made. Even though no new leads to McCrear's whereabouts had been uncovered, Gilchrist was impressed by the Task Force's efforts thus far.

Aside from revisiting CCTV footage around the Thistle Car Park, he assigned his own Constabulary to revisit footage reviewed earlier by DI Barnes at each of the victim's homes, starting with John Moorhouse, the only crime scene from which McCrear had fled in haste – a mistake, he asserted, which might provide some new lead. DS Jessie Janes and DC Mhairi McBride were assigned to lead Fife Constabulary in that task.

And the Task Force in general were energetic and desperate to find the killers before anyone else was murdered. Questions were fired at him at the end of his briefing, which he welcomed, and answered as best he could, although DI Barnes gave him the most trouble.

'If I could take you to task, sir, on why you think we're looking for two, or possibly three killers, albeit part of the same team, as you allege.' She shrugged. 'If it's Tap McCrear, as you seem confident it is, he could've decided to kill Dempsey in his kitchen rather than in the front lounge. There could be any number of reasons. So why do you think someone else might've been involved in Dempsey's murder, sir?'

Gilchrist thanked her, then said, 'We've obtained copies of McCrear's psychiatric reports in prison. Without question, he's OCD. He's meticulous in everything he does, and fanatical about his personal cleanliness. The crime scene in Dempsey's home was messy, dissimilar to other scenes. So the likelihood of McCrear crucifying Dempsey in a cramped kitchen, when the living room had plenty of space, just doesn't work for me.'

'But McCrear wasn't always OCD, sir, was he?'

Give DI Barnes her due, she knew her stuff. 'That's correct, he wasn't. But someone who develops OCD later in life is unlikely to regress to—'

'But he could have. That's my point, sir. We just don't know.'

'No, I suppose we don't. Not for sure. But we're considering likelihoods here, and the likelihood that McCrear all of a sudden lost his OCD tendencies is slim to non-existent.'

'But it can happen, sir.'

'I'm no expert on that, DI Barnes.'

'That's my point, sir,' she said, which brought a smirk to Frazier's face. Before he could respond, she said, 'And I understand, sir, that a report by Doctor Weinstein suggested that you, as the arresting officer in McCrear's case all these years ago, are the most likely person to be his next victim. How do you feel about that?'

He tried to downplay it. 'It's a report,' he said. 'Despite Doctor Weinstein's valued expertise in forensic psychology, I take it only as conjecture.'

But Barnes was having none of it. 'I mean, sir, in terms of your ability to be Deputy Task Force Commander, don't you think it'll hamper it?'

'Not at all. Each and every one of us in this room lives with the daily threat that our lives could be in danger at any moment while carrying out our duties. With that in mind, we are each more aware of our physical frailties, which in turn helps us to be more focused in the day-to-day aspects of our job. In a nutshell,' he concluded, 'the more you are aware of the dangers, the safer you'll be.'

'But again, sir, you don't know for sure whether or not you'll be targeted.'

'Do you?'

That seemed to do the trick. DI Barnes sat back, but left him with the sense that far from convincing her, he'd done the opposite. Truth be told, he wasn't sure he'd convinced himself. If McCrear had him targeted as his next victim, there wasn't much he could do about it, other than to keep an eye out, but more importantly, to focus all resources he had at hand on locating and arresting the man as soon as possible.

He completed his briefing just after 9.40 a.m., relieved it had been well received. And throughout it all, Frazier had sat in silence, flanked by his two DCs, or as Jessie said later, his two sycophants – 'They're probably giving him one.'

'Don't you mean, giving him two?' he joked.

She chuckled. 'Well that might explain why he looks so frazzled.'

The teams gathered their notes. The room emptied. Jessie appeared to be livened by that day's prospects. She'd already contacted Mhairi who'd jump-started the CCTV footage review on Moorhouse's property as a matter of priority – per Gilchrist's instruction.

How could McCrear escape across open fields without being seen? That's what was troubling Gilchrist. He'd studied a map of the area, and worked out that McCrear could have ended up about a mile away from Moorhouse's home. From there, an accomplice could have picked him up. Although he wouldn't have been dropped off there, but at some point much closer to Moorhouse's address. The task set by Gilchrist was for Jessie's team to review footage of all vehicles – cars, vans, buses, even motorcycles – driving into Kilconquhar, and look for discrepancy in the number of passengers.

Back at the North Street Office, Mhairi said, 'I'm not sure I know what you mean by discrepancy in the number of passengers, sir?'

'Let's say McCrear knows the address well, that he's staked it out, and knows where all the CCTV cameras are. After all, it's not like we try to hide them.'

Which was true. Walk through any town in the UK, and if you look up, on the sides of buildings you'll find CCTV cameras on every high street, positioned for maximum coverage, and often controlled remotely from police CCTV centres. Each camera can be turned through 180 degrees to cover the entire length of a street – even 360 degrees in some locations – with the capability to zoom in on anything of interest.

'So what I'm thinking,' he said, 'is that they stop somewhere out of view of CCTV cameras. The killer, let's say it's McCrear, slips out. He's carrying a holdall, or a rucksack, large enough to hide his instruments of torture and forensic coveralls, but small enough not to attract attention. Seconds later, the driver carries on as if nothing's happened.

'So I'm asking you to look for footage that shows two people, say, sitting in the front of the vehicle, then footage from the next camera down the line which shows only one person in the front of the same vehicle.'

'What if he's not sitting in the front to begin with, sir, but in the back?'

'If you were being driven through town, you'd sit in the front. If you didn't, it would make you look more conspicuous, wouldn't it?'

'Unless I was in a taxi, sir.'

'Well, there is that, Mhairi. But we have to start somewhere.' He was pleased by her initiative, and liked that she wasn't afraid to voice her opinion. 'If you come across footage of taxis, then maybe you can check out the back seat, too.'

She grinned. 'Will do, sir. I'll see what I come up with.'

Then to Jessie. 'This is man-hour intensive, so pull in the rest of the Office. I want everyone working on this.'

'Got it.'

'And I'd concentrate on reviewing footage from midday, which is before his daughter, Laura, arrived at his home, through to three, which is about the length of time it would take for McCrear to make his way across open fields.'

'Got it.'

Gilchrist's first solid break came just after 3.30 p.m. when Jessie contacted him, and said, 'I think we might have a hit. How soon can you get here?'

He was still ten miles outside St Andrews, on his way back from yet another meeting in Glenrothes with Frazier. 'With you in fifteen minutes, maybe less, if traffic up front gets a move on.'

'We're in Jackie's office. See you then.'

But traffic worsened, and twenty minutes later he entered Jackie's office – Mhairi fixated on one computer monitor alongside Jessie, while Jackie typed search commands into her computer, her printer clicking away like background clockwork.

'Here we are, sir.' Mhairi worked the mouse, and the recording jumped to settle on a blue Honda Civic cruising along St Andrews

Road just outside Kilconquhar. She zoomed in. 'This is them on their way to Moorhouse's, sir. We can't make out faces, but we have two people seated in the front.' She adjusted the angle. 'There's the registration number.' She read it off and compared it to a number scribbled on a notepad. 'Note the time, sir – 13:54:26. Now watch this.' The screen shifted to another view of the same street, but from a different location. 'At 13:55:48, we have the same car.' She zoomed in on the number plate, and read it out again. 'But only the driver in the car.'

'Show me on a map where we're at.'

Jessie already had one open. 'The two sightings are here, and here,' she said. 'And Moorhouse lives there. Less than a hundred yards away.'

Bloody hell. It was beginning to fall into place. He pushed himself upright, resisted the ridiculous urge to high-five Jessie, who looked ready to do the same. 'Who's the car's registered owner?' he said.

'Meghan Morton.'

'Do we know anything about her?'

'Squeaky clean, sir. Not even a parking ticket.'

For a moment, he almost stalled. 'Find an address for her.'

'Jackie's already got it, sir.'

He took the Post-it from Mhairi, and almost gasped. 'St Andrews?'

'Just round the corner on Market Street, sir.'

A shiver chilled his spine. Whoever Meghan Morton was, she knew Gilchrist, knew where he worked, knew where he lived, knew all his local haunts. Had she been keeping an eye on him over recent days, or weeks? The answer was clear. Of course she had. Market Street was a busy thoroughfare frequented by

Gilchrist more or less on a daily basis. How better to monitor a name on the murder list? How better to plan a murder?

'You all right, sir.'

'Yeah . . .' He forced his thoughts on track, worried that they were missing something. There could be any number of reasons for Meghan Morton to be innocent, and nothing at all to do with McCrear. 'Was the car reported as stolen?'

'No, sir.'

'Check polling records to make sure she hasn't moved. For all we know, DVLA's records could be out of date.'

'Already done that, sir. They're current through the end of last year. And the car's been registered in Morton's name for the last five years.'

Well, that was that. Morton could be involved in this, right up to her neck.

Jessie had her jacket in her hand. 'What's keeping you?' she said.

He frowned, tried to fend off the morbid sense of dread that overpowered him, while his mind fired questions that ricocheted around his head in confusion and indecision. Should he advise Frazier? Organise an arrest team? Apply for a warrant? Arrange for back-up? Maybe even the firearms squad? Could McCrear be at Morton's? And if so, just how dangerous was the man? But going in all guns blazing could result in McCrear – or Morton for that matter – clamming up in interviews, which would get them nowhere—

'Andy?' Jessie stood in the doorway, jacket zipped up, raring to go.

He was about to follow, when Jackie hissed, 'Si . . . si . . .'

'Yes, Jackie.'

'M . . . M . . .'

'Meghan Morton?'

'Uh-huh.' She tapped her keyboard, clicked the cursor. The printer came alive, and a single sheet crept onto the tray. She handed it to him.

He frowned as he took it from her. A marriage certificate? It took a few seconds for him to see the significance of what he was holding. Meghan Morton had married . . . Terence Garson? Christ, this could be the break they were looking for. And in Market Street, right under their noses.

'That's it,' he said. 'We're going in. But before we do, we need to know everything about that address. It's flatted, so how many others are in the building? Are all the flats fully occupied, or are they rental property only? I want to know who owns what, and how long Morton's been at that address. There must be CCTV cameras in the area, too. We need to check these out. So get onto it right away. I want the full works. Everything.'

CHAPTER 31

A phone call to Frazier fired the Constabulary into accelerated action.

Forty-five minutes later, Gilchrist and Jessie strode along Market Street, armed with search warrants for Flats A and C, both produced at the speed of light by Frazier. Jackie had confirmed that both flats were leased in Meghan Morton's name – no sign of Terence Garson anywhere on the lease documents. The property consisted of three flats: Flat A on the ground floor, Flat C on the first floor, which shared a landing with Flat B – currently empty – and owned by the same landlord.

Together, he and Jessie entered the pend that took them through to a communal area which served a number of buildings and provided parking for homeowners – no blue Civic in sight. Two teams of four Kevlar-vested armed police officers each were already there, ready to break into both flats. A quick chat with the commander, and they were all set.

Gilchrist led the way. The communal door was unlocked, and opened with a heavy push against stiff hinges that complained with a rusted squeal. He stepped into a cramped entranceway, which led to a flight of worn stone steps to the common landing on the first floor. The access to the ground floor flat was tight, obliging one team to gather on the landing outside Flat C, while the other straddled halfway up the staircase in readiness to tackle Flat A at the entrance level.

Gilchrist tried to still the pounding in his chest, ran his tongue over dry lips. For the life of him, he couldn't explain why he felt so ill at ease. But they were all there now, and had a job to do. On his signal, both teams went into action.

The stairwell echoed with the hard drumming of doors being thumped with gloved fists, hard enough to crack wood it seemed. *Open up. Police. Open up*. More thumping, followed by, *Police. Open up*.

Another signal from Gilchrist, and one member from each team stepped forward, the Enforcer, a metal handheld battering ram more commonly known as the big key, in hand. The stairwell exploded to the combined thunder of both doors being battered open. One thud, two thuds, and the locks split apart to the cracking sound of the doorframe splintering.

Teams poured into each flat. *Police. Show yourself. Police.*

Gilchrist followed his team into Flat A as they bruised their way into the premises, voices tense in a confusion of shouting, *Clear on the left police bedroom clear show yourself clear on the right.* Then, after an unsettling moment of relative silence, '*All clear,*' leaving only the shuffling and bumping of boots, and the heavy breathing of men still fired up with adrenaline.

In the kitchen, Gilchrist opened the fridge – almost empty. He picked up a carton of milk and shook it. The sides thudded with lumps. Two pieces of cheese had turned green with age. He closed the fridge and opened the waste bin. Crushed beer cans

– Tennent's Super – and a Domino's Pizza box, gave him the slimmest hope of lifting prints. The single bedroom gave nothing away, other than that the occupant lived alone. Crushed pillow, creased duvet cover, suggested a male presence, and certainly not one who suffered from OCD.

'What do you think, sir?'

Gilchrist faced the team commander. 'Looks like it's not been lived in for a number of weeks. And only one person, at that.' He would have the SOCOs go through the flat, but he didn't hold out much hope.

He returned to the front door, taking care to avoid catching his jacket on the splintered frame. From upstairs, an ominous silence told him they'd broken into an empty flat, too. Jessie caught his eye, and he walked up the stairs to meet her.

'Gone,' she said. 'I'm guessing about a month or so. How about yours?'

'The same.' He nodded to the open door behind him. 'Get Jackie onto it. We need to contact the landlord, see if we can get bank details. When was the rent last paid? How was it paid? Cheque, BACS, or cash? How long was the lease? Find out what the landlord knows about Morton. Did he ever meet her?' He raked a hand through his hair in frustration. 'I mean, for crying out loud, we're chasing bloody shadows here.'

'Uh-oh. Here comes trouble,' Jessie said, and slid past Gilchrist back into the flat.

He gritted his teeth as Frazier climbed the stairs, head down, taking his time, like a man about to discharge bad news. When he reached the landing, he looked at the battered door, his eyes taking in the burst lock, the splintered doorframe, before settling on Gilchrist with a hard stare. 'I'm disappointed, DCI Gilchrist.'

'Likewise, sir.'

'All these resources wasted.' He shook his head, as if in despair. 'I have to tell you that this case worries me. On a number of levels.'

Gilchrist thought silence as good a response as any.

'Good teamwork. In fact, *great* teamwork. Good to see these teams working with such precision.' Frazier nodded for several seconds, as if deep in thought, but Gilchrist had a sense of the man's demeanour hardening. 'I thought we'd broken the case today, that we'd make a couple of arrests and put these bastards into custody before they could do any more harm.' He sniffed, cast his gaze down the stairwell.

Gilchrist followed his line of sight.

Two SOCOs in forensic coveralls were dusting the door for prints. He didn't think they would find any, but you never could tell. Another SOCO entered the building with a camera slung over her shoulder. He recognised her from the day before.

'I jumped through hoops of fire to get you these search warrants,' Frazier said. 'Made a couple of phone calls in anticipation of making arrests. And what do we end up with?' He formed an O with his thumb and forefinger. 'A big fat zero. That's what.' His mobile rang at that moment, and he pulled it from his pocket, looked at the screen, then glared at Gilchrist before walking down the stairs to take the call outside.

Jessie reappeared. 'I heard that. What the hell is he about? We've given him the first real lead since the investigation started, and he wants to have your balls on a plate?'

'But we've still come up empty,' Gilchrist said.

'Well, you do have a point.' She grinned, and raised her eyebrows.

Intrigued, he said, 'You look as if you've found something.'

'Not me. But Mhairi. Here.' She held out her mobile to let him read the screen. 'You remember that blue Honda Civic that's vanished off the face of the Earth?'

He frowned as he tried to read Mhairi's text.

'Jackie thought they might have changed its number plate after they scarpered from Moorhouse's. She thought it would be an easy task to use a strip of black tape to change the number seven to a two. So she carried out a search on the ANPR and . . . hey, presto.'

'She found it?'

'With a two on the plate, that number is registered to a Ford Fiesta in Aberdeen, so she knew the plate had been faked. She located a blue Honda Civic on the ANPR pulling into a petrol station in Cupar last night with the same number. I've sent Mhairi to pull the CCTV records from the petrol station. Jackie's been trying to track it, and she thinks she's found where it's at.'

Gilchrist forced his tone level, in anticipation of another disappointment. 'Got an address?' he asked.

She grinned. 'Is the Pope a Catholic?' she said, and skipped down the stairs.

Outside, Frazier was still on his mobile, grim-faced, tight-lipped, staring hard at the ground. Gilchrist turned his back to him, and walked through the pend, Jessie by his side.

'I take it you're not going to advise him of this latest lead,' she said.

'And get chewed out again if it turns up another dead end?' He shook his head. 'He has my number. He can call me.' He stuffed his hands into his pockets, and shivered off a wintry chill. Or maybe it was anger. 'Get Mhairi and Jackie to find out what they can about this latest address.'

'Got it.'

Kennoway lay sixteen miles south-west of St Andrews, about a couple of miles west of the town of Leven on the Firth of Forth. Gilchrist decided to take the B939 which passed the southern edge of Strathkinness, holding his speed between eighty and ninety, and slowing down only where necessary. Pitscottie was little more than a cluster of buildings either side of the road. He ignored the thirty speed limit and thundered through it at sixty. Ceres was more built up, and he was forced to slow down to fifty. Once past the town limits, he accelerated fast, powering up to the ton, only slowing down to sixty as he raced through Craigrothie.

'You ever get done for speeding?' Jessie said.

'Haven't you asked me that before?'

Beyond Craigrothie, he connected with the A916, and this time topped the ton.

Jessie sat beside him in silence, showing interest in her mobile, although he suspected she was not an advocate of his fast driving. When he braked hard, to a sedate forty at the sign for the town of Kennoway, she pressed her hands to the dashboard. Keeping below the speed limit for a change, he followed directions on his satnav. When he turned into a complex of modern bungalows with roughcast and brick facades, and paved driveways that led past well-kept gardens to brick garages with painted doors, Jessie hissed a curse.

'Not what I expected,' she said.

'What were you expecting?'

'Not this. This seems quite tidy. Expensive. A nice place to live.' She peered through the windscreen. 'Why's it called Forth View? I can't see the Forth from here. Can you?'

'Maybe from some houses, you can.'

He indicated right and eased into a side street. There the houses seemed more pristine, gardens more manicured, even exotic. He eyed the street numbers until he found the address, and continued at a slow pace to the end of the road where he did a U-turn and drew to a halt past the entrance to a neighbouring driveway. From there, they had an unrestricted view of the address they were looking for.

Now it was Gilchrist's turn to be surprised. A pair of small palm trees stood in two varnished wooden plant boxes either side of an intricately paved driveway, trunks pruned crisp and clean like the rind of a pineapple. Evergreen bushes, trimmed as square as plastic boxes, lined a gentle incline to a brick garage with two doors. Both doors were closed, but in front of one sat a blue Honda Civic, looking tired and out of sorts, and most definitely out of place, as if it had returned from a long journey in the dark, and been parked there by mistake, sight unseen. Not like the house, where windows sparkled, wood glistened, and gutters and roof tiles were as good as steam-cleaned.

The term OCD flashed through Gilchrist's mind.

'Registration number plate matches,' Jessie said. 'So that's it.' She shifted in her seat, about to unclip her seatbelt.

'Let's wait a minute,' Gilchrist said.

'What for?'

'I think I saw some movement behind the blinds,' he lied.

'You did?' Jessie peered at the house, but from where they were parked, and with the angle of the sunlight, it was impossible to see through the front window. 'Well, they're home, so that's a good thing.'

'Maybe.'

Jessie seemed puzzled by his stillness. 'What's the matter?'

What could he tell her? That now they were here, he was having second thoughts? Would it not have been more prudent to have organised back-up? Not to mention obtaining a search warrant? That if two cars were in the double garage, and one was on the driveway, did that mean there were at least three people at home? And if they were who they were looking for – Tap McCrear, Terence Garson, and this mystery woman, Deeps – could they be armed and dangerous? But in the end, he kept his thoughts to himself, and said, 'Let's give it a few minutes first.'

'If you insist.' Jessie slouched in the passenger seat, and glared at the bungalow.

'Call Mhairi,' he said, 'and see if she's come up with anything on the address.'

He kept his eyes on the house while Jessie made the call. Her voice drifted from his hearing as the warnings of his own instincts sounded out to him, his gut niggling, telling him that something was wrong about this set-up – the Honda Civic with the fake number plates; the abandoned flats in St Andrews. It seemed as if they were chasing shadows, one second there they were, and the next . . . gone, like smoke in fog. Registration numbers altered with black tape that turned a seven into a two. Or white tape to change an E to an F. Or a combination of both that could change numbers to letters and vice versa, with the ease of an illusionist. Of course, you could always fabricate a new number plate, but that involved screwdrivers and the physical swapping of metal plates. Not as simple as tape.

It seemed that nothing was as it appeared any more. How could it be in this digital age in which you could hide your identity under false names, transfer millions of pounds to some foreign account in a different currency at the tap of a key, talk to someone on the other side of the world, face to face, as if they were only next door? Nothing seemed to have any physical existence any more, as if reality existed in the digital ether, a manmade medium you could neither see nor touch, a brand new universe constructed of binary digits, the basic principles of computer language, the simplest of forms – two choices.

On or off. Nothing in between.

Two choices. Not three . . .

He pulled himself upright, and stared through the windscreen. Nothing had moved. Nothing had changed. Or had it? In those last reflective moments had everything changed?

'You're never going to believe it,' Jessie said.

He faced her with a start. 'Believe what?'

'That bastard McCrear. This is his sister's place.'

'His sister?' He shook his head. 'He doesn't have a sister.'

'That's what I said.' She unclipped her seatbelt. 'That's it. Let's go.'

CHAPTER 32

Gilchrist grabbed Jessie's arm, the move so sudden that she bumped her head.

'What?' she said, and slumped back into her seat.

'Close the door.'

She did, then rubbed her sleeve. 'This jacket cost an arm and a leg, so it did.'

'I thought you didn't spend a lot on clothes.'

She stopped rubbing, then smiled. 'Actually, I bought it in a sale. Seventy pounds for twenty. A wee bargain.' She sat back, sniffed, stared through the windscreen. 'Okay. Want to tell me what's got you worked up?'

'I can't help thinking that this is a set-up. McCrear's expecting us. He's waiting for us.' A cold frisson ran the length of his spine at the thought that his name really could be on the murder list. 'Or more correctly, he's waiting for *me*.'

She squinted through the windscreen. 'You said you saw someone inside. Maybe we should call for back-up.'

He didn't want to confess that he'd lied, that he'd wanted an excuse not to approach the address. Not just yet, anyway. 'Could've been a reflection. A passing cloud maybe.'

She eyed the cloud-laden sky. 'Yeah, could've been.' Then back to peering through the windscreen. 'So . . . you think they're in, or not?'

'Does Mhairi have a number for this house?'

'A landline, you mean?'

'What else?'

'Nobody uses these things any more.'

'Give it a try.'

'Hang on,' she said, and worked her fingers and thumbs over her mobile phone like a speed typist, then stared at the screen as if expecting it to spew out an answer. It took Mhairi all of twenty seconds to respond. 'Got it,' Jessie said, and read out the number.

Gilchrist entered it into his mobile, and put the call through the car's speaker system. The double burring of the landline sounded loud enough for the neighbours to hear.

'What're you going to say?' Jessie asked.

He held up his hand for her to be quiet, as he counted the number of rings. If the call wasn't picked up, it would likely go into voicemail after six or seven rings. But twenty rings later, it was still burring away. He ended the call.

'What does that tell us?' Jessie said. 'There's no one in? Or the phone's not set up for messages? Or they're all just sitting around too lazy to pick it up?'

'Are we sure that's the right number?'

'Want me to try?' She tapped her mobile's screen pad, put the call onto speaker, and sat back, phone in the flat of her hand. After ten rings, she ended the call. 'No one's in,' she said. 'Why don't we sniff around first, talk to a few of the neighbours?' She slid her mobile into her pocket. 'Of course, we could apply for a search warrant and come back and do the place in.' She grinned. 'I like that idea.'

Why not, indeed, he thought. They had the Honda Civic sitting in the driveway of a house that was apparently owned by McCrear's sister – even though he didn't have a sister. So who really owned the place?

He nudged Jessie. 'Did McCrear's sister have a name?'

'Hang on.' Back to her mobile, then, 'Jennifer.'

'Jennifer McCrear?' He let the name filter through his senses. Somehow, the sound of it didn't sit right with him. He tried it out in his mind, his thoughts whispering the name.

Jennifer? Jennifer? It sounded too . . . what?

Too proper for a criminal like McCrear to have as a sister?

He would have expected a name like Jenny, perhaps. Or Jen. But not Jennifer.

He eyed the address again, focused on the lounge window for a long moment, before taking in the other homes in the street, left and right, then three opposite. He had to say that McCrear's house had to be the tidiest of them all, and probably the entire estate. He shuffled in his seat, and said, 'Let me call Mhairi and see if she has anything on McCrear's sister.'

But when he got through and asked for a profile on Jennifer McCrear, Mhairi said, 'That's the problem, sir. Jackie's already on it, and she can't find anything on her.'

'Like she doesn't exist?'

'We're not sure, sir, but something's not right.'

He opened the car door – Jessie did likewise – and stepped into a cold easterly wind. *Something's not right*. Where had he heard that before? 'You know where we're at,' he said to Mhairi. 'Get back to me if you come up with anything.'

'Will do, sir.'

He ended the call, and walked towards Jessie.

'How do you want to handle this?' she said. 'Some neighbourly investigation first?'

They'd already placed two calls to the landline, without success. So it was likely that the house was deserted. And with that thought came a sense of urgency to look around the property before anyone returned; maybe take a few photographs, check out the garage, or the Honda Civic on the driveway.

'Let's go,' he said, and strode towards the address.

Up close, the Honda Civic looked scruffier, its paintwork dulled with road grime and hardened spots of bird shit. The driveway had no overhanging trees, so the bird shit told him this was not its normal parking spot, but somewhere else – not locked in a garage, but parked outside overnight in some place under the branches of trees.

'It's not locked,' Jessie said, opening the passenger's door with a click. She leaned in, opened the glove compartment, and removed a compact folder from which she pulled out a well-thumbed owner's manual, and an insurance certificate, which she read. 'The insurance covers Jennifer McCrear as the sole driver.'

Gilchrist glanced around him, the hairs on the back of his neck upright with the oddest sense that someone was watching them. He let his gaze drift around the back garden, hover at windows of neighbouring homes, then back to the Civic. Jessie was scrabbling for something that had fallen between the driver's and passenger's seat.

'What've you got?' he said.

She grunted from the effort of working in too tight a space. 'Thought I had it there, but it's slipped from my grip.'

'Let me have a go.' He pressed a lever, and pushed the seat forward. 'That better?'

'Smart arse.' She held up an RBS bank card, a smile across her face. 'Well well well. Who would've imagined? T. Garson. Valid through June of next year. Bet he doesn't even know it's missing.'

'Have Jackie check it out,' he ordered. He pulled himself away from the stale stench of cigarette ash as Jessie poked her fingers into an overflowing ashtray, and walked to the boot of the car. He opened it, and eyed the interior, taking in the tidy compartment, the dust-free matting, the gleaming metal around the boot lid itself. The faintest aroma of all things floral wafted in the air. The boot space was immaculate, tidy, nothing out of place, not like the rest of the car, telling him that all was not as it seemed. The car could do with being steam cleaned, even stripped back to bare metal and repainted. Or better still, scrapped. Whereas the boot, its rubber linings, and carpet matting could have been brand new—

'Found this in the ashtray,' Jessie said, holding a wrinkled piece of paper that looked as if it had been unfolded from being scrunched into a tight ball. 'Another phone number.'

'Mobile?'

'Landline. Area code 0141. Glasgow. Want me to call it?'

Something warned him to hold back. 'Get Jackie to find the address first.'

She tapped her mobile's screen, then, job done, tugged at her jacket, and eyed the back garden. 'Jackie'll get back to us as soon as. She's good at that.'

Gilchrist felt the vibration in his pocket from his own mobile. He removed it – ID Cooper – and stepped away to take the call. 'Yes, Becky.'

'Sux,' she said.

'Excuse me?'

'Short for suxamethonium chloride, or succinylcholine.'

He was sure he'd heard of it before, but didn't want to show his ignorance by saying the wrong thing. 'And what's that when it's at home?'

'Want me to tell you how I found it?'

He pressed his mobile hard to his ear, glanced at Jessie, and found himself walking out of her earshot. Cooper's husky whisper had failed to disguise the excitement in her tone. She had found something. 'I'm listening,' he said.

'I was puzzled as to why there were no drugs present, or puncture wounds visible on any of the victims. But I found one on Moorhouse—'

'A puncture wound? As in – left by a syringe?'

'Top of the class.'

'So why no puncture wounds on the others?'

'You should be asking why I found a puncture wound on Moorhouse.'

He pressed his lips tight. This was what he disliked about Cooper, teasing him with titbits of information, or innuendo of one sort or another. She used to tease him in all shapes and forms, and he forced thoughts of their past relationship from his mind. 'Okay, Becky, why did you find a puncture wound on Moorhouse?'

'Because there were two.'

'Puncture wounds?'

She sighed. 'Yes, Andy. Two puncture wounds.'

Silent, he waited for her to continue.

'Two because Moorhouse was seriously underweight, and not in good health. Sux is administered by injection into either a vein or a muscle. Injecting into a vein is preferable, but takes a certain level of precision. Into a muscle can be done with a jab. Which is how I expect the others were injected.'

Questions clattered into Gilchrist's mind like hailstones, but he shoved them aside, trying hard to stay with the flow. 'Okay. So the first jab into Moorhouse's arm—'

'Try buttock.'

'. . . into Moorhouse's buttock failed to work. But the second one did.'

'Correct. But not as planned, I suspect.'

'What do you mean?'

'You need to learn to control that impatience of yours, Andy.'

He pursed his lips, looked off to the distance. Jessie was correct. You couldn't see the River Forth. He shifted his mobile to his other ear. 'Well, Becky, you have an irritating habit of making me impatient, but before you start, why don't you explain to me how this succil-whatsitsname works? That way, you'll have a better chance of me not interrupting.'

'Okay,' she said, and he thought he caught the tail-end of a sigh. 'Sux is a fast-acting depolarising neuromuscular block, which in layman's terms means it's a muscle relaxant for intravenous administration as an adjunct to general anaesthesia. It's used to facilitate tracheal intubation during surgery, for example, or mechanical ventilation. It works by relaxing every muscle in the body to the point where the muscles are unresponsive to stimulation. If you're injected with it, in seconds you can't breathe, you can't blink, you can't do anything—'

'So you die?'

'Without assisted ventilation you would die within minutes.' She seemed unperturbed by his interruption. 'You may recall in my PM report on Adam Soutar that I'd noted minor damage to his larynx. I didn't give it much thought at the time, because other than a low level of alcohol, his toxicology was clean. But if he'd been injected with sux, and had to be kept alive for whatever reason, he would have been intubated. In which case, the damage to his larynx could have been caused by a laryngoscope being inserted by someone not particularly skilled in the procedure.'

'Jesus, Becky, are you saying he was paralysed by this sux stuff, then kept alive by artificial means?'

'I'm saying he *might* have been. I can only surmise.'

Gilchrist's mind sparked with questions, but the most demanding one was, 'Once you're injected with this stuff, how long does it last? Hours?'

'No. An average-sized man would be completely paralysed in about twenty seconds, and wouldn't be able to breathe for at least a further five minutes, maybe longer depending on the dosage and the individual's physiology. Recovery would then follow.'

An image of Adam Soutar seared into Gilchrist's mind. If anyone was the physical opposite of Moorhouse, Adam Soutar was. A man the size of Soutar being overcome with a jab in the buttocks just didn't compute. 'There was no evidence of any struggle in any of the victims,' he said. 'It takes about twenty seconds to react, you said. Wouldn't someone put up a struggle in that time? I think I would.'

'Yes and no. As soon as you're injected, you might snap with surprise, or from a nip of pain. But within seconds you'd feel something wrong with your eyes, or your fingers. A few seconds later, you would have difficulty breathing. Panic would set in, as would thoughts of dying. The last thing you'd be thinking of doing would be to attack whoever injected you. Your primary and most basic thought would be trying to breathe.' She seemed to catch her own breath at that moment, then said, 'But the worst of it is, you'd still be wide awake, your other senses all working as normal. Although you couldn't move your eyes,' she added, as if to correct herself.

'My God. It sounds terrifying.'

'Terrifying is one word that fits the bill.'

'But wouldn't it stop the heart?'

'Sux has no direct effect on the myocardium. In someone with high blood pressure, say, or a history of heart problems, it could have an indirect side effect, and cause cardiac arrest. But in a healthy individual it invokes respiratory paralysis.' A pause, then, 'But the difficulty with it from an investigative point of view, is that enzymes in the body break it down quickly, almost immediately, so by the time the body is on the PM table, there's no sux left to test. Testing would prove negative, making it almost impossible to detect, because its metabolites are all naturally occurring molecules.'

'*Almost* impossible . . .?'

She chuckled. 'You never miss a trick, do you? For want of a better word, we got *lucky* with Moorhouse. He was far from healthy, and died from heart failure, most likely within seconds of being injected. Even though sux was present in his body, with his system shut down metabolites were traceable, most notably succinylmonocholine, for which I'd requested a marker on his toxicology.'

At that moment, Gilchrist caught Jessie's eye, and her nod to come and have a look at this. He could think of only one more question to ask, and said, 'If the others were injected with sux, there must be a puncture wound, right?'

'But the condition of the body, the age of the victim, can make it difficult to—'

'So you missed them?'

She hesitated for a couple of beats, then said, 'Yes.'

He thought she sounded deflated, as if reluctant to admit that she'd slipped up, she'd made a mistake, and despite her experience she was only human after all. But he had no time to go into that, and no need to give her a hard time. 'Becky, I've got to go. But I want you to revisit the other victims. If they've been injected with sux, we need to be one hundred per cent certain that a syringe was the murder weapon, and sux was the drug of choice.'

She tutted, as if annoyed. 'I'll do that, Andy. Ciao.'

The line died.

He shoved his mobile into his pocket and walked towards Jessie. He found her at the rear of the bungalow, one foot on the step that led to the back door.

When she saw him, she said, 'How's Queen Becky?'

'She wasn't asking after you, if that's what you're meaning.'

'She find anything worthwhile?'

'Sux,' he said.

'Aye, right. And I bet she's good at it. That's all I'm going to say about that.' Then she nodded to the door. 'What do you think of this?' She poked the door with her finger, and it cracked open. 'Not just unlocked,' she said, and ran the palm of her gloved hand down the edge of the door. 'The lock's been taped back.'

'What?' A silver strip of heavy-duty duct tape about a foot long ran down the door edge, covering the catch, effectively leaving the house open to the elements. Just then, the wind picked up. The door swung about a quarter open, then shivered, as if something on the inside was preventing it from opening fully. He pushed. 'Something's stopping it.' He leaned in as he pressed the door wide to expose a pair of boots and denim-covered legs.

Jessie held up a wallet. 'Removed this from his back pocket,' she said. 'It's Terence Garson.'

'Call it in,' he said.

'Already done that.'

CHAPTER 33

By the time Frazier arrived, the SOCOs had sealed off the driveway, and were setting up forensic analysis of the property and the body. Gilchrist and Jessie had already confirmed the bungalow was deserted, and that whoever had murdered Garson was long gone. Frazier had done his usual, obtaining a search warrant at the speed of light, which he'd slapped against Gilchrist's chest before pacing around the perimeter of the back lawn, mobile to his ear. When he finished his call, he snapped at his coat, snecked a couple of buttons shut, then strode towards Gilchrist and Jessie, looking like an unstoppable force about to meet a moveable object.

Up close, the whites of his eyes were bloodshot, a sign that he was struggling under the strain of the case, and nowhere near as invincible as he portrayed. His breath reeked of mouthwash. 'Okay, DCI Gilchrist,' he said, his voice loud enough to alert the neighbours. 'Once again you're first at the scene of a murder while the rest of my team are running about like chickens with their heads chopped off.' He sniffed hard, squared his shoulders. 'This is becoming a bit of a habit.'

'Running about like headless chickens?' Jessie said.

Frazier glared at her. 'Fancy yourself as a comedian, do you?'

'*Enne*.'

'What?'

'*Enne*. It's comedi*enne*.'

To Gilchrist's surprise, Frazier's lips rearranged themselves into a smile. Then he nodded at Jessie, and said, 'You found it. The body, I mean.'

'Yes, sir.' Jessie had gone from flippant to respectful in a matter of seconds, as if she realised her quip was out of order, and didn't want to spend the rest of her working years dishing out speeding tickets. 'From our initial examination of the deceased, sir, DCI Gilchrist and I suspect that the drug succinylcholine might be the cause of the death.'

'Do you now?'

'Yes, sir.'

'Care to explain, DS Janes?'

'No obvious wounds, sir. No signs of trauma that we can find. Body's not stone cold, and rigor hasn't fully formed, so we're estimating time of death to be sometime mid-morning. Although Doctor Cooper would need to confirm that, sir.'

'Yes, she would.' Frazier seemed to give Jessie's words some thought, then faced Gilchrist. 'Death by succinylcholine is quite the quantum leap. Do you agree?'

For a moment, Gilchrist felt confused. Was he being asked to agree if it was death by succinylcholine, or that their conclusions were a quantum leap? He played safe. 'I've been talking to Doctor Cooper, and she confirmed that Moorhouse's toxicology came back with traces of sux metabolites. So without any clear evidence of trauma, we're fairly confident that the same MO was used, that whoever killed Moorhouse, killed Garson.'

'And the others, too?'

'We believe so, but now we suspect sux, Doctor Cooper is having more toxicology done on the others. She'll get back to us the moment she knows more.' He didn't know if Cooper was going ahead with more toxicology, or if it was too late for further tests, given how quickly sux broke down. But sometimes all you can do is play your cards.

Frazier let it out in a frustrated gush. 'Succinylcholine. The perfect poison, although strictly speaking it's not a poison at all. You can't buy it over the counter. It's used in hospitals. So the killer has to have some connection to the medical profession.'

'We're already looking into that, sir,' Gilchrist lied.

'If memory serves, the first recorded case of someone being found guilty of murder by succinylcholine was in the States in the mid-sixties. But I haven't heard of it being used in the UK.' He looked at Gilchrist as if for confirmation, then eyed the body on the floor. The police photographer had come and gone, and Garson's hands were bagged and tied. 'At times like this, you can't help but feel sorry for him. If it was succinylcholine, he would've known he was dying.' He shook his head at his words of wisdom. 'And there would've been nothing he could do about it.'

Gilchrist followed Frazier's line of sight.

Garson stared at the ceiling, sightless eyes wide open, as if from the shock of knowing he was about to die. A couple of days' growth covered his cheeks and neck like fungus. Grey hair, thinning and tied back with rubber bands in a tight ponytail, exaggerated the roundness of a face that still retained the tell-tale flush of a heavy drinker and smoker. Even in death, Garson's body gave off a taint of cigarette ash.

All of a sudden Frazier turned away, as if he'd seen enough. 'Okay,' he said, focusing on Gilchrist. 'What does this body mean to us? Anything?'

'We're closer to McCrear than we think,' Gilchrist said. 'He's beginning to unravel. Maybe even panic. Whatever team he'd gathered around him, is now breaking up. Why else would Garson end up dead?'

'Criminals fall out with each other all the time,' Frazier said. 'That's the nature of the beast. Maybe McCrear's not unravelling at all. Maybe he's just moving on. Take the flats in St Andrews. Both deserted, abandoned. What does that tell us?'

'It tells me that we're dealing with someone who's smart, maybe smarter than we give him credit for.'

Jessie said, 'I agree with DCI Gilchrist. McCrear's cracking.' She nodded at the body on the floor. 'Garson's murder was never part of the plan. But it also tells me that McCrear thinks on his feet, and isn't afraid to take risks, change his plan.'

Silent, Frazier nodded, contemplating her words. Then he eyed Gilchrist. 'What do we know about Garson?'

Gilchrist struggled to recall Jackie's report. 'In his early forties, sir. Married. Wife is Meghan Morton, hence the flat in Market Street. Separated, or divorced, we don't know yet which. Started out as a brickie's labourer, got fired for drinking on the job. Worked wherever he could find it, but never held down anything for long. Been on the dole for the last ten years.'

'So what's his connection to McCrear?'

'We're still trying to work that out, sir. But we suspect he was the driver.'

'As in . . .?'

'He'd drive McCrear to his next victim, then drive him back. We don't believe he participated in any of the killings.'

Frazier nodded to the Civic. 'That his?'

'His wife's, sir.'

'And this house belongs to McCrear's sister, I'm told.'

'Apparently, sir.'

'Anyone spoken to her yet?'

'That's the problem, sir. We can't find anything on her.'

'She has no criminal record?'

Gilchrist said, 'As far as we're aware, sir, McCrear's never married, and he doesn't have a sister. So she doesn't appear to exist.'

Frazier grimaced. 'So it's a fake name, is what you're saying?'

'It would appear so, sir, but it doesn't make sense—'

'What doesn't?'

'If McCrear was going to use a fake name, why come up with one using his own surname?'

'Mm. Good point.' Frazier seemed lost for words until his mobile appeared in his hand as if by magic. 'Well, there must be a reason for it. Ask around. Find out who the hell she is. And pull out all the stops to find McCrear. Somebody must know where he's at.' And with that, he stepped away, mobile to his ear.

Gilchrist raked his fingers through his hair. He was beginning to see Frazier for what he was – a man who believed that by barking orders and bullying his way through the masses, it was only a matter of time until he climbed to the top of the tree.

'Did you see the way he looked at the body?' Jessie said. 'I thought he was going to faint. You think he's ever attended a post mortem?'

'I wouldn't know. But if he ever does, let's make sure it's not ours.'

'Now there's a thought. Me lying there, stretched out on Queen Becky's table about to be cut up by her.' She made a show of giving a shiver. Just then, her mobile beeped. She eyed the screen. 'Don't you just love Jackie? She found that address in Glasgow. Great Western Road.' She gave a dry whistle. 'Rule of thumb – the bigger the number, the more upmarket the address. So what I'm thinking is, how come a deadbeat – excuse the pun – like Garson has a phone number for a decent address?'

'Who said Garson put the number in the ashtray? We're thinking he's the driver. So it could've been any one of his passengers.'

'No, I don't think so. It's *Garson's*.'

He caught Jessie's emphasis. 'Okay, let's have it.'

'You used to smoke, but you now stay clear of all things nicotine, right?'

'Mostly,' he said, although every once in a while he would catch the whiff of second-hand smoke that would initiate a craving that had him stuffing his hands into his pockets, and walking away in search of fresh air.

'You tell me that smoking's a filthy habit, and smokers are filthy people, so as a non-smoker do you think you're going to scrunch up a bit of paper with a phone number on it, and bury it into a filthy ashtray?' She shook her head. 'Not on your nelly, you're not.'

'Maybe the passenger smoked.'

'McCrear? Obsessive compulsive? Tidier than a virgin nun?'

'Other passengers?'

'No chance. Garson drives McCrear and no one else. End of.'

Gilchrist turned into the wind, breathed in air cold enough to nip his nostrils. What was it about Scotland? Where was summer when you needed it? Or spring, for that matter. Jessie's rationale was flawed. But it did have merit. And did it matter if the number had been put in the ashtray by Garson or one of his passengers? No. What did matter was they now had an address for a property in Glasgow.

He faced Jessie. 'Okay. Let's go and check it out.' As he turned to walk to his car, he caught Frazier signalling to him.

'Uh-oh,' said Jessie. 'This looks like trouble.'

'DI Barnes has just called in,' Frazier said. 'They've found the white van. It was pulled over on the M74 south, outside Baillieston. More than likely heading to England.'

Or anywhere in the south of Scotland, Gilchrist thought. But with Frazier, you just had to chew what he force-fed you, then spit it out later if you had to.

'I want you and DI Barnes to interview the driver right away,' Frazier said to Gilchrist. 'She's been taken to the Cumbernauld Office.'

Gilchrist frowned, confused for a moment. 'She? Did she give a name?'

Frazier flashed a white smile. 'Jennifer McCrear.'

CHAPTER 34

Before heading off to meet DI Barnes at the Cumbernauld Office, Gilchrist instructed Mhairi to team up with Jessie and check out the Great Western Road address. He had a sense that the property was not important, that checking it out was nothing more than a box to be ticked, but he didn't want to take any chances. He tasked Jackie with researching ownership of the property and, if rented out, the letting history. If the note recovered from the Honda's ashtray had indeed been put there by Garson, and Jackie found anything that hinted of even the slightest bit of danger, then Jessie and Mhairi were to stand down, and contact him immediately.

In the Cumbernauld Office, Gilchrist was led into the same open-plan space in which he'd first met Barnes. She was seated at her desk, her attention fixed on the monitor in front of her. On seeing him, she pushed to her feet, jerked a tight smile and, without introduction, said, 'This way.'

He followed her skinny figure – pipe-cleaner jeans, no hips, no shoulders, no shape at all, when it came down to it – along a dingy corridor at the end of which she pushed open a door and stepped into a room without a backward glance.

The interview room in the Cumbernauld Office was your common or garden spartan police room – grey walls, metal table, four chairs and a recording device. Two women were already seated at the table; Jennifer McCrear and the duty solicitor, who was dressed for the part – navy-blue trouser suit, white blouse, diamond rings on each tanned hand, short blonde hair with a black-rooted parting. McCrear on the other hand looked Gothic, with a hint of ethnicity in a pale face exaggerated by jet-black hair, loose-fitting black sweater, black denim jeans. Silver hoops as thick as bracelets looped through and around the cartilage of both ears like metal bindings, as if to lead the viewer's eye away from a row of tiny diamond studs that ran above her top lip like a sparkling Salvador Dalí moustache. Thick-soled studded boots finished off the image.

Gilchrist took his seat next to Barnes with the oddest sense of being out of place.

Barnes clicked on the recorder, stated day and date, added the time, and said, 'Present are DI Ella Barnes, Strathclyde Police; DCI Andrew Gilchrist, Fife Constabulary,' which caused a stiffening in McCrear's posture. Barnes picked up a business card pushed across the table, and pressed on with the introductions. 'Ms Chloe Haddow, solicitor with Parkes Reid and Associates; and Mrs Jennifer McCrear, who was detained this afternoon for driving a suspected stolen vehicle, and who is now being interviewed under caution.' She read McCrear her rights again, then pressed on with the interview.

'You were pulled over this afternoon on the M74,' she said, 'driving a white Ford van registered in the name of Terence Garson. How do you know Terence?'

'I've never met him, so I don't know him,' she said.

'So you stole his van, did you?'

'No. I was given the keys and told to drive it down the M74.'

'You were *told* to?'

'Aye, you know, someone says something, and I listen.'

'You always do as you're told?'

'Only if I feel like it.'

'So who gave you the keys and told you to drive down the M74?'

'My husband.'

'And his name?'

'Tap McCrear.'

Gilchrist raised his hand to interrupt. 'You're saying you're Tap McCrear's wife?'

'That's what I said, aye.'

'And he gave you the keys to the van?'

'Aye.'

'So where's Tap now?'

'Off on a job.'

'Off on a job? What kind of a job?'

'Don't know. He travels a lot, so I don't expect to see him again for a month or so.'

'Overseas, is he?'

'Didnae say. But aye, probably.'

Gilchrist focused on her eyes, struck by how white they were. She returned his gaze with defiance. Lips tight at the edges spoke of a short lifetime of protesting against authority. She could be every bit at home in a police cell as in some rehabilitation centre. And young enough to be Tap's daughter, not his wife. She was lying. Of that Gilchrist was certain. Or probably more correctly, she was spinning a yarn, mixing fact with fiction. Which worked in his favour in a roundabout way – easier to keep track of untruths. But rather than struggle to work out what was truth or not, if you asked why she was here in the first place – arrested while driving a van that Tap must surely have known was on the radar of every police force in the nation – you came up with a different answer.

Best to focus on that, and start off with some facts.

He opened his notebook, made a show of making sure his pen worked. 'What's your maiden name?'

'Bexall.'

He jotted it down. 'Jennifer Bexall?'

'Aye.'

'Any middle names?'

'Smith.'

He smiled. Separating fact from fiction was not difficult. 'We'll check it out,' he said, 'so it's pointless hiding anything from us.'

'Deirdre Theresa.'

'Jennifer Deirdre Theresa Bexall.' He wrote it down. 'Date of birth?' She told him, and a quick mental calculation put her in her mid-thirties, old enough to give Tap a complete step-family. 'And your address before you married Tap?'

She told him – some street in Glasgow, which for all he knew of the city might be round the corner from the address in Great Western Road. He glanced at the recorder to make sure it was taking it all in.

'So . . . Tap's away on a job, to some place you don't know where.' He fixed her with his hardest stare. 'When did you last see him?'

'Yesterday.'

'Morning? Afternoon?'

'Morning. Tap's a morning person. So we shagged first thing.' Her eyes flickered to Barnes. 'He's some man, so he is. And then he left.'

'Have you heard from him since? Has he phoned?'

'Not yet. He said there was no reception where he was going.'

'Now that's interesting,' Gilchrist said, 'because if there's no reception where Tap has gone to, how could he tell you to drive the van down the M74?'

Her eyes widened as she searched for a way out of her lie. 'He told me before he left.'

She seemed pleased with herself, but he didn't challenge her. 'And when did you and Tap get married?'

'Just the other day.'

'The other day,' he repeated. 'Like, yesterday? The day before? When exactly?'

'Sunday.'

'Sunday when and where?'

'At home, about two.'

'So where's home?'

'I've already told youse my address.'

'I'm trying to confirm that you got married at *your* home. Not at Tap's.'

'We got married in my flat.'

'Who officiated?'

'Who offishi-what?'

'Who performed the wedding ceremony?'

'Don't know his name. Some friend of Tap's.'

'A priest?'

'Fuck that. Tap and I are no intae Jesus and all that shite.'

'And where does Tap live?'

She gave him the address in Forth View in which they'd found Terence Garson's body. He jotted a note to remind himself to have the SOCOs check for her DNA in the house. 'So, how long have you and Tap known each other?'

'A while.'

'How long?'

'Can't really say.'

'Ten years? One year? What?'

'About a year.'

'Less than a year?'

'Aye, maybe.'

'We'll check it out, so it's pointless covering for him.'

'About three months.'

'Maybe closer to two months?'

She shrugged. 'Maybe.'

'Maybe closer to one month?'

Something swept through her at that, some emotion that darkened her eyes and had her shifting in her seat with irritation. 'I love Tap, and he loves me. And if we didnae date long enough to keep youse lot happy, who gives a fuck?'

Gilchrist sat back, a signal for Barnes to continue.

'Did you know the van was wanted in connection with a series of recent murders?' Barnes said.

'I wondered why I was pulled over. I wisnae even speeding or nothing. Just minding my own business, driving down the M74—'

'To where?'

'Naewhere. Just driving.'

'Until Tap told you to turn around and drive back?'

'Aye.'

'How was he going to do that if he'd no reception?'

She shuffled in her chair, glanced at her solicitor who raised her pencilled eyebrows for a moment, then returned her attention to her notepad. So much for legal advice. 'Aye, well, he told me no to go too far. Just drive until I got fed up, then drive back.'

'So what was the purpose of you driving the van?'

Gilchrist thought he knew, but he said nothing, just focused on Jennifer's eyes.

She seemed to have recovered from her mini-stumble. 'To send a message.'

Barnes frowned. 'Send a message? What kind of message would driving a van down the M74 send? And who was the message to be sent to?'

'You don't have to answer that,' her solicitor said.

But McCrear ignored her, placed both arms on the table and leaned forward, as if to let Gilchrist know that this was the purpose of her driving the van, knowing she would be pulled over, knowing she would be arrested and interviewed, and that this was the moment she'd been waiting for.

'Tap said to me, so he did, when he was stone cold sober, exact words, he said – I want you to tell that skinny Detective Chief Inspector from St Andrews that he's in my sights, and I'm gonnae get him, I'm gonnae come after him, and that it's nae use hiding, because I'm gonnae get him and I'm gonnae gut him bone dry for what he done to me.'

She sat back.

Gilchrist said. 'Verbatim?'

'Ver-what?'

'Tap's exact words?'

'Aye.'

'Did he give you the name of the skinny Detective Chief Inspector from St Andrews?'

'Andrew James Gilchrist.'

Her lips peeled open to reveal a pretty smile that seemed at odds with the ugliness of Tap's message, and let him see that she could be more than just attractive if she binned the steel hoops and diamond studs. But it raised the question – what on earth did Jennifer née Bexall see in the likes of Tap McCrear? And as he watched her watch him, he knew from the tight smirk that tugged her lips that she'd said all she'd been told to say, that Tap's message had been delivered to him loud and clear, and wouldn't he be so proud of her, the way she'd let him have it? Still, he thought it worth one more question.

'Did Tap have anything to add to that message?' he asked.

She frowned at him, puzzled. 'Is that no enough?' she said.

He nodded. 'Yes, it is,' then excused himself from the interview.

CHAPTER 35

After fleeing the bitter wind on the Fife coast, Jessie found Glasgow almost balmy by comparison – well, temperature in the single figures. It was spring after all. But the wind had dropped to little more than a breeze, and the clouds had shifted to leave the dying embers of a pink sunset. Dusk was settling, and the streets were lighting up for the evening, bringing the busy pubs of Glasgow to coloured life.

Jackie confirmed that the address in Great Western Road was on the books of Wilton Watson & Associates, Property Management Group, and that a one year lease had been taken out on the property two months earlier, and paid for in full in advance by Jenny Bexall. Jessie arranged for her and Mhairi to meet Craig Thurston, a senior employee of Wilton Watson, at the company's main office in Byres Road. She had just driven off the M80 onto the junction of the M8 near Alexandra Park, when her mobile rang.

She handed it to Mhairi. 'Can you answer that?'

Mhairi took the call. 'DC McBride on DS Janes's mobile.'

'Mhairi, Andy here. Where's Jessie?'

'She's driving, sir. We're almost at Glasgow city centre, sir.'

'So you haven't visited that address in Great Western Road yet?'

'No, sir. Jessie's set up a meeting at the property management company, which is where we're heading now.'

A pause, then, 'Can you put the mobile onto speaker?'

'I think so, sir. Hold on.' She fiddled with it, then said, 'I think that's it, sir.'

'Can you hear me, Jessie?'

'A bit tinny, but it'll do.'

'The property in Great Western Road's been leased to Jenny Bexall—'

'Yeah, we've got that.'

'What you might not have is, that Jenny Bexall and Jennifer McCrear are one and the same person. I don't want you to visit that address until I can arrange back-up support from Strathclyde. I'll contact Dainty, and see what we can do at short notice.'

'No problem, Andy. I'll just ream Thurston a new arsehole instead.'

'Who's Thurston?'

'An employee of the property management company, and the person we're meeting. I want to face him eye to eye when I ask how the lease was paid.'

'Why?'

'Jackie says it was paid in advance, and in full. So he's up shit creek for laundering money.'

'*Allegedly*.'

'Whatever.'

'And get the bank details. They could help us find McCrear. I'm on my way from Cumbernauld. I should be with you in about thirty minutes.'

'Bring the cavalry,' Jessie said, and ended the call.

Craig Thurston was not what Jessie expected after speaking to him on the phone. He seemed much younger than his phone voice suggested, and at well over six foot and sixteen stone – as best she could estimate – and in a dark blue business suit that looked as if it had just been collected from the laundry, or maybe purchased that afternoon, he looked every part the high-class property salesman. He welcomed Jessie with a wide smile and firm handshake, and did the same with Mhairi.

'Come in,' he said. 'Come into my office. Can I interest youse in tea, coffee?'

'We're all tea-ed out,' Jessie said, and held out her arm for Thurston to lead the way.

In his office, he adjusted two seats, pulling them out for ease of access, which had Jessie saying, 'We can seat ourselves, thank you.'

Unfazed, Thurston stepped round the desk to take his own seat – a high-backed black leather swivel chair – and faced them with another smile.

'Are these all yours?' Jessie asked, nodding to a display of framed certificates that lined the wall like artwork.

'They are, yes.'

'Looks like you've got a full house.'

'Well, thank you. I do put in the effort to keep myself current with the business.'

'I'm sure you do.'

'And I'm proudest of that one,' he said, waiting for Jessie and

Mhairi to see what he was pointing to. 'Scottish Property Manager of the Year,' he said.

'That's two years ago,' Jessie said. 'What happened since then?'

'Well, not everyone wins one of these.'

'I see.'

Thurston cleared his throat, and forced another smile. 'You've come all the way to Glasgow from Fife, so . . . what can I do for youse?'

'Firstly,' Jessie said, holding out her warrant card – Mhairi did likewise – 'we're detectives with St Andrews CID, following up on a particularly nasty individual by the name of Tap McCrear. You might have seen his name in the papers or heard about him on TV.'

'Oh, my goodness. I do recognise the name. Absolutely shocking.' He frowned at that. 'But what's any of that to do with me?'

Jessie held her notebook up so Thurston could read it. 'This is the address I asked you about on the phone earlier, right?'

He nodded.

'Is it let out as fully furnished?'

'It is.'

'And is it normal for someone to pay a whole year's rent in advance?'

'Not at all. In fact, it's never happened to me before.'

'Did that not worry you?'

'Why would it worry me? I get my commission, and the property's leased for a year.'

'Did you do a walkthrough with Jenny Bexall before you handed over the keys?'

'Well . . .'

'Isn't that normal procedure for furnished rentals? You do a walkthrough with the client, signing off on all the items listed, to make sure nothing's been nicked when the keys are handed back. Is that not how it's done?'

'It is.' He nodded. 'Yes.'

'So why didn't you do that this time?'

'Well . . . I . . .' An idea seemed to come to him. 'There was no need.'

'Why not?'

'Because she put down three months' deposit.'

'In addition to the whole year's rent?'

'Yes.'

'Cash or cheque?'

'Eh . . . I . . . eh . . . cash.'

'How much in total?'

'Fifteen, eighteen thou. I can't remember.'

'Sure you can't. Did she throw in a couple of grand as a tip for you to keep quiet?'

Thurston pursed his lips, as if knowing he was only digging himself deeper.

'Right. That's it. You're coming with us.'

'What?' Disbelief and panic swamped his face. 'You're arresting me? You can't do that. I've done nothing wrong.'

Jessie coughed a laugh. 'Oh yes you have, Sonny Jim. Money laundering. Accepting a bribe. Non declaration of income to your favourite people, HMRC. I'm sure the boys in the know will come up with some other charges that'll get you bombed out of your profession. After all, you haven't exactly performed your professional duties with the utmost integrity.' She nodded to the certificates on the wall. 'These'll mean eff all when you're in jail.

Take one last look at them.' She pushed herself to her feet, then paused. 'But I tell you what. I'm thinking that I might not arrest you. Not just yet anyway. On one condition.'

Thurston swallowed a lump in his throat. 'Anything.'

'You assist us in our ongoing investigation.'

'Of course, of course. I'm here to help. In any way I can.'

'Right. Let's go.'

But by the time Gilchrist had organised back-up support from Strathclyde, and had a search warrant for the flat scanned and printed out, ninety minutes had passed since he and Jessie had spoken. Night had fallen and smothered all vestige of daytime warmth. His breath fogged in the March chill as he eyed the sandstone building. Light spilling from the upper windows more than hinted that someone was home.

DI Barnes had refused to release Jennifer McCrear, and had less than twelve hours remaining before she had to charge her or let her go. Which was fine with Gilchrist. He didn't expect McCrear to be at the Great Western Road flat, but he was proving to be slippier than an eel in a barrel of oil, so he was taking no chances. DCI Dainty Small, Strathclyde Police, stood next to him, his eyes at Gilchrist's shoulder level.

'You ever see that movie *First Blood*?' Dainty said. 'The first Rambo movie.'

'If I did, it would've been years ago.'

Dainty nodded beyond the armed personnel in protective headgear, heavy Kevlar vests, submachine guns held in gloved grips, to where Frazier stood, mobile to his ear, worry etched across his brow. 'Frazier's like that cop played by Brian Dennehy. You remember him? The sheriff who thinks he knows it all, but is next to fucking useless. We'd all get some peace and quiet if they'd just promote that useless fucker, and get him out of our sight.'

'You've never liked him?'

'It's not a question of like or dislike, for fuck's sake. He's a fucking eyesore.' Dainty shuffled his feet, clasped his hands, and blew into them. 'Okay, here we go.'

Frazier had slipped his mobile into his jacket, and was now talking to the armed squad commander. For all the policemen present, Gilchrist was struck by the quietness. Orders were given in hushed voices, and the men shuffled forward in muted silence, and clambered up the front steps to the entrance lobby door, unlocked courtesy of Craig Thurston, who stood close enough to Jessie to give the impression of being handcuffed to her.

The armed squad took the stairs like a dumb conga line. Two police officers followed carrying the big key. Designed for easy handling, once swung it could impart a point force of three tonnes, sufficient to break most domestic locks.

On the top landing, the armed squad lined up against the back wall, allowing enough room for the Enforcer to be used. Silent, using hand signals, the squad leader counted down from three, two, one, and a body stepped forward, swung the Enforcer at the lock. Despite the doorframe cracking, the lock held. Another swing with the big key, and that time the door burst open. Armed officers rushed into the flat, voices loud and fierce with non-challengeable commands – *Armed police show yourself room clear on the left armed police kitchen clear*.

Within a minute, the flat was confirmed as being empty.

Despite Gilchrist being the first detective into the flat – Frazier noticeable by his absence; he'd given commands from the street

– it was Dainty who entered the lounge first and noticed the horror of the place.

'Ah, for fuck's sake,' he said.

Gilchrist stood by Dainty's side, his mind failing for a moment to compute what his eyes were seeing. McCrear had been here. That much was clear. Photographs were pinned to the walls, hundreds of them it seemed, in perfect horizontal and vertical rows, so many that they could have doubled for wallpaper. His gaze shifted to an antique show cabinet, then fell on a white Formica shelf not in keeping with the rest of the furniture. On the shelf, in the cabinet's shadow, sat a collection of ruby- and purple-coloured objects. At first, he thought they were candles, but as he felt himself being irresistibly drawn towards them, with dawning realisation came that first nip of rising bile, which he managed to swallow back, the whisper of Dainty's voice echoing as if from a distance.

'Just when you think you've fucking seen it all.'

CHAPTER 36

It took Gilchrist all of five seconds to recover his composure, by which time Dainty had walked past him and picked up one of the glass jars with latex-gloved hands. He held it up to the light, turning the jar to better see its contents. 'Bastard's fucking printed their names and dates on them. This one's Margaret Rickard's.' He returned the jar containing Rickard's tongue to the shelf, picked up another. 'Adam Soutar's.'

But Gilchrist had turned his attention to the show cabinet beside the Formica shelf. It was manufactured in three distinct sections – glass casements at either end, through which he saw polished shelves stacked mostly with an array of crystal glasses, glittering ornaments that sparkled with light from adjacent table lamps, sets of fine china cups and saucers. Later, Frazier would ask what compelled him to the central section of the cabinet. But Gilchrist had only been able to say, 'Because it looked locked.'

'And this one's Albert Forest's,' Dainty announced, as Gilchrist reached forward, gripped the key in the lock, turned it, felt it stiff from lack of use, then gritted his teeth and gave a hard twist of his hand. The cabinet door opened to reveal three rows of shelves stacked with glass jars, all of them empty.

'That's it,' Dainty said, holding the final jar aloft. 'They're all here.'

Gilchrist reached in and removed one of the jars, and read the label. 'Who's Petra Hampton?' he said.

'One of the jury members,' Barnes said. 'Why?'

He hadn't noticed her creep up behind him, hadn't even noticed her in the collective group on the street. But he handed the empty jar to her, pulled out another one and held it up. 'Gareth Fairfield?'

Barnes took it. 'I believe he was a member of the prosecution team.'

Dainty joined in, removed a jar and read the label, pulled out another jar, then one more. 'Jesus fuck,' he said. 'Bastard's got them all labelled. It's like a fucking to-do list.' He fell silent when he read the next jar, then handed it to Gilchrist. 'If you ever had any doubts, Andy . . .'

Gilchrist read the label – DCI Andrew James Gilchrist – then passed it to Barnes who took it from him without a word. He walked to the window, stared down at the street. A small crowd of around thirty had gathered, and stood in obedient order at the periphery of the taped area. Here and there, mobile phones flashed and lit up the scene. A pair of constables faced the mass like silent guards. From behind him, the Task Force worked in subdued silence, as if stunned by the enormity of the find.

A clap of hands broke the muted atmosphere.

'All right, listen up, everybody.' Frazier stood in the centre of the lounge, turning around in a slow circle as if to make sure he caught everybody's attention. 'I want this place photographed and fingerprinted, and everything bagged and removed to the lab for analysis. DI Barnes will be in charge of this crime scene and everything in it.'

'Yes, sir.'

'DS Lamond?'

'Sir?'

'You're in charge of door-to-doors. Somebody must know something. Did anyone see Tap McCrear entering or leaving this place? Was he alone? Was he with someone? And if so, who? And how did he get here? Car? Bus? Golden chariot, or what? Let me know if you need any resources.'

'On it, sir.'

'DI Phelan?' Frazier spun on his heels until he found her with Mhairi and Jessie, at the wall of photographs, peeling off her face-mask. 'CCTV. Every camera in the area. Check the business premises across the road. I want to see every recording ever taken since this place was rented out.'

'Yes, sir.'

'DCIs Danson and Lorimer. Have your teams track down every person whose name's on one of these jars. When you find them, make sure they're safe. Round-the-clock protection for each of them until we find this Tap McCrear. Interview them. I want written reports. Fully detailed. Nothing missed out.'

With his back still to the room, Gilchrist listened to Frazier rattling off command after command, never missing a beat, never stuttering a wrong word, ordering the collective group into a focused force, as if he were reading from a How-to-Catch-a-Killer booklet. When he heard his own name being announced, he ignored it.

A few seconds later, 'DCI Gilchrist,' the voice gentle, by his ear, then a hand on his shoulder, gripping it, massaging it. 'DI Barnes showed me.'

Gilchrist turned to him, and managed to slip the man's hand from his shoulder.

'How are you holding up?' Frazier said.

He tried a smile, didn't quite pull it off. 'I'm okay. Sure. Fine.'

Frazier's gaze swept around the room. 'I think this is what you call the motherlode.'

'But we're no closer to finding McCrear.' Gilchrist faced the street again. Through the windows in the buildings opposite, shadows in the shapes of people shifted behind closed blinds. On the road below, cars, taxis, vans, buses, stopped and started as they negotiated traffic lights. Despite their gruesome discovery, the world was going about its business, oblivious to the unseen horrors close by. 'Jennifer's the key,' he said to the glass. 'She knows where McCrear is. She has to.'

'Why?' Frazier said.

Gilchrist turned to face him. 'The fact that we're here, standing in a living room that was destined to be a shrine of sorts, tells me she's the key.' He looked around, let his gaze take in the cornicing, roman blinds, heavy velvet curtains, walls in the process of being stripped of McCrear's graphic photos, wallpaper with ghostly dust marks that showed where framed pictures had been removed in readiness for the murderous collage. 'This place was somewhere for him to put his feet up after each killing, to relax, gather his thoughts. We weren't supposed to find these jars. Not now. Not at this stage of his plans. But we did. That's because everything's changed. And it changed with Garson's murder.'

'You seem so sure. Maybe we just got lucky.'

'Garson was murdered this morning, and less than twelve hours later we're in this flat. It's not luck. McCrear had time to clear this place out. But he didn't. He let it lie. Which tells me . . . *one*, that he wanted us to find it, and *two*, that everything's changed.' He took Frazier by the shoulder, led him to a quieter spot at the other side of the room, and said, 'Tell DI Barnes to let Jennifer McCrear go. Release her. We're wasting time if we think she's going to talk. She's of no value to us locked in a cell.'

Frazier narrowed his eyes. 'And we tail her?'

'Put your best men on it. Don't give her any hint that she's being followed.'

'And you think she's going to lead us to McCrear?'

What could he say? That his sixth sense was stirring? That his gut was nipping? That McCrear was steps ahead of Frazier and his team, maybe half-a-dozen – always had been, and always would be? That McCrear was not dumb enough to let his new wife – if that's who she really was – lead the police to his door, that he was too clever for that? Which brought him to the hopeful core of his reasoning – that Jennifer would never lead them to where McCrear was, but she might lead them to where he'd been.

Which was the problem with gut feelings and sixth senses.

Nothing was tangible, let alone provable.

So he said, 'Who knows? But the game's now changed for McCrear.'

'In what way?'

He grimaced for a long second, then said, 'In every way.'

CHAPTER 37

Jennifer McCrear – née Bexall – was released from the Cumbernauld Office the following morning, Gilchrist arguing that she might suspect a set-up if she was released any earlier. Besides, it gave them time to pull in the best surveillance team in the country. Once again showing the extent of his reach, Frazier had a crack team of eight transferred overnight from the London Met, after insisting that every effort be made for them to *blend in* – English banknotes were exchanged for Scottish, and any who couldn't speak with passable Scottish accents were instructed to keep their mouths shut in public.

Back at the North Street Office, Gilchrist assigned a team to find out all they could on Jennifer Deirdre Theresa Bexall. But Jackie was already on it. Once she'd had Bexall's full name and date of birth, she'd pulled up her National Insurance records, accessed her HMRC returns and DVLA records. Despite her alleged close association with McCrear, Bexall appeared to have led a clean life. NI contributions up-to-date. PAYE income tax all in order. No outstanding demands for tax shortcomings or penalties of any kind. No points on her driving licence. No periods of unemployment, up until her not having worked since she left her secretarial job in a local warehouse in January, a period of ten weeks – of course, now she was married to McCrear, her working days were more than likely over. No drink-driving charges. No drugs offences. No markers on the Police National Computer. No cautions or arrests until being pulled over in the white van. Never married – until McCrear, that is. No children. Parents passed away in her mid-twenties. All in all, a mundane crime-free life. Which to Gilchrist's thinking, not only didn't jibe with her physical appearance of hooped earlobes, studded lips and Gothic boots, but strangest of all, that she would associate with, let alone marry, a career criminal like McCrear.

To satisfy his niggling rationale, he insisted on probing deeper.

'We need to check her birth certificate,' he said. 'Is it faked? Has it been forged?'

Mhairi said, 'We already have that, sir, and there's nothing leaps out. It all fits with what she's told us. Middle names, place of birth. Father was a shopkeeper. Mother a domestic help. By all accounts, she is who she says she is.'

'How about her driving licence? Have we matched the photo to the real thing?'

'Yes, sir. And again, nothing leaps out. Sorry.'

'Passport?'

'That too, sir. Everything's in order.'

'Has she been overseas?'

'No stamps in her passport, sir. But that doesn't mean she hasn't visited any European countries.'

Gilchrist pursed his lips in frustration. Bexall's historical background didn't match the visual Gothic image. He was missing something. He just had to be. But what, he couldn't say.

'I want you and Jackie to check her bank statements,' he said to Mhairi. 'Credit cards, too. Does she have a loan of any kind? If so, how much, and who pays it? And anything else you can think of.'

'She inherited her parents' house when they died,' Mhairi said.

'I didn't know that. Where is it?'

'A wee cottage in Largo. Her name's on the title deeds.'

'She doesn't live there now, does she?'

Mhairi scribbled on her notepad. 'I'll check it out, sir.'

'And check out her council tax payments. And get a copy of that bloody marriage certificate.'

'She was married last Sunday, so it's not been registered yet, sir.'

'I don't care whether it's registered or not,' he said, forcing his tone to stay level. 'I need to see evidence of that marriage. Find out who was there. I'm struggling to believe she is who she says she is.'

'Will do, sir.'

He nodded for Jessie to follow him, and together they returned to his office.

He didn't take a seat at his desk, but walked to the window and stared down at the car park in the back. He couldn't put a finger on one specific aspect of what was troubling him, only that everything about Jennifer McCrear – née Bexall – didn't quite . . . what was he trying to say? . . . didn't quite fit.

He turned to face Jessie.

'You don't look happy,' she said. 'Want me to grill her?'

'No. She's under surveillance. Grilling her will only set us back. Let's leave it, and see what they pull up.'

'So you want me to do what, exactly?'

'Find that something we're missing.' He raked his hair with his fingers. 'Why would a clean-living, apparently nice girl like Jennifer Bexall marry someone like Tap McCrear? And when we see this nice girl in the flesh, she looks . . . she looks . . .'

'As rough as a badger's arse?'

'Something like that.' He grimaced, shook his head. 'It doesn't make sense.'

'You know what gets me?' Jessie said. 'The first time we come across her is when we find Garson's body behind the back door. Up until then, she wasn't on our radar.'

'Well, there is that,' he said, then turned to the window again. 'When we first came across Garson, he was driving the white van, and gave us the slip in Stirling. The next time we find the van, she's driving it down the M74, purportedly at McCrear's instruction. Next thing, Garson's found murdered in McCrear's house, with a knack-heap of a Honda Civic in the driveway. Only it's not such a knack-heap, because the boot's clean enough to eat your dinner off.'

'You know what I'm thinking?' Jessie said.

He turned from the window. 'What?'

'I don't think she's married at all. I think it's a story McCrear wants her to tell us. He sent her on a wild goose chase down the M74, knowing she was driving a van that every police force in Scotland and beyond was looking for. He knew she would be pulled over, and she'd be questioned under caution. And I have to ask myself . . . Why? What has he got to gain by setting that up?'

Bexall's words echoed in his mind – *I want you to tell that skinny Detective Chief Inspector from St Andrews that I'm gonnae get him, and I'm gonnae gut him bone dry for what he done to me.* Was that the message McCrear wanted Jennifer to pass on? That he was putting Gilchrist on notice he was targeted as McCrear's next, and possibly final, victim? That McCrear knew the noose was tightening? That his vengeful plan could never have run to the end of its line? That it was now only a matter of time before he was caught, and by Christ, that skinny detective from St Andrews was going to live every second of the remainder of his soon-to-be-terminated life looking over his shoulder, fearful of every shadow, and shitting his pants at the slightest sound? Maybe that wasn't the exact message McCrear wanted passed on *per se*, but as a cold bead of sweat tickled Gilchrist's back, he realised that it didn't matter. Message or not, McCrear had well and truly wriggled into the deepest of Gilchrist's fears.

'. . . Andy?'

He came to with a start, surprised to see Jessie staring at him.

'Earth to Andy?'

'Sorry,' he said. 'I was—'

'On another planet?'

'Thinking about what you said. You're right in one way. But wrong in another. He's using her. Not to pass on messages. But to keep our eyes off the ball.'

'You've lost me,' she said.

Truth be told, he thought he'd lost himself. But sometimes you just had to go with your gut feeling. He'd got it wrong, his instruction to Frazier. Putting a surveillance team on Bexall was going to lead them nowhere. He saw that now. McCrear was too street-smart. He could sit it out in whatever dump or luxury hotel he was holed up in for as long as he needed. His next target was not any of the other names stuck onto glass jars. No, his next target was that skinny detective, and for some reason he needed Jennifer to be free to roam, not to be followed by a crack surveillance team from the London Met.

As long as Jennifer was being followed, the investigation was going nowhere.

No one would find McCrear, and McCrear wouldn't make a move for his next victim.

Stalemate.

Which, when you thought about it, didn't leave Gilchrist many choices, one of which he was not too interested in taking – not just yet, anyway.

CHAPTER 38

In Ninewells, Dundee, Cooper had confirmed which tongues belonged to whom, and checked DNA results against each of the names on the glass jars. As it turned out, there were no surprises. They all matched.

The SOCOs took four full days to complete their forensic examination of the Great Western Road flat, photographing everything, logging each and every piece of furniture, and removing the entire contents of the flat to the lab. A flash-drive found in one of the bedroom side tables caused a momentary stirring of hope. Was this another motherlode moment? But it was found to contain only a dump of jpeg images from a mobile phone – presumed to be McCrear's – many of which matched those stripped from the flat's walls, and none of which provided any greater detail than those taken by the crime scene photographer.

DS Lamond's extensive door-to-door enquiries turned up nothing. McCrear could've been a ghost for all the physical presence he'd left behind. DI Phelan fared no better. CCTV footage captured hundreds of movements in and out of, and around, the building, each tenant verified by a team assigned to the flat. Of those who could not be verified as tenants, none were identifiable as McCrear, and gave no clue that he visited, let alone lived there. Only one staccato black and grey recording captured on the day of Margaret Rickard's murder hinted at Tap's return to store her jarred tongue in the flat.

Gilchrist had hoped they might capture an image of Jennifer and McCrear entering the flat hand in hand – they were allegedly husband and wife, after all – but after studying hours of recordings, it struck him that of all the tenants and visitors entering or leaving the flat, not one of them could be identified as Jennifer Bexall either. Had she ever been there? Did she even know about the flat? Despite his mounting doubts, Gilchrist forced himself to believe that she was still the key to finding McCrear. She just had to be.

But if she was, nothing she did made any sense.

On each of the past four evenings, Gilchrist and Frazier met with DI Nigel Bowen of London Metropolitan Police, the commander of the surveillance team, and were debriefed on that day's events. After each debriefing, Frazier's impatience mounted. On the evening of the fifth debriefing, Gilchrist knew his theory of Jennifer being the key to locating McCrear was being tested almost beyond its limits.

'So she just stays at home all day long and does nothing?' Frazier grumbled. 'No visitors. No phone calls in. No phone calls out. Just spends the day all by herself.'

'This morning she left home at 10:24,' Bowen said, reading from a report with his soft Geordie accent, 'and drove to the local Tesco. She returned home at 11:43 carrying food supplies. She neither engaged with anyone in Tesco, nor made any phone calls while in Tesco, nor did she make any calls or engage with anyone on her way to or from Tesco.'

'What about petrol stations?'

'She hasn't needed to fill up her car yet.'

'And we've no record of her using her mobile phone at all?' Gilchrist said.

Bowen shook his head. 'She hasn't spoken to anyone at all since she was released.'

'She's a woman,' shouted Frazier. 'I don't know any woman who can't go an hour without talking to someone, let alone four whole days.' He slumped back into his chair, and glared at Gilchrist. 'For fuck's sake, we're wasting our time.'

'I disagree.'

'Disagree all you like, DCI Gilchrist, but so far this hunch of yours that she's the key has brought us absolutely fuck all in terms of results.' He pressed the tips of his thumb and forefinger together, held up his hand, and stared hard at him. 'A big fat zero.'

The pressure was getting to Frazier. Lack of sleep, too. Pouches under his eyes had darkened to an unhealthy black. The whites of his eyes could have been sprayed with pepper gas. Where his suits and shirts and ties had looked freshly laundered, they now possessed a second-hand drabness. The press were relentless in baying for updates, and what had once been the highlight of Frazier's day – standing behind a bank of microphones, revelling in the motor-drive clicking of a hundred cameras – was now an event he dreaded. With no obvious advance in his investigation, press conferences were being shortened, almost to the point of non-existence.

But lack of progress was not only evident in Gilchrist's assignment.

Door-to-door interviews had turned up nothing. Same with CCTV footage. And to add to Frazier's misery, DCIs Danson and Lorimer had despatched teams to find and locate every person named on the empty glass jars – all twenty-five of them – and flooded Frazier's desk with enough written reports to capsize a ship. Frazier might like to cover his backside with reports, but the downside to that were the resources needed not only to prepare each report, but to read through them, analyse them, cross-reference them if necessary, then act upon them, either in the form of a new lead or assign them to another pile for filing.

At 8.45 p.m. on the evening of the fifth day, Gilchrist's mobile phone beeped at a text delivery. He opened it up – I'm thirsty. Care to join me? Central at 9?At first, he struggled to work out who'd sent the text, then realised it had to have come from Irene, whose mobile number he hadn't yet entered into his contacts. He eyed the reports on his desk, dropped there courtesy of Frazier. What the man expected him to find in a two-thousand-word document that consisted of nothing more than questions and answers from door-to-doors, he'd no clear idea.

Besides, he was tired. And thirsty.

He texted back – On my way – then powered down his office desktop.

He checked in with Mhairi and Jackie, more to wish them a good evening than to ask if they'd come up with anything new – which neither of them had, as it turned out. Jessie was still at her desk, too, her back to him, her gaze focused on her monitor.

He walked up behind her, and said, 'Anything?'

'Bloody hell, Andy. You gave me a fright.' She returned her attention to the monitor. 'But the answer to your question is . . . I might have.'

He leaned closer, for a better look at her screen.

'Remember those diamond studs on her top lip? Well, I've done a bit of research into them, and as it turns out, not a lot of people in Scotland do these.'

'Crimp them onto the lips, you mean?'

'That's one way of doing it.'

'And another?'

'Like piercing an ear. You just press the stud into the lip and push it through. But that causes a lot of bleeding. And isn't popular. Something to do with lips versus earlobes. Best to press a sanitised needle, preferably red hot, through the lip, which kind of semi-cauterises as it goes through. Then you insert a stainless steel pin into the hole to prevent it from closing naturally, and a few days later you go back to the tattoo parlour to have the diamond studs fitted.'

Gilchrist wasn't sure where Jessie was going with this, so said nothing.

'I'd wasted hours going round a bunch of tattoo parlours showing a photograph of Jennifer Bexall to the tattooists, and getting nowhere. Until tonight.'

'Okay,' he said. 'I'm listening.'

'I'd just about given up, and decided that if I ended up with eff all at the end of today, that was it. It was a dead end. But typical sod's law, in the very last tattoo parlour I visited, some dump in Shettleston in the east end of Glasgow, one of the staff came up with another tattoo parlour that specialised in diamond studs on any part of the body, even . . .' She clenched her teeth. '. . . on your most sensitive parts.' She shook her head at the thought. 'But it's since shut down.'

For a moment, Gilchrist felt confused. Had she found something, or not?

'But I tracked down the owner,' she said. 'And I'm heading to Glasgow to talk to her in the morning.' She clicked her mouse, and the monitor flickered. She pushed her seat back. 'So unless you've got anything else for me, I'm heading home to see my wee boy. If he still knows who I am, that is.' Her screen blacked out, as if to make a point.

Gilchrist helped her on with her jacket. Tiredness seemed to cover her like another garment that hinted of unwashed hair and fried rice. The remnants of a takeaway poked from a plastic bag on the floor beside her desk. They were all working more hours than was good for their health. But you could keep it up for only so long before exhaustion made the mind useless, and the hours pointless.

'I'll see you tomorrow,' he said.

'You bet.'

He smiled at her effort to show enthusiasm, and said, 'Keep me posted.'

She swirled a scarf around her neck. 'You'll be the first to know.'

CHAPTER 39

The Central buzzed. Patrons jostled for space at the bar, and it was all Gilchrist could do to squeeze in at the corner close to the Market Street entrance, through which he was sure Irene would enter. He turned at a gentle tap on his shoulder, surprised to see Irene lean up and peck his cheek with a whispery, 'Hello.'

He breathed her in, revelling in a momentary flush of perfume and freshness, and making him conscious of his own day's worth of sweat and tiredness.

'I've saved us a couple of seats over here,' she said.

The bench seats were occupied by two young couples who cuddled close as if happy with the cramped space. Across the table stood two empty chairs. A quilted jacket, entwined with a red woollen scarf, lay over the back of one. A wine chiller, from which the neck of a bottle of red protruded, perched on the table like a pseudo-ornament.

'I see you've got two glasses at the ready.'

'I didn't know if you preferred a pint. But don't worry, the wine won't go to waste. I said I was thirsty.' She chuckled, and he was taken again by the pull of her eyes as he helped her into her seat.

He removed the bottle from the wine chiller.

'A cheeky little Italian,' she said.

'Saluti,' he said, which other than *Ciao* was about the limit of his Italian. He poured two large glasses, taking the bottle to the halfway mark, then took his seat.

She chinked her glass against his with a 'Saluti', in response, then took a mouthful that reminded him of his daughter, Maureen. Maybe thirsty was not the correct word.

The wine tasted dry and smooth, and left a pleasant taste. 'I'm sorry I left at such short notice the other night,' he said. 'But how did your Leica work out?'

'Excellent.'

'Just like this wine?'

'Naturally.' She took another mouthful, more of a sip that time. 'I'm pleased with the results. I think it's some of my best work yet, if I don't mind saying so. If you're not rushing home, I'd love you to come up and see them.'

He caught a twinkle in her eye over the rim of her glass. 'Have you eaten?' he said.

'Had a cup of soup earlier.'

'That won't sustain you.'

'Got to watch my figure.'

Several responses flashed through his mind, but he said, 'You look fine, in fact better than fine,' which earned him a squeeze on his thigh and a flicker of her eyelashes. 'Can I tempt you with anything?' he tried again, preparing to push himself to his feet.

'If you don't mind, I'll just pick a chip or two from your plate.'

At the bar, he ordered a pint of Belhaven, and a plate of fish and chips, to be shared by two. He watched his pint being poured, then paid the bill. Irene had her back to him, her attention on her mobile as he squeezed himself back into his seat by her side.

'Problems?' he asked, when she put her mobile down.

'Nothing that a bottle of wine can't sort out.'

'Want another one?'

'Good Lord, no. You'll be thinking I'm becoming a right lush.'

'Becoming?' He raised his eyebrows at her, and felt a surge of relief when she smiled at his joke, which he had to confess was perhaps a bit too close to the bone.

'Point taken,' she said. 'But sometimes the wine just goes down too easily.'

'And other times,' he said, raising his pint, 'you just have to say, who cares?' He took his pint down a couple of inches, then returned it to the table.

She turned to face him a bit more, her skirt riding high. But she pulled the hem down, patted it against her knees. 'You're right, Andy. I'm finding that the older I become, the less inclined I am to worry about what others think of me.' She frowned for a moment. 'Is that wrong of me?'

'Can't think why it would be.'

'Have you spoken to Maureen recently?'

He stumbled for a second over her *non sequitur*. 'Not since I met her here with you. I regret to say that I don't speak to her often enough. Jack, too, for that matter.'

'You've been busy, I imagine. With this big investigation, I don't suppose you've got much free time at all.'

'Well, there is that. But it's easy to find excuses. Everyone's busy.'

His fish and chips arrived just then, and he unwrapped one set of cutlery and passed it to Irene. 'I won't need that,' she said. 'I'll just steal your chips with my fingers.'

He pushed his plate her way. 'Help yourself.'

She removed a chip with feminine delicacy, and nibbled it in half. 'Hot hot hot,' she said, sucking air through her mouth, followed by a short sip of wine.

'Better?' he asked.

'I'll need to smother them in sauce to cool them down.'

'Alternatively, you could use a fork.' From the dry smile on her lips, he thought he'd insulted her by referring to her table manners. He stabbed a chip with his fork and waved it in the air. 'Helps cool them down,' he said, relieved once more when she chuckled.

His first mouthful of haddock tasted succulent, and had him wondering why he didn't eat fish more often. But working all hours, snatching a bite here, a nibble there – between reading reports, attending meetings or taking phone calls – and mostly from pizza leftovers or some local takeaway, didn't help matters. He broke off a piece of fish with Irene's fork, which he placed on the side of his plate, handle towards her.

'Try it,' he said. 'It's delicious.'

'Are you trying to fatten me up?'

'Now why would I do that?'

She did as he asked, and nodded when she returned the fork to his plate, and poked at another chip. 'As you said, sometimes you just have to say, who cares?'

The next hour was spent chatting, nibbling, sipping drinks – Gilchrist interchanging wine with beer, while Irene stayed with the wine. He ordered another round of drinks – glass of wine that time – which seemed to vanish after a few mouthfuls. One more after that, and before he realised it, a glance at his watch confirmed it was almost ten-thirty.

'I'd offer to buy you one more,' he said.

'For the road?' she chirped.

'But I'm afraid I've got an early start in the morning.'

Without a word she grabbed her scarf, making him think he'd offended her in some way. But she wrapped it around her neck, pulled her quilted jacket from the back of the chair, and said, 'Well, before you head off, I insist on showing you my latest work.'

Well, what could he say? Nothing that would not offend her for sure. He pushed to his feet, a bit wobbly if the truth be told. 'Well, if you insist. But I can't stay long.'

'Of course not.'

She took hold of his arm and together they stumbled towards the door. Outside, they both seemed to recover their sense of balance. He breathed in the cold night air, realising that the wine must have gone to his head. Overhead, stars hid behind clouds as thick as quilts.

He strode with her arm in arm towards South Street, shortening his stride to fit in with hers, while she tugged tight, pulled herself closer. At the entrance to her home, she released her grip, scraped around the bottom of her bag for what seemed like minutes, before holding up a key for him to see.

'I can never remember where I put it.'

Upstairs in the main lounge, the heat hit him. She peeled off her scarf and gloves and jacket, and threw them over a sofa. Then she strode to the fireplace, and removed a fine-mesh fireguard, which released a wave of hot air. A stab at the open fire with a cast iron poker, and a couple of pine logs from a basket on the hearth placed onto the revived embers lent a smoky ambience to the room. Fireguard back in place, logs crackled and sparked as they caught fire.

'Here,' she said. 'Let me take your jacket.'

He slid his arms free, and said nothing while she hung it with care over the back of a dining-room chair. He hoped she didn't try to offer him a drink, as the heat from the fire was working wonders with the food and alcohol in his system. He'd already had far too much to drink, and still had to drive to Crail. Of course, if the worst came to the worst, he could always stay over at Maureen's, just along the road.

His thoughts were interrupted by Irene reaching for him, and saying, 'Shall we?'

She took hold of his hand, and he let himself be led from the room, up the stairs, with the strangest tingle of excitement that he was allowing himself to be taken advantage of.

On the landing, she said, 'Here we are,' and opened the door to her studio.

She stood back to let him enter first, then flicked a light switch.

A row of down-lighters flush with the ceiling lit up one wall on which a display of eight framed photographs hung in perfect symmetry. He recognised the scenes straight away – the cliffs at The Scores headlined by the orange glow of lighted windows beneath the silver ceiling of a diamond-studded sky. He could tell from the brightness of the lights, and the high definition of the stars, that the image had been taken on a slow shutter speed, clearly using a tripod. Another from the East Sands towards the shore-head, the stone pier some gargantuan arm that reached out to a sea blurred to a surreal stillness – again, another slow shutter speed.

He peered closer, ran the tip of a finger gently over the surface, feeling the texture mildly rippled against his skin. 'You've printed these onto textured paper.'

'I did, yes.'

'They're terrific.'

'For that size, I had to have them professionally printed.'

'That wouldn't be cheap.'

'No, it wasn't.' A pause, then, 'Can I let you into a secret?'

He turned to her. 'If you'd like.'

'I'm thinking of holding an exhibition of my work.'

'Well, why not?' He faced the display again, his gaze settling on the R&A clubhouse and the Links Road taken from – at a guess – some point on the first fairway of the Old Course, or maybe from Grannie Clark's Wynd. Again, the slow shutter speed lent an eerie stillness to the images, brightened by lights from windows in the Hamilton Grand. A silver line cut across one corner like a diagonal crease in the print – a shooting star, which would surely increase the value of the print, if she ever wanted to sell it. Well, he supposed that's what exhibitions were for, some place in which to display your wares for a buyer's interest.

'They're excellent,' he said.

'Do you really think so?'

He faced her then, puzzled by her question. She must surely know her work was as good as that of any professional photographer. Was she searching for more compliments? Did she really doubt herself that much? Then he remembered his son, Jack, when he'd first dared to exhibit his paintings – the uncertainty, the sudden loss of confidence, the worry that his stuff just wouldn't stand up to professional scrutiny.

'I think your work is exceptional, Irene. But I'm not a professional photographer, so it might be in your interests for someone who is to have a look at them.'

She pressed her thumbnail to her mouth, and nodded, letting her gaze drift over the display for a moment. Then she said, 'I'll put on the kettle.'

He was left to close the studio door behind him.

Downstairs, she busied herself at the sink, drumming water into the kettle from the tap, making a show of topping up a porcelain jug with chilled milk from the fridge. He felt as if he'd said something wrong, maybe even let her down in some way.

But what, he couldn't say.

He took a chair close to the fireplace, revelling in the room's dry warmth. The fire had taken hold, and the logs flickered with flames. A hiss came from somewhere in the burning mass, followed by a squirt of smoke – trapped dampness freed by the flames. He thought he heard the teapot being filled, a cup rattling in its saucer.

Or maybe a spark hitting the fireguard, as exhaustion pulled him down.

CHAPTER 40

He struggled from the depths with the memory of being on a swing as a child.

'Andy . . .?'

His shoulder moved again.

'Andy . . .?'

He opened his eyes.

Irene smiled down at him. 'You said you had an early start.'

'I do, yes, thanks.' He pulled himself upright, surprised by how tight his muscles felt, how stiff his back was. He puzzled over the fire being out, and at the faintest smell of toast in the room. It took him a few confusing seconds to work out where the blanket had come from, and why Irene was wearing her dressing gown.

'I didn't know how early a start you had in mind,' she said. 'But it's six-thirty, and I thought I'd better waken you.'

He peeled the blanket free, and sat upright. 'What . . . what time is . . .?'

'You fell asleep. I tried to waken you, but you were out for the count.'

He dug his thumb and forefinger into the corners of his eyes, forced his mind to pull itself awake, his body into gear. 'I'm sorry, I must . . . I must've dozed off.' He ran his hand down his face, around his chin, felt the roughness of a day's growth.

'I've made a pot of tea,' she said. 'And some toast. But you're more than welcome to have a shower. I have a spare razor, too, if you'd like a shave.' She returned his enquiring gaze. 'I bought it for Jamie,' she said. 'Somehow I can't part with it.'

He nodded, held onto the arm of the chair, and stood.

His world shifted for a moment, threatened to tilt on its axis, then steadied. He ran his tongue over his teeth, worked it around his mouth to try to shift the parrot-cage taste.

'I've got a spare toothbrush, too. Still in the box,' she added.

He nodded. 'Where . . .?'

'Follow me.'

This time she led him along a narrow hallway to a high-ceilinged bedroom in the back, and showed him to a bathroom that still possessed the warmth and humidity from an early morning shower. She opened a cupboard crammed full of towels, and from the bottom shelf removed a plastic container with a toothbrush in it, then an up-to-date Gillette razor that looked as if it had never been used.

'Towels over there,' she said. 'Soap and shampoo on the shelf in the shower. It's easy to operate. I'm sure you'll figure out how it works.' She gave him a quick peck on the cheek. 'I'll leave you to it. And see you at breakfast?' She was almost out of the bedroom, when she said, 'Are you a marmalade or a bacon person?'

'Marmalade sounds perfect.'

'Me, too,' she said, and left him with a wide smile.

He waited until he heard the echo of footsteps along the hallway before slipping out of his clothes. He felt a thousand per cent better after brushing his teeth, and found a bottle of mouthwash with which he duly gargled his throat. He couldn't find shaving soap, and settled for working up a lather from a bar of hand soap in the hand basin. Not perfect, but good enough for a half-decent shave. As Irene had said, the shower was indeed simple to operate. He turned the heat up as high as he could bear, and lathered himself from head to toe.

Showered, shampooed, shaved and towel-dried, he put his clothes back on – which spoiled the fresh cleanliness he'd felt – and made his way through to the kitchen.

The TV was on BBC One, the sound muted. Nothing about the ongoing investigation for the Fife serial killer; something to do with the stock markets in the USA.

'Would you like me to turn it up?' Irene said.

'It's fine as is.'

'I forgot to ask. Tea or coffee?'

'Tea, please.'

'With only a touch of milk,' she said. 'I remembered.'

He patted his pockets for his mobile, then looked around the room for his jacket.

As if reading his mind, she said, 'I hung it up in the cupboard in the hallway,' then added, 'Let me,' and stepped out of the living room. A few seconds later, she was back, his leather jacket in hand.

'Thank you.' He removed his mobile from the inside pocket to find he'd missed two calls – one from Frazier last night, and one from Jessie that morning. He frowned at Jessie being up so early. He checked his messages to find five texts – two from Mhairi, one from Jackie, and two from Frazier. The man could be nothing more than a pest at times.

He checked Frazier's texts first, both the early side of midnight, and both with the same short message – Call me. He tutted as he switched to voicemail.

Where the hell are you, DCI Gilchrist? I've been trying to reach you. He walked towards the window, pressed the mobile hard to his ear, hope rising. Had his team come up with something? Had they found that missing lead to McCrear? But whatever hopes he had were dashed in the following instant. *I've pulled all surveillance units off Jenny Bexall. Five days and she's done nothing and led us absolutely nowhere, except up the garden path. She's not the key any more. If you'd replied to my texts you might've been able to argue the toss. She's no longer part of our line of enquiry. She's finished. And so will you be, if you don't call me first thing.* The message ended.

Gilchrist hissed a curse. Well, what could he expect? Ever since he'd suggested the idea to Frazier, he'd had a real sense that the man had not fully bought into it. Pulling in a top surveillance team from the London Met had raised his hopes for a short while, but with Jenny Bexall appearing to be nothing more than an innocent wife waiting for her husband to return from some overseas trip, he was on a loser. And even as these thoughts ran through his mind, he knew it made no sense.

She was the key to opening the door that would lead them to McCrear. She knew where he was. And she knew how to contact him. She just had to. Why else would she know not to put a step wrong for days on end? Why else would she make no phone calls, send no texts, talk to no one, live the life of a domestic hermit? Because McCrear had warned her she would be killed if she didn't do as she was told came the simple answer. She'd done as he'd instructed – drive the van, be pulled over, be questioned under caution, and pass on that vile message to that *skinny detective from St Andrews*.

He whispered a frustrated curse, and looked down on South Street. At that level, the view was partially blocked by trees that lined the street. Bare branches hinted at the coming of spring, the tiniest of buds pressing through the bark. Cars moved with care in and out of parking spots, with few vacant spaces even at that time of the morning.

Back to his mobile, and Jessie's voicemail.

On my way to Glasgow to meet that numpty that does these diamond studs. I woke up this morning feeling flat about it all. It's probably going to be a waste of time. I was hopeful last night, but in the sobering light of dawn, I'm not so sure. But as you say, if it's a lead, it's worth following. I'll keep you posted, Andy, but I have to tell you that this punter, McCrear, is getting on my nerves. I'll call if I come up with anything. Cheers.

He exited his messages, and checked his texts.

Both of Mhairi's texts had come in just before midnight, too. The first text confirmed that Jennifer Bexall had two bank accounts with RBS – current and savings – with a small balance in each. He read on – At the start of this year, her savings a/c had a balance of £18,474.82, but substantial withdrawals since then have left a current balance of £98.47. He faced the window again. What had Jenny spent over £18,000 on? A new kitchen? A new car? But neither of these computed for him. She didn't look the type on which money would be, or had been, lavished. Maybe McCrear was responsible for the depletion of her savings. Now, that would make sense. A criminal like McCrear locks onto his new girlfriend, Jenny, bleeds her accounts dry, then dumps her?

But he didn't do that. He married her. *Allegedly.*

Again, nothing seemed to fit.

He opened Mhairi's second text, which was more of the same, only this time referring to Jenny's credit cards – Spending history since the card was opened ten years ago, confirms she paid off her balance every month. She lived within her means, with the largest balance of £845.65 for a holiday in Greece paid up over two months, the only time she ever failed to clear the balance, until now. Today her balance is £12,342.68 in debt, run up since the start of the year, and no payments made to her card this year.

Gilchrist puffed up his cheeks, and let it out in a gush. Almost £31,000 gone in less than four months? On what? But being associated with McCrear would do that to you, he thought. One day you're fine, the next you're up to your ears in debt. But even so, why would Jenny allow that to happen? For someone whose life, up until she met McCrear, had been led in a tidy and orderly fashion, and within her financial means, the change was so dramatic it didn't set off an alarm bell or two, it set off a whole factory load of klaxons.

Something was going on. But whatever it was, he couldn't see it.

He opened Jackie's text, this one about Jenny's marriage certificate – Can find no record of any marriage certificate being registered. Maybe too soon? But checked the place where the marriage was supposed to have taken place, and none of the neighbours know anything. Did she marry McCrear? Don't think so. What do you want me to do now? What indeed. He exited his messages, and thought of calling Frazier. But what was the man going to say to him, other than give him a rollicking for wasting police resources. Instead, he called Bowen – the surveillance team leader – and got through on the first ring.

An authoritative voice said, 'DI Bowen.'

'Andy Gilchrist here. I've just heard you've been pulled off the case.'

'Sorry, Andy. Nothing's cooking. But I tell you, what she's doing isn't natural. I think you're right. There's something going on with her. But I couldn't convince Frazier. He's under pressure over costs now, and he wasn't impressed.'

Well, there he had it. Detective Superintendent Rommie Frazier, hotshot rising star SIO, throwing money at the case as if there were no limits, in the belief that it would be only a matter of time – the emphasis being on *short* time – before the case was solved, and another gold star was stamped on his CV. With McCrear lying low, and no one any the wiser where he was, the case was dragging on, and with every passing day, maybe even hour, Frazier's stock was tumbling.

'Where are you?' Gilchrist asked, hoping that he might have a face-to-face debriefing with Bowen and his surveillance unit.

'In Edinburgh. Just about to board the train to London.'

Well, that was that.

'I'll email our final report to Frazier by midday today,' Bowen said.

Gilchrist asked to be copied in, then thanked him, and ended the call.

From behind, Irene said, 'Your toast is getting cold.'

'Oh, I'm sorry.'

'Want me to zap your tea in the microwave?'

He wanted to say that he didn't have time for tea or toast, but he'd overstayed his welcome last night, and spoiled a pleasant evening by being discourteous enough to fall asleep. The least he could do was spend a few minutes with her over breakfast.

'That would be lovely,' he said.

At the breakfast bar, he made a show of buttering a slice of toast, spreading a dollop of marmalade onto it, while Irene heated up his tea. The microwave beeped, and she placed the mug in front of him. 'I'm always leaving cups of tea lying around, and a quick zap in the microwave heats it up. Some people don't like it, but I never mind.'

'That's what I do, too,' he said, and took a sip, followed by a bite of toast. 'This tastes lovely,' he managed to say with his mouth full. 'Is it homemade?'

'All my own work.' She seemed pleased. 'Would you like a jar to take away?'

Again, he was about to refuse, but said, 'That's very kind of you.'

'I'll get one right now.'

She had just opened one of the kitchen cupboards, when he said, 'I feel awful about last night, Irene. Why don't I repay you for my bad manners and my inability to stay awake, and take you out for a meal? Tonight, if you're free. But after work, of course. And I can pick up the marmalade then.'

She beamed a smile. 'If I didn't know any better, I'd say you're vying for two jars of marmalade.'

'You caught me,' he said. 'Two it is.' He chuckled as he pushed his stool back. 'But I really must go. And thanks for being the perfect host last night, and for not tossing me out the front door. It really was unforgiveable, falling asleep like that. And again, I'm sorry.'

'Not at all.' She followed him down the stairs and unlocked the door for him.

He turned to give her a peck on the cheek, but she took hold of his arms, and gave him a hug. When she released him, she said, 'You don't have to take me out tonight, if you don't want to.'

'But I would really like to,' he said, the realisation that he was speaking from his heart taking him aback for an instant. And with that thought, he smiled. 'I look forward to it. You choose the restaurant. I'll call later, and we can set a time. But let's say, seven, just in case I fall asleep again.'

She chuckled at that.

He leaned down and kissed her on the cheek.

Then he stepped outside.

CHAPTER 41

Jessie pulled her Fiat 500 to a stop, half-on half-off the pavement.

It had taken her almost two hours to drive to the housing estate in Bishopbriggs on the northern suburbs of Glasgow. She'd given her son, Robert, the address last night, and he'd googled it and printed out street maps for her, which he'd marked up and enlarged the closer to the address. She'd never been good at reading maps, and was sure she would take a wrong turn once she came off the M80. But Robert's final zoomed-in printout was helpful, and the address hadn't been difficult to find, even though she had the feeling she would take a wrong turn on her way back onto the M80.

The semi-detached house could have been built in the seventies, and looked cared for, as if someone had spent a bit of money on it without breaking the bank. Double glazing had been put in, but the peeling sealant around the window frames told her it had been done years ago. Solar panels on the roof spoiled the tiles, but matched other homes either side.

Up close, the letterbox was speckled with rust, the door handle dulled from use.

She pressed the doorbell, and stood back at the echoing sound of footsteps within.

The door opened with a sticky slap to reveal a barefooted man stripped to the waist, in pyjama shorts that had seen better days. Every square inch of his torso – arms, legs, even his neck – was covered in more tattoos than a family of yakuza gangsters. Brown feathered eagles flew across his shaved chest to attack his nipples with yellow talons. Green boa constrictors slithered their way around his arms and neck, open mouths set to strike at the jugular. Some other animal, a dragon of sorts, peeked out the top of his shorts, and had her concentrating on his face.

'Seen enough?' he said.

'What are you? A walking advert?'

He flexed his pecs, causing the talons to shift their grip.

'Is she in?'

'Who?'

'The tattooist of Bishopbriggs.'

'You don't look like the tattooing kind.'

'Correct.' She thrust out her warrant card. 'She's expecting me. So go get her, sonny, before I arrest you for disturbing the peace.'

'Disturbing the what?'

'The peace. *My* peace.'

'She's in the conservatory in the back.'

'Good, I'll talk to her there.'

She pushed past him and strode along the hallway, through a narrow kitchen and into a glass conservatory. Even before she entered the room, a wall of heat hit her. 'Bloody hell,' she said. 'Who pays your heating bill?' This to an Asian woman lying on a sunbed wearing only a black thong that left nothing to the imagination. A pair of nipples no larger than bee stings stood proud, despite the heat. Jessie'd already had Jackie confirm that Yuki Kimura wasn't married. Like her partner, every square inch of her body, except for her hands, face and feet, was covered with tattoos, more decorative than the call-of-the-wild display on her partner. Jessie thrust out her warrant card. 'DS Jessie Janes. We spoke on the phone yesterday.'

Yuki set aside the magazine she'd been browsing through, and stared at her with a look of amazement. '*You're* interested in diamond studs?' She seemed disappointed.

Jessie ignored the question, and said, 'You used to run a tattoo parlour in Shettleston,' letting Yuki know she was several steps ahead of her.

'All legit.'

'I never said it wasn't.' She caught Yuki's flicker of a glance to the side, and realised her talon-nippled partner had entered the conservatory and was standing behind her. Samurai warriors couldn't have crept in with more stealth. 'Do you mind if I take this off?' she said, unbuttoning her jacket. 'I'm melting in here.'

Yuki watched Jessie unravel her scarf and remove her jacket, then said, 'So what's your interest in diamond studs?'

'Before we go there.' She faced the man. 'Who are you?'

'Stu.'

'Stu what?'

'Just Stu.'

Jessie didn't press for a surname, but instead turned back to Yuki. 'Why did you shut down your parlour? Run out of space?' she joked, nodding to her tattooed body.

'I'd had enough. I didn't like the clientele any more.'

From her days in Strathclyde Police, Jessie knew which areas were rough, and which weren't. 'Shettleston too low class for you?'

From behind, Stu said, 'Too many people wanting a cut of the action, if you get my meaning.'

Jessie faced him, all of a sudden struck by how powerful he was. Stu flexed his muscles, and the eagles fluttered their wings. 'Steady on, Tarzan. Don't be getting any ideas.'

'Glasgow's full of gangsters,' he said, as if she hadn't spoken. 'Everybody and their brother wants something for nothing. We refused to pay protection money, so they burned the place down. Insurance paid for the rebuild, but they burned that down, too. And that was it. We'd had enough. So we moved. To this place.'

'Retired?'

'Not quite. We run a website that brings in some cash. So we get by.'

'What? Selling tattoos?'

'Ideas.'

Jessie turned back to Yuki, who'd pulled herself upright, and now sat with her bare feet on the floor. She reached for a glass of water – or maybe it was gin or vodka – and in doing so, revealed that the thong was not a thong, but a lookalike tattoo.

'Bloody hell,' Jessie said. 'Are you starkers?'

'It's good, isn't it?' She ran her hand over the tattoo. 'You can't tell, can you?'

'Just keep your legs together and you'll be all right.'

Yuki smiled, and for whatever reason, Jessie found herself warming to the pair of them. They'd had it tough, tried to ride it out, but in the end the Glasgow gangsters were as mean and cruel as any others. 'From what I've heard, your tattoo parlour was one of the more reputable ones.'

'The best,' Yuki said. 'It was always what I wanted to do. Ever since I was a little girl.'

'Growing up in Japan?'

Yuki frowned. 'You know that?'

'I did my homework.' She waited for a moment. 'Was your father a member of the yakuza? Is that where your love of tattoos started?'

'He was. But he died. Was killed. And yes, I loved his tattoos.'

'I'm sorry,' Jessie said, but she needed to move on with her enquiry. 'I understand you kept drawings and photographs of your work.'

'Most of my records were destroyed in the fires.'

Jessie pursed her lips to smother her curse. *Shit.* Not what she'd expected. She'd been banking on Yuki's records helping her confirm Jennifer Bexall as a client. Now, she felt that line of enquiry closing down in front of her. She reached into her jacket, and retrieved an envelope from the inside pocket. She peeled it open, and removed a photograph.

'Do you remember doing this?'

Yuki studied the image of Jennifer Bexall, pulled the photo to her for a closer look. 'Yes I do. Seven diamond studs. One of my first.' She handed the photograph to Stu.

He took it. 'What's happened to her? Is she dead?'

'Why do you say that?'

'Why else would you be here?'

Jessie let her question float between them unanswered, then turned back to Yuki. 'What else can you tell me about her?'

Yuki reached for her glass, took a sip, then returned it to the table. 'I remember she didn't want to be numbed. She was the only client I ever had who refused to have an injection for that procedure.'

'Scared of needles?'

'Not at all. I'd say she was more of a masochist.'

Jessie rubbed her upper lip with her fingers and thumb, cringing from the thought. 'It would bleed, too, I'm sure.'

'It does, but I use a specialised needle clamp that's extremely hot, and cauterises the skin as it pierces, so it keeps bleeding to a minimum. It's quick, too. In and out. No more painful than a bee sting.'

'Ah,' Jessie said. 'So, being a masochist she must've been disappointed.'

'No. She refused that, too. Said she wanted it done the old-fashioned way.'

'Bloody hell.'

'Exactly.'

All of a sudden, Jessie was aware of movement behind her. 'Will you stop sneaking around like a Ninja warrior,' she snapped. 'You're making me nervous.'

Without a word, Stu handed the photograph back to her, then opened a manila folder. 'You're in luck,' he said. 'Mandeep's file was one of those not destroyed in the fire.'

'Mandeep?' Jessie said. 'Who's Mandeep?'

Stu handed her the folder. 'Mandeep Wilson. Isn't that who you're asking about?'

Jessie snatched the folder from him, and flicked through the medical questionnaire and standard consent form, until she came to a set of before and after photographs of the person who called herself Jennifer Bexall. She held onto her anger for as long as she could.

But it was no use.

'That fucking *bitch*.'

CHAPTER 42

Back in her Fiat, Jessie settled down to contemplate her options. What she'd just found out was explosive in how it would affect the ongoing investigation. Her immediate problem was that she didn't know for certain if Mandeep Wilson was a real person, or just a name she'd given Yuki when she'd had her lips studded. Jennifer McCrear née Bexall could have changed her name to Mandeep Wilson for any number of reasons, none of which were clear to Jessie at that moment. So, first things first, she would find out all she could about this Wilson slash Bexall, and take it from there.

She phoned Mhairi, and spent five minutes explaining in detail that morning's events, after which they both agreed that before they let this bombshell loose – if it did indeed turn out to be a bombshell – Jackie would do some research. And if Mandeep Wilson and Jennifer McCrear née Bexall were the same person, they would bypass Frazier – they were both up for that – and report directly to Gilchrist as soon as possible but not before Jessie's return to the North Street Office. Which seemed as good a plan as any.

It took Mhairi forty minutes to call back with Jackie's findings, by which time Jessie had crossed the River Forth at Kincardine, and was sitting at the tail-end of a trail of fourteen cars and vans stuck behind a tractor, its oversized tyres spitting dollops of dirt as it travelled up the road at a little over thirty miles an hour.

'She goes by the name of Deeps, not Mandeep. The name threw us for a while, but Jackie's something else, so she is. Once we got over that wee hurdle, this is where it gets complicated. Are you sitting down?'

Jessie eyed the traffic ahead. 'Regrettably.'

'Mandeep Wilson's birth name is Mandeep McSherry. She was born thirty-seven years ago in Port Glasgow to a single mother of Indian descent who couldn't afford the cost of another child. So she handed her over to her sister, Roshni, who effectively adopted her and raised her as if she was one of her own. But apparently her childhood was not good, and her adoptive father, Archie Wilson, was accused of sexually abusing her when she was only ten. Archie and Roshni then split up, after which Roshni took to the bottle and died two years later, having choked on her own vomit. Mandeep was fostered out to another family, this time in Birmingham, England, but that, too, didn't work out. She was a wild child, and by the age of fifteen, she'd spent a total of twelve months in a number of juvenile detention centres. Then it gets worse.'

'Jeez oh,' Jessie said, and flexed her grip on the steering wheel.

'She got in with a bad crowd, and started having sex and experimenting with drugs, which in turn landed her in a backstreet abortion clinic at the age of sixteen. She claimed she'd been raped, and the Crown Prosecution Service brought action against three men, all in their twenties, who claimed they were innocent.'

'As they would,' Jessie interjected.

'But they got off on some technicality, and walked out of court bragging and jesting. Two weeks later, Mandeep was back in court charged with serious assault on one of the three men. It made the national news back then, and her face was all over the telly. By the time she went to trial, she was only seventeen, and the man she'd attacked had been stabbed to death in a separate incident. But the CPS took the unusual decision to drop the case.'

'So she's had a tough upbringing, is what you're telling me.'

'And then some. Hang on.' The line dulled, as Mhairi conversed with someone in the background, then came back. 'We're still looking into it. But Jackie's just handed me a printout from the PNC, and Mandeep Wilson features on it big-time.'

'How the hell didn't we pick up on this when we had her in custody?'

'Because everyone thought she was Jennifer Bexall.'

'Have you seen photographs of Mandeep Wilson?'

'It's her, Jessie. No doubt about it.'

'But what about Bexall's driving licence and passport photographs?'

'Forgeries. Good ones. Expensive, too.'

'That's it,' Jessie said. 'Get someone to arrest that bitch right now, and bring her in for some serious questioning.'

'Maybe we should . . . maybe we need to run it past Andy first?' Mhairi said, her voice unsure.

Jessie almost told her to forget Andy, just get on with it, then decided against it. With Frazier nipping at everybody's heels, they were all up against it, none more so than Andy. No, she thought, if this was as big a break as she thought it was, Andy could use all the legs-up he could get.

'Have you heard from him?' she said.

'Haven't seen him this morning. I think he's been in with Frazier, probably getting a new arsehole fitted.'

Jessie coughed out a laugh. Not like Mhairi to come up with chatter like that. 'Here's how I think we should handle it,' she said. 'You and Jackie keep digging, find out whatever else you can about this Mandeep Wilson. I'll be in the Office in about another hour.' She eyed the cars ahead. 'Maybe two hours, unless someone can nuke this bloody tractor up ahead. Then we'll have a meeting with Andy, and let him take it from there. Sound good?'

'Perfect.'

Frazier faced Gilchrist, eye to eye. Nervous energy that looked as if it could turn to anger seemed to emanate from his being in a show of raised veins, pursed lips, clenched jaw. And dead eyes. That's what Gilchrist took note of most of all; eyes that levelled with his in a cold reptilian stare.

Then Frazier looked off over Gilchrist's shoulder, held his gaze on something beyond his line of sight, then came back a changed man. 'I couldn't care less if you agree with me or not, DCI Gilchrist. What you don't seem to appreciate, and repeatedly fail to understand, is that we have a chain of command, which is how authority has to work in times like this. And whether you like it or not, I'm above you in that chain of command.' He took a deep breath, then said. 'Is that. Under. Stood?'

'It is.'

'Good.'

'But it doesn't oblige *me* to agree with *you*. You should never have terminated the surveillance on Jennifer McCrear without first talking to me.'

'You didn't answer your phone.'

'Not my fault. You could have waited.'

Frazier levelled his eyes at Gilchrist again. From the hint of a smirk at the corners of his mouth, it seemed that the nervous energy of moments earlier had been put on hold. 'Has anyone ever told you, DCI Gilchrist, that you can be an annoying fuck?'

'I've been known to get under people's skin.'

'Well, now we understand each other, I'm through with you, Gilchrist. I'm back in charge of the investigation. If you don't like it, take it up with whoever the hell you want.'

Silent, Gilchrist watched Frazier stride from his office.

It took all of five minutes for Mhairi to appear in the doorway.

'Yes, Mhairi. Come in.'

She took a few tentative steps into his office. 'We thought the ceiling was going to come down, the racket that was going on.'

'Well, thankfully it didn't.'

'But are you all right, sir?'

Gilchrist tried to give her a smile of reassurance, but he was still smarting at the way in which Frazier had spoken to him. Still, he'd been there before with disagreements with authority, and he'd have to put the usual face on it. 'I'm fine,' he said.

'I couldn't help but overhear the end of your meeting, sir, which sounds like you might not have to report directly to Detective Superintendent Frazier any more.'

'Which has its upsides,' he said, and tried another smile.

'Well, with that in mind, sir, Jessie shouldn't be long. She's on her way back from Glasgow, with information that we now don't have to share with Detective Superintendent Frazier. Unless you think otherwise, sir.' She sided up to him, and handed him a print-out of Mandeep Wilson's PNC records.

For a moment, he failed to make the connection. 'Who's Mandeep Wilson?' he said.

'The mystery woman known as Deeps.'

By the time Jessie stepped into his office, he'd already set the ball rolling.

They drove the sixteen miles to Kennoway in no time at all, Gilchrist behind the wheel, Jessie seated next to him. The first phase of his plan was not to let anyone else know what they were about to do. The second phase was to have Mhairi and Jackie continue with their research and find out what they could about Mandeep Wilson. And the third phase was to arrest this Jennifer slash Mandeep on suspicion of perverting the course of justice, and obstructing a murder investigation. Once in custody, they would attempt to glean what they could from her, without letting her know they'd uncovered her true identity, the worry being that once she knew, she would clam up and respond to every question thereafter with No comment, or even stonewall silence.

Jessie had other ideas. 'She's led us a right merry dance, that one has. She's known all along exactly what she was doing. I'm going to make sure the cuffs hurt when I put them on.'

'That'll get you nowhere,' Gilchrist said.

'But it'll make me feel a hundred times better.'

'Sometimes softly softly's the way to go,' he said, as he eased into Forth View. He turned at the end of the cul-de-sac, checked out the house on the way back, then parked round the corner, out of sight.

A stiff breeze rose as he and Jessie strode up the driveway. The Honda Civic still stood at the entrance to the garage, taking up space, and pulling down the neighbourhood. Again, they went to the back door, and Gilchrist stood back while Jessie rapped it. After thirty seconds, he sent her to the front of the house to try the door there, while he continued to thump the back door with the heel of his hand.

But two minutes later, after ringing doorbells and peering through windows, he came to the conclusion that no one was home. The surveillance team's reports had noted that trips to Tesco for groceries had been done in the Honda Civic. But there it was, parked on the driveway, and no Jennifer slash Mandeep in sight.

He checked the driver's door – unlocked – and pulled it open. No keys in the ignition, nothing obvious lying around. No empty coffee mugs, McDonald's wrappers, which might suggest some other avenue to search.

Jessie shoved her hands into her pockets. 'What now, Kemosabe?'

'Check with some of the neighbours. Ask if they noticed anyone leaving the house, or if she took a taxi, or maybe was picked up by someone.'

Jessie said, 'It's odd, don't you think, that the very day the surveillance unit is pulled off, she goes missing.'

'We don't know she's missing yet.'

'Excuse me for being dumb, but ever since she was under surveillance, she always drove the Civic. And now it's parked in the driveway, she's nowhere around. Unless she's hiding in the boot.'

Which had Gilchrist sucking in his breath, and walking to the back of the car.

CHAPTER 43

But the boot was empty, and none of the neighbours had noted anything. No taxis to pick anyone up, no cars, vans, motorcycles or vehicles of any kind at the door, and no one could recall seeing anyone leaving the house.

'Penny for your thoughts,' Gilchrist said to Jessie.

'She's done a runner.'

He couldn't disagree. But the timing of it all worried him. 'Why now?' he said. 'Why, on the very day the surveillance was pulled off, does she leave?' He eyed the Civic, then the house, trying to work out when and how she'd left the property. 'Maybe she has someone on the inside. How else would she know the surveillance unit was pulled off?'

'Jesus,' Jessie hissed. 'You're thinking McCrear's got a contact in the Constabulary?'

'Well, that's the million-dollar question.'

'The two-million-dollar question might be – is this bitch now with McCrear?'

'Let's hope we can find the two-million-dollar answer . . . before . . .'

'Before what?'

He shrugged. What could he say? That his gut was telling him that Mandeep Wilson, in cahoots with Tap McCrear, was making a mockery of the investigation? That she'd fooled them into believing she was Jennifer Bexall, a person she was nothing like at all? He turned away, felt frustration shift to anger. Jesus *Christ*. Just as well they'd kept this from Frazier. The man would have more than a field day. He'd have a bloody funeral parade.

Jessie said, 'Do you think there's even the slightest chance that she's stepped out to do a bit of shopping?' A pause, then, 'Okay okay, it was just a thought. A stupid one, I agree. But a bit of lateral thinking from time to time never hurt anybody.'

Gilchrist said, 'Sorry.'

'You're forgiven.'

'But it really is so bloody annoying. Just when we thought we were onto something solid for the first time in days . . . poof, it's gone.' He gave her shoulder a gentle squeeze. 'You did a fine piece of detective work today, Jessie. I'll make sure it gets noted.'

'I think for the time being, mum's the word. Let's see if Jackie's turned up anything else. Who knows, she might come up with another address for her.'

Despite Mhairi and Jackie spending the rest of the afternoon digging deep, they found nothing to lead them down a fresh path. It seemed that Wilson had vanished into the night, simply left home in the early hours of that morning to a destination unknown. But at the end of the day, Gilchrist found himself still struggling with the coincidental fact that she'd done so the instant the surveillance unit was pulled off her.

Should he bring these matters to Frazier's attention, or keep them to himself? He had a professional duty to keep him up-to-date with new developments. But as Frazier was more intent on making Gilchrist the scapegoat for his stalling investigation, it didn't seem right that the man should benefit from their day's efforts – even though it'd been mostly wasted.

By 7.30 Gilchrist had reached a decision. He rationalised that as Frazier had pulled the surveillance unit off Bexall slash Wilson, then she was of no interest to his investigation. He would have to be notified some time, and tomorrow was as good a time as any.

Decision made, he reached for his leather jacket. The day was done, and so was he. He was adjusting his jacket collar when he stopped. 'Shit shit *shit*,' he said, then removed his mobile.

At that instant, Jessie appeared in the doorway, notebook in hand. 'Something I said?'

'I've forgotten I'm meeting Irene.'

'Sounds like a date.'

He pressed the phone icon in Contacts, and noticed Jessie's notebook. Had she come to his office to tell him something new? 'Anything I need to know?'

She closed her notebook. 'It's late,' she said. 'And I'm knackered. It's nothing that can't wait until the morning. I'm going to head off home—'

'Irene. Andy here. I'm sorry, I got tied up for a bit.' He nodded in response to Jessie's toodle-do wave. 'But I'm finished now. Are you still up for having a bite to eat?'

'And a drink?'

'Or three?'

She laughed, a whispery sound that pulled him closer to her. 'I thought we'd go to the Doll's House,' she said. 'It's just around the corner. Do you want to meet me there?'

'No,' he said. 'I'll pick you up at your home. I should be there in about five minutes. Does that work?'

'It does. I'll see you then.'

He returned his mobile to his pocket, feeling light-hearted, despite the long day. The thought of a few drinks and a nice meal in the company of an attractive woman was just the pick-me-up he needed. But before leaving, he stuck his head into Jessie's office.

'You were going to tell me something?'

'It's nothing we'll be doing anything about tonight, so *go*,' she said, and shooed him away. 'You're late for your date. Tomorrow all will be revealed.'

When he stepped from the Office, the temperature had dropped, the night darkened. He shivered off a chill as he upped his collar, then stuffed his hands into his pockets, and set off up College Street. He strode past the Central Bar, its night-time hubbub oddly subdued. As he crossed Market Street, a cold drizzle filled the air like a winter mist. By the time he turned into South Street and passed the Criterion – strangely quiet for that time of night – rain glistened off his leather jacket like oil.

He crossed South Street, and twenty seconds later stood outside Irene's door. Light spilled from the upper windows into the dank night. His breath puffed in the frigid shadows, as his subconscious picked up the metallic click of a car door closing – or maybe opening. He was about to remove his hands from his pockets to ring the doorbell, when he sensed, rather than heard, movement behind him. Then something nipped his left biceps, as sharp as a bee sting. His reflexes had him slapping at it, and turning to fend off the attack. But his range of vision seemed limited somehow, as if what he was searching for was shifting beyond his peripheral range.

He tried to shout at the shadows, force a warning into the night, but he managed only a strangled grunt as if his tongue and throat had become one. His world tilted, shifted on its axis, and he realised with mounting terror that he couldn't breathe. His chest and lungs felt as if they'd collapsed, at the same time all strength seemed to vanish from his legs.

A strong hand gripped him by the nape of his neck, and a voice as hard and cold as an Arctic wind, said, 'I've been waiting years for this.'

CHAPTER 44

They moved with incredible speed.

At least that's how it felt to Gilchrist. One minute he was upright, the next horizontal in the back of some car – a Volvo estate with the seats folded forward, his brain was able to tell him. And that's what was so terrifying about it; not just the silent swiftness of the attack, but his ability to understand what was happening, and the inescapable conclusion that he was about to die within the next few minutes.

For try as he might, he could pull in no air. He could be underwater, in some hellish nightmare, holding his breath. All he had to do was wake up and inhale for all he was worth. He tried. He really did. But nothing worked. Not his lungs, his mouth, his lips, his eyes. Only his heart, which was pumping in his chest like a wild animal, rhythmic drumming in his ears, pounding away as it searched for every molecule of oxygen from his circulatory system with which to remain alive. He was utterly helpless, staring at the black carpet-like material on the floor, unable to blink, unable to move and, most frightening of all, unable to inhale a single breath of life-saving air. And still, his heart pumped hard and fast, as if knowing it was in its final death throes.

His body rolled over onto its side as the car cornered, too fast, he thought, which might attract attention. How had they been able to abduct him in town, with a busy public bar along the street? Had no one seen anything, heard anything, done something, raised an alarm? But he would have heard the clamour of their alarm, surely. He would have heard someone shout out. But no one seemed to have noticed a thing, his attack carried out with almost professional precision.

These thoughts flashed through his mind with the speed of a lightning strike, but even though just over a minute had passed since the attack, he could tell from the steady darkening of his vision that he was about to black out from lack of oxygen. And once he did, he knew there would be no coming back.

That would be it. Life over. Lights out.

If he could have, he would have smiled at the irony of that thought – lights out – because that's what it felt like. That's what he knew was coming. A gradual darkening of his senses, until all that would be left was blackness. And complete silence.

Then hands were by his head – small hands, hard hands – lifting it up, turning it one way until something pressed hard against his lips and a metal contraption clattered against his teeth as it was pushed into his mouth and shoved with careless expertise beyond the back of his throat. More fumbling, then a cool rush of air, which brought him back to life.

'You'll be paralysed for ten or fifteen minutes,' the voice said, a woman's voice he'd heard before. He tried to pull it from the depths of his memory, but his brain was working on keeping him alive, and whomever it belonged to, he was unable to recall.

'Don't try to fight it,' she said. 'You can't.' Another rush of air filled his lungs as he felt himself slide forward as the car braked sharply.

'Fuck's sake,' the driver shouted. 'D'you see that fucking lunatic.' A horn blared, but Gilchrist couldn't tell if it was from the car he was in, or from another on the road.

'Fucker.'

Another blare, longer that time.

'Never mind them,' the woman said. 'You'll get us noticed. Just drive, will you?'

Her hands pulled him off his side, rolled him onto his back, and he caught a glimpse of something rubbery, like a ball she was squeezing, and with each press of her hands air was pumped into his lungs. He'd seen the contraption used once before – an Ambu bag, as best he could recall – a simple rubber balloon-shaped device, which when pumped by hand forced air into lungs through intubation.

Which told him what had happened.

Succinylcholine. That's what he'd been injected with. Cooper had been right in her description of its symptoms. But what she'd been unable to describe with any real degree of accuracy was the utter terror and mind-numbing helplessness of being paralysed without the ability to breathe. Waterboarding would be less terrifying.

Another rush of air, for which he was grateful.

On and on the journey into the countryside went, not a word being spoken. Only the steady thrumming of the car's engine, the rumbling of its suspension, and the steady press of air being supplied. He couldn't say how long it had been since he'd been injected, but it had to be in the five-to-ten minute range, for he was recovering some sensation of movement. He could bend a finger, move his tongue, just a little. He was still unable to breathe, but in a few minutes he might. Another rush of air gave him the strength to move his eyes, and recognise Jennifer . . .

Or was it Mandeep Wilson?

As if sensing his impatience, she shouted, 'How much longer to go?'

'Another five minutes or so.'

She leaned over him then, and stared at his eyes, moving her head from side to side. 'He's coming round,' she said.

'Well, sort him out, for fuck's sake. What d'you want me to do?'

Gilchrist's peripheral vision watched her delve into a bag and fumble about inside. Then she held up a syringe and a glass vial that contained a clear liquid into which she inserted the tip of the needle, and drew the contents down.

His mind screamed at her not to do it – *No, no, no, don't, I'm not going to fight, just let me recover* – but to no avail. She pierced his arm with the syringe, and another bee sting burned him. She pressed the plunger, and he felt all sense of movement evaporate, as good as clicking a switch. The steady release of air from the Ambu bag kept him company as the journey rumbled on.

A short time later, the car braked hard, took a sharp left, mounted a kerb or something similar, and crunched its way along what sounded like a gravel driveway. It drew to a halt, and the engine died, and hands were at his head again, removing the tube from his mouth.

He lay there in mounting horror as the driver's door clicked, then the rear door opened and Wilson clambered out, leaving him alone to die in airless silence. He listened to the hard sound of feet crunching stones, then fade from his hearing. The metallic rattle of a door being unlocked barely reached his fading senses.

Surely this was not what they intended – drive him here to let him die in the back of a car. They would not have gone to all that bother to do that, and he held onto that hope as his sight diminished from lack of oxygen, and blackness enveloped him. The rhythmic thumping of his heart, its steady beat, the only sound in his head that told him he was alive and could somehow live through this, seemed to falter as it missed a beat, fluttered for a moment as it pumped its last, then faded into . . .

He was drifting free, floating through the black void of space, weightless, powerless, helpless. Stars shifted around him, gathering in their intensity, until they clustered into shapes that took the form of faces. Maureen smiled at him. Jack was there, too. And there was Gail, his late wife, his first real love, cradling a baby in her arms, the joy of that singular moment something he would never experience again. As the sound of his failing heart faded from his senses, lifelessness slithered in, and took over his being.

CHAPTER 45

'You're not dead yet, Gilchrist.'

The man's voice came at him from the darkest depths of his consciousness.

Had he been dreaming? Was he dreaming now?

'You're not going to die until I want you to die, you smarmy fuck, and by Christ I'm gonnae have a grand old time sorting you out good and fucking proper.'

No dream. A nightmare. A living nightmare. One he could call his very own.

He'd been intubated again, and life flooded his system in cool clean oxygen to the steady clicking of some machine he was hooked up to, a more permanent arrangement than the handheld Ambu bag in the back of the car. But the recent dose of succinylcholine had not yet metabolised in his body, and he could do nothing other than stare at the ceiling.

He felt hands on his feet, fingers untying his shoelaces, then removing them. His socks were next, then his belt on his jeans, and his fly unzipped. He realised everyone in the Task Force had made a mistake in their analysis of the crime scenes. The folded clothes had not been prepared by each victim, but by the killers. And it struck him as odd that they'd all slipped up on that, too, the unarguable fact that there had to be two killers, which made sense now – Wilson to administer the succinylcholine and intubate each victim, and McCrear to get on with the more enjoyable task of nailing them to the floor.

It was up in the air as to which one of them cut out the tongues.

'This is the bit that always surprises me,' McCrear said. 'How everyone's different in their private areas. It's the men that surprise me the most, because not one of them ever has a cock that's big enough to match their ego. And you're no fucking different, Gilchrist.'

He was aware of the floorboards shifting beneath him, and he caught a glimpse of a knife in a gloved hand as McCrear moved around him like a butcher studying a carcass and deciding which part he was going to cut into first. Which, when he thought about it, was probably what McCrear was actually doing.

Gilchrist's leather jacket was pulled off him, with a little bit of effort, he had to say. Then fingers fumbled around his shirt buttons, and undid them, one by one. Removing his shirt was done with some care, as if Wilson didn't want to rip the material. But her action caused his body to rock to his left, then his right, during which he was offered sight of a man wearing forensic coveralls, standing off to the side. He'd recognised McCrear from his voice, although he looked larger in the flesh than Gilchrist remembered from years ago.

As if on cue, McCrear came over to him, forensic-booted feet only inches from his head. Then he leaned forward to intercept his line of sight. 'See this, Gilchrist?' The blade shone like polished steel as McCrear turned it from side to side, as if to afford a view of every aspect of its razor-sharp edge. 'I'm going to use this to cut off your balls. I'd love to shove them down your throat, but I think I'm gonnie keep them in the same jar as your tongue.'

Then Wilson leaned down beside him, and he felt another bee sting on his arm. As his senses shimmered from reality again, both McCrear and Wilson slipped from sight, leaving him to lie there, fearing what was about to happen, listening only to the steady clicking of the oxygen pump. He couldn't say how long he lay there, alone, terrified – ten, fifteen minutes, maybe more – but the introduction of music, almost too faint to catch, then the hard clatter of metal on wood, and the sound of something heavier sliding off a smooth surface, had his senses on full alert.

'Right,' said McCrear. 'The waiting's over. Let's get down to business.'

'Want me to give him another dose?' Wilson said.

A hand passed in front of his eyes, then just as quickly vanished. 'Naw, he's still out of it. I'm never sure how much feeling they lose—'

'None at all,' Wilson snapped. 'I keep telling you that. They can see. They can hear. They can feel, all as normal. They just can't breathe or move anything.'

'Aye, so you keep telling me. But I'm no sure I believe it or not.'

'He'll be coming to in another five minutes or so. Maybe best to dose him again.'

'I said naw. I want this bastard to feel the pain.'

The floorboards shivered as McCrear dropped to his knees, took hold of Gilchrist's left arm and tugged it wide, so that it lay outstretched on the carpet.

'I was saving you for last, but then that stupid fucker Terry went and fucked it all up. So this is when payback starts, you cocky wee bastard. And just to tell you how I'm gonnie do it, I'm gonnie start by nailing your hands to the floor, then I'm gonnie hammer a nail in every six inches up each of your arms. And once you're well and truly fucking nailed, I'm gonnie do the same with your legs.'

The pain when the first nail was driven through his palm sent a shockwave through his body. His mind screamed in agony as the sensation of his fingers and hand being scorched in flame seared the length of his arm, and seemed to ricochet around his brain in electric jolts.

And he was helpless to do anything about it. Now he knew why none of the victims' hands or feet showed any sign of resistance against the nails driven through them. With their systems flooded with succinylcholine all they could do was let their lungs accept the oxygen being supplied to them, while their brains reacted to the sheer agony of the process.

The floorboards shifted again. 'Did you ever work out why we cut out their tongues?' A pause, then, 'I didn't hear you. What's that you said? Oh, you think it's because I'm a sick fuck, is that it?' McCrear coughed a laugh as he shifted his position. 'Well, I'm not as sick a fuck as you think I am. I just do the heavy grafting, the lifting of the bodies from the car, or wherever, and setting them on the floor. Then I hammer in the nails, which is a piece of piss, really. Couple of thumps, and that's it. Nothing to it.'

Gilchrist's sight had misted over with tears, which told him that the sux might be wearing off. Even so, try as he might, he could move nothing. He couldn't even blink away the tears. The floorboards thudded as McCrear sank to his knees again. Then rough fingers gripped his right arm, stretched it wide. The prick of the nail-head as it pierced his skin was nothing compared to the flash of pain that erupted in his hand to the sound of a heavy thud, and shot along his arm with a force that should have concussed his brain. The floorboards shifted as McCrear pushed to his feet. Gilchrist felt as if he'd been left staked to a Catherine wheel, fire in his arms, waiting for the world to spin round and round in a dizzying end.

'As I was saying, we cut out their tongues because we have to keep topping up the succinyl stuff, and that's where we inject it. Just to keep you lot guessing. Mandeep here's a vicious wee cunt, aren't you, Deeps?'

'If you say so.'

'Oh, I say so, Deeps. And she's the sick fuck, Gilchrist. No me.'

Molten metal could be coursing through his veins. He couldn't see past a fog of tears, felt their slippery warmth as they ran down his cheeks. Terror froze his heart as rough hands gripped his left leg and pulled it wide.

'Deeps tried to go straight a while back, once she realised she needed money to buy drugs and stuff. They say money can't make you happy, but they don't tell you that you can do fuck all without it. Aye, money makes the world go round right enough. So Deeps went and got herself a job in a doctor's surgery. A real job. Earning money. Not enough to keep her happy. There's never enough for that, no matter what they tell you.'

'So, about the tongues,' Deeps said. 'You're about to learn something.'

But what Gilchrist was learning was that you didn't just feel pain, you heard it. He was learning that pain sounded like blood screaming through your brain, beating like war drums that echoed in the deepest part of your mind in time with your palpitating heart.

'Show him, Deeps.'

Amidst the deafening sound of pain, Gilchrist could make out the metallic clatter of something being scraped – metal against leather, perhaps. Then Deeps came into his line of sight, holding up for him to see what looked like two suede brushes clipped together. Only they weren't suede brushes; the heads were too small, and the metal strands too sparse.

'I made it myself,' she said, showing him a plastic tube that ran from the back of the brushes, and led to a jar of clear liquid. 'It's what I used to inject more succinylcholine. The tongue is as good a muscle as any. Better in fact. More direct to the brain.'

Gilchrist's brain was in too much turmoil for him to work out the intricacies of the brushes and the tubing, although he was beginning to have a horrifying sense of what was about to happen.

'You open the mouth,' she said. He was helpless to object as her fingers prodded and prised his mouth open. He felt the intubating tube being pressed to one side, and something hard and cold take its place. 'And you clamp the tongue like this.'

It could have been a hundred fire ants stinging his tongue in unison.

'Now, if I wanted to, I'd press this button here, and a dose of sux would be injected into your tongue. But don't worry, I'm not going to give you any more. My brother won't let me do that. He wants you to feel all the pain he can give you.'

Brother? Was that what she'd just said? She and McCrear were brother and sister?

'But it also doubles as a clamp for pulling the tongue out . . . like this.'

His head lifted off the floor from his tongue being pulled by the metal clamp.

'And all the easier for slicing it off,' she said.

Even though he couldn't move, he felt his eyes widen at the sight of a scalpel in her hand. His mind roared in silence for her to stop, drowning out the noise of the pain from his burning limbs.

But it was McCrear's voice that shouted, '*Deeps.*'

The scalpel wavered inches from his outstretched tongue. 'What?' she snarled.

'We spoke about this.' A hand moved her arm, pulled the scalpel away from his face. 'I want his balls first. I told you that.'

'Does it fucking matter what gets cut off first?'

'It does, aye. It fucking matters to me.'

'You've still to nail the bastard's feet.'

'Well, you can do his balls first, then I'll do his feet. Would that keep you happy, you crazy fucking witch?'

The clamp was released, and his tongue slipped back into his mouth, along with a wave of blood that threatened to choke him. He was conscious of liquid sliding down the back of his throat. But even so, he couldn't cough, and knew that if the intubating tube was removed, it would be only a matter of seconds before his lungs filled and he drowned in his own blood.

Cooper's words came back to him, the echo of her professional authority lost in a cacophony of other voices cast up to him from his memory in a flurry of final living thoughts. He'd often heard it said that in the moment before you die, your entire life passes before your eyes in a flash. Well, he was about to find out.

Warm fingers took hold of his cold testicles.

'You're about to lose your manhood, Gilchrist.'

Then silence, as his testicles were stretched, ready to be hacked free.

'That's it, Deeps. Give them one long slice.'

CHAPTER 46

For one confusing moment, Gilchrist couldn't understand what the sharp crack was, a hard thud like metal hitting wood, followed by wood splintering, glass shattering, floorboards shuddering and the roaring of a thousand voices shouting *Police don't move down down put that weapon down now police don't move now now.*

Among the uproar, he heard McCrear shout, 'Get the fuck—' before a Taser crackled and his body thudded to the floor with a thump that shook the walls. A flicker of someone moving fast through his line of sight could have been a shadow, or his imagination, but another Taser crackled and Wilson crashed to the floor, taking a side table and a set of ornaments with her.

Other figures moved past him, thumping the floor by his head as voices shouted out names and formal detention declarations – *you're being detained under Section 14 of the Criminal Procedure Scotland Act 1995 on suspicion of the murders of . . .*

Then Jessie was by his head, hands on his face, shouting in his ear, 'Andy, Andy, can you hear me?' She turned away, and screamed, 'Fuck's sake, call the paramedics right now. Someone.

Anyone. Now.' Then she was back at him, turning his head, looking into his eyes, fingers tugging at the tube in his throat.

But he was helpless to resist, couldn't even tell her to leave the tube alone, that if it was removed he wouldn't be able to breathe.

Then another woman's voice said, 'I've got it, Jessie,' and if he could, he would have breathed a sigh of relief at Mhairi's calm demeanour. She tilted his head to one side, then the other, all the while keeping her eyes focused on his fixed gaze. A light shone in his left eye, then his right, and clicked off. 'He's showing signs of coming out of it. He'll maybe recover some movement in a few minutes. Meanwhile, we have to keep him intubated.' She reached for the oxygen supply, and checked a pressure gauge. 'We have enough to keep him going.'

'Didn't know you had a medical degree,' Jessie said.

'I once wanted to be a nurse. Besides, my uncle's an anaesthetist in Ninewells.'

This was all good news to Gilchrist, but he still couldn't shift any of the blood from his bleeding tongue, which continued to flow down his throat. It didn't matter how well he was intubated. If his lungs were filled with blood, he would drown.

As if reading his mind, Mhairi prised his lips apart, and said, 'Shit. His tongue's bleeding.' She removed a tissue from her pocket, and pressed it against the tube and dabbed at the blood. When she removed the tissue, she said, 'Badly.'

'What does that mean?' Jessie said.

'Get him over onto his front.'

'How do we do that? His hands are nailed.'

Mhairi leaned to the side, fiddled with one hand. Then tried the other side, and did the same. 'This one,' she said, and took hold of his left hand. 'If you can hear me, sir, this is going to hurt. But only for a moment.' She slipped her hand under the back of Gilchrist's, then pressed upwards.

Fire erupted in his hand, flared the length of his arm.

'It's moving.' Mhairi pressed some more, as the nail-head sank deep into his palm. 'Again.' Deeper still.

All of a sudden, his hand was pulled free, leaving behind a bloodied nail that glistened red with scraps of tattered skin.

'Turn him over,' Mhairi shouted, lifting his left arm high as Jessie pushed at his back.

On his front, right hand still nailed to the floor, his body over his arm, the awkward angle had his shoulder complaining. The tube down his throat had shifted, too, so that his mouth twisted as if he suffered from Bell's palsy. A pair of hands gripped his head, adjusted it so that he lay face down on the carpet, leaving him with the oddest sensation of draining. Blood flowed from his mouth, pooled around his chin and face, that simple action causing his throat to spasm, and he choked a cough.

'He's coming out of it,' Mhairi said, pumping both hands against his back.

He coughed again while oxygen rushed into his lungs.

The clamour of running feet announced the arrival of the paramedics. 'What do we have?' the lead paramedic asked, kneeling on the floor.

Jessie pushed to her feet and walked to the side. She would let Mhairi explain.

On the settee, she noticed Gilchrist's clothes, neatly folded in the reverse order of his undressing. She removed his leather jacket from the pile, unfolded it, and placed it with care over his buttocks and thighs.

Outside, the driveway was already taped off. Not that there were any neighbours to interfere with the crime scene. It was standard protocol. She counted four patrol cars, blue lights flashing, parked at odd angles either side of the driveway, as if abandoned. Six police cars, all unmarked, sat at the far end of the property, as if they'd not been allowed to come to the party. As she walked into the night, she breathed in the cold air.

If it hadn't been for Jackie's ability to research the case, and being able to establish where Jennifer Bexall had once lived before she vanished – most likely murdered by Wilson and McCrear – she knew for a fact that they would have been too late to save Gilchrist. She closed her eyes at that thought, but an image of Gilchrist's naked body, hands and feet nailed to the carpet, tongue cut out and stored in a jar somewhere, jolted into her mind like an electric shock.

She opened her eyes, and the image vanished.

She shivered off a chill, then pulled out her mobile.

Her call was answered on the first ring.

'Have you found him?'

'We have, yes, and he's . . . he's all right, Maureen.'

'Thank God,' she said. 'I was so worried. I thought . . . I thought . . .'

'Me, too. But he's safe now.' She didn't think Maureen needed to hear the details of her father's injuries, not just at that moment, anyway. 'If you hadn't called when you did, we wouldn't have got here in time.' She pressed her mobile to her ear as Maureen let out a sob. 'Sometimes we have to rely on Joe Public lending us a hand. So well done, Maureen.'

'Where is he? Can I speak to him?'

Jessie couldn't fail to catch the tension in her voice, the realisation that if her father couldn't talk to his daughter himself, then there had to be something wrong. 'He can't talk to you at the moment, Maureen. He's . . . he's been drugged, so he's kind of out of it. But the instant he comes around, you'll be the first to know.'

'Thanks, Jessie. I'll pass on the good news to Irene.'

The line died, and Jessie returned her phone to her pocket. She hadn't met this Irene, the woman Gilchrist was on his way to meet earlier that night, and the woman who alerted them to Gilchrist's kidnapping; she'd just happened to look out her window to see him being manhandled into a car. She'd been unable to say what kind of car it was, but quick enough to take a note of the number plate. Rather than call 999, Irene then phoned Maureen in the belief that she would be able to contact someone in the know directly – which she had. She'd phoned Jessie. And those precious minutes gained, due to Irene's quick action, had saved Gilchrist's life.

So, yes, she definitely wanted to meet Irene, and when she did, she would buy her a bottle of her favourite champagne – provided she drank, of course. But if you thought about it, she would surely have to like a few wee drinks, if Andy had anything to do with it.

She chuckled at that.

She'd buy Andy a drink, too. Just as soon as he'd recovered.

She wrapped her scarf around her neck and walked to her car.

She had a report to complete, so it was going to be a long night.

CHAPTER 47

The Caribbean sun warmed his face and worked wonders on his stiff neck. A breeze stirred, and the raft on which he was sunbathing rocked in the gentle swell. A woman's voice whispered in his ear, a voice he thought he recognised, but for the life of him couldn't place. He knew who she was, he was certain of that. Again, she spoke, louder that time, calling out to him. He struggled to turn around to see where she was . . . and . . .

'Dad . . .'

She came into focus as slowly as mist clearing.

'They said I should let you sleep.' Warm fingers brushed his arm, sweeping up and down, as if to check he was still there, still alive. 'But I had to see you, to know that you're all right.'

He smiled at her, but his lips felt tight. He tried to say *I'm fine*, but it could have been someone else mumbling for him.

Her hand caressed the side of his face. 'How do you feel?'

He thought he said *Okay, I'm okay*. But it came out like a stuttered gasp.

Then the mist returned, and she faded from sight as darkness enveloped him again.

'Looks like he's coming to.' A man's voice, someone he knew.

He opened his eyes, and winced from the burst of clinical brightness. Somewhere in the background, someone coughed, a gurney rattled. By his side, feet shuffled, bodies shifted, making him turn his head to search for the source. But his muscles refused to work the way they should.

'He's still under sedation. So you only have a few minutes. No more.'

More shuffling, a chair scraping. The bed rocked, then two faces swam into view.

He thought Frazier looked refreshed, as if he'd just stepped out of the shower. His skin glistened, his eyes shone. Gone was the pained tiredness that had haunted him for days.

'I'll keep this short, Andy, but Tap McCrear and Mandeep Wilson are now safely in police custody, and are both singing like canaries, each willing to sell out the other. And the house in Largo was the motherlode. They'd been planning it together for years.'

Confusion clouded Gilchrist's mind. Did they know Wilson and McCrear were sister and brother? What house in Largo? And how could they have been planning it for years if McCrear had been out of jail for only nine months? He thought he saw the answer to that, but his logic seemed bogged down, as if it needed oiled. And Frazier's voice, too, was rambling on and folding into the background. For all Gilchrist was catching, it might as well have been a foreign language he was listening to.

'. . . and in light of the gallant effort both you and DS Janes have put into this case, I'm commending the pair of you for the

Queen's Police Medal. Do you have anything you would like to say, DCI Gilchrist?'

He lifted his hand, surprised to see it wrapped with bandages as large as a horse's hoof. 'Water,' he managed.

'Oh, yes, of course. Let me see. Where is it?'

'Here you are, Andy.'

He recognised Smiler's voice, and before he could speak a plastic cup pressed against his lips. Perfume as fresh as spring flowers lifted off her hand as water poured over his tongue and swept the tackiness from his mouth, soothed the dryness in his throat.

She removed the cup. 'Thanks,' he said.

'I think we should go now. Let you sleep.' She touched his shoulder, gave the gentlest of squeezes, then stepped back from the bed. He tried to watch them leave, but his peripheral vision swept in on him again, and his last thought was that Frazier looked disappointed.

'Ah, sleeping beauty awakens.' Jessie's face appeared before him.

He thought she looked pale and tired, more tired than he'd ever seen her before.

'How do you feel, Andy?'

He rolled his head from side to side. 'Stiff.' His voice sounded hoarse. He tried to clear his throat, but winced from the pain. Returning to reality will do that to you.

'You'll be sore for a while. Here. I bought you this. Your favourite. But then I thought you might find it hard to swallow, so I kind of nibbled away at it.' She unfolded a napkin, and held out a broken piece of blueberry muffin. 'Sorry.'

He almost laughed. 'That's very kind of you,' he managed to

say. 'But my tongue's nipping . . . and my throat's too sore.' He grimaced to make his point.

'Well, in that case, waste not want not.' She scoffed what was left of the muffin.

Whatever drugs they had him on seemed to be diminishing, and he moved his tongue, worked up some saliva, and tested his voice. 'I have a vague . . .' He licked his lips, and tried again. 'I have a vague memory . . . of Frazier . . . and Smiler being here.' Much better, although his tongue felt swollen, and stung as if he'd licked fresh jalapeños. 'I didn't catch it all . . . but I think a house . . . in Largo . . . was mentioned.' He paused. 'Or maybe I imagined it.'

Jessie dabbed the napkin at her mouth, then gave a wide-lipped smile. 'Any bits stuck in my teeth?'

'No . . . you're fine.'

Another dab at her mouth. 'You didn't imagine it. Largo was where Jennifer Bexall lived, the *real* Jennifer Bexall, before her identity was stolen by Mandeep Wilson. She lived in a wee cottage about a mile and a half outside town. Used to be her parents', but they died, and she inherited it.'

He thought he knew the answer, but had to ask. 'Was that where I was taken to?'

'Got it in one.'

'But . . .' he said, and this was the bit that troubled him, '. . . how did you know I was there?'

'We got lucky. Really lucky. Or I should say, *you* got lucky.' She pulled her chair closer to his bed, as if to confide in him. 'Emergency services took three 999 calls in the space of a few minutes, reporting someone being overpowered in South Street, then driven off in the back of a car. And this is where eyewitnesses are so unreliable. The car could have been anything from a green Volvo estate to a grey Ford Mondeo. The callers' names were taken, and details logged in, but before our Office was notified, I got a call from Mo, who'd got a call from Irene, who'd witnessed the whole thing from her living-room window.'

'Did Irene give details of the car?'

'Yes and no. She said it was an estate car, but didn't know the make and model. She did however write down the number plate. And this is where you really lucked out. Frazier turned up at the Office a few minutes after you'd left to meet Irene, and cornered me at my desk. You remember I told you I had something that could wait until the morning?'

He nodded. 'What was it?'

'Jennifer Bexall's address in Largo.'

'How did you . . .?'

'Jackie found out that the mailing address on her bank and credit card statements had been changed to a PO Box number earlier in the year, around about the time her finances all started going haywire, money bleeding from her accounts like a slashed artery. Jackie being Jackie managed to find the address before it was changed, which turned out to be Jennifer's wee cottage. When I explained all of this to Frazier, he was convinced it had to be where McCrear was hiding out.'

'Ah.' It was all he could think to say.

'Don't know if you've ever watched a whirlwind in action, but bloody hell, when that man wants something, it gets done in a hurry. I'm listening to him rattling off commands like he's setting up World War III, when out of the blue I get that call from Mo. She tells me she's just off the phone with Irene, and she gives me a registration number, and tells me Irene told her that's the plate of the car that took you. Even before Glenrothes forwarded the 999 calls to us, we had it tracked through ANPR, heading in the general direction of Largo. As soon as I mentioned that to Frazier, that was enough for him. Off he went, and within ten minutes he's mobilised half the Constabulary with authorisation to use firepower as necessary.'

Her lips pressed together as she stared at his bandaged hands for a long moment. When her gaze returned, her eyes glistened. 'I tell you, Andy, when we burst that door down, and I saw you lying there . . .' Her voice faltered. She sniffed, ran a finger under her eyes. 'I honestly thought we were too late.'

Truth be told, he'd thought it was all over, too – goodnight, and lights out. He reached out to her, to thank her for acting so quickly, for saving his life, but she couldn't suppress a grin that turned into laughter at the sight of his oversized bandages.

He laughed, too. 'They want to keep me under observation overnight.'

'Did no one tell them you never do as you're told?'

'Well, there is that, I suppose.' He watched her dab her eyes again, and when she seemed to recover, he said, 'Did you find anything in the house? In Largo, I mean.'

She nodded. 'The SOCOs are still going through it. By the time they finish, it'll be picked clean. But one of the bedrooms appears to be some sort of shrine – curtains over the windows, a hundred candles if there was one, jewellery dangling from the furniture, and that St Christopher's medallion we looked for. We'll be asking family members to ID each piece, but I've no doubt they're trophies. Oh,' she said, as if she'd just remembered something. 'And jars. Loads of them, like the ones we found in that flat in Great Western Road. If they'd got away with killing everyone named on these jars, I think they weren't going to stop, but just carry on.'

He closed his eyes, but the image of his name printed on a jar had him opening them again. He let out his breath, felt his heart palpitate at the thought of how close he'd come to being a statistic, just another number, one more victim of a murder spree.

'When you were lying on the floor, they had you hooked up to a mechanical ventilator to keep you breathing while they got on with their business. And in one of the cupboards, we found two rolls of heavy-duty bubble wrap, which we think, although we don't know for sure yet, is what they wrapped the ventilator in when they transported it as they went from house to house killing folk. We also found two more cars that they used, different ones for different murders. We were able to track them on stored ANPR footage at the time of each murder.'

Gilchrist closed his eyes for a moment, as he tried to shove that thought away.

'And we found over a dozen syringes, and jars of a clear liquid that Queen Becky's already confirmed is suxilwhatsitsface, and enough of it to paralyse an entire army. Anyway, you look as if you're about to drop off.'

He forced his eyes wide. 'Sorry.'

'No, I've overstayed my welcome.' She pushed her chair back. 'I'd better be getting back. Frazier wants me to interview McCrear again. I told him I'd be happy to do that if he gave me a set of jump leads. If it was up to me, I'd plug the bastard in, and leave him to it.'

'Deeps,' he said. 'Mandeep Wilson. Is she McCrear's sister?'

'No way. You can't believe a word that comes out of her mouth. DNA's already confirmed they're not related. And as for their marriage? Complete and utter sham. Partners in crime is what they were.' She surprised him by leaning forward and pecking his forehead. 'They tell me that no nerves or tendons were damaged in your hands, so once the bandages come off in a few days, you should make a full recovery.'

'Good enough to play the piano?'

'Better still, good enough to hold a pint.'

She gave him a toodle-do wave, then walked from the room.

CHAPTER 48

4.48 p.m., four days later
Elmbank Cottage, outskirts of Largo

Gilchrist crouched at the edge of the open excavation. 'Is it her?' he said.

Without taking her eyes off the human remains, Cooper said, 'There you go again, Andy, asking questions I can't possibly answer as things stand.' She brushed latex-covered fingers over the skull, not yet fully skeletonised – Jennifer Bexall hadn't been in the ground long enough for that to happen – and leaned forward for a closer look. Another brush with her fingers, and bared teeth took shape through the dirt. She widened the jaw and removed some soil from the skull's mouth. 'Jennifer's dental records show she had all her teeth, but she also had a rare supernumerary premolar between her right maxillary first and second premolars.' She peered intently at the jaw. 'She also had a couple of silver fillings in her lower molars, which I can't confirm until I have the remains back in my lab and the skull cleaned.'

'Anything else . . .?'

'For God's sake, Andy, why don't you go and have a pint, and I'll call you when I'm finished here?'

If there had been a pub close by, he might have taken her up on that. But Elmbank Cottage was over a mile from the nearest dwelling, let alone public bar. He pushed to his feet, tried to slide his hands into his pockets, but his bandaged hands were still tender, so he stood, arms by his side. Just then he caught the faintest whiff of second-hand smoke. He looked around the garden and found it – the digger driver, standing by a stone dyke that marked the property boundary, relaxing in the late afternoon sun, his task done for the day. He'd been called in to clear shrubbery and excavate the top three feet, after which the Victim Recovery Unit had used hand trowels to dig deeper, taking care not to destroy evidence, in particular, human remains. When Wilson told them where Jennifer Bexall's body was buried – in an attempt to pass her murder onto McCrear – Gilchrist had been sceptical. But Frazier on the other hand went for it flat out. Jessie had been correct – whirlwind in action was as good a description as any.

About an hour ago, at exactly 3.32 p.m., the first signs of a woman's jacket had been uncovered, and the North Street Office notified. Although his hands were still bandaged – no longer horse hooves, but palms covered, fingers and thumbs free to move – they were bruised and painful enough to make driving difficult, and certainly not recommended. So Jessie had driven him to the exhumation site in her Fiat 500.

Rather than stand over Cooper, or fight the urge to have a cigarette, he chose to give her some breathing space, and himself fresh air, so went looking for Jessie. He found her at the front of the cottage, mobile to her ear. When she saw him, she spoke into her phone, then ended the call.

'Everything okay?' he asked.

'That was Mhairi just telling me that Tap McCrear says Wilson's the psycho, and that she killed everyone on the murder list. Not him.'

McCrear's words echoed through his mind – *I'm not as sick a fuck as you think I am. I just do the heavy grafting, the lifting of the bodies* – which told him that McCrear could be telling the truth. But in the eyes of the law, that didn't matter. 'It's his murder list, right?'

'He's not denying that, although his solicitor is suggesting it was some innocent list he drew up so he could come to terms with his past.' Jessie shook her head. 'I mean, do they really think we're that stupid?'

'Clearly.'

'Uh-oh, here comes trouble again.' Jessie turned her back to him, and tapped her mobile's screen.

Gilchrist strode towards Cooper, who'd lowered her coveralls from her face, and was running her fingers through her hair, which was lengthening, he had to say, but nothing like her tumbling locks of last year. He thought her short hair and fringe didn't suit her, although he would never risk telling her that.

'Anything?' he said.

'As opposed to nothing?'

Silent, he returned her gaze.

'I've carried out an initial comparison of the teeth in the skull to Jennifer Bexall's dental records, and I'm fairly confident that the remains are Jennifer's.'

For a moment, Gilchrist experienced an odd mixture of elation and despair – elation at having found Jennifer, despite the fact she'd never been reported missing; and despair at the loss of such a young life, only thirty-three. But unlike Cooper, Gilchrist was more than fairly confident. The fact that Wilson had accused McCrear of murdering Jennifer and burying her body in the back garden of her remote cottage, nailed it for him. When you thought about it, who else could it have been? Still, you never could tell.

He let out his breath in a frustrated gush. 'Thanks, Becky.'

Silent, she held his gaze, as if waiting for him to ask another question.

He obliged with, 'But you'll be one hundred per cent confident they're Jennifer's remains only after you match her DNA, correct?'

'Well done, Andy.' She slipped off her latex gloves. 'And before you ask, it'll take me at least a couple of days before I get the results back. But rest assured, you'll be the first to know.'

He smiled at that, and was about to walk off and join Jessie when he said, 'Last week, you were going to tell me something. But we were interrupted. I had the impression at the time that it might have been important to you.'

It took her a few seconds to search her memory. 'It wasn't important then, and it still isn't important now, but I thought you might like to know that Max has filed for divorce.'

This was the problem he had with Cooper, being fed tantalising personal tidbits, but not knowing how he was expected to respond, as if she were setting him a test. Should he be happy that her husband had finally filed for divorce? He knew Cooper had to be happy. She'd complained about her marriage for as long as he'd known her. And infidelity by both parties emphasised the depth of the breakup. Or should he be sad? Sad she'd failed in her attempts to revive her relationship with Max? Or even sad she'd missed the chance of a new relationship with himself, despite the fact that they were clearly at odds with each other.

In the end, he settled for the truth. 'I'm sorry to hear that, Becky. I really am. I'd hoped you and Max might've been able to work things out.'

Her blue eyes held his for several seconds, before she said, 'Ever the diplomat,' then turned and walked to her car, a gleaming Range Rover parked off the country lane, sitting by itself, remote from other vehicles, which somehow emphasised how unapproachable and lonely she would always be.

He watched her go, watched her click her remote fob, watched the rear hatchback pop open, and wondered if she would give him a backward glance, maybe even a parting wave.

But that wasn't Cooper's way.

With heavy heart, he strode off in search of Jessie and a lift back to the Office.

Despite his best efforts to leave the Office that night before 8 p.m., he found himself running late. Too many interview statements to read, reports to write, and general debriefing meetings, had him striding hard and fast across Market Street, mobile to his ear.

'I'll be with you in five minutes,' he said.

And he was.

He thought Irene looked pleased to see him, despite his failure to take her out for their promised meal to the Doll's House over the last few days. Being nailed to a floor, hospitalised, then every free minute after that, it seemed, taken up with meetings, press conferences, and witness interviews, would do that to you.

'I finally made it.' He pecked her cheek, the air redolent of her perfume.

'And not a moment too soon. I'm starving.'

'Hungry.'

'Excuse me?'

'You're hungry. Famine victims are starving.' The words were out before he could stop himself, a snappy routine he'd once had with his children, years ago, when they were much younger. 'I'm sorry,' he said. 'It's a weak joke that's fallen flat.'

She chuckled, and said, 'But you're right. I'll have to remember that.' To his surprise, she removed a spare scarf from under her arm, reached up and wound it around his neck. 'A present,' she said.

'For what?'

'You'll see.' Then she slipped her arm through his, and he found himself being tugged closer. Together they crossed South Street as a tight couple, and when they reached the Criterion, she stopped.

'What's wrong?' he said.

'Nothing.' She slid her arm free. 'I fancy a drink *al fresco*. Don't you?'

'Ah,' he said. 'The reason for the scarf?'

'Exactly.' She pulled a chair to her, and sat at the table. Despite the March chill, they were not alone. Another couple were seated at the far end of the set of tables. But they were smokers, and his heart sank at the thought that Irene might have taken up the habit.

He sat down next to her. 'Can I get you something to drink?'

'I rather fancy a glass of wine, if you don't mind.'

'My pleasure. Red? White?'

'Red, of course.' He pushed his seat back to stand, and she said, 'Can you make it a cheeky little red?'

'A *little*?'

She chuckled. 'Go on then. Make it a large.'

As he walked past her to enter the bar, their hands grazed and, despite the bandages, he felt her fingers run along his. Inside, the Criterion did not carry many wines, mostly beers and spirits. He placed the order – a bottle of red if you've got it, yes, that'll do – and watched Irene through the window. He thought she looked relaxed, comfortable in her own skin, as if she was happy with all she had in life, and nothing could ever faze her.

When he placed the wine on the table, and filled both glasses with a good measure, he said, 'I asked for the cheekiest red they had.'

She laughed at that, and they chinked glasses, and huddled close as they took that first mouthful. She licked her lips, and said, 'Very cheeky.'

'But definitely not little?'

'*Definitely* not.'

He glanced at his watch. 'I should call the restaurant and let them know we're running late.'

'I wouldn't bother,' she said, and eyed him over the rim. 'I've already called and put the reservation back an hour.'

He raised his eyebrows and his glass. 'I can see you're one to watch.'

'The problem is, by the time we finish here, we may have to put it back another hour.'

'I'm in no hurry,' he said, and meant it.

It felt nice being in the company of a woman again, and oddly comfortable, too. As he watched her watch him, he couldn't help but be pulled in by her eyes. She sipped her wine, raised her glass and they chinked together again, a silly ritual that brought a smile to her face. The wine was going down well, and seemed to be staving off a chilling wind – or maybe that was the scarf. It didn't take long before he had to top up their glasses again, surprised to find the bottle almost emptied.

'Oh, well,' he said, and tipped the last of it into Irene's glass.

They spent the next twenty minutes sipping wine, talking about life in St Andrews versus Crail, his plans for renovating Fisherman's Cottage, her plans for turning one of her five bedrooms into a working photographic studio. When the conversation drifted to his son, Jack, and his art gallery in Edinburgh, he sensed her grief at the loss of her own son, Jamie, and he shifted the topic to when and how Irene and Maureen first met.

At a rare gap in the conversation, Irene lifted her close-to-empty glass to her lips, and held it there for a moment, as if savouring the bouquet. Her eyes seemed to twinkle from light spilling from the bar. 'I'm enjoying this,' she said.

'A rare vintage from the Criterion's cellar,' he joked.

'No, this. Having a chat. You and me. It's lovely.'

Well, what could he say? Nothing, came the answer. Well, not quite nothing. 'It is lovely,' he said. '*You're* lovely,' he added, then hid behind a sip of wine.

She waited until he returned his glass to the table. 'I'm thinking . . . why don't we postpone the reservation? For another day. If you don't mind, that is.'

He frowned. 'Is something the matter?'

'Not at all. I'm thinking we should have another bottle of wine.'

'Certainly.' He pushed his chair back. 'Same again?'

'No.' She clasped his arm. 'Thank you. I'm finding it a bit chilly. So why don't we head to *chez moi* and have another bottle there?'

'*Al fresco, chez moi*. You'll be telling me you speak Chinese next.'

She laughed at that, a husky rush that had him leaning closer to peck her lips.

'I take it that's a yes?' she said.

'*Certamente,*' which really was stretching his Italian.

He helped her to her feet, and she surprised him by shuffling with his scarf, tucking it this way and that, adjusting it until it was just so, while he looked into her eyes and revelled in her closeness.

When she was done, she said, 'Shall we?'

Without a word, he put his arm around her waist.

And together they walked to her home.

ACKNOWLEDGEMENTS

Writing is indeed a lonely affair, but this book could not have been published without the help and advice from the following: Jon Miller, formerly of Tayside Police, and Alan Gall, retired Chief Superintendent, Strathclyde Police, for police procedure; Gordon Boyle BDS for all things to do with teeth; Andy Forman LBIPP for invaluable advice on photography; Peggy Boulos Smith and Al Zuckerman of Writers House, New York, for encouragement when it was needed most; Howard Watson, once again for professional copyediting to the nth degree; at Little, Brown: Rebecca Sheppard, Senior Desk Editor, Sean Garrehy, Art Director, Brionee Fenlon, Marketing Executive, John Fairweather, Senior Production Controller, for working hard behind the scenes to give this novel the best possible start; and in particular Krystyna Green, Publishing Director, Constable, for placing her trust in me once again. And finally Anna, for putting up with me, believing in me, and loving me all the way.